MW00570301

THE ULTIMATE
Werewolf

Other ULTIMATE MONSTER
Books from Dell
THE ULTIMATE DRACULA
THE ULTIMATE FRANKENSTEIN

THE ULTIMATE
Werewolf

BYRON PREISS, EDITOR
▼▼▼

DAVID KELLER, MEGAN MILLER, & JOHN BETANCOURT
ASSOCIATE EDITORS

ILLUSTRATED BY
MICHAEL DAVID BIEGEL

BOOK DESIGN
BY FEARN CUTLER

A BYRON PREISS BOOK
A DELL TRADE PAPERBACK

A Dell Trade Paperback

Published by Dell Publishing a division of Bantam Doubleday Dell Publishing Group, Inc., 666 Fifth Avenue, New York, New York 10103

If you purchased this book without a cover you should be aware that this book is stolen property. It was reported as "unsold and destroyed" to the publisher and neither the author nor the publisher has received any payment for this "stripped book."

Design: Fearn Cutler

Associate Editors: David Keller, Megan Miller, John Betancourt

Copyright © 1991 by Byron Preiss Visual Publications, Inc.

"Introduction" © 1991 The Kilimanjaro Corporation
Adrift Just off the Islets of Langerhans: Latitude 38° 54' N Longitude 77° 00' 13" W" © 1991 The Kilimanjaro Corporation
"Wolf, Iron, and Moth" © 1991 Philip José Farmer
"Angels' Moon" © 1991 Kathe Koja
"Unleashed" © 1991 Nina Kiriki Hoffman
"The Mark of the Beast" © 1991 Kim Antieau
"At War with the Wolf Man" © 1991 Jerome Charyn
"Day of the Wolf" © 1991 Craig Shaw Gardner
"Moonlight on the Gazebo" © 1991 Mel Gilden
"Raymond" © 1991 Nancy A. Collins
"There's a Wolf in My Time Machine" © 1991 Larry Niven
"South of Oregon City" © 1991 Pat Murphy
"SpeciaL Makeup" © 1991 Kevin J. Anderson
"Pure Silver" © 1991 A.C. Crispin and Kathleen O'Malley
"Close Shave" © 1991 Brad Linaweaver
"Partners" © 1991 Robert J. Randisi
"Ancient Evil" © 1991 Bill Pronzini
"And the Moon Shines Full and Bright" © 1991 Brad Strickland
"Full Moon Over Moscow" © 1991 Stuart Kaminsky
"Wolf Watch" © 1991 Robert E. Weinberg
"The Werewolf Gambit" © 1991 Agberg, Ltd.
"Selected Filmography" © 1991 Leonard Wolf

All rights reserved. No part of this book may be reproduced or transmitted in any form or by any means, electronic or mechanical, including photocopying, recording, or by any information storage and retrieval system, without the written permission of the Publisher, except where permitted by law.

The trademark Dell is registered in the U.S. Patent and Trademark Office.

ISBN: 0440 50354-X

Printed in the United States of America

Published simultaneously in Canada

October 1991

10 9 8 7 6 5 4 3 2 1

RRH

THE ULTIMATE
Werewolf

CONTENTS

INTRODUCTION
▼▼▼

CRYING "WOLF!"
▼▼▼

HARLAN ELLISON

THAT was one helluva year, 1941. Life on this planet was savagely altered for all time, for every human being, in ways too obscure and too terrible to predict. We began to metamorphose— to change shape and purpose—to become beasts of a different kind than had ever roamed the Earth before.

Looking in the mirror will not reveal the face of the creature. We look about the same. But that's only because the full moon isn't shining. Try the mirrors of television, advertising, newspaper reports, crime statistics; or look out your window at the color of the sky, the litter in the street, the graffiti on the wall. It started in earnest in 1941.

In that year, powerful influences were hardwired into our society. We went to war in the most massive assemblage of force and brutality since 1237 and the beginning of the Mongol conquest of most of the civilized world. 1941 was the sneak attack on Pearl Harbor, the full-bore entry of America into World War II, the proclamation on my eighth birthday—May 27th—by President Franklin Delano Roosevelt of a state of national emergency; it was the year the human race poured fusel oil on the conflagration and four years later added to the flames with the power of the split atom.

And the world of fantasy literature was changed forever in that year. But no one seemed to notice.

In 1941 movies were at the height of their mesmeric power over the American public. We were coming out of the Depression, millions were still on the road, selling pencils, working for what they called "coolie wages"—and radio, pulp magazines, and movies were the only inexpensive diversions. Despite the false courage embodied in Shirley Temple songs and Busby Berkeley kick-turn-kick-turn assurances that *We're in the Money*, scrounging up a dime for a Saturday matinee double-bill was no less than hardscrabble for most Americans.

But, oh, what a pull on every one of us; to be drawn into those gorgeous palaces of dreams. 1941 was arguably the best year for cinema before and since. In that twelvemonth before the world pitched headlong into darkness, here is a *partial* list of the more than four hundred motion pictures produced by Hollywood:

The Maltese Falcon
Citizen Kane
Dumbo
Sergeant York
Major Barbara
How Green Was My Valley
The Lady Eve
Here Comes Mr. Jordan
The Stars Look Down
Suspicion
The Little Foxes
Meet John Doe
Ball of Fire

Leonard Maltin gives four stars to seven of those, and three and a half to the remaining six. What a lineup! Films so influential that even today, when critics are polled, at least three off that list perennially find placement among the top ten of all time. But there was one more, that went unnoticed, that altered the world of fantastic literature as surely and positively as Hitler altered the world at large sorely and negatively. Was it the John Lee Mahin-scripted, Victor Fleming-directed version of Robert Louis Stevenson's classic *Dr. Jekyll and Mr. Hyde,* starring Spencer Tracy, Ingrid Bergman, Lana Turner, and Sir C. Aubrey Smith . . . a film on which hundreds of thousands of dollars were spent for a lavish production by MGM, the most prestigious studio of its day? In fact, no.

It was a minor, only-passingly-noted, "B" (for *bottom*) second feature on a double-bill. It was from a studio hardly known as the House of Influential Cinema. It was made on a parsimonious budget; and though it boasted such outstanding thespic talents as Claude Rains, Ralph Bellamy, Warren William, and Bela Lugosi (in a cameo role), it was by no means a *big* film, or even a film that Universal pushed very hard. It was intended to come, and to go; to make a few bucks, and to fill the hole in a Saturday matinee that came immediately after a Charles Starrett "Durango Kid" western.

It has been fifty years since that intentionally disposable chunk of celluloid trash was tossed out onto the movie screens of America, like an unwanted infant wrapped in newspaper and flung into a dumpster. And if you check any exhaustive reference on the Oscars (such as ACADEMY AWARDS: *The Ungar Reference Index*) you will discover that in no category did that film get a nomination.

Yet fifty years later, even with the plethora of period films committed to videocassette, aired late night on local channels, run and rerun on cable—even specialty channels such as American Film Classics—and screened in the dwindling number of revival theaters or in film schools or museum cinema programs, you will likely never see *Dive Bomber, Aloma of the South Seas, Son of Monte Cristo, or Las Vegas Nights* . . . all of which received Oscar nominations in one or another category.

But I'll bet you an eyeball that somewhere in these here great Yewnited States, today, tonight, tomorrow, an enraptured audience is watching Lon Chaney, Jr., as *The Wolf Man*. A film created as a throwaway fifty years ago, exquisitely scripted by Curt Siodmak, directed by George Waggner, moodily art directed in the horrorstory equivalent of *film noir*; a film that forever cast into the American idiom the timeless words of Madame Maria Ouspenskaya:

"Even the man who is pure in heart
"And says his prayers by night
"May become a wolf when the wolfbane blooms
"And the moon is pure and bright."

Before the seventy-one minutes of *The Wolf Man* were unleashed on generations of kids whose spines creaked and whose hair trembled as they watched tragic Lawrence Talbot metamorphose into a blood-hungry beast thing, the werewolf was barely considered fit fodder for fantasy. Yes, there had been a 1913 silent, *The Werewolf*, two or three French films featuring lycanthropy, and the excellent *Werewolf of London* with Henry Hull in 1935, but that was just about the totality. The potboiler picture no one thought would last more than a couple of weeks, has not only endured, it has skewed imaginative literature in its own image for half a century. More than any previous rendition of the werewolf mythos, *The Wolf Man* created an entire genre.

Purposely, I'll not rehash the litany of the werewolf theme in classical literature: Dumas-*pére's* THE WOLF LEADER in 1857, Captain Marryat's "The White Wolf of the Hartz Mountains" in 1839, or even the first known introduction of the werewolf antetype in English fiction—the 13th century court romance by Marie de France, "Lay of the Bisclavaret". Nor will I dwell at length on images of the werewolf in phenomenological anecdote . . . though it wouldn't hurt you to look up Freud's *Notes Upon a Case of*

Obsessional Neurosis (1909) in which the father of modern psycho-analysis treats the case of a wealthy young Russian whose history is now commonly referred to as being that of the "Wolf Man."

Those who want irrefutable documentation of the longevity, fecundity, and legitimacy of the werewolf motif in literature are commended to three excellent essays: "Images of the Werewolf" and "The Werewolf Theme in Weird Fiction", both by Brian J. Frost, each exhaustive and breathtakingly lucid, and both available in Frost's frequently-reprinted 1973 paperback anthology, BOOK OF THE WEREWOLF (Sphere Books Ltd.); and Bill Pronzini's 1978 essay on the form in his anthology WEREWOLF!

I choose to sidestep Sabine Baring-Gould and Guy Endore (who was a terrific gentleman, whom I was privileged to know) and Montague Summers, to suggest that for all its weighty and unchallengeable credentials, the man-into-wolf story never really came into its own until Lon Chaney, Jr. assayed the role of Curt Siodmak's Lawrence Talbot and . . .

. . . talk about casting a role perfectly: do you know about the *amazing* thing that happened when Lon Chaney, Jr. was born?

Creighton Tull Chaney was delivered, *stillborn*, on February 10th, 1906. His father grabbed him up, rushed out into the frigid Oklahoma night, broke the ice on Belle Isle Lake with a small hatchet, and plunged the baby into the freezing water, bringing him to life. Man was *born* to play that part.

And the younger Chaney was properly proud of his perform-ance as the Wolf Man. Though he received inordinate acclaim for his roles in *High Noon* and *The Defiant Ones*, and will always be remembered as Lenny to Burgess Meredith's George in the film of Steinbeck's *Of Mice and Men*, Chaney always doted on how well he'd performed as Lawrence Talbot. He always said that others had set the models for The Mummy, Frankenstein, Dra-cula . . . but *he* had created the image of the Wolf Man, for all time, for all those who came after him.

And it is that 1941 film, I submit, that is the impetus for the book you now hold. No matter how many spectacular werewolf stories had been written and published before the house lights went down and the opening credits rolled for the first time (and I've always suspected that when Jack Williamson sat down to write DARKER THAN YOU THINK for *Unknown* in 1939, when it was published in late 1940, when it was expanded for book publication in 1948, it was the final moment of *non*-filmic influence in the werewolf genre), thereafter no one could go to the form free of the tormented face of Lawrence Talbot.

It was that film, in that tortuous moment of human existence before we plunged so totally into the bestial existence whose results we see around us today, that the world of imaginative literature absorbed completely. *The Wolf Man* has become so thoroughly an icon, that almost no one notices (and no one has noted in print) that the only element of Accepted Werewolf Lore now endemic to *every* saga of lycanthropy that predates the film, is the business about the full moon.

The pentagram, seeing it in the palm of the next victim, silver used to kill, half-man/half-beast . . . it was all cobbled up by Siodmak.

So it is appropriate that on this more-or-less 50th anniversary of the first shape-change of Lawrence Talbot into the rending, ripping, frightful creature the entire world now identifies as The Wolf Man, that this book should pay homage to a "little trash movie" that has sown its seed of entertainment with such delicious profligacy.

For this book was born on a freezing night in 1906, on the shore of an Oklahoma lake, where the son of a great actor-to-be was immersed in the waters of posterity. Lon Chaney, Jr. changed for us in 1941; and we've been changing ever since.

The question remains: who among us are the *real* beasts?

ADRIFT JUST OFF THE
ISLETS OF LANGERHANS:
LATITUDE 38° 54′ N
LONGITUDE 77° 00′ 13″ W
▼▼▼

HARLAN ELLISON

WHEN Moby Dick awoke one morning from unsettling dreams, he found himself changed in his bed of kelp into a monstrous Ahab.

Crawling in stages from the soggy womb of sheets, he stumbled into the kitchen and ran water into the teapot. There was lye in the corner of each eye. He put his head under the spigot and let the cold water rush around his cheeks.

Dead bottles littered the living room. One hundred and eleven empty bottles that had contained Robitussin and Romilar-CF. He padded through the debris to the front door and opened it a crack. Daylight assaulted him. "Oh, God," he murmured, and closed his eyes to pick up the folded newspaper from the stoop.

Once more in dusk, he opened the paper. The headline read: BOLIVIAN AMBASSADOR FOUND MURDERED, and the feature story heading column one detailed the discovery of the ambassador's body, badly decomposed, in an abandoned refrigerator in an empty lot in Secaucus, New Jersey.

The teapot whistled.

Naked, he padded toward the kitchen; as he passed the aquarium he saw that terrible fish was still alive, and this morning whistling like a bluejay, making tiny streams of bubbles that rose to burst on the scummy surface of the water. He paused beside the tank, turned on the light and looked in through the drifting eddies of stringered algae. The fish simply would not die. It had killed off every other fish in the tank—prettier fish, friendlier fish, livelier fish, even larger and more dangerous fish—had killed them all, one by one, and eaten out the eyes. Now it swam the tank alone, ruler of its worthless domain.

He had tried to let the fish kill itself, trying every form of neglect short of outright murder by not feeding it; but the pale, worm-pink devil even thrived in the dark and filth-laden waters.

Now it sang like a bluejay. He hated the fish with a passion he could barely contain.

He sprinkled flakes from a plastic container, grinding them between thumb and forefinger as experts had advised him to do it, and watched the multicolored granules of fish meal, roe, milt, brine shrimp, day-fly eggs, oatflour and egg yolk ride on the surface for a moment before the detestable fish-face came snapping to the top to suck them down. He turned away, cursing and hating the fish. It would not die. Like him, it would not die.

In the kitchen, bent over the boiling water, he understood for the first time the true status of his situation. Though he was probably nowhere near the rotting outer edge of sanity, he could smell its foulness on the wind, coming in from the horizon; and like some wild animal rolling its eyes at the scent of carrion and the feeders thereon, he was being driven closer to lunacy every day, just from the smell.

He carried the teapot, a cup and two tea bags to the kitchen table and sat down. Propped open in a plastic stand used for keeping cookbooks handy while mixing ingredients, the Mayan Codex translations remained unread from the evening before. He poured the water, dangled the tea bags in the cup and tried to focus his attention. The references to Itzamna, the chief divinity of the Maya pantheon, and medicine, his chief sphere of influence, blurred. Ixtab, the goddess of suicide, seemed more apropos for this morning, this deadly terrible morning. He tried reading, but the words only went in, nothing happened to them, they didn't sing. He sipped tea and found himself thinking of the chill, full circle of the Moon. He glanced over his shoulder at the kitchen clock. Seven forty-four.

He shoved away from the table, taking the half-full cup of tea, and went into the bedroom. The impression of his body, where it had lain in tortured sleep, still dented the bed. There were clumps of blood-matted hair clinging to the manacles that he had riveted to metal plates in the headboard. He rubbed his wrists where they had been scored raw, slopping a little tea on his left forearm. He wondered if the Bolivian ambassador had been a piece of work he had tended to the month before.

His wristwatch lay on the bureau. He checked it. Seven forty-six. Slightly less than an hour and a quarter to make the meeting with the consultation service. He went into the bathroom, reached inside the shower stall and turned the handle till a fine needle-spray of icy water smashed the tiled wall of the stall. Letting the water run, he turned to the medicine cabinet for his shampoo. Taped to the mirror was an Ouchless Telfa finger bandage on which two lines had been neatly typed, in capitals:

> THE WAY YOU WALK IS THORNY, MY SON,
> THROUGH NO FAULT OF YOUR OWN.

Then, opening the cabinet, removing a plastic bottle of herbal shampoo that smelled like friendly, deep forests, Lawrence Talbot resigned himself to the situation, turned and stepped into the shower, the merciless ice-laden waters of the Arctic pounding against his tortured flesh.

▼▼▼

Suite 1544 of the Tishman Airport Center Building was a men's toilet. He stood against the wall opposite the door labeled MEN and drew the envelope from the inner breast pocket of his jacket. The paper was of good quality, the envelope crackled as he thumbed up the flap and withdrew the single-sheet letter inside. It was the correct address, the correct floor, the correct suite. Suite 1544 was a men's toilet, nonetheless. Talbot started to turn away. It was a vicious joke: he found no humor in the situation; not in his present circumstances.

He took one step toward the elevators.

The door to the men's room shimmered, fogged over like a windshield in winter, and re-formed. The legend on the door had changed. It now read:

INFORMATION ASSOCIATES

Suite 1544 was the consultation service that had written the invitational letter on paper of good quality in response to Talbot's mail inquiry responding to a noncommittal but judiciously-phrased advertisement in *Forbes*.

He opened the door and stepped inside. The woman behind the teak reception desk smiled at him, and his glance was split between the dimples that formed, and her legs, very nice, smooth legs, crossed and framed by the kneehole of the desk. "Mr. Talbot?"

He nodded. "Lawrence Talbot."

She smiled again. "Mr. Demeter will see you at once, sir. Would you like something to drink? Coffee? A soft drink?"

Talbot found himself touching his jacket where the envelope lay in an inner pocket. "No. Thank you."

She stood up, moving toward an inner office door, as Talbot said, "What do you do when someone tries to flush your desk?" He was not trying to be cute. He was annoyed. She turned and stared at him. There was silence in her appraisal, nothing more.

"Mr. Demeter is right through here, sir."

She opened the door and stood aside. Talbot walked past her, catching a scent of mimosa.

The inner office was furnished like the reading room of an exclusive men's club. Old money. Deep quiet. Dark, heavy woods. A lowered ceiling of acoustical tile on tracks, concealing a crawl space and probably electrical conduits. The pile rug of oranges and burnt umbers swallowed his feet to the ankles. Through a wall-sized window could be seen not the city that lay outside the building but a panoramic view of Hanauma Bay, on the Koko Head side of Oahu. The pure aquamarine waves came in like undulant snakes, rose like cobras, crested out white, tunneled and struck like asps at the blazing yellow beach. It was not a window; there were no windows in the office. It was a photograph. A deep, real photograph that was neither a projection nor a hologram. It was a wall looking out on another place entirely. Talbot knew nothing about exotic flora, but he was certain that the tall, razor-edge-leafed trees growing right down to beach's boundary were identical to those pictured in books depicting the Carboniferous period of the Earth before even the saurians had walked the land. What he was seeing had been gone for a very long time.

"Mr. Talbot. Good of you to come. John Demeter."

He came up from a wingback chair, extended his hand. Talbot took it. The grip was firm and cool. "Won't you sit down," Demeter said. "Something to drink? Coffee, perhaps, or a soft drink?" Talbot shook his head; Demeter nodded dismissal to the receptionist; she closed the door behind her, firmly, smoothly, silently.

Talbot studied Demeter in one long appraisal as he took the

chair opposite the wingback. Demeter was in his early fifties, had retained a full and rich mop of hair that fell across his forehead in gray waves that clearly had not been touched up. His eyes were clear and blue, his features regular and jovial, his mouth wide and sincere. He was trim. The dark-brown business suit was hand-tailored and hung well. He sat easily and crossed his legs, revealing black hose that went above the shins. His shoes were highly polished.

"That's a fascinating door, the one to your outer office," Talbot said.

"Do we talk about my door?" Demeter asked.

"Not if you don't want to. That isn't why I came here."

"I don't want to. So let's discuss your particular problem."

"Your advertisement. I was intrigued."

Demeter smiled reassuringly. "Four copywriters worked very diligently at the proper phraseology."

"It brings in business."

"The right kind of business."

"You slanted it toward smart money. Very reserved. Conservative portfolios, few glamours, steady climbers. Wise old owls."

Demeter steepled his fingers and nodded, an understanding uncle. "Directly to the core, Mr. Talbot: wise old owls."

"I need some information. Some special, certain information. How confidential is your service, Mr. Demeter?"

The friendly uncle, the wise old owl, the reassuring businessman understood all the edited spaces behind the question. He nodded several times. Then he smiled and said, "That *is* a clever door I have, isn't it? You're absolutely right, Mr. Talbot."

"A certain understated eloquence."

"One hopes it answers more questions for our clients than it poses."

Talbot sat back in the chair for the first time since he had entered Demeter's office. "I think I can accept that."

"Fine. Then why don't we get to specifics. Mr. Talbot, you're having some difficulty dying. Am I stating the situation succinctly?"

"Gently, Mr. Demeter."

"Always."

"Yes. You're on the target."

"But you have some problems, some rather unusual problems."

"Inner ring."

Demeter stood up and walked around the room, touching an astrolabe on a bookshelf, a cut-glass decanter on a sideboard, a sheaf of the London Times held together by a wooden pole. "We are only information specialists, Mr. Talbot. We can put you on to what you need, but the effectation is your problem."

"If I have the modus operandi, I'll have no trouble taking care of getting it done."

"You've put a little aside."

"A little."

"Conservative portfolio? A few glamours, mostly steady climbers?"

"Bull's-eye, Mr. Demeter."

Demeter came back and sat down again. "All right, then. If you'll take the time to write out very carefully precisely what you want—I know generally, from your letter, but I want this precise, for the contract—I think I can undertake to supply the data necessary to solving your problem."

"At what cost?"

"Let's decide what it is you want, first, shall we?"

Talbot nodded. Demeter reached over and pressed a call button on the smoking stand beside the wingback. The door opened. "Susan, would you show Mr. Talbot to the sanctum and provide him with writing materials." She smiled and stood aside, waiting for Talbot to follow her. "And bring Mr. Talbot something to drink if he'd like it . . . some coffee? A soft drink, perhaps?" Talbot did not respond to the offer.

"I might need some time to get the phraseology down just

right. I might have to work as diligently as your copywriters. It might take me a while. I'll go home and bring it in tomorrow."

Demeter looked troubled. "That might be inconvenient. That's why we provide a quiet place where you can think."

"You'd prefer I stay and do it now."

"Inner ring, Mr Talbot."

"You might be a toilet if I came back tomorrow."

"Bull's-eye."

"Let's go, Susan. Bring me a glass of orange juice if you have it." He preceded her out the door.

He followed her down the corridor at the far side of the reception room. He had not seen it before. She stopped at a door and opened it for him. There was an escritoire and a comfortable chair inside the small room. He could hear Muzak. "I'll bring you your orange juice," she said.

He went in and sat down. After a long time he wrote seven words on a sheet of paper.

▼▼▼

Two months later, long after the series of visitations from silent messengers who brought rough drafts of the contract to be examined, who came again to take them away revised, who came again with counterproposals, who came again to take away further revised versions, who came again—finally—with Demeter-signed finals, and who waited while he examined and initialed and signed the finals—two months later, the map came via the last, mute messenger. He arranged for the final installment of the payment to Information Associates that same day: he had ceased wondering where fifteen boxcars of maize—grown specifically as the Zuñi nation had grown it—was of value.

Two days later, a small item on an inside page of the *New York Times* noted that fifteen boxcars of farm produce had somehow vanished off a railroad spur near Albuquerque. An official investigation had been initiated.

The map was very specific, very detailed; it looked accurate.

He spent several days with Gray's *Anatomy* and, when he was satisfied that Demeter and his organization had been worth the staggering fee, he made a phone call. The long-distance operator turned him over to Inboard and he waited, after giving her the information, for the static-laden connection to be made. He insisted Budapest on the other end let it ring twenty times, twice the number the male operator was permitted per caller. On the twenty-first ring it was picked up. Miraculously, the background noise-level dropped and he heard Victor's voice as though it was across the room.

"Yes! Hello!" Impatient, surly as always.

"Victor . . . Larry Talbot."

"Where are you calling from?"

"The States. How are you?"

"Busy. What do you want?"

"I have a project. I want to hire you and your lab."

"Forget it. I'm coming down to final moments on a project and I can't be bothered now."

The imminence of hangup was in his voice. Talbot cut in quickly. "How long do you anticipate?"

"Till what?"

"Till you're clear."

"Another six months inside, eight to ten if it gets muddy. I said: forget it, Larry. I'm *not* available."

"At least let's talk."

"No."

"Am I wrong, Victor, or do you owe me a little?"

"After all this time you're calling in debts?"

"They only ripen with age."

There was a long silence in which Talbot heard dead space being pirated off their line. At one point he thought the other man had racked the receiver. Then, finally, "Okay, Larry. We'll *talk*. But you'll have to come to me; I'm too involved to be hopping any jets."

"That's fine. I have free time." A slow beat, then he added, "Nothing but free time."

"*After* the full moon, Larry." It was said with great specificity.

"Of course. I'll meet you at the last place we met, at the same time, on the thirtieth of this month. Do you remember?"

"I remember. That'll be fine."

"Thank you, Victor. I appreciate this."

There was no response.

Talbot's voice softened: "How is your father?"

"Goodbye, Larry," he answered, and hung up.

▼▼▼

They met on the thirtieth of that month, at moonless midnight, on the corpse barge that plied between Buda and Pesht. It was the correct sort of night: chill fog moved in a pulsing curtain up the Danube from Belgrade.

They shook hands in the lee of a stack of cheap wooden coffins and, after hesitating awkwardly for a moment, they embraced like brothers. Talbot's smile was tight and barely discernible by the withered illumination of the lantern and the barge's running lights as he said, "All right, get it said so I don't have to wait for the other shoe to drop."

Victor grinned and murmured ominously:

> "*Even a man who is pure in heart*
> *And says his prayers by night,*
> *May become a wolf when the wolfbane blooms*
> *And the Autumn moon shines bright.*"

Talbot made a face. "And other songs from the same album."

"Still saying your prayers at night?"

"I stopped that when I realized the damned thing didn't scan."

"Hey. We aren't here getting pneumonia just to discuss forced rhyme."

The lines of weariness in Talbot's face settled into a joyless pattern. "Victor, I need your help."

"I'll listen, Larry. Further than that it's doubtful."

Talbot weighed the warning and said, "Three months ago I answered an advertisement in *Forbes*, the business magazine. Information Associates. It was a cleverly phrased, very reserved, small box, inconspicuously placed. Except to those who knew how to read it. I won't waste your time on details, but the sequence went like this: I answered the ad, hinting at my problem as circuitously as possible without being completely impenetrable. Vague words about important money. I had hopes. Well, I hit with this one. They sent back a letter calling a meet. Perhaps another false trail, was what I thought . . . God knows there've been enough of those."

Victor lit a Sobranie Black & Gold and let the pungent scent of the smoke drift away on the fog. "But you went."

"I went. Peculiar outfit, sophisticated security system, I had a strong feeling they came from, well, I'm not sure where . . . or when."

Victor's glance was abruptly kilowatts heavier with interest. "*When*, you say? Temporal travelers?"

"I don't know."

"I've been waiting for something like that, you know. It's inevitable. And they'd certainly make themselves known eventually."

He lapsed into silence, thinking. Talbot brought him back sharply. "I don't know, Victor. I really don't. But that's not my concern at the moment."

"Oh. Right. Sorry, Larry. Go on. You met with them . . ."

"Man named Demeter. I thought there might be some clue there. The name. I didn't think of it at the time. The name Demeter; there was a florist in Cleveland, many years ago. But later, when I looked it up, Demeter, the Earth goddess, Greek mythology . . . no connection. At least, I don't think so.

"We talked. He understood my problem and said he'd undertake the commission. But he wanted it specific, what I required of him, wanted it specific for the contract—God knows how he would have enforced the contract, but I'm sure he could have—he had a *window*, Victor, it looked out on—"

Victor spun the cigarette off his thumb and middle finger, snapping it straight down into the blood-black Danube. "Larry, you're maundering."

Talbot's words caught in his throat. It was true. "I'm counting on you, Victor. I'm afraid it's putting my usual aplomb out of phase."

"All right, take it easy. Let me hear the rest of this and we'll see. Relax."

Talbot nodded and felt grateful. "I wrote out the nature of the commission. It was only seven words." He reached into his topcoat pocket and brought out a folded slip of paper. He handed it to the other man. In the dim lantern light, Victor unfolded the paper and read:

GEOGRAPHICAL COORDINATES
FOR LOCATION OF MY SOUL

Victor looked at the two lines of type long after he had absorbed their message. When he handed it back to Talbot, he wore a new, fresher expression. "You'll never give up, will you, Larry?"

"Did your father?"

"No." Great sadness flickered across the face of the man Talbot called Victor. "And," he added, tightly, after a beat, "he's been lying in a catatonia sling for sixteen years *because* he wouldn't give up." He lapsed into silence. Finally, softly, "It never hurts to know when to give up, Larry. Never hurts. Sometimes you've just got to leave it alone."

Talbot snorted softly with bemusement. "Easy enough for you to say, old chum. You're going to die."

"That wasn't fair, Larry."

"Then help me, dammit! I've gone farther toward getting myself out of all this than I ever have. Now I need *you*. You've got the expertise."

"Have you sounded out 3M or Rand or even General Dynamics? They've got good people there."

"Damn you."

"Okay. Sorry. Let me think a minute."

The corpse barge cut through the invisible water, silent, fog-shrouded, without Charon, without Styx, merely a public service, a garbage scow of unfinished sentences, uncompleted errands, unrealized dreams. With the exception of these two, talking, the barge's supercargo had left decisions and desertions behind.

Then, Victor said, softly, talking as much to himself as to Talbot, "We could do it with microtelemetry. Either through direct micro-miniaturizing techniques or by shrinking a servo-mechanism package containing sensing, remote control, and guidance/manipulative/propulsion hardware. Use a saline solution to inject it into the bloodstream. Knock you out with 'Russian sleep' and/or tap into the sensory nerves so you'd perceive or control the device as if you were there . . . conscious transfer of point of view."

Talbot looked at him expectantly.

"No. Forget it," said Victor. "It won't do."

He continued to think. Talbot reached into the other's jacket pocket and brought out the Sobranies. He lit one and stood silently, waiting. It was always thus with Victor. He had to worm his way through the analytical labyrinth.

"Maybe the biotechnic equivalent: a tailored microorganism or slug . . . injected . . . telepathic link established. No. Too many flaws: possible ego/control conflict. Impaired perceptions. Maybe it could be a hive creature injected for multiple p.o.v." A pause, then, "No. No good."

Talbot drew on the cigarette, letting the mysterious Eastern smoke curl through his lungs. "How about . . . say, just for the sake of discussion," Victor said, "say the ego/id exists to some extent in each sperm. It's been ventured. Raise the consciousness in one cell and send it on a mission to . . . forget it, that's metaphysical bullshit. Oh, damn damn damn . . . this will take time and thought, Larry. Go away, let me think on it. I'll get back to you."

Talbot butted the Sobranie on the railing, and exhaled the final stream of smoke. "Okay, Victor. I take it you're interested sufficiently to work at it."

"I'm a scientist, Larry. That means I'm hooked. I'd have to be an idiot not to be . . . this speaks directly to what . . . to what my father . . ."

"I understand. I'll let you alone. I'll wait."

They rode across in silence, the one thinking of solutions, the other considering problems. When they parted, it was with an embrace.

Talbot flew back the next morning, and waited through the nights of the full moon, knowing better than to pray. It only muddied the waters. And angered the gods.

▼▼▼

When the phone rang, and Talbot lifted the receiver, he knew what it would be. He had known *every* time the phone had rung, for over two months. "Mr. Talbot? Western Union. We have a cablegram for you, from Moldava, Czechoslovakia."

"Please read it."

"It's very short, sir. It says, 'Come immediately. The trail has been marked.' It's signed, 'Victor.' "

He departed less than an hour later. The Learjet had been on the ready line since he had returned from Budapest, fuel tanks regularly topped-off and flight-plan logged. His suitcase had been packed for seventy-two days, waiting beside the door, visas and passport current, and handily stored in an inner pocket. When he departed, the apartment continued to tremble for some time with the echoes of his leaving.

The flight seemed endless, interminable, he *knew* it was taking longer than necessary.

Customs, even with high government clearances (all masterpieces of forgery) and bribes, seemed to be drawn out sadistically by the mustachioed trio of petty officials; secure, and reveling in their momentary power.

The overland facilities could not merely be called slow. They were reminiscent of the Molasses Man who cannot run till he's warmed-up and who, when he's warmed-up, grows too soft to run.

Expectedly, like the most suspenseful chapter of a cheap gothic novel, a fierce electrical storm suddenly erupted out of the mountains when the ancient touring car was within a few miles of Talbot's destination. It rose up through the steep mountain pass, hurtling out of the sky, black as a grave, and swept across the road obscuring everything.

The driver, a taciturn man whose accent had marked him as a Serbian, held the big saloon to the center of the road with the tenacity of a rodeo rider, hands at ten till and ten after midnight on the wheel.

"Mister Talbot."

"Yes?"

"It grows worse. Will I turn back?"

"How much farther?"

"Perhaps seven kilometer."

Headlights caught the moment of uprootment as a small tree by the roadside toppled toward them. The driver spun the wheel and accelerated. They rushed past as naked branches scraped across the boot of the touring car with the sound of fingernails on a blackboard. Talbot found he had been holding his breath. Death was beyond him, but the menace of the moment denied the knowledge.

"I have to get there."

"Then I go on. Be at ease."

Talbot settled back. He could see the Serb smiling in the rearview mirror. Secure, he stared out the window. Branches of lightning shattered the darkness, causing the surrounding landscape to assume ominous, unsettling shapes.

Finally, he arrived.

The laboratory, an incongruous modernistic cube—bone white against the—again—ominous basalt of the looming prominences—sat high above the rutted road. They had been climbing steadily for hours and now, like carnivores waiting for the most opportune moment, the Carpathians loomed all around them.

The driver negotiated the final mile and a half up the access road to the laboratory with difficulty: tides of dark, topsoil-and-twig-laden water rushed past them.

Victor was waiting for him. Without extended greetings he had an associate take the suitcase, and he hurried Talbot to the sub-ground-floor theater where a half dozen technicians moved quickly at their tasks, plying between enormous banks of controls and a huge glass plate hanging suspended from guy-wires beneath the track-laden ceiling.

The mood was one of highly charged expectancy; Talbot could feel it in the sharp, short glances the technicians threw him, in the way Victor steered him by the arm, in the uncanny racehorse readiness of the peculiar-looking machines around which the men and women swarmed. And he sensed in Victor's manner that something new and wonderful was about to be born in this laboratory. That perhaps . . . at last . . . after so terribly, lightlessly long . . . peace waited for him in this white-tiled room. Victor was fairly bursting to talk.

"Final adjustments," he said, indicating two female technicians working at a pair of similar machines mounted opposite each other on the walls facing the glass plate. To Talbot, they looked like laser projectors of a highly complex design. The women were tracking them slowly left and right on their gimbals, accompanied by soft electrical humming. Victor let Talbot study them for a long moment, then said, "Not lasers. *Grasers*. Gamma Ray Amplification by Stimulated Emission of Radiation. Pay attention to them, they're at least half the heart of the answer to your problem."

The technicians took sightings across the room, through the glass, and nodded at one another. Then the older of the two, a woman in her fifties, called to Victor.

"On line, Doctor."

Victor waved acknowledgment, and turned back to Talbot. "We'd have been ready sooner, but this damned storm. It's been going on for a week. It wouldn't have hampered us but we had a freak lightning strike on our main transformer. The power supply was on emergency for several days and it's taken a while to get everything up to peak strength again."

A door opened in the wall of the gallery to Talbot's right. It opened slowly, as though it was heavy and the strength needed to force it was lacking. The yellow baked enamel plate on the door said, in heavy black letters, in French, PERSONNEL MONITORING DEVICES ARE REQUIRED BEYOND THIS ENTRANCE. The door swung fully open, at last, and Talbot saw the warning plate on the other side:

CAUTION
RADIATION
AREA

There was a three-armed, triangular-shaped design beneath the words. He thought of the Father, the Son, and the Holy Ghost. For no rational reason.

Then he saw the sign beneath, and had his rational reason: OPENING THIS DOOR FOR MORE THAN 30 SECONDS WILL REQUIRE A SEARCH AND SECURE.

Talbot's attention was divided between the doorway and what Victor had said. "You seem worried about the storm."

"Not worried," Victor said, "just cautious. There's no conceivable way it could interfere with the experiment, unless we had another direct hit, which I doubt—we've taken special precautions—but I wouldn't want to risk the power going out in the middle of the shot."

"The shot?"

"I'll explain all that. In fact, I *have* to explain it, so your mite will have the knowledge." Victor smiled at Talbot's confusion. "Don't worry about it." An old woman in a lab smock had come through the door and now stood just behind and to the right of Talbot, waiting, clearly, for their conversation to end so she could speak to Victor.

Victor turned his eyes to her. "Yes, Nadja?"

Talbot looked at her. An acid rain began falling in his stomach.

"Yesterday considerable effort was directed toward finding the cause of a high field horizontal instability," she said, speaking softly, tonelessly, a page of some specific status report. "The attendant beam blowup prevented efficient extraction." Eighty, if a day. Gray eyes sunk deep in folds of crinkled flesh the color of liver paste. "During the afternoon the accelerator was shut down to effect several repairs." Withered, weary, bent, too many bones for the sack. "The super pinger at C48 was replaced with a section of vacuum chamber; it had a vacuum leak." Talbot was in extreme pain. Memories came at him in ravening hordes, a dark wave of ant bodies gnawing at everything soft and folded and vulnerable in his brain. "Two hours of beam time were lost during the owl shift because a solenoid failed on a new vacuum valve in the transfer hall."

"Mother . . . ?" Talbot said, whispering hoarsely.

The old woman started violently, her head coming around and her eyes of settled ashes widening. "Victor," she said, terror in the word.

Talbot barely moved, but Victor took him by the arm and held him. "Thank you, Nadja; go down to target station B and log the secondary beams. Go right now."

She moved past them, hobbling, and quickly vanished through another door in the far wall, held open for her by one of the younger women.

Talbot watched her go, tears in his eyes.

"Oh my God, Victor. It was . . ."

"No, Larry, it wasn't."

"It was. So help me God it *was!* But *how,* Victor, tell me *how?*"

Victor turned him and lifted his chin with his free hand. "Look at me, Larry. *Damn it,* I said *look at me:* it wasn't. You're wrong."

The last time Lawrence Talbot had cried had been the morning he had awakened from sleep, lying under hydrangea shrubs in the botanical garden next to the Minneapolis Museum of Art, lying beside something bloody and still. Under his fingernails had been caked flesh and dirt and blood. That had been the time he learned about manacles and releasing oneself from them when in one state of consciousness, but not in another. Now, he felt like crying. Again. With cause.

"Wait here a moment," Victor said. "Larry? Will you wait right here for me? I'll be back in a moment."

He nodded, averting his face, and Victor went away. While he stood there, waves of painful memory thundering through him, a door slid open into the wall at the far side of the chamber, and another white-smocked technician stuck his head into the room. Through the opening, Talbot could see massive machinery in an enormous chamber beyond. Titanium electrodes. Stainless steel cones. He thought he recognized it: a Cockroft-Walton pre-accelerator.

Victor came back with a glass of milky liquid. He handed it to Talbot.

"Victor—" the technician called from the far doorway.

"Drink it," Victor said to Talbot, then turned to the technician.

"Ready to run."

Victor waved to him. "Give me about ten minutes, Karl, then take it up to the first phase shift and signal us." The technician nodded understanding and vanished through the doorway; the door slid out of the wall and closed, hiding the imposing chamberful of equipment. "And that was part of the other half of the mystical, magical solution of your problem," the physicist said, smiling now like a proud father.

"What was that I drank?"

"Something to stabilize you. I can't have you hallucinating."

"I wasn't hallucinating. What was her name?"

"Nadja. You're wrong; you've never seen her before in your life. Have I ever lied to you? How far back do we know each other? I need your trust if this is going to go all the way."

"I'll be all right." The milky liquid had already begun to work. Talbot's face lost its flush, his hands ceased trembling.

Victor was very stern suddenly, a scientist without the time for sidetracks; there was information to be imparted. "Good. For a moment I thought I'd spent a great deal of time preparing . . . well," and he smiled again, quickly, "let me put it this way: I thought for a moment no one was coming to my party."

Talbot gave a strained, tiny chuckle, and followed Victor to a bank of television monitors set into rolling frame-stacks in a corner. "Okay. Let's get you briefed." He turned on sets, one after another, till all twelve were glowing, each one holding a scene of dull-finished and massive installations.

Monitor ;1 showed an endlessly long underground tunnel painted eggshell white. Talbot had spent much of his two-month wait reading; he recognized the tunnel as a view down the "straightaway" of the main ring. Gigantic bending magnets in their shock-proof concrete cradles glowed faintly in the dim light of the tunnel.

Monitor ;2 showed the linac tunnel.

Monitor ;3 showed the rectifier stack of the Cockroft-Walton pre-accelerator.

Monitor #4 was a view of the booster. Monitor #5 showed the interior of the transfer hall. Monitors #6 through #9 revealed three experimental target areas and, smaller in scope and size, an internal target area supporting the meson, neutrino and proton areas.

The remaining three monitors showed research areas in the underground lab complex, the final one of which was the main hall itself, where Talbot stood looking into twelve monitors, in the twelfth screen of which could be seen Talbot standing looking into twelve . . .

Victor turned off the sets.

"What did you see?"

All Talbot could think of was the old woman called Nadja. It *couldn't* be. "Larry! What did you see?"

"From what I could see," Talbot said, "that looked to be a particle accelerator. And it looked as big as CERN's proton synchrotron in Geneva."

Victor was impressed. "You've been doing some reading."

"It behooved me."

"Well, well. Let's see if I can impress *you*. CERN's accelerator reaches energies up to 33 BeV; the ring underneath this room reaches energies of 15 GeV."

"Giga meaning billion."

"You *have* been reading up, haven't you! Fifteen *billion* electron volts. There's simply no keeping secrets from you, is there, Larry?"

"Only one."

Victor waited expectantly.

"Can you do it?"

"Yes. Meteorology says the eye is almost passing over us. We'll have better than an hour, more than enough time for the dangerous parts of the experiment."

"But you *can* do it."

"Yes, Larry. I don't like having to say it twice." There was no hesitancy in his voice, none of the "yes but" equivocations he'd always heard before. Victor had found the trail.

"I'm sorry, Victor. Anxiety. But if we're ready, why do I have to go through an indoctrination?"

Victor grinned wryly and began reciting, "As your Wizard, I am about to embark on a hazardous and technically unexplainable journey to the upper stratosphere. To confer, converse, and otherwise hobnob with my fellow wizards."

Talbot threw up his hands. "No more."

"Okay, then. Pay attention. If I didn't have to, I wouldn't; believe me, nothing is more boring than listening to the sound of my own lectures. But your mite has to have all the data *you* have. So listen. Now comes the boring—but incredibly informative—explanation."

▼▼▼

Western Europe's CERN—*Counseil Européen pour la Recherche Nucléaire*—had settled on Geneva as the site for their Big Machine. Holland lost out on the rich plum because it was common knowledge the food was lousy in the Lowlands. A small matter, but a significant one.

The Eastern Bloc's CEERN—*Conseil de l'Europe de l'Est pour la Recherche Nucléaire*—had been forced into selecting this isolated location high in the White Carpathians (over such likelier and more hospitable sites as Cluj in Rumania, Budapest in Hungary and Gdańsk in Poland) because Talbot's friend Victor had selected this site. CERN had had Dahl and Wideroë and Goward and Adams and Reich; CEERN had Victor. It balanced. He could call the tune.

So the laboratory had been painstakingly built to his specifications, and the particle accelerator dwarfed the CERN Machine. It dwarfed the four-mile ring at the Fermi National Accelerator Lab in Batavia, Illinois. It was, in fact, the world's largest, most advanced "synchrophasotron."

Only seventy per cent of the experiments conducted in the underground laboratory were devoted to projects sponsored by CEERN. One hundred per cent of the staff of Victor's complex was personally committed to him, not to CEERN, not to the Eastern Bloc, not to philosophies or dogmas . . . to the man. So thirty per cent of the experiments run on the sixteen-mile-diameter accelerator ring were Victor's own. If CEERN knew—and it would have been difficult for them to find out—it said nothing. Seventy per cent of the fruits of genius was better than no per cent.

Had Talbot known earlier that Victor's research was thrust in the direction of actualizing advanced theoretical breakthroughs in the nature of the structure of fundamental particles, he would never have wasted his time with the pseudos and dead-enders who had spent years on his problem, who had promised everything and delivered nothing but dust. But then, until Information Associates had marked the trail—a trail he had previously followed in every direction but the unexpected one that merged shadow with substance, reality with fantasy—until then, he had no need for Victor's exotic talents.

While CEERN basked in the warmth of secure knowledge that their resident genius was keeping them in front in the Super Accelerator Sweepstakes, Victor was briefing his oldest friend on the manner in which he would gift him with the peace of death; the manner in which Lawrence Talbot would find his soul; the manner in which he would precisely and exactly go inside his own body.

"The answer to your problem is in two parts. First, we have to create a perfect simulacrum of you, a hundred thousand or a million times smaller than you, the original. Then, second, we have to *actualize* it, turn an image into something corporeal, substantial, material; something that *exists*. A miniature *you* with all the reality you possess, all the memories, all the knowledge."

Talbot felt very mellow. The milky liquid had smoothed out the churning waters of his memory. He smiled. "I'm glad it wasn't a difficult problem."

Victor looked rueful. "Next week I invent the steam engine. Get serious, Larry."

"It's that Lethe cocktail you fed me."

Victor's mouth tightened and Talbot knew he had to get hold of himself. "Go on, I'm sorry."

Victor hesitated a moment, securing his position of seriousness with a touch of free-floating guilt, then went on, "The first part of the problem is solved by using the grasers we've developed. We'll shoot a hologram of you, using a wave generated not from the electrons of the atom, but from the nucleus . . . a wave a million times shorter, greater in resolution than that from a laser." He walked toward the large glass plate hanging in the middle of the lab, grasers trained on its center. "Come here."

Talbot followed him.

"Is this the holographic plate," he said, "it's just a sheet of photographic glass, isn't it?"

"Not this," Victor said, touching the ten-foot square plate, "*this!*" He put his finger on a spot in the center of the glass and Talbot leaned in to look. He saw nothing at first, then detected a faint ripple; and when he put his face as close as possible to the imperfection he perceived a light *moiré* pattern, like the surface of a fine silk scarf. He looked back at Victor.

"Microholographic plate," Victor said. "Smaller than an integrated chip. That's where we capture your spirit, white-eyes, a million times reduced. About the size of a single cell, maybe a red corpuscle."

Talbot giggled.

"Come on," Victor said wearily. "You've had too much to drink, and it's my fault. Let's get this show on the road. You'll be straight by the time we're ready . . . I just hope to God your mite isn't cockeyed."

▼▼▼

Naked, they stood him in front of the ground photographic plate. The older of the female technicians aimed the graser at him, there was a soft sound Talbot took to be some mechanism locking into position, and then Victor said, "All right, Larry, that's it."

He stared at them, expecting more.

"That's it?"

The technicians seemed very pleased, and amused at his reaction. "All done," said Victor. It had been that quick. He hadn't even seen the graser wave hit and lock in his image. "That's *it?*" he said again. Victor began to laugh. It spread through the lab. The technicians were clinging to their equipment; tears rolled down Victor's cheeks; everyone gasped for breath; and Talbot stood in front of the minute imperfection in the glass and felt like a retard.

"That's it?" he said again, helplessly.

After a long time, they dried their eyes and Victor moved him away from the huge plate of glass. "All done, Larry, and ready to go. Are you cold?"

Talbot's naked flesh was evenly polka-dotted with goosebumps. One of the technicians brought him a smock to wear. He stood and watched. Clearly, he was no longer the center of attention.

Now the alternate graser and the holographic plate ripple in the glass were the focuses of attention. Now the mood of released tension was past and the lines of serious attention were back in the faces of the lab staff. Now Victor was wearing an intercom headset, and Talbot heard him say, "All right, Karl. Bring it up to full power."

Almost instantly the lab was filled with the sound of generators phasing up. It became painful and Talbot felt his teeth begin to ache. It went up and up, a whine that climbed till it was beyond his hearing.

Victor made a hand signal to the younger female technician

at the graser behind the glass plate. She bent to the projector's sighting mechanism once, quickly, then cut it in. Talbot saw no light beam, but there was the same locking sound he had heard earlier, and then a soft humming, and a life-size hologram of himself, standing naked as he had been a few moments before, trembled in the air where he had stood. He looked at Victor questioningly. Victor nodded, and Talbot walked to the phantasm, passed his hand through it, stood close and looked into the clear brown eyes, noted the wide pore patterns in the nose, studied himself more closely than he had ever been able to do in a mirror. He felt: as if someone had walked over his grave.

Victor was talking to three male technicians, and a moment later they came to examine the hologram. They moved in with light meters and sensitive instruments that apparently were capable of gauging the sophistication and clarity of the ghost image. Talbot watched, fascinated and terrified. It seemed he was about to embark on the great journey of his life; a journey with a much desired destination: surcease.

One of the technicians signaled Victor.

"It's pure," he said to Talbot. Then, to the younger female technician on the second graser projector, "All right, Jana, move it out of there." She started up an engine and the entire projector apparatus turned on heavy rubber wheels and rolled out of the way. The image of Talbot, naked and vulnerable, a little sad to Talbot as he watched it fade and vanish like morning mist, had disappeared when the technician turned off the projector.

"All right, Karl," Victor was saying, "we're moving the pedestal in now. Narrow the aperture, and wait for my signal." Then, to Talbot, "Here comes your mite, old friend."

Talbot felt a sense of resurrection.

The older female technician rolled a four-foot-high stainless steel pedestal to the center of the lab, positioned it so the tiny, highly-polished spindle atop the pedestal touched the very bottom of the faint ripple in the glass. It looked like, and was, an actualizing stage for the real test. The full-sized hologram had been a gross test to ensure the image's perfection. Now came the creation of a living entity, a Lawrence Talbot, naked and the size of a single cell, possessing a consciousness and intelligence and memories and desires identical to Talbot's own.

"Ready, Karl?" Victor was saying.

Talbot heard no reply, but Victor nodded his head as if listening. Then he said, "All right, extract the beam!"

It happened so fast, Talbot missed most of it.

The micropion beam was composed of particles a million times smaller than the proton, smaller than the quark, smaller than the muon or the pion. Victor had termed them micropions. The slit opened in the wall, the beam was diverted, passed through the holographic ripple and was cut off as the slit closed again.

It had all taken a billionth of a second.

"Done," Victor said.

"I don't see anything," Talbot said, and realized how silly he must sound to these people. Of *course* he didn't see anything. There was nothing to see . . . with the naked eye. "Is he . . . is it there?"

"You're there," Victor said. He waved to one of the male technicians standing at a wall hutch of instruments in protective bays, and the man hurried over with the slim, reflective barrel of a microscope. He clipped it onto the tiny needle-pointed stand atop the pedestal in a fashion Talbot could not quite follow. Then he stepped away, and Victor said, "Part two of your problem solved, Larry. Go look and see yourself."

Lawrence Talbot went to the microscope, adjusted the knob till he could see the reflective surface of the spindle, and saw himself in infinitely reduced perfection

staring up at himself. He recognized himself, though all he could see was a cyclopean

brown eye staring down from the smooth glass satellite that dominated his sky.

He waved. The eye blinked.

Now it begins, he thought.

▼▼▼

Lawrence Talbot stood at the lip of the huge crater that formed
Lawrence Talbot's navel. He looked down in the bottomless pit
with its atrophied remnants of umbilicus forming loops and protu-
berances, smooth and undulant and vanishing into utter darkness.
He stood poised to descend and smelled the smells of his own
body. First, sweat. Then the smells that wafted up from within.
The smell of penicillin like biting down on tin foil with a bad
tooth. The smell of aspirin, chalky and tickling the hairs of his
nose like cleaning blackboard erasers by banging them together.
The smells of rotted food, digested and turning to waste. All the
odors rising up out of himself like a wild symphony of dark colors.

He sat down on the rounded rim of the navel and let himself
slip forward.

He slid down, rode over an outcropping, dropped a few feet
and slid again, tobogganing into darkness. He fell for only a short
time, then brought up against the soft and yielding, faintly springy
tissue plane where the umbilicus had been ligated. The darkness
at the bottom of the hole suddenly shattered as blinding light
filled the navel. Shielding his eyes, Talbot looked up the shaft
toward the sky. A sun glowed there, brighter than a thousand
novae. Victor had moved a surgical lamp over the hole to assist
him. For as long as he could.

Talbot saw the umbra of something large moving behind the
light, and he strained to discern what it was: it seemed important
to know what it was. And for an instant, before his eyes closed
against the glare, he thought he knew what it had been. Someone
watching him, staring down past the surgical lamp that hung

above the naked, anesthetized body of Lawrence Talbot, asleep on an operating table.

It had been the old woman, Nadja.

He stood unmoving for a long time, thinking of her.

Then he went to his knees and felt the tissue plane that formed the floor of the navel shaft.

He thought he could see something moving beneath the surface, like water flowing under a film of ice. He went down onto his stomach and cupped his hands around his eyes, putting his face against the dead flesh. It was like looking through a pane of isinglass. A trembling membrane through which he could see the collapsed lumen of the atretic umbilical vein. There was no opening. He pressed his palms against the rubbery surface and it gave, but only slightly. Before he could find the treasure, he had to follow the route of Demeter's map—now firmly and forever consigned to memory—and before he could set foot upon that route, he had to gain access to his own body.

But he had nothing with which to force that entrance.

Excluded, standing at the portal to his own body, Lawrence Talbot felt anger rising within him. His life had been anguish and guilt and horror, had been the wasted result of events over which he had had no control. Pentagrams and full moons and blood and never putting on even an ounce of fat because of a diet high in protein, blood steroids healthier than any normal adult male's, triglycerol and cholesterol levels balanced and humming. And death forever a stranger. Anger flooded through him. He heard an inarticulate little moan of pain, and fell forward, began tearing at the atrophied cord with teeth that had been used for just such activity many times before. Through a blood haze he knew he was savaging his own body, and it seemed exactly the appropriate act of self-flagellation.

An outsider; he had been an outsider all his adult life, and fury would permit him to be shut out no longer. With demonic purpose he ripped away at the clumps of flesh until the membrane gave, at last, and a gap was torn through, opening him to himself. . . .

And he was blinded by the explosion of light, by the rush of wind, by the passage of something that had been just beneath the surface writhing to be set free, and in the instant before he plummeted into unconsciousness, he knew Castañeda's Don Juan had told the truth: a thick bundle of white cobwebby filaments, tinged with gold, fibers of light, shot free from the collapsed vein, rose up through the shaft and trembled toward the antiseptic sky.

A metaphysical, otherwise invisible beanstalk that trailed away above him, rising up and up and up as his eyes closed and he sank away into oblivion.

▼▼▼

He was on his stomach, crawling through the collapsed lumen, the center, of the path the veins had taken back from the amniotic sac to the fetus. Propelling himself forward the way an infantry scout would through dangerous terrain, using elbows and knees, frog-crawling, he opened the flattened tunnel with his head just enough to get through. It was quite light, the interior of the world called Lawrence Talbot suffused with a golden luminescence.

The map had routed him out of this pressed tunnel through the inferior vena cava to the right atrium and thence through the right ventricle, the pulmonary arteries, through the valves, to the lungs, the pulmonary veins, crossover to the left side of the heart (left atrium, left ventricle), the aorta—bypassing the three coronary arteries above the aortic valves—and down over the arch of the aorta—bypassing the carotid and other arteries—to the celiac trunk, where the arteries split in a confusing array: the gastroduodenal to the stomach, the hepatic to the liver, the splenic to the spleen. And there, dorsal to the body of the diaphragm, he would drop down past the greater pancreatic duct to the pancreas itself. And there, among the islets of Langerhans, he would find, at the coordinates Information Associates had given him, he would find that which had been stolen from him one full-mooned night of horror so very long ago. And having found it, having assured himself of eternal sleep, not merely physical death from a silver bullet, he would stop his heart—how, he did not know, but he would—and it would all be ended for Lawrence Talbot, who had become what he had beheld. There, in the tail of the pancreas, supplied with blood by the splenic artery, lay the greatest treasure of all. More than doubloons, more than spices and silks, more than oil lamps used as djinn prisons by Solomon, lay final and sweet eternal peace, a release from monsterdom.

He pushed the final few feet of dead vein apart, and his head emerged into open space. He was hanging upside-down in a cave of deep orange rock.

Talbot wriggled his arms loose, braced them against what was clearly the ceiling of the cave, and wrenched his body out of the tunnel. He fell heavily, trying to twist at the last moment to catch the impact on his shoulders, and received a nasty blow on the side of the neck for his trouble.

He lay there for a moment, clearing his head. Then he stood and walked forward. The cave opened onto a ledge, and he walked out and stared at the landscape before him. The skeleton of something only faintly human lay tortuously crumpled against the wall of the cliff. He was afraid to look at it very closely.

He stared off across the world of dead orange rock, folded and rippled like a topographical view across the frontal lobe of a brain removed from its cranial casing.

The sky was a light yellow, bright and pleasant.

The grand canyon of his body was a seemingly horizonless tumble of atrophied rock, dead for millennia. He sought out and found a descent from the ledge, and began the trek.

▼▼▼

There was water, and it kept him alive. Apparently, it rained more frequently here in this parched and stunned wasteland than appearance indicated. There was no keeping track of days or months, for there was no night and no day—always the same even, wonderful golden luminescence—but Talbot felt his passage down the central spine of orange mountains had taken him almost six months. And in that time it had rained forty-eight times, or roughly twice a week. Baptismal fonts of water were filled at every downpour, and he found if he kept the soles of his naked feet moist, he could walk without his energy flagging. If he ate, he did not remember how often, or what form the food had taken.

He saw no other signs of life.

Save an occasional skeleton lying against a shadowed wall of orange rock. Often, they had no skulls.

He found a pass through the mountains, finally, and crossed. He went up through foothills into lower, gentle slopes, and then up again, into cruel and narrow passages that wound higher and higher toward the heat of the sky. When he reached the summit, he found the path down the opposite side was straight and wide and easy. He descended quickly; only a matter of days, it seemed.

Descending into the valley, he heard the song of a bird. He followed the sound. It led him to a crater of igneous rock, quite large, set low among the grassy swells of the valley. He came upon it without warning, and trudged up its short incline, to stand at the volcanic lip looking down.

The crater had become a lake. The smell rose up to assault him. Vile, and somehow terribly sad. The song of the bird continued; he could see no bird anywhere in the golden sky. The smell of the lake made him ill.

Then as he sat on the edge of the crater, staring down, he realized the lake was filled with dead things, floating bellyup; purple and blue as a strangled baby, rotting white, turning slowly in the faintly rippled gray water; without features or limbs. He went down to the lowest outthrust of volcanic rock and stared at the dead things.

Something swam toward him. He moved back. It came on

faster and as it neared the wall of the crater, it surfaced, singing its bluejay song, swerved to rip a chunk of rotting flesh from the corpse of a floating dead thing, and paused only a moment as if to remind him that this was not his, Talbot's, domain, but his own.

Like Talbot, the fish would not die.

Talbot sat at the lip of the crater for a long time, looking down into the bowl that held the lake, and he watched the corpses of dead dreams as they bobbed and revolved like maggoty pork in a gray soup.

After a time, he rose, walked back down from the mouth of the crater, and resumed his journey. He was crying.

▼▼▼

When at last he reached the shore of the pancreatic sea, he found a great many things he had lost or given away when he was a child. He found a wooden machine gun on a tripod, painted olive drab, that made a rat-tat-tatting sound when a wooden handle was cranked. He found a set of toy soldiers, two companies, one Prussian and the other French, with a miniature Napoleon Bonaparte among them. He found a microscope kit with slides and petri dishes and racks of chemicals in nice little bottles, all of which bore uniform labels. He found a milk bottle filled with Indianhead pennies. He found a hand puppet with the head of a monkey and the name *Rosco* painted on the fabric glove with nail polish. He found a pedometer. He found a beautiful painting of a jungle bird that had been done with real feathers. He found a corncob pipe. He found a box of radio premiums: a cardboard detective kit with fingerprint dusting powder, invisible ink and a list of police-band call codes; a ring with what seemed to be a plastic bomb attached, and when he pulled the red finned rear off the bomb, and cupped his hands around it in his palms, he could see little scintillas of light, deep inside the payload section; a china mug with a little girl and a dog running across one side; a decoding badge with a burning glass in the center of the red plastic dial.

But there was something missing.

He could not remember what it was, but he knew it was important. As he had known it was important to recognize the shadowy figure who had moved past the surgical lamp at the top of the navel shaft, he knew whatever item was missing from this cache . . . was very important.

He took the boat anchored beside the pancreatic sea, and put all the items from the cache in the bottom of a watertight box under one of the seats. He kept out the large, cathedral-shaped radio, and put it on the bench seat in front of the oarlocks.

Then he unbeached the boat, and ran it out into the crimson water, staining his ankles and calves and thighs, and climbed aboard, and started rowing across toward the islets. Whatever was missing was very important.

▼▼▼

The wind died when the islets were barely in sight on the horizon. Looking out across the blood-red sea, Talbot sat becalmed at latitude 38° 54′ N, longitude 77° 00′ 13″ W.

He drank from the sea and was nauseated. He played with the toys in the watertight box. And he listened to the radio.

He listened to a program about a very fat man who solved murders, to an adaptation of *The Woman in the Window* with Edward G. Robinson and Joan Bennett, to a story that began in a great railroad station, to a mystery about a wealthy man who could make himself invisible by clouding the minds of others so they could not see him, and he enjoyed a suspense drama narrated by a man named Ernest Chapell in which a group of people descended in a bathyscaphe through the bottom of a mine shaft where, five miles down, they were attacked by pterodactyls. Then he listened to the news, broadcast by Graham MacNamee.

Among the human interest items at the close of the program, Talbot heard the unforgettable MacNamee voice say:

"Datelined Columbus, Ohio; September 24th, 1973. Martha Nelson had been in an institution for the mentally retarded for 98 years. She is 102 years old and was first sent to Orient State Institute near Orient, Ohio, on June 25th, 1875. Her records were destroyed in a fire in the institution sometime in 1883, and no one knows for certain why she is at the institute. At the time she was committed it was known as the Columbus State Institute for the Feeble-Minded. 'She never had a chance,' said Dr. A. Z. Soforenko, appointed two months ago as superintendent of the institution. He said she was probably a victim of 'eugenic alarm,' which he said was common in the late 1800s. At that time some felt that because humans were made 'in God's image' the retarded must be evil or children of the devil, because they were not whole human beings. 'During that time,' Dr. Soforenko said, 'it was believed if you moved feeble-minded people out of a community and into an institution, the taint would never return to the community.' He went on to add, 'She was apparently trapped in that system of thought. No one can ever be sure if she actually *was* feeble-minded; it is a wasted life. She is quite coherent for her age. She has no known relatives and has had no contact with anybody but Institution staff for the last 78 or 80 years.' "

Talbot sat silently in the small boat, the sail hanging like a forlorn ornament from its single centerpole.

"I've cried more since I got inside you, Talbot, than I have in my whole life," he said, but could not stop. Thoughts of Martha Nelson a woman of whom he had never before heard, of whom he would *never* have heard had it not been by chance by chance by chance he had heard by chance, by chance thoughts of her skirled through his mind like cold winds.

And the cold winds rose, and the sail filled, and he was no longer adrift, but was driven straight for the shore of the nearest islet. By chance.

▼▼▼

He stood over the spot where Demeter's map had indicated he would find his soul. For a wild moment he chuckled, at the realization he had been expecting an enormous Maltese Cross or Captain Kidd's "X" to mark the location. But it was only soft green sand, gentle as talc, blowing in dust-devils toward the blood-red pancreatic sea. The spot was midway between the low-tide line and the enormous Bedlam-like structure that dominated the islet.

He looked once more, uneasily, at the fortress rising in the center of the tiny blemish of land. It was built square, seemingly carved from a single monstrous black rock . . . perhaps from a cliff that had been thrust up during some natural disaster. It had no windows, no opening he could see, though two sides of its bulk were exposed to his view. It troubled him. It was a dark god presiding over an empty kingdom. He thought of the fish that would not die, and remembered Nietzsche's contention that gods died when they lost their supplicants.

He dropped to his knees and, recalling the moment months before when he had dropped to his knees to tear at the flesh of his atrophied umbilical cord, he began digging in the green and powdery sand.

The more he dug, the faster the sand ran back into the shallow bowl. He stepped into the middle of the depression and began slinging dirt back between his legs with both hands, a human dog excavating for a bone.

When his fingertips encountered the edge of the box, he yelped with pain as his nails broke.

He dug around the outline of the box, and then forced his bleeding fingers down through the sand to gain purchase under the buried shape. He wrenched at it, and it came loose. Heaving with tensed muscles, he freed it, and it came up.

He took it to the edge of the beach and sat down.

It was just a box. A plain wooden box, very much like an old cigar box, but larger. He turned it over and over and was not at all surprised to find it bore no arcane hieroglyphics or occult symbols. It wasn't that kind of treasure. Then he turned it right side up and pried open the lid. His soul was inside. It was not what he had expected to find, not at all. But it *was* what had been missing from the cache.

Holding it tightly in his fist, he walked up past the fast-filling hole in the green sand, toward the bastion on the high ground.

> We shall not cease from exploration
> And the end of all our exploring
> Will be to arrive where we started
> And know the place for the first time.
> —T. S. Eliot

Once inside the brooding darkness of the fortress—and finding the entrance had been disturbingly easier than he had expected—there was no way to go but down. The wet, black stones of the switchback stairways led inexorably downward into the bowels of the structure, clearly far beneath the level of the pancreatic sea. The stairs were steep, and each step had been worn into smooth curves by the pressure of feet that had descended this way since the dawn of memory. It was dark, but not so dark that Talbot could not see his way. There was no light, however. He did not care to think about how that could be.

When he came to the deepest part of the structure, having passed no rooms or chambers or openings along the way, he saw a doorway across an enormous hall, set into the far wall. He stepped off the last of the stairs, and walked to the door. It was built of crossed iron bars, as black and moist as the stones of the bastion. Through the interstices he saw something pale and still in a far corner of what could have been a cell.

There was no lock on the door.

It swung open at his touch.

Whoever lived in this cell had never tried to open the door; or had tried and decided not to leave.

He moved into deeper darkness.

A long time of silence passed, and finally he stooped to help her to her feet. It was like lifting a sack of dead flowers, brittle and surrounded by dead air incapable of holding even the memory of fragrance.

He took her in his arms and carried her.

"Close your eyes against the light, Martha," he said, and started back up the long stairway to the golden sky.

▼▼▼

Lawrence Talbot sat up on the operating table. He opened his eyes and looked at Victor. He smiled a peculiarly gentle smile. For the first time since they had been friends, Victor saw all torment cleansed from Talbot's face.

"It went well," he said. Talbot nodded.

They grinned at each other.

"How're your cryonic facilities?" Talbot asked.

Victor's brows drew down in bemusement. "You want me to freeze you? I thought you'd want something more permanent . . . say, in silver."

"Not necessary."

Talbot looked around. He saw her standing against the far wall by one of the grasers. She looked back at him with open fear. He slid off the table, wrapping the sheet upon which he had rested around himself, a makeshift toga. It gave him a patrician look.

He went to her and looked down into her ancient face. "Nadja," he said, softly. After a long moment she looked up at him. He smiled and for an instant she was a girl again. She averted her gaze. He took her hand, and she came with him, to the table, to Victor.

"I'd be deeply grateful for a running account, Larry," the physicist said. So Talbot told him; all of it.

"My mother, Nadja, Martha Nelson, they're all the same," Talbot said, when he came to the end, "all wasted lives."

"And what was in the box?" Victor said.

"How well do you do with symbolism and cosmic irony, old friend?"

"Thus far I'm doing well enough with Jung and Freud," Victor said. He could not help but smile.

Talbot held tightly to the old technician's hand as he said, "It was an old, rusted Howdy Doody button."

Victor turned around.

When he turned back, Talbot was grinning. "That's not cosmic irony, Larry . . . it's slapstick," Victor said. He was angry. It showed clearly.

Talbot said nothing, simply let him work it out.

Finally Victor said, "What the hell's *that* supposed to signify, innocence?"

Talbot shrugged. "I suppose if I'd known, I wouldn't have lost it in the first place. That's what it was, and that's what it is. A little metal pinback around an inch and a half in diameter, with that cockeyed face on it, the orange hair, the toothy grin, the pug nose, the freckles, all of it, just the way he always was." He fell silent, then after a moment added, "It seems right."

"And now that you have it back, you don't *want* to die?"

"I don't *need* to die."

"And you want me to freeze you."

"Both of us."

Victor stared at him with disbelief. "For God's sake, Larry!"

Nadja stood quietly, as if she could not hear them.

"Victor, listen: Martha Nelson is in there. A wasted life. Nadja is out here. I don't know why or how or what did it . . . but . . . a wasted life. Another wasted life. I want you to create her mite, the same way you created mine, and send her inside. He's waiting

▼ 45 ▼

for her and he can make it right, Victor. All right, at last. He can be with her as she regains the years that were stolen from her. He can be—*I* can be—her father when she's a baby, her playmate when she's a child, her buddy when she's maturing, her boyfriend when she's a young girl, her suitor when she's a young woman, her lover, her husband, her companion as she grows old. Let her be all the women she was never permitted to be, Victor. Don't steal from her a second time. And when it's over, it will start again. . . ."

"*How*, for Christ sake, how the hell *how*? Talk sense, Larry. What is all this metaphysical crap?"

"I don't *know* how; it just is! I've been there, Victor, I was there for months, maybe years, and I never changed, never went to the wolf, there's no Moon there . . . no night and no day, just golden light and warmth, and I can try to make restitution. I can give back two lives. *Please*, Victor!"

The physicist looked at him without speaking. Then he looked at the old woman. She smiled up at him, and then, with arthritic fingers, removed her clothing.

▼▼▼

When she came through the collapsed lumen, Talbot was waiting for her. She looked very tired, and he knew she would have to rest before they attempted to cross the orange mountains. He helped her down from the ceiling of the cave, and laid her down on soft, pale yellow moss he had carried back from the islets of Langerhans during the long trek with Martha Nelson. Side by side, the two old women lay on the moss, and Nadja fell asleep almost immediately. He stood over them, looking at their faces.

They were identical.

Then he went out on the ledge and stood looking toward the spine of the orange mountains. The skeleton held no fear for him now. He felt a sudden sharp chill in the air and knew Victor had begun the cryonic preservation.

He stood that way for a long time, the little metal button with the sly, innocent face of a mythical creature painted on its surface in four brilliant colors held tightly in his left hand.

And after a while, he heard the crying of a baby, just one baby, from inside the cave, and turned to return for the start of the easiest journey he had ever made.

Somewhere, a terrible devil-fish suddenly flattened its gills, turned slowly bellyup, and sank into darkness.

WOLF, IRON, AND MOTH
▼▼▼

PHILIP JOSÉ FARMER

LESS than Man, more than Wolf, he ran.

More than Man, less than Wolf, he ran howling with ecstasy through the forest.

He had no memory of being Man any more than he would remember being Wolf when he again became Man.

Whenever the storm clouds were torn apart briefly by the howling wind, the full July moon was revealed. It seemed to him, though vaguely, that his howling worked the magic that rent the clouds. But he had no conception of magic. He lacked words and The Word.

Lightning as white as cow fat crashed. Thunder like the death cry of a bull bellowed. Being Wolf, he did not think of these comparisons. The tips of the trees danced under the whiplash of the winds and seemed to him to be alive. He sensed that the thunder and lightning were the orgasms of Earth Herself locked in frenzy with the moon, though this feeling had no link to human thought and image. Being Wolf, he had no words to voice such feelings. Words could never image forth Wolf feelings.

He ran, and he ran.

Where a man would have seen trees, bushes, and boulders, he saw beings that had no names and were not connected or grouped by word or thought. They had in his mind no species or genus but were individuals.

The vegetation and the boulders he passed moved, changing shape slightly with each of his leaps, seeming to have their own life and mobility. Perhaps, they did. Wolf might know what Man could not know. Man knew what Wolf could not know. Though they occupied the same physical world, they lived in separate mental-emotional continuums.

A is A. Not-A is Not-A. Therefore, never the twain shall meet. Not in the world of the mind. But werewolves . . . what are they? A plus not-A makes B?

He ran, and he ran.

Rain came from nowhere; he did not know that it was from above. Its nature changed when it dashed against the ground and splashed on his fur and into his eyes and on his nose. Raindrops had become something else, just wetness. He had no name for wetness. Wetness was a live being. It veiled his sight and his sense of smell. But the wind had carried the scent of lightning-frightened cattle to him before the rain absorbed the thousands of billions of scent molecules whistling by.

He floated over a wire fence and was among the cattle. He did bloody work there. The half-deaf farmer and his half-deaf wife and their stoned sons in the house a hundred feet away did not hear the loud cries of cattle-terror. The thunder, lightning, and booming TV censored the noise from the pasture. The wolf ate undisturbed.

▼▼▼

"I've never seen a man gain weight so fast or lose it so fast," Sheriff Yeager said. "Seems to me it goes in a cycle too, regular as prune juice. You gain twenty or more pounds in a month.

Then, come full moon, you seem to lose it overnight. How do you do it? Why?"

"If questions were food, you'd be fat," Doctor Varglik said.

Throughout the physical examination, the sheriff's pale-blue but lively eyes had fixed on the huge wolf skin stretched across the opposite wall of the room. It lacked the legs and the head, but its bushy tail had not been cut off.

"It doesn't seem natural," Yeager said.

"What? The wolf skin? It's not artificial."

"No, I mean the incredibly rapid fluctuations in your weight. That's unnatural."

"Anything in Nature is natural."

The doctor removed the inflatable rubber cuff from Yeager's arm. "One twenty over eighty. Thirty-six years old, and you got a teenager's blood pressure. You can get off the table now. Drop your pants."

From a wall-dispenser, Varglik drew out a latex glove. The sheriff, unlike most men during this examination, did not groan, grimace, or complain. He was a stoic.

While he was bent over, he said, "Doctor, you still didn't answer my question."

The son of a bitch is getting suspicious, Varglik thought. Maybe he knows. But he must also think he's going bananas if he sincerely believes that what he's not so subtly hinting at is true.

He withdrew the finger. He said, "Everything checks out fine. Congratulations. The county'll be satisfied for another year."

"I don't want to be a nuisance or too nosey," Sheriff Yeager said. "Put it down to scientific curiosity. I asked you . . ."

"I don't know why I have such a phenomenally rapid weight loss and gain," Varglik said. "Never heard of a case like mine in a completely healthy man."

The wall mirror caught him and Yeager in its mercury light. Both were thirty-six, six feet two inches tall, lean, rangy, and weighed one hundred and eighty pounds. Both lived in Wagner (pop. 5000 except in tourist season), set along the south shore of Pristine Lake, Reynolds County, Arkansas. Yeager had an M.A. in Forest Rangery, but, after a few years, had become a policeman and then a sheriff. Varglik had an M.D. from Yale and a Ph.D. in biochemistry from Stanford. After a few years of practice in Manhattan, he had given up a brilliant and affluent career to come to this rural area.

Like most people who knew this, Yeager was wondering just why Varglik had left Park Avenue. The difference between Yeager and the others was that he would be checking out or had already checked out the doctor's past.

Despite their many similarities, they were worlds apart in one thing. Varglik was the hunted; Yeager, the hunter. Unless, Varglik thought, I can reverse the situation. But when did A and not-A ever exchange roles?

The doctor had removed the gloves and was washing his hands. The sheriff was standing in front of the wolf skin and looking intently at it.

"That's really something," he said. His expression was strange and undecipherable. "Where'd you shoot him?"

"I didn't," Varglik said. "It's a family heirloom, sort of. My Swedish grandfather passed it on down. My mother, she's Finnish, wanted to get rid of it, I don't know why, but my father, he was born in Sweden but raised in upper New York, wouldn't let her."

"I'd've thought you'd've put it up on the wall above the fireplace mantel in your house."

"Not many people'd see it there. Here, my patients can see it while I'm examining them. Makes a good converstational piece."

The sheriff whistled softly. "He must've weighed at least a hundred and eighty. Hell of a big wolf!"

The doctor smiled. "About as big as the wolf that's terrorizing the county. But what would a wolf be doing in the Ozarks? Hasn't been one here for fifty years or more."

Yeager turned slowly. He was smiling rather smugly and without any reason to do so. Unless . . . Varglik's heart suddenly beat harder. He should not have been so bold. Why had he mentioned the wolf? Why steer the conversation to it? But, then, why not?

"It's a wolf, all right! I don't know how in hell it got here, but it's not a dog!"

"O.K." Varglik said. "But it had better be caught soon! The cattle, sheep, and dogs are bad enough! But those two kids!" He shuddered. "Eaten up!"

"We'll get him, though he's damned elusive so far!" the sheriff said. "Tomorrow morning, most of the county police, thirty state troopers, and two hundred civilian volunteers will be beating the bush. We're not stopping until we flush him out!"

Yeager paused, glanced sideways at the skin, then turned his head to face Varglik. "The hunt won't stop, day or night, until we get him!"

"Even the tourists are getting afraid," Varglik said. "Bad for business."

The sheriff turned to the pelt again. "Are you sure it's not artificial and you're not putting me on?"

"Why?"

"I don't know for sure. A minute ago, while I was looking at it, it suddenly seemed to glow. I thought my eyes were playing tricks on me. It had, still has, a light, very dim but a definite glow. I . . ."

"Aha!"

Yeager jumped a little. He said, "Aha?"

Varglik was smiling as if he were trying to conceal something behind it. His mirror image showed that too plainly. He uncreased his face.

"Sorry. I was thinking of the results of an experiment I made recently in my lab. I suddenly saw the answer to something that's been puzzling me. I apologize for not giving you my complete attention. It's rude."

Yeager raised his eyebrows. He was as aware as the doctor that the explanation was dragging one leg far behind it. But he said nothing. He put on his Western hat and started toward the door. Hebe, Varglik's receptionist and nurse, appeared in the doorway.

"Phone call for you, Sheriff."

Yeager went into the front office. Varglik followed him to the office door and listened. Evidently, the wolf had gotten to Fred Benger's cattle last night and had killed four and crippled five. The Bengers had not heard anything, and the parents had not discovered the slaughter until they had returned from shopping in town. From Yeager's questions and his responses, Varglik deduced that the two sons were supposed to have put the cattle in the barn in the evening before milking them. But they had fallen asleep—passed out was closer to the truth—before the storm started. Old Man Benger's threats to kill his sons screamed from the phone. But he, like everybody in the county, knew that they were on drugs and were not to be trusted.

"I'll be right out," the sheriff said. "But don't tramp around the pasture and mess up the tracks."

He hung up and charged out of the office.

"The bastard knows!" Varglik muttered. "Or he thinks he knows. But he must also be suffering great doubt. He's very rational, not the least bit superstitious. He's struggling as much as I once did to believe this."

For years, both in his Manhattan office suite and in this Ozark office, the wolf skin had hung where his patients could see it and he could observe their reactions. Yaeger was the first to see its glow! The first to comment on it, anyway. Only one kind of person could see the light. His father would call the person *Kväl-lulf*. The Evening Wolf. His mother would name him *Ihmissusi*. Man-wolf.

He went into the reception room to tell Hebe that he was lunching in his office. Hebe was gone. At the stroke of twelve noon, she had fled, a daylight Cinderella running away from the ball, the answering machine turned on, waiting for her to come back at one. If he ate in, he was supposed to monitor incoming calls. Today, he would let the machine do the work.

In his private office, he sat down and opened a box containing three beef sandwiches, two orders of French fries, a monumental salad, three bottles of beer, and a jar of honey. A huge bite of sandwich in his mouth, he opened a brown-covered envelope that had come in today's mail. Hebe, following his orders, had set it aside unopened for him. She must be wondering, of course, what the envelope that came every four months contained. Probably thought it was some kinky sex magazine, *Hustler* or *Spicy Onanist Stories* or *The Necrophile Weekly* with an updated list of easily accessible mortuaries and a centerfold of this month's lovely female corpse.

The glossy-paper magazine he pulled out was WAW, a very limited-distribution publication. How had the editors of the Werewolf Association of the World known about him? His letter of inquiry to WAW had been answered with a cryptic note. *We have ways.* The magazine, though in English, was published and mailed from Helsinki, Finland. A small section was devoted to articles about the problems of Asiatic weretigers, African werecrocodiles, South American werejaguars, and Alaskan and Canadian werebears and mountain lions. One article on the extinction of the Japanese werefox concluded that overpopulation and pollution and the consequent loss of forest space had caused its demise. The last line of the article was grim. *The situation in Japan may soon be ours.*

Another writer, under the obviously false byline of Lon Chaney III, gave the results of his survey-by-mail of werewolf sex habits. The sampling showed that 38.3 percent of male and female lycanthropes were unconsciously influenced by their lupine phases. When in their human phase, they preferred that the female be on all fours and that the male use the rear approach. They also tended to howl and yelp a lot. This had led to trauma in 26.8 percent of the nonlycanthrope partners.

One of the most interesting articles speculated that the genes for lycanthropy were recessive. Thus, a werewolf could be born only to parents each of whom had the recessive genes. But the son or daughter had to be bitten by a werewolf before the heritage was manifested. Or the offspring had to obtain a skin taken from a dead werewolf. Hence, the extreme scarcity of lycanthropes.

Having gobbled down all the solid food, his belly packed and yet still feeling hungry, Varglik spooned out the honey from the jar into his mouth while he read the Personals column.

WM, single, 39, handsome, vivacious, affluent coll. grad, loves Mozart, old movies, long walks in the evening, seeks young, lovely, coll. grad, polymorphous-perverse WF. Children no problem, won't eat them. Photo exch. req. Write c/o WAW.

Jane, come home. I love you. All's forgiven. You may use the cat's litterbox. Ernst.

The magazine articles were serious scientific papers. But, surely, the WAW staff was making up most of the Personals column. Maybe to relieve the grimness of their lives. After all, being a lycanthrope was no fun. He should know.

Having read the magazine, he put it through the shredder. It hurt his bibliophile soul to do that, but the publisher's urgings to her subscribers to destroy their copies after reading them made good sense. On the other hand, the publisher might be keeping a small inventory of every issue hidden away, knowing that they could become quite valuable collector's items. His doubts about her intentions were probably unfounded. But being a lycanthrope, like being a dweller in the Big Apple, made one downright paranoiac. He had double reason to know that it was better to be suspicious than to be sorry.

It was also best to always play it safe. But the lycanthrope ejaculated all caution when the full moon was up. That had been yesterday. It did not matter. Two nights on either side of the full moon exerted almost as strong an influence. He was as helpless against the tug possessing him—soon to be a flashflood—as the moon was against the grip of its orbit.

Unable to fight the forces of change, not even knowing how to do it, he had once tried to cage himself during the metamorphosis. When its time was near, he had locked himself in a windowless room of his Westchester house with a side of beef as fuel for the re-transformation back into Man. Then he had pushed the key through the lock so that it fell on a paper in the hall just outside the door. As soon as he had felt the change beginning, a shudder running through him even more sweet and powerful than sexual arousal, he had smashed the furniture and bitten off the doorknob and howled so mightily that he would have awakened the entire neighborhood if his house had not been so isolated.

He had no memory of his agonies during his frenzied attempts to escape to freedom. But the wrecked room and the wounds in his arms, legs, and buttocks where he had bitten himself were just as good evidence as if he had taped the drama. When he regained consciousness as a man, he was so crippled and weak from loss of blood that he had almost not been able to pull back under the door the paper holding the key.

Somehow, he had gotten up, unlocked the door, put on his clothes, cut and torn them over the wounds, and phoned a physician friend to come to his house to attend the wounds. The doctor had obviously not believed his story about being attacked by a large dog while walking in the woods, but he had not said so.

Since the police could not find the dog, Varglik had had to take a series of painful rabies shots.

That was his first and last attempt to cage himself.

A diligent and experienced detective, the sheriff would have found out about the supposed attack. A few phone calls or letters to New York would be enough. He would also have learned about the dogs and horses slain in the area, though the scenes of the killings were twenty miles from Varglik's house. Yeager would have learned about the mutilation-murders of two hikers and two lovers in the woods. The police suspected that the killer was a man who had butchered the four so that they would appear to have been killed and partly eaten by wild dogs. Yeager would tend to believe that the killer was neither man nor dog.

"It must drive him nuts to have to believe that," Varglik muttered. "Welcome to the funny farm, Sheriff."

Whatever Yeager did or did not believe or intend to do, Varglik could do nothing about what was going to happen to his persona. He could control where he would be when the inevitable happened.

At six p.m., he left his office. The wolf skin, rolled up, was in the attaché case he carried. He waited in his house, eating a huge supper and afterwards munching on potato chips, until 10:30 p.m. Then he drove his car through town, watching behind him, going in an indirect route, stopping now and then to check for possible shadowers. Within thirty minutes he was on a gravel country road deep within the county just north of Reynolds County. After ten minutes, he pulled into a sideroad and stopped the car in the darkness of an oak grove. The only sounds except for his accelerating breathing were the shrillness of locusts and the booming of frogs in a nearby marsh. Then, the whine of mosquitoes zeroing in on him.

Hastily, he opened the car trunk, removed the skin, doffed his clothes, and put them through the open window into the front seat. His breath sawed through his nose. He panted. His body seemed to be getting warm, and it was. The fever of metamorphosis was nearing its peak.

The wolf skin was draped over his shoulders when he stepped out from under the shade to stand in the full shower of moonlight. Though he was not holding the skin, it clung like a living thing to his back.

The moonlight beams, pale catalytic arrows, pierced him. His blood thumpthumped. The great artery of his neck jumped like a fox caught in a bag. He reeled, and he fell through a cloud of shining silvery smokepuffs. His head and neck hairs rose; the curly pubic hair straightened out. An exquisitely pleasureful sensation rippled through him. He swelled like the throat sac of a marsh bullfrog. His nose ran; the fluid oozed over his lips, which were puffing outward.

Without his will, his arms lifted and straightened. His legs expanded as if blood had poured through the skin. His bowels contracted and expelled his feces with the sound of an angry cat spitting. He emptied his blade in a mighty arc. Then his penis became enormous and lifted toward the moon until it had almost touched his belly and seemed to his darkening senses to howl shrilly.

Howling deeply with his mouth, he fell hard backwards on the ground. The wolf skin was still fastened to him as if it were a giant bloodsucking bat. He felt forces shooting through the ground and then through him like saw-topped oscillograph waves, chaotic at first then organizing themselves into parallel but curving lines. They shook his body until he had to claw deep into the dirt with his outstretched hands to keep from falling off the planet.

He shot out his spermatic fluid, again and again, as if he were mating with Mother Earth Herself. His human spermatozoa were gone, and his glands were already pouring Wolf fluid into his ducts.

After that, he knew nothing as Man.

Only the moon saw his hair and skin melt until he looked like a mass of jelly that had been formed into the figure of a man. After a minute or so, the jelly quivered, and it kept on quivering for some time. It shone as pale and semisolid as lemon jello. Or as some primeval slug that had crawled out of the earth and was dying.

But it lived. The furious metabolic fires in that jelly had already devoured some of the fat that Varglik had accumulated so swiftly. The fires would eat up all of it and then attack some

of the normal fat before the process was completed. In the dawn
of Varglik's awareness of what he was heir to, he had tried to
diet. He reasoned that if he lacked the fat, he would lack the
energy needed to carry out the metamorphosis. But the sleeping
Wolf in him had defeated him. Varglik could no more stop eating
great quantities of food then he could stop sweating.

The jelly darkened as it changed shape. The arms and legs
shrank. The head become long and narrow, and newly formed
teeth shone like steel spears. The buttocks dwindled, and from
the incipient spine, now a dark line in the mass, a tentacle
extruded. This would become the tail, smooth at first, then hairy.
Other darknesses appeared in his head, trunk, legs, and arms.
These were at first swirling, the cells shifting as they were re-
formed by the magnetic lines generated by the Wolf in him.

The wolf did not become conscious until the change was
completed. The wolf skin had become a living part of the living
jelly and then of the metamorphosis. That completed, what had
fallen as two-legs rose as four-legs. He shook himself as if he had
just emerged from swimming. He sat down on his furry haunches
and howled. Then he prowled around, sniffing at the feces and
the fluids. He investigated the car despite its repulsive and overpowering stench of gasoline and oil.

A moment later, he was running through the woods. He ran
and ran. He loped through a world that had no time. He saw the
bushes and trees and rocks he passed as living beings which
moved. He saw the moon as an orb that had not existed until
then. He had no concept of a changeless moon rising from above
the Earth in its orbit. It was a new thing. It had been born with
him.

But the wolf knew what it wanted. Flesh and blood. And,
being a werewolf, it desired human flesh above all flesh. Yet, like
all creatures two-legged or four-legged, it ate what it could. Thus,
he bounded over a fence and gripped the throat of a barking
watch-dog and carried it over the fence into the woods where he

slew and ate it. That was not enough. He needed more prey to kill to thrill his nerves with ecstasy and to fill his belly for fuel for the change back into Man. He ran on until he came to a pasture on which horses grazed or slept. He killed a mare and disemboweled her and began tearing at the flesh until the aroused farmers came at him with flashlights and guns.

Then, in his wide circuit through the woods, he crossed a moonlight-filled meadow because sheep scent drifted across it to him. As he got close to the edge of the woods, he smelled, along with sheep, that flesh he most lusted for. A man stepped out from the darkness of the trees, the moon shining on the rifle barrel. He lifted it as Wolf leaped snarling at him.

▼▼▼

Sheriff Yeager had not joined the hunting party just north of Benger's farm. Instead, outtricking his prey's every trick to detect a shadower, he had followed Varglik to the oak grove. He had sat in his car down the road until the wolf-howl had told him that what he had expected to happen had happened. After ten minutes, he had gotten out of the car and cautiously approached the grove. He was just in time to see the bushy tail disappearing into the dark woods.

Using his flashlight, he followed the pawprints in the wet earth. After a while, he heard distant shots. Guessing from which direction they came, he cut at an angle through the woods. Just before he got to the meadow, he saw the enormous wolf loping across it. He waited until the beast was almost ready to plunge into the forest, and he stepped out. His rifle cartridges contained no silver bullets. That was bullshit. A high-velocity .30-caliber lead bullet would kill any animal, man included, weighing only one hundred and eighty pounds. The werewolf might seem to be of supernatural origin. But it was subject to the same laws of physics and chemistry as any other animal.

The bullet entered the gaping mouth, bounced off the roof of the mouth, tore down the throat, and angled into the liver. The wolf was dead and so was Varglik. Nor was there a change into the human body such as shown in so many movies. The cells were dead, and the transformation principle could not act on the cells. The wolf remained Wolf.

Yeager did not want questions or publicity. He skinned the carcass and dug a grave and buried the wolf. In the process of re-metamorphosis, the skin would have fallen off, he supposed, separating from the body and other parts of the skin. But it remained whole now, the process of change having been erased with the end of life.

▼▼▼

Now, the pelt was stretched out against the stone of the fireplace in the sheriff's house. Every night, its light seemed to Yeager to be getting brighter. He considered destroying it. He knew or thought he knew what he would do soon if the skin stayed within his sight or within the reach of his hand. He had to burn it.

The hungry wolf will try to get at the meat even if it sees the trap. An iron filing does not will not to fly to the magnet. The moth does not extinguish the flame so that it will not be incinerated.

ANGELS' MOON
▼▼▼

KATHE KOJA

HE thought he might be an angel. Angels had transformations, he was reasonably certain of that: from man to spirit and back again, it was in the Bible. *Fear not*, they said when they changed.

On his back, not quite staring up at the ceiling, arms at his long sides like a patient on a table. His hair was short and blond and dirty. He was dirty all over, no wash since winter; there was no more water upstairs in the pipes and he had no idea how to turn it back on. Memory of the change, creep and stutter, rolling up his body like the movement of some relentlessly disfiguring disease. Leprosy. Did people still get leprosy, or was it one of those things of which the world was permanently rid, old scourge conveniently crisped to nothing by the microwave heat of medical science?

One of the two windows was broken, small rectangle kicked to chips and sullen cracks. He had tried to seal the pieces retrieved with duct tape, dull silver like the surface of a nickel. The wind still found purchase, there was no way to keep it completely out. Still he didn't mind the cold. There were worse things than weather.

Exploratory scratch at his chin; he had not shaved since the

angelic change, but his beard had not grown at all. The hair on
his arms, his chest, his legs and groin, all seemed the same, but
then it was hard to tell, it wasn't the kind of thing you would
notice. Maybe it was a little coarser, but then again that could
be imagination. At first he had tried to tell himself it was all
imagination, some manifestation of his inner illness, some new
unbearable loss. First the poems, then the words, and now
humanity entire, forced transcendence on a specimen already so
weakened that mere living was a challenge unhealthy in its force.
He remembered waking, frightened, naked on the cement floor,
compulsively counting his toes and fingers as if he might have
dropped one changing back.

But wolves had ten toes, too; he knew that from the book he
had gotten from the library. Had stolen, really; ashamed but it
was so, he had no library card and no money to buy a book like
that; and he had to have it. He had to find out what he was like
when swept by angelic change, and there was no one to tell him,
no way to ask. So with clumsy dread he struck the book down
his shirtfront, where it lay thumping arrhythmic counterpoint
against the beat of his heart as he bicycled home. Snow chivvied
him, made it hard to ride, to keep the bike straight, but could
not increase his hurry. Snow on his bed from the broken window,
drifting small and dusty across the slick gray paint of the concrete
floor. He had to put the book aside to tape the window shut
again, but as soon as that was done he sat down to read; no
bathroom, he did not even eat; he had a greater hunger.

At once he found that most of these words were as well beyond
him, too long and hard, like roads made up entirely of stone,
and in his anger he pounded at his forehead: stupid, stupid, he
should have stolen a children's book, something easy. But at least
there were pictures. For an hour or more he studied them, the
yellowish cool of the short-lashed eyes, the firm muscled landscape of their pelts. Despite himself he felt a shameful pleasure
in their strength; if he was really so, then he was something to

be proud of. He fell asleep with the book on his chest, tucked back inside the wilting flannel of his shirt as if it were a living thing whose heat he must protect to the limits of his own.

▼▼▼

The room was ten by ten, a basement storage area for the abandoned building above, the origin of which he could not guess. It was not precisely a house, but if it had once been a business then it was a small business indeed. When he first came, he had cleaned it out, piled the scatter of boxes and containers neat as a puzzle in the far corner. None of the boxes held anything he could use—plastic squares of various colors, some tiny metal pieces that looked like the atom genesis of machines—but he would not discard them, in case the owners one day came looking.

The bed was a twin-sized mattress, mildew-bleached and only a little rank, balanced carefully atop its plywood boxspring and four blue plastic milk crates which he had weighted with rocks selected for their potential immobility as well as their size. He had three other milk crates which were chairs and table, or sometimes pantry when he had food enough to warrant storage: stale chewy saltines, cereal which he ate by hand, or his favorite, raisins, they would keep forever. He also had a boombox with one speaker and no batteries; he had to save the batteries for the camping-out light, although sometimes he would filch their power to listen for a precious hour to the Top 40 station; he loved the bright thump and screech he found there, he could repeat word for word the DJs' promos. He had three shirts, two summer and one winter, and two pairs of socks which he wore together; when he was not wearing the shirts he kept them rolled into neat balls; he liked their shapes, like little animals curled and burrowed against the cold. Sometimes it got so cold in his room that he could not bend his hands.

When he was changed, though, no weather could touch him,

nothing disturb that heedless fierce insouciance. Dirty winds, thrown bottles, broken glass scattered on the pavement, the bravado snarl of lesser dogs: less than nothing. It was hard to remember, at first, how things felt, but he was getting better at it, the angel-time memories bright with sparkling dread. Each time it happened, and it had happened three times so far since the first gibbous wax of autumn, he found the memories both easier and more fantastical, as if waking drowsy and bemused from a dream of kings and terrors to find in one hand a scepter and in the other a bloody ax. He knew that all of it should have frightened him more, been more horror than horrible pleasure—another brick in the highrise tower of self-loathing—but knew also that this terror's edge was born blunted from other, blacker troubles. Once the worst has happened, perspective changes to reflect the new reality, and evil, like pain, is more relative than ever.

▼▼▼

Sitting on a parking block in the co-op lot, carefully peeling the secret sweet layer of foil from a candy bar found like a jewel on the sidewalk outside the store. The smell released from paper was nearly overpowering, rich as gas in his nose. Since becoming an angel he had found his sense of smell raised to a disturbing level of precocity, his appetite provoked now by ant-crawling dog-chewed hamburger rinds as well as more pedestrian treats, like candy bars. Yesterday he had had an almost unbearable impulse to eat a dead bird.

Chewing slowly at the candy, letting it melt unto dissolution between his sore teeth, he was aware of the people around him, passing on the sidewalk, parking their cars, loitering outside the store. A complex threnody of scents: the sour explanations of old men, dusty fart of a starting car's exhaust, cigarette smoke, flat stink of grease, unexpected flower of menstruating women, tumbled skein of food odors as the store door opened again. Young woman, red shoes, an odor like unease beneath the false mask of perfume that never covered entire. She paused to step past him; he was sitting on the parking block next to her car.

"Excuse me," she said, rote courtesy, but responded to his smile. Looked at him, as people rarely did; the mad, or even mad-appearing, are anonymous by virtue of false perception, fear of potential danger; don't make eye contact, he might do something. Still their mutual smile held until something, some thought, fluttered under her skin to break the pleasant tension into wariness and he began, slowly, to wrap the uneaten candy back in its wrinkled jacket of foil, prefatory to flight.

She was not smiling at all, now.

"You're Ethan Parrish," she said, and he bowed his head.

▼▼▼

Ethan?

What.

Ethan, it's important we do this.

Scowl, the pick and flutter of his fingertips against the grainy wale of his oversize corduroys, and the waistline cinched with a woman's chain belt, cheap goldtone and flashy buckle filigree. She could smell the unfresh odor of his clothing from where she sat, carefully not across the desk from him, too distancing, too formal, too authoritarian. Instead she sat in the chair not quite next to him, legs calm together at her ankles, expensive shoes. The micro recorder open on the table did not disturb him; he liked to pick it up and watch, hypnotic smile as if the tiny whorling of the wheels mimicked in some more orderly way the grind and whirl of his own thoughts.

We were talking, her voice soothing, prompting, her gaze on his dirty hair, the sagging socks, about what you used to do, before. You were a writer, weren't you.

So uncomfortable he could barely speak. Her office was so hot, and all this *red*: carpet and chairs, the pictures on the wall, all as red as a chambered heart. The stryofoam cup of coffee sat untouched and lightly steaming on the desktop before him. The first half hour had been all smiles, coffee and bustle, over and over her pleasure at finding him, really uncanny, it was not a part of town she visited often (he could believe that) but a meeting with a hospital administrator had run late, she had stopped at the first grocery she saw, and. And.

She was looking at him to answer; for a moment the question stayed beyond him, then returned with its shiver of shame.

I was a poet.

I know. I've read your work, it's brilliant. You're an extraordinarily brilliant man. But you stopped writing a lo—— Her pause elongated in the larger silence, as if she had offended, done something bawdy or cruel. You were hospitalized for awhile, she said finally. At Bridgemoor.

I didn't like it there. All I did was lose things.

What do you mean?

I mean I *lost* things, I couldn't find them any more. I lost all the words and all I had were the, the pictures, the *images*, you see? That's all I had so I had to hang onto them.

Is that why you left the hospital?

Yes. Frowning; was it there that the angel-change had begun, come to him in the night like another kind of nurse? He used to remember; it seemed like. But she was waiting, again, for another answer. Yes. They were trying to medicate me too much. They do it to keep you quiet but I was quiet already. So I left. It wasn't really that hard, they don't watch you as much as they think they do. Plus they think because you're crazy, you're dumb.

You're not crazy, Ethan.

His pale shrug. What difference does it make now?

Firmly, A *lot* of difference. To a lot of people. I'm not going to give up on you, Ethan. No matter what it takes. Taking out her card, making a business of placing it in an envelope and the envelope within his reach. I'm keeping my eye on you! And her vigorous nod, smile, more answer to her own inner torment than his: sweet, beautiful and sick, those eyes, that tender bruise of a smile as he gathered up his dirt-scabbed hat, his book, a ninth-grade biology workbook, the hard words laboriously underlined with the fading green of a cracked felt-tip pen, his poetry was taught in graduate courses at the university from which she had received her degree and he could no longer understand a simple word like predator.

▼▼▼

Claws on the sidewalk, hard against his hard pads. Shiver of hair about his ears, pointed to the moon, cacophony of smells inside his wise nostrils. He had just ripped a small mongrel cat to rags, for no reason, all reasons. Nothing spoken, in this world, and everything understood.

Except the human smell, sometimes, caught inside—inside!—his own aroma: *that* was disquieting, but in the way of his kind he did not mull or worry it, worried instead the cat's carcass, dropped both to bend, lick silver from a puddle of ice. Noises in the alley, and with the long empty grin of his kind he padded off, heavy nails too short to click warning against the pavement, short with use, and use, and use.

▼▼▼

At the co-op grocery the woman behind the counter stopped him as he picked up his irregularly-donated rations—broken boxes of Hi-Ho crackers, a crushed can of cocktail peanuts, hothouse tomatoes lounging on the voluptuous edge of rot. He could not recall her name past the S that began it but her smell had the unhappy power to drive him out of the store at vulnerable moments.

"Hey," she said. "I gotta note for you."

Frightened, he stepped back, feet choosing flight before his heart could make an opposing decision. "Wait a minute," she said, misunderstanding. "I'll read it to you if you want." Leaning across the counter, she opened the note—flat white rectangle, short dashing slant of letters.

He was out the door before she had finished the first sentence entire; he knew where it came from by the scent. Pity and kindness no small disguise but no match in the end for his wariness, developed by necessity, more honed perhaps even than his sense of smell, and underneath it all he smelled the cage. Again. It always started out this way, started nice, warm like a blanket with the soul of a net. For your own good, they would say, she would say, with her red shoes and her wide, pained smile. You're a brilliant man. Hold still.

That night he lay small and frightened, all his clothing stretched over him like a blind of rags, praying now for the change to come, take hold and stay forever, remove him from contention with this end of the world which he could never hope to navigate without disaster and place him, like a jewel in prongs of waiting silver, in that other, colder, simple place where everything was two things: hot or dead.

In the morning, crosslegged and weary, eating one by sumptuous one the cocktail peanuts, he made decisions. First and most stringent, he must give up the co-op grocery, which meant his shopping would now be confined solely to dumpsters. Very well, he was prepared to make sacrifices. If by some terrible miscarriage of luck she found his basement home—and now, this moment, how good it looked, milk crates and camping light, boombox and bed, how sorrowful and dear—then he must find another nest, this one deeper, less visible to light and the curiosity of strangers who mean so ruinously well.

But. Would the missing words come looking, here and leave if he was not? That was insupportable; the last unbearable thing; he shook the thought away with the small frantic motions of a man putting out a fire inside his own head. Surely they were more resilient than that. Surely they could find him wherever he

went, if they came looking. But they would never come looking
to a hospital, he was sure at least of that.

So. Made almost light with resolution, the acceptance of a
plan of action, he curled back on the bed to seek the sleep denied
by last night's worry, found it at once and at length and lay in
the gray luxury of its trench, dreaming of a time beyond angel
time when thoughts were not words and words were not pain,
ache perpetual in their terrible insubstantiality where once they
had been so close and concrete, a time when no one cared to
find him or even knew that he was; even himself.

When he woke it was to a fragile restoration, body sleep-rich
and possessed of a well-being so rare and giddy it deserved, he
thought, celebration. Slotting the batteries in the boom box, turning it on, and up, loud so the small room reverberated, pushy
music and his own flat-footed dance, slapping a hand against the
outer wall in time to the beat's demands, louder still and in the
smiling second's worth of silence between song and patter, a different noise.

Broken sounds. A man's voice, brusque, walking back and
forth, the scrabble of kicked plastic. "Hey!" and in that echo
rabbit-heart, he shut off the boom box before realizing that was
the surest signal of all. "Hey," again, more sure this time; and
he bent, breathless, hinge-spined to grab everything at once, realizing he could not both run and carry, wondering in a weakening
flash of greater terror if there was time, or room, to run at all.
The shadow of the net and he dancing, blind and stupid, in its
fall, no wonder he had lost his words, he did not deserve to have
words.

"Hey, anybody down there?" Heavy-set, bright flashlight, blue
uniform: it was the uniform, finally, that sent him bursting empty-
armed up the stairs, madder than a wardful of patients, long
springing limbs like desperation as he swung past the utility
worker—not a policeman after all—and out into the street. Running and trying to breathe through the open mouth that could

only weep loud tears, horrible tears, he had to fall at last from sheer airlessness and did, lay curled in a burned-out doorway to find, when he could breathe enough to think, to take inventory, that he had only one shirt on, socks but no shoes. One heel was gouged, splintered glass he at once picked out with clumsy finger-tips. Sweat-slippery, hair crimped wild by sleep and wet to the roots, standing on comical end like fear's caricature. Shivering already in the negative chill of thirty low degrees as he gathered himself in the best fold he could make of flesh shaken by adren-alin exhaustion, pressed into the cold welcomeless embrace of the doorway's rectangle.

By numb rote he reviewed what he could remember of shel-ters, rejected each in turn as risks too bold to take. It would be dark in perhaps three hours. He could hide, in the dark. Until then, wait, and he did, camouflaged by the obvious disguise of need into something no one would look at, searching or not.

▼▼▼

His dreams, afire.

Angel time?

I see my own face in the moon.

And awake all at once, under its ice, naked in the parking lot of the co-op grocery—how?—cold beyond sensation's grasp into some primal sluggishness; still not deep enough to hide in, still life without words, only the spaces unoccupied, as if his body lay pocketed with the emptiness of missing organs: liver, heart, brain, soul. Driven to his knees by that endless irretrievable loss, so vast that it transcended even grief, it was too large for grief, it was at last too large for his body so he dropped to all fours, limbs twisting against the asphalt, mouth a mere empty howl as if scourged breathless by pain. It would never be the same. They would never come looking, those missing words, and with what resources he had left he could never make right. All gone, this time, but hurt and the ragged ghost of hunger.

Dazed in the gripe and flex, the cold on his body, he tried to rise and predictably fell, the cut on his heel bleeding again, slow cold blood. His breath was beautiful under the moon. An empty tortilla-chip bag blew against his side, scaring him so he cried out, loud, the exquisite gasp of breath again and as if in punishing response he heard cars, somebody's angry laugh and he tried to judge the moon, was it truly angel time? It was hard to see in the dark, harder than it should have been, but still it was flesh and not fur. Not time yet. He got up, paralytic slowness, all his responses deadened by the underwater cold, tried to move across the lightless street to the memory of the alley beyond. And in the motion the sound of a motor, his slow startle, one too many and somebody's laugh now a bellow, his running stagger a full-length moonlit sprawl and

    oh God

    the blessed flash of fur, *yes*, telescoping legs and arms into limbs that hit the ground running, *yes*, the one skin in which he could hide forever, the rhythm of safety in the sound of his claws grabbing purchase on the street into an immediate dazzle like lightning, growl like the biggest wolf in all the world, too big for even such a rib-scarred veteran as he; and past impact the taillights of the swerveless car reflecting on the scored and icy concrete the wordless husk, the rorschach blood of angels.

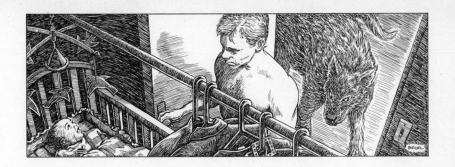

UNLEASHED

NINA KIRIKI HOFFMAN

THE baby, Joe, was still nursing when Amelia felt the change
coming on, the first stirring of appetite for the forbidden, the faint
current of unnatural strength, the hint that she would become
the thing she feared and hated. She glanced toward the apartment's living-room window. Its white curtains were parted, showing that night had arrived as gently as first snow, shadows lodging
among the buildings in drifts, melted in spots by the yellow
warmth of the street lights. Now that she was thinking of it, she
could taste the cool metal of twilight in the autumn air. Soon
the moon would crest the hill above town. For the first of its
three nights full, the moon would work on her weakly; she could
resist change for a little while. But not all night.

Where was the babysitter?

Gently, Amelia pulled Joe free and tucked her breast back
into her bra, buttoning her shirt. Rising from the folding metal
chair, she carried the baby to the closet where she had set up his
crib three months before.

Pregnancy had protected her from the moon change, and she
had thought nursing would, too. She had prayed that this frightening mother-change in her body had driven out the other,

unwelcome change entirely. For a year it had. Just in case, since Joe's birth she had arranged for a babysitter each full moon. Of course, the first time she really needed a sitter, the sitter was late.

Whom could she call? She glanced over her shoulder at the phone. The sitter first. Then, maybe, the man who had moved into the apartment downstairs two weeks ago. Amelia usually had trouble talking with strangers, especially men, but something about this man—his smell, perhaps, a musty, stale-sweat-in-body-hair scent that she would have dismissed as unclean, save for its strange attractiveness—had reassured her. They had spoken by the mailboxes three times. He had patted Joe's head with a gentle hand, and Joe had not minded.

What would Mother think of her even considering calling a strange man to look after her child?

Blast that thought. If Mother were alive and knew Amelia had a child at all, she would disown her daughter.

She put Joe in his crib and wound up the music-box mobile above it. By the light of a shell nightlight, plastic cardinals and bluebirds spun to the tune of Brahms' lullaby. The baby stared up at the birds. Amelia tucked the blanket in around Joe.

He was such a good baby. Gentle, quiet, undemanding. Just the way she had been as a baby, according to her mother. The way she had been all through girlhood.

She kissed Joe's forehead.

Change gripped her breasts, flattening them against her chest, her body shifting to absorb and redistribute tissue. She backed out of the closet and lay on the rag rug in the tiny living room, her eyes clenched shut, her mind grappling with the change, holding it at bay. When the hunger woke to fullness in her, would Joe be safe?

▼▼▼

Kelly Patterson sat on the dirty laundry in his armchair and looked at his apartment. In the two weeks since he had moved in, he had managed to get it as messy as any other place he had lived—

crushed beer cans mingling with wadded potato chip bags and filthy socks on the floor, an assortment of dirty shirts and jeans draped across most of the furniture, and a couple of crumpled TV dinner trays on the lamp table, right next to the rings left on the wood by wet cans. Sawdust he carried home from the construction site in the cuffs of his pants and in the waffles on his workboots mixed with everything else, but its clean wood scent couldn't compete with the odor of decay, which was almost a color in the air, spiced but not diminished by the scent of soured beer.

By morning it would all be cleaned up and he would have to start over. No matter how much he challenged his animal self, it always rose to the challenge and exceeded it.

Kelly scratched a stubbled cheek. The night Sonya-the-sudden had bitten him—he had forgotten that she had asked him not to come by that night, and he had an album he was convinced she should hear—the night she had bitten him, he had visualized a lot of scenarios, but never one to match this reality. Who would ever guess that somewhere inside his sloppy self lurked a finicky creature?

Maybe he should stop teasing himself, leave the place neat once and see what his alter ego would do when housekeeping didn't get in its way. Adult-onset lycanthropy. It was still so new and weird. There were lots of experiments he hadn't tried yet. Like, what would he do in the woods? Maybe he should throw a couple blankets, kibble, and a dog dish into the Jeep, drive out into the woods and check it out—if not tonight, tomorrow. But he had never had any woods sense. What if he got lost? Lost, forty, and naked in the early morning. An ugly thing to contemplate.

He sighed. He stood up and went to the curtains, parted them a crack to check the progress of the night.

There was a thump from upstairs, then a drumming of heels. What was going on with Amelia-the-mouse? Mouse brown hair, mouse dark eyes, alive with the mouse wish to be invisible. Had someone come to visit her, and were they having a go? He had tried to imagine a man who could be the father of her baby, and failed; Amelia was a walking wall of don't-touch-me, though some of the shrug-off softened when he talked to her about the kid. Who could get close enough? Though there was something about her that tempted a person . . .

There was another sharp heel thump on his ceiling, and a low cry that sounded more desperate than satisfied. He straightened out of his habitual slouch, staring up, wondering if she needed someone or something.

The hot silver fire ran through him, starting from his heart and flowing out to his extremities, traveling like flame along gas lines. His fingers tightened on the curtain. He drank a long breath in, feeding the silver fire. Smells sharpened and sounds intensified; he knew that somewhere in the room was a rat he would soon enjoy catching and eating. He could hear it chewing on leftover pizza in the corner.

A floor away, he could hear Amelia, moaning his name. His first name. Something had to be wrong with her; he couldn't imagine her ever calling somebody male and older then she was by their first name, not under normal circumstances.

He chomped his lip, the pain waking him of change, dousing the silver fire. It was First Night, the loosest night of change; he could overmaster it, at least for a while. He gripped the knob of his front door. For a while. What if change caught him in Amelia's place? Scare her out of her skin. She'd get him in trouble, no question.

"Kelly!" she cried.

He opened his door and glanced out. Across the hall, Peter-the-snoop was peeking out. Peter waggled his eyebrows at Kelly and slid his door shut. Kelly sighed and ran for the stairs.

▼▼▼

Amelia had the phone's handset in her fist, but she couldn't dial the phone, not with change gripping her. Anyway it was too late.

If the sitter hadn't left her building yet, she'd never get here in time.

Soon change would consume Amelia, and she would lose all her normal feelings, her restraints, her cares and concerns. She would go prowling, looking for victims. Before that happened, she must get help for Joe.

Her lower body locked, and the little tail began to grow between her legs. Clenching her fists, locking her elbows, she forced the tail back inside her.

"Kelly!" she cried.

Change whispered through her mind: Kill inhibitions. Mate with impulses. Take the night and make it yours. Your feet are made for wandering, and desire is your master.

The doorknob rattled, turned.

She panted short harsh breaths. She could feel her hips slimming, her shoulders changing. Her skin simmered as hair sprouted on chest and arms and legs and back.

Kelly, messy Kelly, slipped into the apartment. " 'Melia?" He knelt beside her.

She unclenched a fist long enough to grip his arm. "Joe," she said, her voice already low and harsh with change. "Will you watch Joe for me?"

"I, uh," he said. His face looked funny, and his smell had changed, though it was still just as enticing. she could feel the racing heat in him against the palm of her hand. "Okay—" he said, on a rising note.

She cried out. All her muscles locked, holding her still while the rest of change happened and she became the monster.

▼▼▼

It was going to happen. Kelly was going to change in front of somebody for the first time since Sonya had talked him through it. And this time it wasn't going to matter, because—

He wondered who or what had bitten Amelia.

What she was turning into didn't seem to be an animal. Its outline was human.

She shuddered and panted and sweated in front of him, her face twisted in pain and revulsion.

Change didn't hurt him like that. For him, it was as good as sex.

Amelia writhed. He felt he should be watching her, maybe soothing her somehow—a wet towel on the forehead? What?— but his own silver change pulsed through him, and he could no longer hold it off.

▼▼▼

Grinning, Adam sat up. Then he glanced down at his lap and frowned. Damn Amelia, the stupid bitch. Why hadn't she changed into his clothes? How could she let him wake up still in a skirt? Didn't she even *care* how he felt? He grabbed handfuls of skirt and ripped it off his body, enjoying the strength in his arms. And this blouse, so obviously feminine, pastel pink, soft and wimpy like the bitch—it had to go too.

Something warm was behind him. He narrowed his eyes. What had happened since last time? He turned and discovered a big black pointy-eared dog standing, staring at him with yellow eyes. Something funny about its paws—they were too big—but before he could get a good look at them, it leaned toward him. An edge of its black lip lifted, showing a canine. It made no sound.

"Shoo," he said. His voice wavered.

It took a step toward him.

He stood up, the shreds of skirt scattering around his feet. He stripped the shirt off and dropped it, then skinned out of Amelia's cotton underpants.

"Didn't know she got a dog," he said to the dog. He wasn't sure how it would behave toward him, either. Did he still smell enough like her to confuse it? He held out a hand to it, and it sniffed him, then backed up one step. "Look, I'll get out," he said. "Just gotta get some clothes first."

The dog sat, its gaze fixed on him.

He went to his closet, the one where she had kept a grudging wardrobe for him. But the clothes were gone. Baby music came from fake birds above a topless cage, and muted light from something orange on the floor. The closet smelled like milk and talcum powder and pee. "Christ!" There was a baby in the cage, a little baby who looked up at him with big eyes. How could she have a baby? A baby in his closet. A baby and a dog! He would have to do something drastic to her. She couldn't keep switching things around on him while he was sleeping. It wasn't fair.

He took a step toward the crib and the big dog growled, low in the back of its throat. He glanced at it. The hair on its spine was standing on end. He shrugged and headed for the bedroom, where he found his clothes in her closet shoved over against the wall, crowded out by her own. Dumb bitch. She'd wrinkled his favorite shirt. He slapped his thigh, wondering if she could feel it. It hurt him too much to try again.

The dog was watching him from the bedroom door. It showed him its pointed tooth again. He dressed hurriedly. "All right, all right," he said, "I'm going out! Just a minute." He found the black socks in her underwear drawer, and his loafers (she hadn't polished them in more than a month. How could that be?) in the closet among a jumble of her shoes. The dog growled when he rifled her purse. "I need money to go out, don't I?" he demanded. The growl lowered, but it kept coming. Adam ignored it. Amelia had twenty-six dollars in her wallet, and a smudy driver's license with a short-haired photo of her on it. If he got stopped, he always said he was a male impersonator. He looked enough like her to pass, which was an uncomfortable thought. She was so unattractive. But most of that was the way she carried herself, always flinching, eyes downcast; her wardrobe was full of dark, neutral colors.

He took her keys. As he walked past the growling dog, he
kicked out at it, but missed. Its growl rose to a bark. It snapped
at his leg, then backed off, following him at two paces until he
reached the door. "Goodnight, sucker," he said as he locked the
door from outside. "I hope you drank two gallons of water."

The little dark man with glasses was peeking out his door in
the downstairs apartment, the way he always was. Adam made
kissy lips at him. Anybody was fair game on Adam's nights—the
more disgusting and repulsive the better. The little man ducked
inside and slammed the door, and smiled.

▼▼▼

Amelia lay quiet, her eyes shut. His hateful clothes were tight
around her hips, across her breasts, and she smelled alcohol and
at least two different perfumes on Adam's shirt; the castor-oil scent
of lipstick came from his collar where it nudged her cheek. She
could feel the sickness gathering in her stomach and knew that
soon she would need to dash to the bathroom to throw up everything: the knowledge of what the monster had done the night
before (she couldn't really remember, but she knew it was awful),
and the remnants of whatever he had eaten and drunk.

She gulped twice.

She realized there was a strange sound in the room.

Breathing.

Terror stilled her breath, her heart. Her hands clutched the
sheet.

The breathing went on, undisturbed.

So he had done it. He had finally brought his prey home.
She had a horrible moment wondering what might be in her
stomach besides normal food and drink. Her gorge rose. She
couldn't hold back any longer. She stood up in a rush, locked
herself into the bathroom, and made it all the way to the toilet
before she lost it.

When she had finished retching and loosened all the most

torturous buttons on Adam's clothes, she rinsed her face in the sink. Something nagged at her. There was something she was forgetting, but she couldn't think, not with some stranger in her bedroom. She got her oversize red terrycloth robe from the hook on the bathroom door and put it on over her half-undone clothes, then peeked around the door.

A man was sleeping curled in her bed, a naked man. A long lanky leg lay folded on top of the quilt, and a long arm curled around his dark head; the rest of him was drawn up around his stomach. He breathed softly, not snoring the way she expected all men to snore.

What was she going to do?

Get some decent clothes, dress quietly, grab her purse and flee the apartment. Maybe if she waited long enough the man would leave, and then she could get back in and lock up. But he knew where she lived . . .

And what about—

What about Joe?

The baby's morning wail of hunger rose just then. Amelia watched, wide-eyed, as the man in her bed yawned and stretched, then turned to look at her.

It was Kelly, Mr. Patterson from downstairs. He knew who she was: was her first frozen thought.

Joe, used to being taken care of any time he made a sound, wailed a little louder.

Mr. Patterson sat up and yawned into the back of his wrist. "He's probably hungry," he said. "I couldn't find anything to feed him last night."

"What are—what are—" She hid her eyes with her sleeves.

"Well, excuuuse me," said Mr. Patterson. A minute later, he said, "You can open your eyes again. I'm covered by a sheet."

Hot tears streaked down Amelia's cheeks. She lowered the sleeves of her robe and glanced at him to see if he was lying, but he wasn't. He had a sheet up around his waist, shielding her from seeing the monster part of him. "Why aren't you wearing any clothes?" she asked, a little girl's voice coming from her mouth.

"Don't you remember anything about last night?"

Tearblind, she shook her head.

"Wait a second, that didn't come out right. Nothing happened between us last night, Amelia. Except you wanted somebody to take care of the baby on Change Night, and I guess I was the only person you could think to call."

"Change Night?" she whispered.

"Moon Night, some call it."

"Curse Night." She licked a tear off her lip and peered at him through salt haze. "How do you know about Curse Night?" He smelled like something she wanted for breakfast, and she didn't understand that at all.

"I change too."

Joe wailed a little louder. Amelia stuffed her sleeve into her mouth and bit down. What kind of monster had she left the baby with last night? She dashed through the living room and into Joe's closet. He was red-faced and teary, but when she picked him up he settled down immediately. He didn't even smell wet. She went to the metal chair and sat, settling Joe on her thigh and offering him a breast. He sucked as if he were starving.

Mr. Patterson walked out of the bedroom, wearing the sheet like a toga. He glanced at her nursing Joe, shielded his eyes with a hand, and bent to pick up some clothes lying folded on the rug. "What bit you?" he said. He turned his back to her.

"I don't know." She heard the despair in her voice and wished she could unsay it. Her mother had taught her never to let a man hear her despair.

"How long have you been changing?"

"Since I was twelve." She hesitated. "It stopped while I was pregnant with Joe."

"How old are you now?"

"Twenty-one."

"Do you know what you change into?"

She shuddered. "A monster," she said, and then, whispered, "Him."

"Do you remember being him? I remember being my other self. I'm not as different, somehow, as you are."

"I can't remember anything he does. I just know it's disgusting."

"Oh," said Mr. Patterson. He didn't say anything more for a little while. "I'm going to dress in your bathroom, all right? I think the less Peter-the-snoop has to talk about, the better."

While he was gone she got an extra diaper and draped it over Joe as he nursed so that no secret part of her showed. Her despair was so strong she hurried about it getting into the milk and hurting Joe.

In a couple minutes Mr. Patterson came out. With him dressed and herself covered she could look at him again. "Mr. Patterson," she said in a low voice. Her worry about Joe made her strong enough to speak.

"Yes, Amelia."

"What do you change into?"

"A wolf. Kind of a wolf, anyway. Much more normal than your change, I imagine."

"I left the baby with a wolf?" The warmth of Joe against her chest, his hot mouth on her breast, reassured her. "How could I?"

He lifted his eyebrows, but didn't answer.

Of course, her monster self would do anything.

"How did you change his diapers?"

"It was tricky," said Kelly. He glanced at the clock above the card table where she ate all her meals. "Got to get to the site, Amelia. Gotta pick up a few things from my apartment and get to work. I'll be home after five—three hours before moonrise, more or less. We can talk then." He put his hand on the doorknob.

Joe, warm and dry, lay in her arms. "Mr. Patterson. Thanks," said Amelia. She lowered her eyes.

She locked and bolted the door behind him, not sure if she wanted to talk to him ever again. He had seen the worst part of her—if it was really part of her, and not some alien creature that took her over three nights a month, which was what she told herself, how she lived with it.

Maybe, if she worked fast, she could load everything she really needed into her VW bug and get away, far away. There was still a little left of her mother's legacy, enough for first-and-last-plus-damage-deposit and another six months of low rent and generic groceries. After that Joe would be old enough to go to daycare, and she could get back to temping.

But there was still the problem of getting a sitter for Joe before tonight.

Joe was sleeping against her breast. She transferred him gently to his crib and closed the closet door almost all the way, then went to the phone.

What had happened to that girl who was supposed to come last night, anyway? Amelia had left Joe with her a few times before when she had to go shopping and couldn't take Joe. She had found the girl's number on the bulletin board at the laundromat, and the girl had been clean and prompt and had no objections to the idea of staying with the baby overnight if necessary. The nights Patty had come when Change hadn't happened, Amelia had gone out to a movie and then come home, dismissing Patty early.

She checked the pad of paper by the phone and called the number. "Patty?" she said when a young voice answered.

"Patty's not here," said the voice, breathless. "There was an accident."

"Goodness, is she hurt?"

"Yeah, pretty bad. Yesterday she hit a car with her bike! She got a concussion. She had to go to the hospital."

"Oh, I'm so sorry! Will she be okay?"

"We think so," said the voice. It sounded uncertain.

"I'm sorry," Amelia said again. It didn't seem like the right time to ask the voice to recommend another babysitter. "I'm sorry," she said again. "Goodbye."

"Goodbye," said the voice.

She couldn't trust Joe with someone she had never met, and that included . . . him. Adam.

She wished she knew the phone number of the place where Mr. Patterson worked. She glanced toward the closet where Joe slept, then sat on the floor, elbows on the seat of one of the chairs, chin propped on hands. She had to think.

▼▼▼

Kelly was carrying a sack full of Chinese take-out when he knocked on Amelia's door after work. The door opened a crack and she peeked out, then widened the opening just enough for him to slip inside. He glanced at her as she bolted the door behind him, and got a shock. She had done something to her long brown hair—pinned it up somehow, the Search for Sophistication. She was wearing makeup—too much of it—and a nightgown. A flannel nightgown, but the hem was torn off above her knees, and she had rolled the sleeves up to mid-forearm, and left the buttons at the throat undone.

He began to have a sinking feeling.

She looked at his face, then dropped her gaze. Her pinkened lower lip trembled. "I was afraid—" she said.

He went to the table and took the white cartons out of the sack, with napkins and two pair of chopsticks. "Have you eaten yet?"

"No, Mr. Patterson."

"Come on over and sit down. Call me Kelly. You did last night."

"Last night I was desperate."

"You look pretty desperate now."

She sat down in her second chair. She wouldn't meet his eyes. "I had this great idea," she said in a small voice. "When it turned out my babysitter was in an accident. I thought . . ."

He handed her a pair of chopsticks and a carton of shrimp fried rice. Savory steam rose from the opened carton. She set the carton down and stared at the chopsticks, still safe in their red paper sheath. "I mean, I could ask you to sit with Joe again, but you must have other things to do with your time. So I thought . . ." she said.

He opened a couple more cartons, waiting.

"I know how to get rid of Adam now," she said.

"How?"

"Get pregnant." Her glance darted up to meet his, then dropped. After a silence, she said, "I don't know how it happened last time. How or who. But I thought . . ."

Kelly swallowed. He let a minute go by. "You know that's not a long-term solution? You don't want to spend the rest of your life pregnant, do you?" She had an attractive scent; he had noticed it every time he came into contact with her. It spoke to him even when all the rest of her was posted No Trespassing. So he knew that what she was asking him wasn't impossible, but it would probably be damned uncomfortable for both of them. "Besides, you can't just plan on getting pregnant. Sometimes it takes time and work."

Her eyes closed. She had done the lids in silver, and her lashes in black. Too much of everything, but the hand that had applied the makeup had been steady and skillful.

"Can you support two kids?"

She took a deep breath and let it out. She looked like a little girl playing Mommy. She opened her eyes and stared at him, and she looked like a wood sprite. "I don't know," she said. "There's welfare, isn't there?"

"But look," he said, leaning a little closer to her across the gently steaming food. "You can't disrupt your whole life just because you want to—you want to get rid of this little fraction of it. Three nights out of thirty, and you've got all your days free. What is it? Five percent of your month, that's all. You can live with it." It was a set speech. He had heard it from Sonya-the-sudden. That seemed so long ago. He wondered why he had been so upset about the whole thing. It worked out fairly well, as long as he focused during change on thinking that what he really needed to do in the night was guard his apartment and take care of it. He hadn't done much exploring yet, but he figured there was plenty of time for that.

"You don't know what he does," she said, her eyes tearbright.

"Acts like an asshole," Kelly said.

"Much worse things than that."

"How do you know?"

Her lips thinned. She looked away.

"You *do* remember."

"I do his laundry."

He reached across the table and touched her hand. "Amelia, do you remember?"

"No," she said, and her face tightened. In a whisper, she said, "Maybe." Louder, "Everything he does, he does just to torture me. He knows all the things I hate and he does them all. Things I can't even think of. Things that make me throw up. Things my mother told me would make God strike me dead on the spot."

Her mother? How'd her mother get into this? "Still, just three nights out of twenty-nine or so days."

"Would you say that if I told you I murdered people on my Curse Nights? Just three people a month?"

"Uh—no, nope, I guess you're right."

She looked toward the window. It was still light out. In the streets below children played a game that involved shouts, racing footsteps, and the slap of a ball against asphalt or wall.

"Mr—Kelly, will you help me?"

"I still don't think this is your final answer, Melia."

"Maybe I can find some other answer, if I just have this . . . breathing room."

▼▼▼

Before moonrise they sat naked side by side on her living room rug and waited, not sure how change would take them. Joe had been fed and diapered and put to bed, the birds circling above him. The lullaby played faintly from the closet behind them. "I don't know," Amelia said. She had her knees up and her hair down, concealing everything a bathing suit would have covered, though he had seen and touched most of her already. "Maybe if I just start acting more like—like him, he won't come anymore. Maybe if I like doing what he did, he wouldn't do it anymore because he couldn't hurt me that way."

"Do you think that's possible? That you could like it?"

She slanted a look at him. "You smell good," she said. A silence. "I almost liked it," she said. "I'm not supposed to. I know I'm not supposed to. Mother said . . . But I think—"

Silver flame flared through him. It was Second Night, the night of no refusal. For an instant he tried to resist; but resistance made it hurt. He relaxed into it.

Moonlight spilled into the room through the open window. Wolf and woman stared at each other. She lifted a hand, and he nosed it. She stroked his head. "I think I can learn," she said.

THE MARK OF THE BEAST
▼▼▼

KIM ANTIEAU

BUSHES and saplings grabbed me as I hurried through the starless moonless forest. M. Garnier had warned me to return to the chateau before dark, yet I had foolishly hunted until dusk and now I was lost. I stopped for a breath and shouldered my musket and game bag. Once night falls, Garnier had told me, the beasts come out.

In the distance, a wolf howled, a lonely cry which made my bones ache. I started forward again. The surrounding night reached into me. I felt like a child, untouched and alone in a darkness filled with malevolent shapes, instead of the man I was, sent from my father's house to shake the melancholy which had gripped my soul these many months. Now I was far from the world I had known all my life. Far from the world most men knew. The forest whispered to me in a language I could not comprehend. Some manner of beast awaited me behind each shadow. I shuddered.

"I will never find my way back," I said out loud.

My voice startled an owl off its perch in an old oak, and the air quivered as the bird fluttered its huge wings.

Near me, leaves crackled. Bushes shook. What thing sought me out in these woods? My heart pounded in my throat.

Suddenly, a small hand grasped my hand.

"This way," a woman whispered. She led me through blackness, and I welcomed her guidance. The forest parted as she moved ahead of me, like the sea parting before the bow of a ship. Leaves and ferns stroked my arms, calming my racing heart. For the quarter of an hour that the woman held my hand, the forest became familiar, like the woods surrounding my own distant home.

Then suddenly, the woman's hand pulled away from mine, and she was gone. I stepped out onto the lawn of the chateau.

"Jean-Jacques? Is that you?" Louis Garnier became a shadow in the entryway, framed by the dim gold light of an inside fire. "At last! I was afraid the beasts had gotten you. My old friend Rieux would have never forgiven me if I had allowed his only begotten son to come to harm!" Garnier motioned me inside. "Come," he said as I came toward him, "show me what you have killed this day."

▼▼▼

The following morning was bright and cool. After I dressed in a shaft of warm sunshine, I joined Garnier downstairs for breakfast.

"Have you recovered from your adventure last night?" he asked.

"Yes," I said, sitting across from him. "It was strange. I have lived in the Auvergne district all of my thirty years and I have never gotten lost before." I took a breast of quail from the platter and began to eat.

"Don't let it trouble you," Garnier said. "The Apcon forest is unlike any other place. Not many journey this far into it. Even our good King Francis does not venture here often!" He laughed heartily. Then he looked beyond me and the laughter died.

"Good morning," a familiar voice said quietly. My savior from the forest! I turned. I wanted to thank her then and there, but something about her timid gaze kept me silent.

"Marie," Garnier said. "Please, join us. Jean-Jacques Rieux, this is my wife, Marie. She was resting yesterday when you first arrived."

I stood and bowed slightly. Marie returned the bow and then sat next to her husband. She was small with golden hair pulled away from her face and curled so that it fell down her back in a way I had not seen in other women. She was more a girl than a woman, perhaps eighteen. I glanced at Louis Garnier. He could have been her father.

"Her parents were killed when she was a child," Garnier said. "They were distant relations of mine. I took Marie when they died."

"My husband is a generous man," Marie said. Garnier glanced at her and then down at his food again. Marie picked up her goblet with her child's hand and sipped the water slowly.

"How long can you stay with us?" Garnier asked me.

"Though the week if that is convenient for you and Mme. Garnier," I said. "I wish to be far from the world for a time."

Marie twisted the heart-shaped ring on her little finger. She did not look at either of us, yet I sensed she was intensely interested in the conversation.

"No inconvenience," Garnier said, his voice merry. "It will be good for Marie to have someone around closer to her own age. In this forsaken place, she has only me and her wretched Gypsy as companions."

Marie looked at Garnier and smiled. "Yes, it will be good to have M. Rieux stay." She reached out to touch her husband's arm, but he quickly moved it out of her reach.

"Hurry and eat, my dear," Garnier said. "You have lessons. I must go into the village today, but I will want to hear your recitations when I return."

"I am finished," Marie said. She had not eaten anything. "If you will excuse me?" I nodded. Marie quietly left the room.

"Troubled child," Garnier said.

"How so?"

"You cannot see?" he said. "She has the mark of the beast on her."

"I'm afraid I do not understand." I had seen no birthmark on her. No sign of the devil.

"Her parents were killed within this Godless forest," he said, "by a man-wolf. Marie almost died, too. She was mauled by the beast."

"Are you saying her parents were killed by a werewolf?"

Garnier pushed away from the table. "Yes, such things live in these forests. We convicted a man only last week for crimes he committed while he was in the shape of a wolf. I go to town today for his execution."

I had heard stories of werewolves, but I had regarded such tales as mere gossip—a way to damage a man's good name.

"These are treacherous times," Garnier said, his voice rising. "The plague devastated our village ten years ago. As we try to rebuild, we have witnessed a degradation of moral character which must be stopped. The man we are hanging raped and killed a young girl! A rope will snap the devil out of him. It will break the beast's back."

"What does this have to do with your wife, sir?"

"My wife is an emotional . . . sensual girl. She must be on her guard or the beast she carries within her will be unleashed." He looked out the window at the forest. "I married her so no one else would."

I stared at him, not understanding how he could speak so about his own wife.

He sighed and slapped the table. "Well, enjoy yourself today. I will return before dark."

As Garnier left the room, Marie wandered into view outside. An older woman with shiny black hair followed her. They talked in friendly whispers. Marie laughed and touched her companion often. When she bent to sniff a rose, she saw me watching. She bowed slightly. I nodded. Perhaps later I would get an opportunity to talk with her.

Clouds covered the chateau soon after Garnier rode away. The rainfall was heavy and I was in no mood to hunt. Instead, I explored the chateau. I walked about for some time admiring the woodwork and paintings. Then I grew hungry and wanted to return whence I had come. I soon realized I was lost. I wandered down a long empty corridor cursing myself. First the forest and now the chateau.

I heard laughter coming from one end of the passage and I went toward the sound.

"Raynie! That's cold!" Marie's voice.

I stopped at the entrance to the room. The two women had their backs to me. A fire burned in a huge stone fireplace. Near to the fire, Marie sat on the polished stone floor, naked, her knees drawn up toward her breasts. Her eyes were closed as the old woman stroked her back with a wet cloth. Tiny pools of water around her buttocks and feet reflected the fire and her whiteness. I remained still, startled by the beauty of the scene. I watched the cloth move up and down. With her other hand, the old woman stroked Marie's hair.

"This reminds me of when I was a child," Marie said. "When you would take me to the river. Remember?"

The old woman nodded. She leaned forward. Her hand moved up over Marie's shoulder until the cloth and her fingers cradled Marie's small breast.

I nearly gasped. Marie's mouth opened slightly. The pleasure was so apparent in her features that I almost became ill. Garnier had been right. The fire illuminated her lustful features. She *was* a sensual creature.

The woman's hand moved again. Marie giggled.

"That tickles!"

I stared at Marie. She was merely a young woman enjoying the innocent caresses of her servant.

I stepped away from them and leaned against the wall. It was I who was lustful, I who had seen what was not there, I who had stared at another man's wife while she bathed!

"I cannot bear Louis's coldness," Marie whispered. "He thinks I am some kind of monster."

"Shhh, child, you are not a monster."

"I want to be touched. Loved. Is that wrong?" Her voice trembled. "I remember when your people used to visit us once a year." Her voice became happy again. "How we danced! Each person held me in his arms for a moment before whirling me forward. I am sorry Louis won't allow them on his land anymore."

"We will sneak away to see them sometime soon," Raynie said. "They have only just arrived, did I tell you?" Raynie's voice was gentle and affectionate, stroking away her mistress's despair.

I hurried from the women, down the passageway and the stairs, and somehow found my way back to my own room.

Garnier was late getting home. We ate alone. I was both disappointed and relieved that Marie did not join us.

"He cried out for forgiveness," Garnier said, describing the hanging. "We told him to beg the Almighty Lord for mercy."

"Tell me," I said, watching the reflection of the candle flames in the side of my goblet, "how did you know this man was a werewolf?"

"He confessed."

"Convenient."

"Easier, yes," he said. He picked up a pheasant leg and began pulling off the meat. "We caught a werewolf in his wolf shape once. Someone shot him and he immediately became a man again. Injury sometimes makes them revert, but death *always* makes them become what they truly are—men who have strayed."

We ate in silence for several minutes. Then Garnier said, "I must excuse myself to listen to Marie's recitations of the holy word. Tomorrow we will go hunting."

"Yes, I look forward to that."

I sat in the near dark sipping my wine. I shrugged away visions of the hanged man, and instead thought of Marie by the fire. How could Garnier see the mark of the beast on her? She seemed to be an innocent. Only a girl.

Suddenly, I heard shouts. A moment later, I heard muffled sobs. Raynie ran past the dining room. I followed her into the passageway. She stood near the closed doors with her head in her hands. Garnier's shouts grew louder. Raynie looked up at me.

"Is he hurting her?" I asked.

"Do you mean is he beating her? No, he does not touch her." She moved toward me with sudden familiarity. I stepped back. "He never touches her. He pretends he has no desires, yet he leaves her several nights a week for his whores. When he returns, he is more brutal than ever because they could not satisfy him." Her eyes were intense. "You saw her. You know the only beast in her is the one he will bring out!"

I backed up against the wall. Did this woman know I had been watching them? Did she know I had seen her naked mistress? I felt hot and ashamed.

"He pushes her as only a monster would," she said.

The doors flew open. Raynie disappeared around a corner. Garnier strode by me. When the sound of his footsteps had faded, I went into the room. Marie was by the fire. At first I thought she was stretched in front of the flames, languishing like a cat before the heat. Then I realized she was sobbing. I knelt next to her. Without looking at me, she moved closer. I reached out to touch her.

Raynie came in then. I dropped my outstretched hand and moved out of the way as she took Marie in her arms. I hurriedly left the room and went upstairs. I lay in bed, sleepless, wondering what I could do to help Mme. Garnier.

The next morning, Garnier was out behind the chateau examining his roses when I came downstairs.

"There you are," he called as I walked across the lawn toward him. "Did you eat? I must apologize for last night. I'm afraid Marie is not a very obedient girl, but we should not have quarreled with guests in the house. It is the influence of that old Gypsy." He bent slightly and broke off a rose blossom from its bush. "Not quite the right shade of red." He tossed away the flower. "So I sent the woman back to her Gypsies. She left this morning before Marie awakened. I thought it would be easier that way."

A scream interrupted our conversation. The scream became a wail.

"Excuse me," Garnier said. "My wife has awakened and discovered her loss." He walked toward the chateau.

I picked up the rose blossom he had cast aside and pocketed it. I waited several minutes to see if my host would return. I wanted desperately to run inside to see if Marie was well. Instead, I listened to the surrounding forest. The voices of the birds and insects seemed to blend together in a peculiar soothing song. After a while, I realized the animal world was being accompanied by the tinkling tones of a harpsichord. I followed the sound around the chateau and in through the front door. I walked down the corridor until I reached the room where Marie and Garnier had argued the night before. Now, Garnier sat in a chair near the fire with a curious smile on his lips. By the window, Marie sat at the harpsichord. She stared ahead without expression, yet I sensed she was in agony. Each note brought a tear to her eye that would tip over to her cheek and down her face until it disappeared onto the instrument; for a moment, I was certain her tears were bringing the song to our ears rather than her fingers.

"Is this not pleasant?" Garnier asked. "Please, join us."

Reluctantly, I sat in a chair by the door. As I watched Marie and listened to each high note, I was reminded of my night in the forest and the cry of the lonely wolf howling to an empty sky. I longed to take Marie in my arms and stroke her lovely hair and ease her pain. I had to act somehow; I could no longer stand by and watch this innocent be so cruelly treated. I stood.

"That is enough, Marie," Garnier said abruptly "It was lovely." His tone was conciliatory. "Rieux and I will go hunting now. Will you join us for supper later?"

Marie smiled, her tears gone. "Of course," she said. "Enjoy your afternoon."

"Come, young man," Garnier said. I glanced at Marie. She was still smiling. Perhaps I had imagined the tears.

▼▼▼

We had bagged several quail and pheasant by midday. At that time, we stopped along a stream to eat the bread and cheese we had brought. Garnier was friendly, yet I found it increasingly difficult to hold my tongue regarding his treatment of his wife.

"You think I am cruel," he said quite unexpectedly. "Well, you do not understand women." He laughed. "Perhaps you do. You have never married, have you?"

I shook my head.

"Marie . . . there are things about her you do not know. Ways she makes people feel." He tore off a chunk of bread from the loaf. "You are my friend's son, so I will caution you. I can tell she has caught your fancy. Do not be left alone with her. She will try to seduce you."

"M. Garnier!" I cried. "She is your wife. Must you speak of her so? Must you assume that I would allow myself to be seduced?" I stood and began pacing the banks of the stream. "Perhaps I have come at a bad time. I will leave tomorrow."

"My friend Rieux will be displeased if you leave with this impression of me," Garnier said. "I wish you would stay a while longer."

I did not want to offend my father's friend, although I was certain my father would be shocked by Garnier's manner. I sighed. "I will stay another day and night, and then I really must return home," I said. "Now, shall we continue on our way?"

We remained in the forest until mid-afternoon and then we returned to the chateau, hot and tired from our excursion. We gave the game bags to the kitchen staff and then went our separate ways for a rest. I lay in the cool darkness of my room and wished I could say something to Garnier which would change his attitude toward Marie. Perhaps he was right, I thought as I closed my eyes. Perhaps I was merely captivated by a young girl who was trying to entice me. No, I turned onto my stomach; Marie was merely attempting to save herself from a loveless man.

I drifted into sleep. I dreamed Marie came into my chamber. She put her small hand on mine. I kissed the tiny heart-shaped ring on her smallest finger.

"You can save me," she whispered. She lay next to me on the bed, naked except for some kind of sheer garment which covered her entire body.

"Save me," she whispered.

I reached for her.

Garnier shook me awake. I sat up quickly and looked around. Marie was not there. I sighed, relieved.

"A man was torn to pieces outside the village," Garnier said. "They are certain it was a man-wolf. We're going hunting."

I hurried downstairs with Garnier. Outside, in the near night, several men waited, torches held high. Dusk? Apparently I had slept for hours.

"Stay in pairs," Garnier called. "Shoot to kill."

I glanced back at the house as we started toward the forest. Marie stood in the music room, looking out at us. I felt her hand on my arm once again, heard her pleas. "Save me." I stepped into the forest and followed the light of Garnier's torch.

The men talked loudly. Garnier's face was alight with the joy of an adventure, or lust for the kill. I remembered too well my hours of wandering alone in this forest. I did not look forward to meeting a wolf, werewolf or otherwise. As we went further into the forest, we broke up into pairs. Garnier and I walked in silence. Once we heard the cry of a wolf coming from a great distance. An owl talked to us as we passed by it. A full moon ascended. And still we walked.

Suddenly, when the forest was completely silent, when I could hear only the breathing of my companion, something huge and black leaped out of the darkness, howling as it knocked Garnier to the ground. Garnier screamed. I heard bones crunch, like a chicken leg being snapped, as the beast closed its jaws around Garnier's arm. I jumped on the animal and tried to pull it off Garnier. It shook me away easily, but the effort caused it to release Garnier. Then it turned on me. I smelled blood on its breath. Garnier struggled to reach his musket. Using its huge black head, the beast rammed me up against a tree. Then it attacked Garnier again, furiously, enraged, it seemed. I saw a flash of moonlight on steel. The animal screamed in agony and then it was gone, disappearing into the darkness.

I dropped onto the ground next to Garnier.

"Are you injured?" I asked. I still smelled blood.

"Yes, my arm is broken. But I've got a prize!" He held up something in the darkness which I could not quite see. "I sliced off a piece of its devil's paw." He dropped the thing into his game bag.

"I'll take you back to the chateau," I said. "Can someone there attend to your wounds?"

"Yes," he answered, his breathing ragged.

I picked up the smoldering torch, the muskets, and the game bags.

"Come. Lean on me," I told him.

The journey back to the chateau was a long one. Garnier was hardly alert enough to give directions. We met no other men, though we heard shots in the distance several times. Every sound in the forest was now a warning to me that the beast was returning. I longed for Marie's guiding hand.

Finally, we stood on the moonlit lawn of the chateau. Garnier collapsed. I ran to the house and awakened the servants. Within minutes, they had carried their master up to his rooms and were seeing to his wounds. I picked up the game bags and muskets and took them into the house.

The stench of blood on my own clothes was sickening, so I returned to my bed chamber to retrieve other garments. I dropped the soiled clothes into a corner and put on fresh ones. Then I sat on the bed and opened the game bag to get a look at the severed paw of the monster who had attacked us.

I tilted the bag toward the light. In a pool of black blood there lay not a paw of some unknown beast but two fingers from a human hand. I threw down the bag and quickly moved away from it. Two small fingers: one with a tiny heart-shaped ring on it.

I felt ill. "Save me," she had begged in my dream. "The only beast in her is the one Garnier will bring out," Raynie had said.

I picked up the bag and left the room. Quietly, I went up several flights of stairs and down the corridor until I found Marie's room again. She lay on her bed, her eyes closed, her face ashen. Her left hand was wrapped in gauze. Raynie stood at her side.

I held out the bag to Raynie. She came to me and looked into the bag. She shook her head.

"She doesn't know what happened," Raynie said. "It's never happened before, but I was afraid it would. That's why I came back."

"I don't believe you," I said. "Garnier said a man was killed earlier today by a werewolf."

"It was not her," Raynie said. "Please, she was driven to it! He married her and then did not love her. It was cruel."

"He was right all along," I said. "She does have the mark of the beast on her."

"And the beast is M. Garnier!" she cried. Marie moaned. Raynie went to her and stroked her arm. "You cannot tell anyone of this," she said. "They will kill her. First they will torture her and then kill her! Please, you cannot tell them!"

"Garnier will find out," I said. "He will see the ring. He will see her hand!"

"Raynie?" Marie whispered. "It hurts."

"I know, child," she said. "Shhh." She moved away from the girl and touched my arm. "She is in great pain. I must return to the caravan and get some medicine for her. Can you stay with her?"

I heard the snarls of the beast, smelled the blood again. I gazed at Marie. How could they be one and the same?

"I will stay," I said.

Raynie went back to Marie and leaned over her. "M. Rieux will stay with you while I'm gone. I will return before morning."

She kissed the girl's forehead and then she left. I sat in a chair near the bed.

Marie's eyes were closed as she reached for me. Her fingers curled around mine. "Save me," she whispered. "Please."

"Rest," I said. "You are safe."

As the candle burned down and the moon moved across the sky, I waited for Raynie with Marie's hand in mine. Near the end of the night, I fell asleep. I awakened to find Garnier bent over his game bag. His right arm was wrapped and tied to his neck. He looked at me with a self-satisfied smile.

I gently pried Marie's fingers from my own.

"It was Marie who tried to kill me," Garnier said.

"Be quiet," I said, coming toward him. "You'll wake her. Shouldn't you be resting?" I put my hand on his arm to lead him away. He shook me off and stepped closer to the bed. I moved in front of him.

"This is none of your concern," he said, looking beyond me.

"You made it my concern," I said.

"I will report it to the council tomorrow," he said. "She will be executed."

"And that certainty does not trouble you?" I asked.

He looked at me. "No," he said. "She as troubled my sleep with her lustful longings, she has troubled my waking hours with her lustful looks. She should have died in that forest with her parents. It would have been easier."

"Easier for whom? She only wanted your affection," I said. "You are her husband!"

"She will die for this." He turned and strode from the room. I hurried after him.

"Garnier," I called. "Please, stop." I caught up with him at the top of the stairs. "You mustn't do this. Have you no feeling for her?"

"I feel her teeth in my arm," Garnier said. "Now leave be." He turned. I grabbed his arm. As he pulled away, he lost his balance. I tried to catch him, but he fell away from me and tumbled down the stairs. Seconds later, he lay at the bottom of the stairs, his head askew, both arms flung out at odd angles. I ran down to him. As I knelt by him, he sighed once and then was still.

"Louis?"

I looked up. Marie was at the top of the stairs. I raced up to her and put my arms around her.

"Don't look," I said. "It was an accident."

"He's dead?" she asked.

"Yes." She fell against me. She felt like a child in my arms. "It will be all right," I said.

Someone screamed. I looked toward the sound. At the bottom of the stairs, one of the servants stood. She held her fist in her mouth as she gazed at her master. I gasped. Where Garnier had been, there was now the huge mangled body of some beast which resembled a wolf.

"My God," I whispered.

Raynie was at my elbow, taking Marie away from me.

"We all become what we truly are in death," Raynie said. "He did not love her well."

Marie leaned heavily on Raynie as they went back to her room. "I have brought something to ease your pain," Raynie whispered.

▼▼▼

I buried the wolf, Marie's two fingers, and the heart-shaped ring all in one grave before sunrise. I knew Garnier's relatives would descend upon Marie and the chateau as soon as they learned of his death. Marie said she wanted to leave with Raynie. I gave them my horse so no charge of theft could be brought against them. Marie and I said our farewells at dawn. I took her wounded child's hand in mine and kissed it.

"I am sorry," I whispered.

She squeezed my fingers. "Thank you," she said. She released my hand, and the women rode off to join the Gypsies. That was the last time I saw Marie. The story was later told that M. Garnier had been killed by a werewolf, and the attack had left him blood-ied, battered, and changed; Mme. Garnier had returned to her people.

I traveled back to my father's house.

Months later, I met a woman called Joy who reminded me of bright days and laughter beyond all earthly considerations. We married. When we had children, I held them close and stroked their fine golden hair and told them they were jewels of inestima-ble value. I often dreamed of Marie and Garnier. I would awaken cold and sweaty, afraid of the darkness and the beasts within. One night when I awakened in terror, I told my wife about the dreams. She kissed me and pulled me out of bed. "Dance with the beasts," she said. "Don't be frightened by them." We laughed and danced together in a shaft of silver moonlight that fell across our floor.

Afterward, the dreams stopped. From that time forward, when I thought of Marie, I imagined her dancing in the arms of some-one who knew how to embrace the beast and love her well.

AT WAR WITH
THE WOLF MAN
▼▼▼

JEROME CHARYN

THE mayor was going out of her mind. She didn't need another Wolf Man scare. Tourism was down thirteen percent. Manhattan was becoming a ghost town toward midnight. If *this* Wolf Man continued to strike with such alarming regularity, then Her Honor would have to go into the street and sing love songs to a vanishing New York. The first Wolf Man had added a festive touch to the city. He was a starving actor who wore a crazy mask and bit women on the neck without leaving a hint of blood. He came and went with the holiday season. But the new Wolf Man made his own seasons. He had claws and big yellow teeth and ran away with enormous pieces of flesh. Surgeons had to sew people together after the Wolf Man struck. Whatever witnesses there were claimed he had the clearest blue eyes under a great maw of fur, a kind of whisker that extended to his forehead like some extraordinary foliage. The blue eyes were intelligent. But the Wolf Man clawed without mercy. Nineteen men and women lay in the hospital because of him. Half were lingering in a life-support system, the eyes all yellow, the faces like waxen masks.

Becky Karp blamed the whole affair on Isaac Sidel. He was her police commissioner, and Isaac hadn't slowed the Wolf Man's walk across Manhattan.

"Isaac, do something, or my whole administration will sink."

"I'm doing what I can. I have my deputies out on the street day and night."

"It's not good enough," she screamed at Isaac, who looked like a woolly bear with sideburns. "I want a special werewolf patrol, with an ace psychologist who can talk about all the implications . . . what's that word again?"

"Lycanthropy," Isaac said.

"Yes, lycanthropy. We need a spokesman, Isaac. Someone who can calm the public, who can give the right definitions, take a scientific approach. Not a policeman like you. You're too primitive, Isaac. I want a scientist on this case. Either you pick one, or I will."

"Then I'll resign," Isaac said.

"You won't resign. You're too interested in the Wolf Man . . . it's sink or swim, Isaac. Get me a scientist."

Isaac marched out of City Hall with reporters on his back, nibbling like little vampires. What could he say? He'd captured the other Wolf Man, Harvey Montaigne, because Isaac had discovered his modus operandi. There was something theatrical about Montaigne in all the tracks he left, that desire to play at harming people, as if he were caught in some perpetual Halloween, and was waiting for Isaac, who stumbled upon him in a hotel room, lonely and depressed, a couple of days after Christmas.

"How'd you find me?" Harvey Montaigne had asked.

"By chance."

"I've seen you on the tube. Your sideburns are too big. How'd you find me?"

But Isaac wouldn't give his secrets away. While his own detectives scoured the city, looking for some maniac in a mask, Isaac had gone through hundreds of theatrical bills, until he happened upon a bill that belonged to a small theatre company in Queens, the Corona Players, which was offering an ensemble production of "The Monster Hours, a Musical by Many Hands." It wasn't simply that the Corona Players had a Wolf Man in their ensemble. They also had a Frankenstein and a Dracula. And these monsters were played "by Many Hands," which bothered Isaac. Because there was a terrible sadness built into the idea of monsters shaking their musical bones in some obscure corner of Queens. And so Isaac trespassed upon the anonymity of the Corona Players, interviewed Harvey's mother, who was the head cashier, and broke the case.

He was called the number-one detective in the world, Sidel, who reached outside his own Department to bring in Harvey Montaigne. And now the public expected him to sustain his own magic and have another success. But this Wolf Man didn't wear a mask. He took wicked bites out of people's throats, he chewed on their flesh. He held to Manhattan, but that wasn't much of an MO. The Wolf Man might decide to cross a bridge one afternoon and start a whole other life.

And Isaac was hounded by reporters, foreign and domestic, because the Wolf Man was international news, a totem of our times, the beast within the belly of the beast. Isaac gave no interviews. But he couldn't shuffle between Headquarters and City Hall without being noticed.

"Isaac, is this another Harvey Montaigne?"

"No comment."

And he withdrew into the red maze of One Police Plaza. But Becky had already found a scientist for *her* werewolf patrol. He was a professor of psychology at Brooklyn College who specialized in lycanthropy and other kinds of cannibalism. He was much younger than Isaac, a mulatto from Los Angeles who'd migrated to Bedford-Stuy. He looked like a cherub. His name was Walter Gunn.

"Let's get one thing straight, Professor Gunn."

"Walter will do," the cherub said. "I don't like formalities when I'm on a case."

"You've worked for other police departments?"

"As a consultant, yes. You don't think your Wolf Man is the only one around, do you, Commissioner?"

"Call me Isaac."

"Then don't fuck with me. I didn't ask for this assignment."

"You're a civilian," Isaac said.

"So are you."

"But I still have a badge and a gun. Let Becky Karp play her politics. I give the orders around here. If you're her spy, Walter, then say so. I'll respect that. You can sleep on my carpet and collect your honorariums. Just leave me alone."

"Yeah, you're the boy who found Harvey Montaigne. But this one isn't Harvey. He eats human flesh."

"I don't believe in werewolves, Walter. And if this mother is a cannibal, then I'll kick his ass."

"He eats flesh, Isaac. The victims will die of blood poisoning or pernicious anemia, and you'll have more than a curio on your hands. You'll have a killer, whoever or whatever he is. You need me, Isaac, or you'll never get near him."

"Then what's your guess?"

"The Bangor Wolf. He came down from Canada and he's been causing havoc ever since."

"Is he some trapper who started hallucinating in the woods?"

"All I know is he's a werewolf."

"Whiskers and all that shtick. Did they run saliva tests on this Bangor baby's victims?"

"Yes, they found human spittle and human blood. But Bangor is human, Isaac. That's the whole point. He only has certain characteristics of a wolf."

"Blame it on the moon," Isaac said.

"Or some deep psychosis. It doesn't matter. Bangor has fur on his face and unholy blue eyes. He's down from the north woods, I'm telling you. And he's nesting in Manhattan."

"Then why haven't you volunteered this information until now?"

"I did. But your detectives wouldn't believe me."

"So you went to Becky Karp."

"No. Her Honor came to me."

"Grand," Isaac said, imitating his Irish forebears at the NYPD. "Nesting in Manhattan. But I thought he has a fondness for woods."

"He does. I'd say he's living in Central Park."

"And he won't foul his nest. So he waltzes into the side streets whenever he wants a meal. But he seems to have a fondness for lower Manhattan. Nine of his hits have been below Fourteenth Street. What does he do, Walter? Hail a cab? Or does he hop around after midnight, stealing clothes from the best boutiques?"

"No. He uses the subway system."

"A straphanger, huh?"

"A man can move awful fast in those tunnels, Isaac. There are abandoned lines and everything. All he'd have to do is wear a long coat and step down into the tracks."

Isaac began to look at the cherub. "You've done your homework . . . I shouldn't have been so gruff."

"You're a police commissioner. You have to be suspicious."

"Don't compliment me, Walter. I'm a son of a bitch."

▼▼▼

The Wolf Man knocked down a widow on Madison and Twenty-ninth, ate off half her neck. But the widow wouldn't die. She lingered like the others until Isaac felt he inhabited this same half-world between the living and the dead. Whiskers. Blue Eyes. Homo lupus, the wolf who walked upright.

Isaac avoided the slow-eyed detectives from the Central Park precinct. They could catch their own case. He brought in a squad of men who looked like state troopers. They pummeled through the grass. They knocked open abandoned caves in the northern heights of the Park. They poked around in the Harlem Meer, frightening users of crack. Isaac worked with an enormous blueprint. He was like some pirate searching for the secret treasure of a Wolf Man's droppings. There were no signs of the Wolf Man's nest. Isaac broke up a small smuggling ring that operated out of an old abandoned fort. He arrested half a dozen crack dealers and a rapist. But Isaac wanted the Wolf Man.

He went into the bowels of Manhattan with two engineers from the Metropolitan Transit Authority. He rode in a little electric car. It was like Coney Island under the ground. One of the engineers kept socking at rats' heads with a shovel. They entered a subway line that had been closed in nineteen twenty-six. Isaac had to get out of the little car, because there was no electricity on this line. He was given a pair of boots and a miner's lamp that he wore over his brain. The old subway station was intact. And Isaac marveled at the different-colored tiles, mosaics that spelled out Beaver Street and Cherry Street on this phantom line. Isaac was a little jealous. His own dead uncles and aunts might have been among the human cargo seventy years ago. A piece of his own history had eluded Isaac, the expert on Manhattan.

He made thirty arrests. He collared a gang of pickpockets that had used the Cherry Street station as their private sanctuary. There were no signs of the Wolf Man. Isaac grew more and more depressed.

He visited Harvey Montaigne, who lived at a half-way house run by the Federation of Jewish Philanthropies. He wasn't sure what this earlier Wolf Man could divine for him, but Isaac needed Harvey somehow.

"Have you been acting again?"

"No. I couldn't seem to pick up on my career."

"I could have talked to a couple of producers."

"Yeah, and I'd have to play the Wolf Man for the rest of my life."

"You shouldn't have gone around biting people. I had no choice. Someone could have been killed. A cop might have seen you in your mask and shot your head off . . . Harvey, I need your help."

"That's a laugh," the Wolf Man said.

"I'm not kidding. What's your opinion about this Wolf Man?"

"I have no opinions."

"But you have to feel something. I mean, it has to touch you somewhere. Another Wolf Man."

"He's a perfect stranger to me."

"But who do you think he is?"

"One more actor, Mr. Isaac, in a fucking world of actors."

▼▼▼

The Wolf Man struck again. He had his own cosmology. The moon could wax or wane around him. He was always out on the street with that furry head and bottomless blue eyes. And Isaac began to wonder if the Wolf Man was some horrible visitation upon the city itself, as if all the monstrosities of Manhattan had taken flesh.

But he didn't have time to ponder. Becky's scientist had been hit by a bus. Isaac brought him flowers at Mount Sinai Hospital. Walter Gunn's lips had turned entirely blue. He lay like some discarded man inside intensive care. Isaac had to use all his influence to enter Walter's tiny closet.

"I saw the Wolf Man," Walter said, puffing out his blue lips.

"Why'd you go tracking him on your own?"

"Because you wouldn't believe that he hibernates in Central Park."

"Bears hibernate," Isaac said. "Not wolves."

"Our man hibernates whenever he's in the mood."

"And he gets up periodically to eat some human flesh . . . Walter, we combed Central Park. We searched every cave. We didn't find his fucking nest."

"But I caught him coming out of the Park."

"How can you tell it was the Bangor Wolf?"

"The whiskers, Isaac, and the eyes."

"Was he wearing clothes?"

"A dirty pea coat, dark pants, shoes without socks."

"No socks? Are you sure?"

"His pants were rolled up. He didn't have shoelaces. He didn't have socks. He rushed past me. I tried to follow him and . . ."

Walter shut his eyes and never opened them again. He was the first fatality in the war against the Wolf Man.

Isaac returned to Central Park with a complement of detectives and trained dogs. The dogs devoured rabbits in the north woods. The detectives tore through every patch of ground. Isaac called off the search. He sat in his office at One Police Plaza like some melancholiac. He wouldn't take calls from Becky Karp. He set up his miniature chessboard and replayed the opening gambits of Bobby Fisher, the former world champion who was hibernating in his own north woods.

He allowed only one visitor, Harvey Montaigne, who'd walked out of his half-way house in a pair of slippers and a flannel robe. "Mr. Isaac, I'm sorry I was so glib. I want to help."

"It's too late."

"I want to help."

Harvey Montaigne wore his flannel robe in Isaac's limousine. People mistook him for a medium Isaac had hired. They forgot he was the former Wolf Man. Isaac visited the catacomb of old abandoned subway stations with Harvey Montaigne. They heard the beat of water over their heads. They discovered more and more stations until Isaac realized there was a whole New York he knew nothing about. He existed at the scratchy surface of things. The interior had never been his.

Harvey caught a cold. Isaac fed him Bufferin and brought him home to the half-way house. He had his aides look for any other reference to the Bangor Wolf. There were none. He faxed all the police chiefs of Maine. No one could recall any previous sightings of the Bangor Wolf.

▼▼▼

The moon turned a marble color and was eaten up in the sky. Isaac slept in his office. Hairs grew on his face. He was one more hibernating man. He got a call from Central Park. The Wolf Man had been spotted. Isaac didn't even get out of his chair. Fifty patrol cars converged upon the Park. Sharpshooters were arriving from Tactical Services. The dogs were taken out of the kennels at the Police Academy. And Isaac sat.

He looked at his own hairy face and left One Police Plaza. He entered the catacombs through a door near the tracks of Becky's own subway station at City Hall. Isaac walked a half mile under the ground and arrived at the Cherry Street station of the old Kings County line. He had his pocket flashlight and a small, collapsible shovel with a very sharp blade. My man likes a direct north to south line, with only a little bit of a bias, Isaac muttered to himself. He knew Bangor would escape the sharpshooters and the dogs.

Isaac whistled to himself and waited.

He heard the trudge of feet against the tracks.

He put out the light and opened the shovel's neck. Ah, he said. Should have brought my baseball bat. But the shovel had been more convenient.

He saw the blueness of the eyes, caught the heavy breathing. He couldn't tell if the Wolf Man had been wounded or not. Isaac would have to depend on surprise. His heart was pounding.

I'll have to wait until I can feel his whiskers.

He held the shovel in that high, classic stance of Joe DiMaggio and walloped the Wolf Man over the head.

The Wolf Man dropped without a groan. Isaac shoved the light in his eyes. The Wolf Man was all whiskers. He looked shorter than

Isaac. He slept like a little boy without his socks. His teeth weren't yellow. He had long fingernails, but he didn't have claws.

▼▼▼

It was Isaac who carried him out of the catacombs, who brought him to the Elizabeth Street police station, read him his rights while the Wolf Man was still groggy. And that was Isaac's last moment of peace. There were reporters all over the place. Becky Karp arrived in her chauffered limousine. She had a press conference on the steps of the precinct. "Ain't he the best?" she said, pointing to Isaac, who stood outside the cage where the Wolf Man sat, hair up to his eyes.

"You can't become a wolf man in the city of New York without getting zapped by Isaac Sidel."

And Isaac was feeling more and more guilty. Perhaps he shouldn't have used a shovel. But if there had been detectives around from the tactical unit, they would have shot out the Wolf Man's teeth. No one, not even a wolf man, should have been subjected to this: sitting in a cage like a circus freak, while there was a fury of faces all around him.

Her Honor entered the precinct. She was still angry at Isaac, because he'd stopped sleeping with her. Isaac was in love with Margaret Tolstoy, an undercover girl for the FBI *and* the KGB.

"Is that him?" Becky said, growling into the cage. The Wolf Man blinked.

"Becky," Isaac said, "leave the guy alone."

"Guy? That's a fucking monster, not a guy."

"Yeah, but if you tamper with him, some judge will put him back in the street."

"Over my dead body . . . Isaac, have dinner with me."

"Can't," Isaac said.

"Ah, it's that Roumanian slut, Madame Tolstoya. She's been jerking you off, Isaac. She has a hundred boyfriends."

"Becky, do you have to discuss my personal life in public?"

"You have no personal life. You're my police commissioner."
And she disappeared from Elizabeth Street.

Isaac took the Wolf Man out of the cage and brought him
into the interrogation room. It was the last chance Isaac would
have to talk with the Wolf Man, who had no Social Security
card or driver's license in his pockets, no identity papers. The
blue eyes seemed to converge somewhere beyond Isaac's narrow
ken.

"I can help you," Isaac said.

The Wolf Man would belong to the courts once he was
arraigned.

"I can help you."

The Wolf Man wouldn't take cigarettes or a sandwich from
Isaac.

"If the D.A. starts getting rough, call me . . . day or night,"
Isaac said, shoving his card into the Wolf Man's shirt pocket.

▼▼▼

The Wolf Man did become a child of the courts. He sat in his
own ward at Bellevue. No one could discover his name. He didn't
seem to have a past outside his little history of chewing on people.
Then a woman came forth and identified the Wolf Man as her
son, Monroe Tapler, who'd grown up as an incorrigible in Jersey
City and had moved to Manhattan at the age of twenty-two and
lived in the streets. Papers began to appear in psychological jour-
nals on the subject of Monroe Tapler as sociopath "in our mean,
modern season."

Isaac wrote to the editor of one such journal.

Dear Sir,
    In regard to the article, "Pathology of the Lycanthrope,"
in your November number, I would like to say that your
author is skating on very thin ice. Monroe Tapler may have

bitten people at nine or ten, but that would not necessarily make him a wolf man. I'm afraid your author should have moved from psychology to myth. The Wolf Man is closer to our collective unconscious than he is to any sociopathic chart.

Sincerely, Isaac Sidel

The letter started a controversy. But Isaac was sick of the whole thing. His whiskers grew longer and longer. He began to look like the Wolf Man. And one night, while he was in his tiny apartment on the Lower East Side, he had a visit from Margaret Tolstoy, she who slept with Mafia chieftains all across America while she busted up gangs for the FBI. She was over fifty, Isaac's age. But he couldn't take his eyes off her. She was wearing a blond wig in her latest avatar. Her cheeks were flushed. Her eyes looked like huge green marbles. She removed a pair of scissors from her handbag without saying a word and chopped off Isaac's beard.

"Now you're human," she said.

Isaac stared into the mirror. He had white stubble all over his face.

"Come to bed," she told him. He lay down next to Margaret Tolstoy. She rubbed the fur on his chest.

"My little Wolf Man," she said, and she made love to him until most of his melancholy was gone.

DAY OF THE WOLF
▼▼▼

CRAIG SHAW GARDNER

THE animals knew.

In the city, he didn't have to worry about that. Cats, birds, rodents: all stayed out of his way. Dogs would go wild sometimes when he was near, especially as it grew close to the full moon. But other dogs, small nervous things that yipped at the heels of anything that moved, were so domesticated that they were almost as blind as their human masters.

In the city, he could be one of those famous faceless millions. No one needed to know his name, or his business. And if there was a little extra violence on the streets, no one came looking for him. It was easier, these days, for his sort to survive.

But the violence became so bad that even city people had to pay attention. There were too many dying in the wrong ways, too many bodies found with claw and teeth marks. Even those bored by drug turf wars and drive-by shootings took notice. And, once they noticed, they started to ask questions.

He had known he would have to leave the city eventually. No place was safe forever. But he had lived within the tall buildings for too long.

He had forgotten about the animals.

He was going by the name Sam now. Not that anybody had asked his name.

There was a gun pointed straight at him. The gun barrel glinted in the early morning sunlight. The moon, still visible above the horizon, was perfectly round, perfectly full. The first of three nights, he thought. Two more nights to go. If only it could be night again, and everything would change.

Sweat poured down his face. He was breathing so heavily from his exertion that his mouth was open. He could taste the salty drops of sweat on his tongue. They had him cornered, against the back wall of a neighbor's garden. There were maybe a dozen of them, spread out in a half-circle. He had nowhere else to run. He thought the revolver was a forty-four.

"Wait a moment," said one of the well-dressed men. His hunting jacket alone must have cost hundreds of dollars. "You can't shoot him."

The man holding the gun started to shake. "What do you mean, I can't shoot him? Jenny's dead!"

"You can't kill him," said the first man, his voice still calm. "Not with that."

But the man with the gun got more upset with every passing word. "She had her throat ripped out! She was only twelve, god-damn it. That thing over there only looks human." He glanced down then at the revolver in his hand, almost as if he couldn't believe it was there himself. For a moment his voice became quieter, almost resigned. "It has to die."

"I'm not arguing with you, John," the first man said. "That thing has to die. But if that's what we think it is, regular bullets won't kill it."

Someone laughed nervously in the crowd. And the way John looked at Sam, he knew the gunman wasn't buying the argument.

"To hell with your silver bullets!" John screamed, his voice shifting to the falsetto as it again filled with emotion. His gun hand shook with his rage. "I'm going to shoot his fucking face off!"

He cried out as he pulled the trigger, as if the bullet came not from the gun but from somewhere deep inside him.

Sam flinched as the first bullet flew into the trees over his head.

▼▼▼

If he was careful, he didn't have to hurt anyone.

That was the first of the lies.

He had tried so hard to believe that, after what he had become. He had wanted so desperately, despite everything he saw in front of him, despite all the blood and all the death, to have some sort of control.

But no matter how hard he tried, other people came, and were touched by him. And other people died. So many now, that there was no way to count them all.

The only thing that made it worse was the second lie. Like the first, it was a lie he had told only to himself:

He could stop himself at any time.

The two times he had gotten up the nerve to kill himself, he'd learned a single lesson. It didn't matter if he had slits in his wrists or a hole in his skull. He could bleed for hours or writhe for days in semi-conscious agony. But this thing that lived inside him would always make him whole again.

Not that it made him well. He could never be well again, after what had happened. But, as much as he could hurt inside, he could not die.

So he lived, and tried to keep to the edges of society, where nobody looked you straight in the eye, and he hoped and prayed no one would ever come close enough for him to jeopardize again.

But that was the first lie all over again.

▼▼▼

There was a long silence after the gunshot, the kind of quiet you never hear in the city. It was as if the explosion had frozen everyone in shock. Sam had been through this before. He could guess what went through all those normal minds. Before that gunshot, every person in that mob probably had thought of himself as a good soul, a good neighbor. What were they doing here? What were they doing to another human being?

A woman's voice broke the silence. "Arnie? Joe? Carl? Mr. Reinbeck? What's going on here? What's the matter?"

Parts of the mob shifted. Some men turned their heads to watch the woman run toward them across the lawn. Others looked away.

"Debbie," a man in the crowd called, "I thought I told you to stay at home."

"You can tell me a lot of things, Arnie," Debbie answered defiantly. "But when people start shooting guns, I want to see what's going on in my neighborhood."

"Your neighborhoods!" Arnie exploded. "Since when does freeloading in my spare bedroom make this your neighborhood?" His eyes jerked back to Sam, his expression half anger, and maybe half shock that the anger could make him forget what he was here for.

"Arnie, it doesn't matter about the neighborhood," another man interrupted. "She's right." It was the same man who'd asked John to give up the gun. "We have no business doing this ourselves. Let's get the sheriff."

"The sheriff?" John demanded. "He'll never believe what happened!" He waved the gun at his target again. "He killed my Jenny! He ate part of her, for god's sake. How many more are you going to let him murder?"

The gun went off again. Sam felt a shot of fire, then clear, cold pain, as the bullet entered the soft flesh of his upper arm.

The woman screamed and ran to his side. He realized he had lost his balance when he saw she was using her weight to help keep him on his feet.

"Debbie!" Arnie screamed, his face almost as deep a red as the fluid pouring from Sam's arm. "If you get in the way one more time, I swear—"

"What are you going to do, Arnie?" She called out to the crowd: "What are all of you going to do? You're all animals!"

He couldn't help himself. He started to laugh.

It was always the animals.

▼▼▼

So he moved on before they came for him. It didn't matter that they never ever knew exactly what they were looking for. There was always the chance that they'd stumble upon him anyway. He always moved on when he felt that shift coming, like an animal who senses a change in the weather. In all the years since this had begun, he had changed. Most of all, he had learned how to survive.

And he'd learned, after a time, to savor this new life. He had managed to make certain investments over the years—some monetary, some personal, some legal, some not so legal—but all of them kept him comfortable. After a while, he had grown to appreciate his solitary existence as he watched the world go by, so close to all the others, yet so different from every one of them. He had started to collect things, some relating to his childhood, so long ago, others that commented on his curse. And he had started to make little changes in the world around him.

He was careful, for a time, to only go after those who he felt deserved his touch; pushers and pimps and the like. Once, when he was feeling foolhardy, he had taken a particularly obnoxious small-time politician. He might live forever—he hadn't aged since it happened, close to fifty years go—but he held death in his hands.

Then the world changed again, and even the city became dangerous. So dangerous that people started to take back the streets in order to survive, and the police started to count the corpses. But where could he go next?

He had tired quickly in his early years of living out in the wilds, far beyond civilization. And now even the jumped-up pace of the inner city seemed to pale. He'd grown restless with both extremes. It was time for something in the middle, someplace that had never seen the likes of him. Not a mountain resort, nor farm country; they'd expect wild animals in places like that, and there would be people who knew how to handle the unexpected.

But where else was there? Perhaps his years of survival had made him reckless, but he knew where he wanted to go.

So, before the next full moon, he grabbed his Big Bad Wolf Big Little Book—a cornerstone to both his collections—a suitcase full of clothes and bank books, and headed for one of the bedroom communities outside of town.

No one expected his sort of thing in the suburbs.

▼▼▼

The woman's presence changed the chemistry in the yard, but it didn't stop the violence. He had yelled out at the pain. Some might have mistaken the sound for a growl.

The others rushed forward. He felt a dozen hands on him. Some lashed out, connected with Sam's stomach, his chin, his groin. Some tried to pull their neighbors away. Debbie shouted at them to leave him alone.

He no longer had the anger to strike back at them, or the energy to tell them to stop what they were doing. He had used up everything he had in trying to escape them. Now he was nothing but tired, and all he could do was wait for this latest drama to end.

"Look, there's one way to prove this thing!" one of the men

said in a louder voice. "The moon is still full tonight. If what John says is true, we'll know then, right?"

"Yeah, right," other voices agreed one after another. "Lock him up. Reinbeck's tool shed. We'll see tonight."

John had stayed behind the rest of the crowd. "Maybe you're right," he said now as he walked forward. "I'm not a murderer. But I'm staying outside the shed until we know." He grabbed Sam's chin, and lifted his head so that he looked straight into John's eyes. "And I'm holding on to my gun."

They pushed Sam into the dark shed as the summer sun rose over the subdivision, and slammed the door behind him. He heard something heavy clank and bang against the other side; probably a padlock. He decided to sleep. There was nothing he could do that would change tonight.

▼▼▼

He woke to a sound of a key in the padlock outside.

The door swung open, and Debbie stepped inside. The door slammed shut behind her, propelled by other hands.

"I thought you'd like something to eat," she said, waving a picnic basket at the prone Sam. A picnic basket? Just like Little Red Riding Hood. He wondered if she saw the humor in that. He'd laugh all over again if he wasn't feeling so lousy. "Besides, somebody should look at your arm." In her other hand she held a damp sponge and a first-aid kit.

This Debbie, then, actually cared what happened to a stranger. He looked up at her. She was dressed simply, in worn jeans and a blouse with a faded floral print. Her clothes didn't speak of money like the wardrobes of the other women he'd seen in the neighborhood.

She smiled reassuringly. She didn't know what was going to happen.

She didn't deserve to be here like the others. But then, who was he, even now, to know what people deserved?

He had fallen in love with a woman once, soon after the change had come over him. It had shown him the true extent of his transformation, and it had been the biggest mistake he ever made.

And the woman? She still had to be alive, if you could call it that. She hadn't been able to handle what had happened. Somehow, though, he had learned from it, and survived.

He managed to push himself up to a sitting position. "You shouldn't have touched me," he said.

"Well, it's too late now, isn't it?" she said, taking his bloody arm. "Somebody had to stand up against all those men." She pulled the ragged cloth of his shirt away from the wound, and brought the damp sponge up to clean off the clotted blood. "I don't know what's gotten into them. You'd think this was the middle ages."

She stopped and looked more closely at the area of his skin she had just cleaned with her sponge. "This wound isn't as bad as I thought."

They never were, was his silent reply. He didn't have the energy, or maybe it was the emotion, for an explanation.

"It doesn't look like it was more than a scratch." She looked up at him. Her face was very close to his. She was young, maybe in her twenties. Of course, everyone looked young to him. She wasn't bad to look at, either. How long had it been since he had kissed a woman?

"That makes me feel a little better," she went on. "I can't imagine them locking you up like this, not even letting you see a doctor."

To his own surprise, he found he wanted to smile. "That sort of thing happens," he replied. "I seem to bring that out in people."

She continued to stare into his eyes. "Are you what they say you are?"

"No, not exactly," he answered as honestly as he could. "What about you? What brings you to this fine community?"

She blushed at the question. Yes, she seemed very young. "The story of my life is far too boring. A bad marriage, a job lost thanks to the recession. And here I am, trapped in the suburbs, living with my brother Arnie. I never should have moved in here. He treats me like a child, or his own personal maid! You're the first interesting thing that's happened in the six months since I got here." Her smile broadened then to show her teeth.

She considered herself an outsider, too, then; but she didn't know the meaning of the word. He shook his head. "I'm afraid you're a little bit too trusting."

She laughed softly. "What's to be scared of? Even if the whole world's turned upside down, and you're what they say you are, that won't happen until the full moon tonight."

There was something about her eyes, and that way she kept on smiling, that made him want her to be the first to know in a long time. "No, you don't understand. It's too late. Everything is already—"

He stopped. How could he possibly explain? He didn't have the words.

He looked deeper into the woman's eyes and remembered Lorraine.

▼▼▼

They were the liberators, a fancy name for a bunch of frightened kids who somehow ended up as soldiers marching through France, chasing the last remnants of the Third Reich.

It had been a great patriotic march, and it had been hell. When they weren't scared, they were tired. And if they weren't either of those, they were dead. They had lost half their battalion in nameless villages across the blasted countryside. And that day, that goddamned day, Stuart Samson was tired, and scared, and sick of nothing but K-rations. But he was also horny as a bastard.

And that day they had liberated a brothel.

Most of the whores had fled during the battle. The locals explained they had been good French girls, from the local farms, forced into service by the German occupiers. Stu and a couple of the other boys had joked about the women who were gone, wondering why they hadn't stuck around to show their gratitude. Even the Lieutenant had joined in on the laughter.

And then Stu had found that cell in the basement. And in that cell was Lorraine.

What had brought him to do it? What had he been feeling then? Even now, Sam remembered. He hadn't been angry. Or scared. Or happy. Or sad. He was nothing. That was what those endless weeks and months and years of war had done for him; killed the feelings inside. Or so he had thought then. He hadn't felt anything or wanted anything for a long time—until Lorraine.

And Stuart Samson knew what he wanted to do with her.

The other guys had found other things to do, elsewhere in the building. Even the lieutenant had pulled the cigar out of his mouth to mention, "Boys will be boys." Then he was gone, too.

So Stuart Samson went in alone, closing and locking the door behind him. A hero needed to have a little fun, didn't he?

She screamed at him in German. Hell, he didn't understand German. He bet his lieutenant wouldn't, either.

There was something about her—he'd thought about this a lot in all of the years since—something primal. If he had had any doubts about what he was doing before he got in there, they were all gone when he got that close.

Sam remembered it even now. In that moment, he had realized that all his anger, all of his fright, all of the hundred emotions that he had thought he had lost had only been locked deep inside him, waiting for the right moment to burst out, and that moment was now. Maybe that sudden rush of emotion should have made him back away, but, somehow, it only served to increase his desire.

He had to have her.

He undid his belt, pulled down his fly.

She should be goddam grateful. It wasn't like she wasn't used to it. And this was the last time she'd ever have to do this sort of thing. But, right now this liberator needed to liberate something from between his legs.

She fought him at first. But then she started to laugh. At first he thought the bitch was enjoying it.

Later on, he realized she was laughing at what Stuart had brought on himself.

▼▼▼

She kissed him.

It startled him. He didn't realize how deeply he had been lost in his memories.

"No," he said. He was different now.

"Don't argue," Debbie insisted. "I can see that you want to."

He found himself kissing her back. Why should he pull away from her now? It was too late for her, too late for this whole place. Why not just enjoy it?

He thought again about Lorraine.

He pushed himself away. "There's things you don't understand," he began, "about what's going to happen to this town—"

She laughed harshly at that. "Do you think I care at all about this whole damn town? A bunch of self-important men who think they have it made, because they live in this crummy place? And their wives aren't any better, let me tell you, with their holier-than-thou attitude about some woman who couldn't hold onto her man." She giggled; an innocent sound, like the laugh of a little girl. "Let's just do it to spite them all."

He kissed her, then. If that's the way she wanted it. They were the two outsiders, together. They kissed some more, and then they made love on the dirty floor of the shed.

It had been nearly fifty years since he had made love. Fifty years since he had discovered who he really was, and what happened to those who got too close.

Afterwards, he remembered Lorraine's laughter. But there was nothing now he wanted to laugh about.

Why had he let it happen?

Debbie and he were both outsiders. Surely, that was an easy excuse. But he had made sure they would always stay that way. This was the only way that would make a difference.

He sighed. Feelings had come and gone again, leaving him nothing but tired.

▼▼▼

He had tried to stop it from happening again.

He had moved into his new suburban home without much of a fuss. The Realtor had a bit of difficulty when he wouldn't shake hands, but he had used the old excuse of a "skin condition." It wouldn't do to wear gloves in the summer, especially when he was trying to appear as normal as possible. In certain parts of the city, you could wear pretty much what you wanted. But this new place had its advantages, too. Here in the suburbs, he thought, you could stay invisible, as long as you mowed your lawn.

So he had moved into his new place without touching anyone, flesh on flesh. And he would stay anonymous, hopefully for many years, in that house at the end of the street.

The boy and girl had been playing in his back yard the evening before, but they were so quiet he hadn't known they were there, until he had heard the screams. High, piercing animal sounds. Not thinking, he had rushed out to see what was the matter.

The two kids had cornered a raccoon, and what they thought was a cute animal with a mask had shown them nothing but teeth and claws. The two kids screamed then, and the boy ran right into him.

He realized what had happened. There was no way he could take back his touch. Maybe if he got the boy inside the house, he could keep death away.

But he was too frightened. He didn't reason with the kids, but only grabbed. The boy and girl, already upset with the raccoon, panicked at what must have seemed like the bogeyman to them. They ran into the woods that bordered his backyard. He had gone after them, calling to them, but night had fallen fast, and he had gotten lost among the trees.

A half hour later, the full moon had risen in the sky. And with that, he knew, the little girl—Jenny, that was her name—didn't have a chance.

He cursed himself. He lost all track of time as the moon fled across the sky toward morning. The woods were silent around him. The animals kept away. The crashing he finally heard was the search party, as they discovered Jenny's corpse. After that, the search party had turned into a mob.

▼▼▼

There was a pounding on the door.

"Debbie!"

The voice shocked them out of their languor.

"I'll be out in a minute, Arnie!" she called through the door as she quickly slipped back into her jeans.

"What's going on in there?" the angry voice demanded. "Is he doing anything to you?"

"My brother," she whispered as she rolled her eyes heavenward. "This man is hurt in here!" she answered in a louder voice. "What could he do?"

She looked back at Sam as she buttoned her blouse.

"What happens to us?" she asked. "Especially after you turn into a wolf?"

"I won't turn into a wolf," he said. "And neither will you."

She kissed him lightly one final time and banged on her side of the door. "What's the matter, Arnie? Why don't you open the door?"

Arnie did what his sister asked. Sam saw a brief flash of daylight, then the door slammed again, as if the very sight of him might corrupt those outside.

And what about Debbie? It might have been the second most foolish thing he had ever done in his life. But she had touched him. And now she was safe. Safe, and changed.

Somehow, though, he doubted she would thank him.

▼▼▼

It had grown dark in suburbia, and soon they would see the moon.

The door opened, and in the dimness, he could see three men in the doorway. One of the three held a Coleman lantern. With that light, he could see that the other two men carried guns.

John smiled over his forty-four. "We're ready for you now, whatever you are." He waved at the man on the far side of the lantern. Sam recognized him as the fellow who had spoken reason earlier that morning. "Mark here has managed to make some silver bullets."

"Three of them," Mark agreed. "Melted down some old jewelry, including a couple of crucifixes. And I felt damned stupid doing it."

"Now all we have to do is wait," said the man with the lantern, whom Sam recognized as Arnie. "If you do turn yourself into some kind of monster, it'll be the last time it ever happens."

He wondered if he should tell them. But they wouldn't listen, any more than he had, almost fifty years ago.

"What's that?" John shook his head. "Damned flies."

"Flies?" Mark asked. "Where?"

"I hear 'em too," Arnie agreed. "God! What a noise. It's making me itch all over."

The moon was rising.

John started to shake convulsively. Arnie dropped his lantern.

"What's the matter?" Mark called. But neither John nor Arnie could talk in coherent sentences.

Soon they began to growl, and change.

Mark yelled at them to stay away. It wouldn't do any good; Sam knew. The transformation always left the new wolves very hungry. Mark shot them both, using all three bullets in the process.

He glanced once, open-mouthed, at the unchanged Sam. Then he ran from sight.

He screamed a moment later as Sam heard a new chorus of growls. Mark would have needed a lot more than three bullets to stop all the wolves.

It was time for Sam to go. He would stop by his new house and pick up the important things.

The neighborhood outside was as bad any he had ever seen, city or country. Those he had touched were busy killing those he had missed, ripping apart their neighbors with claws and teeth and eating their fill. A wolf cub, the same boy who had killed Jenny the night before, growled as he gnawed on a dead man's leg.

Stuart Samson walked on. He was beyond asking for forgiveness. He was beyond finding fault. He survived.

Debbie stood in the midst of it all, and watched the carnage in shock. But the wolves wouldn't touch her, for he had loved her, and given her his gift, just as Lorraine had given it to him all these years ago.

Two wolves looked up from their meal as he walked forward. Both cried in fright and ran from him as fast as their new paws could carry them, their tails between their legs.

The animals always knew.

MOONLIGHT ON THE GAZEBO

▼▼▼

MEL GILDEN

IT was a beautiful night for an execution, warm and fragrant with summer flowers. Though, in his shaggy brown bathrobe, Cornelius Miller looked a little as if his Transformation had already begun, the full moon would not be up for nearly twenty minutes. Besides, if the Transformation really had begun, Miller would not have been outside the gazebo joshing with Mayor and Mrs. Grimes. The best sort of people walked by and nodded at them in greeting. The men tipped their flat straw hats. Nearby, a uniformed officer stood at ease near one of the gazebo's two entrances.

The natural amphitheater in which the gazebo was the central and main attraction was lit by hundreds of torches that stood at odd angles where people had thrust them into the turf. Light and shadow shivered, giving the scene a nervous quality it would have possessed in any case.

At the top of the natural amphitheater, just beyond the outside row of seats, a swarthy foreign-looking person in clothes too color- ful to be in good taste turned the handle on a hurdy-gurdy, loudly playing "The Man On the Flying Trapeze" in a monotonous sing-songy way. A monkey on a leash begged coins from the crowd.

A man in white carried a small ice chest from a harness slung around his neck while he bellowed, "Ice cream!" He wound his way through the crowd of people dressed in their best, trying not to be run down by children who, for this occasion, were allowed to be a little wilder than was usually considered proper.

Mayor Grimes stopped the man in white and said, "Ice cream, Mr. Miller? How about you, Mrs. Grimes?"

Miller smiled shyly and shook his head, but Mrs. Grimes said that she would be delighted. Like her husband, she was a substantial and stately person. An explosion of purple ostrich feathers complemented the beauty of her large purple hat and of her purple silk dress. Mayor Grimes was outfitted all in pearl gray. Miller was thin and rangy. He might have been suffering through the early stages of a terrible wasting disease, but he wasn't.

While Mrs. Grimes used a wooden spoon to take refined globs of ice cream, Miller waved at Allegra Idaho, a delicate woman in the front row who wore the palest blue, from her wide-brimmed straw hat to her satin shoes. Allegra lowered her eyes for a moment and then waved back, her hand like the wing of a bird.

As the time approached, parents reeled in their children and everyone found seats. A big man and his six children noisily evicted seven people who had been sitting in the front row since early that evening.

"Nice night, Mr. Tivley," said one young man who hurried out of the way of a small blonde Tivley girl.

As he settled himself, Mr. Tivley said, "Any night when justice is done is a nice night."

Allegra Idaho glanced at the late-comers and shook her head.

"We'll be starting soon," Mayor Grimes said as he studied the crowd. He popped open his big turnip pocketwatch and nodded.

Miller glanced at the clear summer sky and made an affirming noise. He glanced at Allegra Idaho and she nodded encouragement.

Mrs. Grimes wished him luck, and the mayor pressed the traditional gold coin into his palm. Mr. and Mrs. Grimes sat down in the seats that had been saved for them, and Mr. Grimes and Mr. Tivley shook hands. Cornelius Miller stood at his entrance, alone but for the company of the single uniformed policeman. Miller slipped the coin into a bathrobe pocket.

The policeman took his work seriously. As he opened the outer barred door and Miller stepped inside, the policeman barely looked at him. The outer door closed with the click of a catch. Miller now had a single barred door behind him and one in front of him.

The crowd hissed and booed as Chief O'Mara walked forward leading a tumbrel in which knelt a very worried man dressed in prisoner's stripes. The tumbrel was pushed by three of O'Mara's men. The eyes of the prisoner, staring straight ahead, were ringed with red. He had the surprised, unhappy and dazed appearance of a man who had been hit on the back of the head with a baseball bat. No one had bothered to comb his hair, which was long and a luminous golden color in the torchlight.

Chief O'Mara unlocked the outside door of a small cage directly opposite the small cage in which Miller stood. Two policemen grabbed the prisoner while the third unlocked the shackle around his neck. As they forced him into the small cage, the prisoner struggled a little, but without energy or hope, the way a sick old cat might struggle on its way to an inevitable bath.

The door was slammed and the crowd became silent. The hurdy-gurdy stopped in mid-phrase. A very young child asked a parent what was going on. The parent hissed and the child settled right down. The policemen backed away from the cage. The prisoner started to whimper and moan.

Two men stood ready. The one in the shaggy brown bathrobe, calmly; the one in the stripes whimpering, clutching the bars of the door he'd just come through, his knees a trifle bent as if his legs would not support his weight. A light wind shook the leaves, making the sound of grain rushing down a chute.

The waiting continued for a long time, stretching like a rubber band. When the rubber band was tight and in danger of breaking, a white shape peeked through the arms of the trees. Then it rose slowly over the trees like a silver serving plate.

As the full moon drifted higher, Cornelius Miller shed his bathrobe. It dropped at his feet and he stood there buck naked, but no more offensive than a statue in a park. His Transformation began slowly. Then an intake of breath came from the audience as if from one throat. The crowd sat frozen, the only movement being by individuals leaning this way or that to get a better view.

Miller's reddish brown hair spread across his body in waves while his limbs changed. His face grew into a muzzle. His ears lengthed into demonic points. Soon the growling in one cage nearly blotted out the sounds of distress in the other.

A policeman at each cage pulled the inner door aside on tracks. Miller-the-Wolf trotted forward and stiffened, his ears up, his nose pulsing. The prisoner glanced over his shoulder, then tried to climb his outer door and to melt through the bars. He shouted for help.

Miller-the-Wolf growled and took another step. The prisoner, finding himself to be more solid than smoke, turned around. He shouted for help again, slinging a string of spit down his stubbly chin. He pleaded for mercy, for help, for release.

Miller-the-Wolf leaped at the same time the prisoner shrieked. Miller-the-Wolf tore into the prisoner's neck and blood spurted. Soon the prisoner stopped struggling and Miller-the-Wolf dragged the carcass into the center of the gazebo where he settled down to pull meat from bone. He paid no attention to either the polite applause or the sound of crying children.

Much later, Cornelius Miller returned to his human form and collapsed next to the messy remains of the prisoner. It would not take an expert to be certain the prisoner was dead, but Doc Kelly's signature on a paper made the pronouncement official.

Doc had no hair under his bowler, and he smiled most of the time, as if his work pleased him. The smile comforted some and disconcerted others. He and Mayor Grimes supervised as Chief O'Mara and his men loaded Miller onto a stretcher. Doc threw the brown bathrobe over him. At Miller's hotel, Doc made sure that he was properly tucked in.

▼▼▼

The remainder of that night, an entire day, and most of the following morning had passed when Miller awoke. He moved slowly under the covers, then opened his eyes. After a while he got out of bed, moving carefully. He poured a glass of water from the pitcher on the night stand, swished his mouth and spit the water into a bowl. He did this a few times, and then just sat on the bed with the half-full glass in his hand.

Miller got dressed and went downstairs, still moving like a man made of sticks. In the lobby he found Doc Kelly waiting for him in a big wing chair. Smoke rose from a cigar in a silver stand next to him.

Miller sat in a wing chair across from him and said, "Hello, Doc."

"Hello, Cornelius. Justice was done."

Miller nodded and said, "Thank goodness. Too many months without an execution was making me crazier than a snake with the mange." He patted the arms of his chair. "I'm going to dinner. Want to come?"

"Delighted," Doc said and smiled in a way that may not have meant anything. He said, "You haven't seen this," and threw that morning's Mill River *Rambler* into Miller's lap.

The headline said ALLEGRA IDAHO HELD.

"What's this?" Miller said, surprised and horrified.

"Read the story."

"Tell me," Miller said. "My head is full of hay."

"Allegra was arrested yesterday for malpractice."

"What does that mean?" Miller said hotly.

"Manor Tivley's hen house burned down. They say it's her fault."

"She wouldn't do that."

"Maybe not on purpose. That's why they're calling it malpractice."

Miller stood up, seemingly too fast, because he swayed a little and touched the arm of the chair. "I'm going to see her."

"I'll be keeping office hours. Come by when you want that dinner."

After giving Doc Kelly a curt nod, Miller marched out of the hotel and across the wide porch. The day was hot, as summers always were. "Justice was done," said a fat man rocking in the thick shade. "Thanks," Miller said and kept moving. He nearly tripped himself as he ran down the steps into the sunshine.

Nobody much was out on the street except a few kids still in knickers, too excited about summer vacation to stay out of the sun. From the porches of big wooden houses that sprawled on their wide lawns like self-satisfied white cats, people nodded at him. Some offered him lemonade. He waved and was polite but kept moving.

City Hall was a three-story brick building on the town square. He galloped up the steps and went along the cool dim hallway to its end where he entered the office of the chief of police.

Miller walked up to the counter and said, "Hello, Casey," to the young uniformed man behind a desk.

"Justice was done," Casey said, looking uncomfortable.

"I'd like to see Allegra."

A thick brown door with a pebbled glass window opened and Chief O'Mara stood in front of it. "Here to see Allegra?" he said. He was solemn.

Miller nodded and said. "Want to search me?"

O'Mara looked at the floor and puckered his lips. "I don't think that will be necessary."

Casey led Miller through another door and down a hallway much dimmer and cooler than the one outside. Ev Dinks, the town drunk, slept loudly in one cell. Casey and Miller stopped in front of another. In it, Allegra Idaho sat on her bunk reading a book. She wore a light summer dress with a flower pattern, certainly clothing she had brought from home. Her normally thin face was even thinner, and in that light had the appearance of a death mask. She looked up and smiled, as if doing it through pain.

"Brought you a visitor," Casey said and stood there like a kid at his first dancing class.

"So I see," Allegra said.

"Can I talk to her alone?"

"Sure," said Casey, relieved. "I'll be outside if you want anything."

When Casey was gone and the only sound in the block was of Ev Dinks's snoring, Allegra Idaho threw aside her book and came to the front of the cell where she hugged Miller as best she could through the bars. The hug was not a great success, and soon both she and Miller backed away.

"What is this?" Miller said.

"Manor Tivley's accused me of burning down his hen house."

"What really happened?"

"His hen house really did burn down."

"Can't you be serious for a minute?"

Allegra sat down on her bunk and said, "Manor's son, Irvin, had a terrible cold. Home remedies didn't work and Doc Kelly couldn't do much for him so they sent for me. Well, Irvin had evidently attracted a minor imp someplace—"

"I'm not surprised. That Irvin will come to a bad end."

"A bad end. Didn't you read all this in the *Rambler?*"

"No. Doc told me a little. I want to hear the story from you."

She looked at the barred window high in the wall. Somebody

walked by whistling "The Man On the Flying Trapeze." Without turning to Miller, she said, "I did my exorcism. The imp left Irvin and got into the hen house."

"Didn't he use silver nails to build it?"

"Manor claims I never advised him to use silver instead of iron."

Miller grumbled, "Cheapskate," and leaned against the wall waiting for Allegra to go on. She said, "So the imp made the chickens lay eggs that exploded when Manor's youngest girl, Edwina, tried to collect them."

"She all right?"

"Minor burns. Threw a good scare into her."

"So Manor claims the loss of the hen house is your fault."

Allegra nodded.

"Nobody can believe that."

Allegra shrugged. "I'm in here. Somebody believes it that much. Manor holds deeds on half the property in this town."

Miller shook his head and said, "Malpractice. When's the trial?"

"Next week."

"We'll get you a good lawyer."

"I've seen Art Simms."

"All right. Let me know if there's anything I can do."

Miller walked out of City Hall and suddenly sagged. He did not quite fall down, but he sank onto a step and stayed there for a few minutes while he wiped the back of his neck with his handkerchief.

He went and had dinner with Doc Kelly at the Cornhusker Room. Not even Doc spoke much and neither of them finished what was on their plates.

▼▼▼

Three days later Manor Tivley's youngest girl, Edwina, died in a fire that consumed only her and her bed. The tragedy was obviously the work of infernal forces. Manor claimed it was the work of the same imp Allegra Idaho had exorcised; therefore the death of his little girl was Allegra's fault even though she had been in jail at the time and had absolutely no motive for wanting to harm the little girl.

Allegra's malpractice trial became a murder trial. Like any other unusual event that might occur in a given summer, the trial of Allegra Idaho was treated as a popular entertainment.

When he heard what had happened, Cornelius Miller's first thought struck him like a thunderbolt, and he ran to Doc Kelly's office to share his revelation. Doc was sitting on the buttoned leather couch in his waiting room reading a dogeared copy of *Liberty* magazine.

"Sit down," said Doc. "You look as if you're about to have a stroke. I'll get you some water."

Miller shook the newspaper in Doc's face and said, "My God! If Allegra is convicted of murder, I myself will be the instrument of her execution."

Doc read the paper while Miller paced before him. Doc looked up and said, "You can refuse."

"Yes," said Miller slowly. "But avoiding my responsibility would only make things worse. If I refuse to enter the gazebo with Allegra on the night of the full moon, Mayor Grimes will hire someone else to perform the execution."

"If he can find someone else."

"He will have no trouble finding one of the itinerant were-wolves that are always ready to take up the judicial slack for a fee." Miller shook his head and flung himself onto the couch. "And to think I had almost screwed up my courage to the point where I could ask her to marry me."

"Well, you can't marry her now. It would be scandalous." Doc Kelly watched Miller from the tip of his eye.

"You know me better than that. I have been Allegra's beau for two years. Scandal means nothing to me where she is concerned."

Doc Kelly smiled. "Yes, I know you better than that." He patted Miller on the back and said, "Your only hope as well as Allegra's is that justice prevail."

Miller laid his head on the arm rest and said, "We have the chance of a flea on a hot griddle."

It seemed that Miller was right. Though Art Simms did his best, things went badly for Allegra right from the start. Everybody agreed on the facts. Only their interpretation was open to question. Iron nails rather than silver had been used in the construction of the hen house; had Allegra Idaho advised Manor Tivley properly or not? Edwina Tivley had died in infernal fire; was the cause the same imp that Allegra had exorcised from Irwin? And if it was, did that make Edwina's death Allegra's fault? The skein was tangled, no question. The fact that Manor Tivley was a powerful man in town did not hurt his case. Allegra Idaho was just one more country witch.

Cornelius Miller and Doc Kelly spent the morning in the hot courtroom and then, along with many other members of the audience, took dinner at the Cornhusker Room.

Debate over Allegra Idaho's fate continued. Men conducted their arguments with knives and forks while their womenfolk looked on either with disapproval or with faint cynical smiles or with adoration, as was their habit. Strong-willed women spoke up occasionally, and their comments were met with similar reactions from the men, though the most frequent reaction was a jocular sarcasm.

Miller shook his head over his untouched steak, and for the hundredth time since they'd been seated, said, "We must do something."

Doc Kelly nodded while he chewed. He was one of those rare men who could chew and smile at the same time without looking ridiculous. He swallowed and said, "Talk to Manor. Maybe you can convince him to drop the charges."

"Bad joke, Doc."

"I suppose." Even now the smile did not entirely leave Doc's lips. "Manor's not exactly famous for straining the quality of his mercy."

Though he had three cut already, Miller cut another strip off his steak. He waved it about in the air on the end of his fork as he said, "This is all my father's fault."

"How so?" said Doc.

"I wanted to be a lawyer, but my father was not confident of my intellectual abilities. Still, he was a practical man—perhaps terminally practical—and he wanted to make certain that I could always make a living. When I was thirteen he took me to George Sewell, the local werewolf, and paid him to bite me. It was over in an instant and did not hurt much, and at the next full moon I turned into a wolf."

"How did that strike you?"

"I was terrified. My human part was shunted to a back room of my brain while my animal instincts and appetites reigned over me. I was a living example of Stevenson's ideas in that Jekyll and Hyde story of his."

"You can't blame your father for Allegra's problem with Tivley."

"I suppose not." Miller actually ate something and sipped his iced tea. Neither of the spoke for a while.

Doc Kelly said, "How does the Transformation strike you now?"

Miller started as if he'd forgotten Doc Kelly was there, then stared at him very hard. He said, "Not so bad after you know what to expect. Of course even on the full moons when no executions are needed you spend most of the night in a locked gazebo." He shook his head. "A cow or a goat or a crate of chickens does not satisfy all a werewolf's hungers." He threw down his silverware, causing people at nearby tables to glance at him. He said, "We must do something about Allegra."

"Art Simms is doing his best."

"Yes. And if that's not good enough, come the next full moon I'll be tearing apart the woman I love."

▼▼▼

Allegra Idaho was found guilty of murder by a jury of her peers. "Yes," said Miller to Doc, "peers who owe money to Manor Tivley." Miller momentarily considered murdering Tivley, but his anger soon cooled into a sort of black funk. He spoke to no one.

He visited Allegra once. They looked at each other through the bars with slack puffy faces. She said, "Goodbye, Cornelius. I don't want to see you any more."

"Marry me, Allegra."

Allegra managed a thin smile and said, "One might speak of your bad timing, Cornelius."

"But I love you."

"Yes. And I love you. But looking at you reminds me of how I'm going to die."

"Would you rather someone else—?"

"No. I don't want strangers chewing on me."

Miller went to his hotel room and stayed there. He refused to eat, refused to answer any knock. Mayor Grimes came to the door, and through it offered to hire another werewolf. Miller said nothing but, "No, thank-you." The mayor waited for more and after a while went away. Sometimes Doc Kelly came in uninvited and sat with Miller. Miller's constant refrain was, "We must do something." Doc's constant question was, "What?"

Three days before the execution, when Doc Kelly said, "What?" Miller's eyebrows went up. He looked at Doc Kelly and smiled in a way that more suited a wolf than a man. He leaped to his feet, cried, "Yes. Yes, of course," and ran from the room.

Doc sat on Miller's bed smoking one cigar after another. The smoke gathered in clouds near the ceiling and was sucked out through the top of the open window. Miller came back half an hour later rubbing his hands and grinning. "It's perfect," he said. "Perfect."

"What is?"

"Let's go to the Cornhusker Room. I'm famished."

"What did you do?"

"Let's eat," Miller said.

Over crispy fried chicken, Miller said, "I can't tell you what I did because I don't want you to be an accessory, or whatever it is you'd be. You'll know what I did when you see it happening. But will you do me a favor?"

"Of course."

"When it happens, try to stir up as much confusion as you can."

"How will I know—?"

"You'll know. Trust me."

▼▼▼

The evening was almost as warm as the day had been. In his brown bathrobe, Cornelius Miller stood alone just outside the small cage at his end of the gazebo. He glanced again and again at the clear sky. The crowd around the gazebo was large and many people had taken seats early, including Manor Tivley and his family; they sat in the front row in their best clothes, grim vengeful expressions on their faces. Latecomers had spread blankets at the lip of the amphitheater.

The mayor looked at his turnip pocketwatch and strode to Miller. He gave Miller the traditional gold coin and watched him enter the cage. Miller gripped the outer door as he looked over the crowd. He nodded to Doc Kelly and Doc nodded back. Then Miller faced the arena of the gazebo.

Chief O'Mara and three of his men brought Allegra Idaho on the tumbrel. She was chained but standing, looking very much like a queen who had the misfortune to be a member of the wrong family. Instead of hissing, the crowd became silent, allowing the squeaking of the tumbrel wheels to be heard. O'Mara escorted Allegra into the cage and locked the door behind her. He bowed without mockery and backed away. Allegra stood across the gazebo facing Cornelius Miller. Neither of them made any sign they knew the other was there.

The moon, a silver ghost, peeked through the branches of a tree. It rose and Miller dropped his bathrobe. The policemen pulled open the inner doors of the two cages. Miller and Allegra Idaho stepped forward and faced each other across the battered ground.

Miller's Transformation began slowly. Instead of shying away, Allegra Idaho suddenly tored off her dress, revealing reddish brown hair rolling in waves across her body. Sounds of protest and surprise swelled among the crowd. Among the frightened shrieks, Manor Tivley shouted, "It's a flagrant affront to the law!" Others cried out agreement.

Mayor Grimes ordered Chief O'Mara to stop Allegra Idaho from Transforming. O'Mara shook his head and laughed pityingly. "You want a wizard, sir, not a police chief. But I assure you they'll never escape the gazebo." The mayor was about to hurl another demand, but like everyone else, he became distracted by what was happening behind the bars.

Allegra Idaho's ears lengthed and her limbs changed. Opposite her, Cornelius Miller was going through the same transformation. When they were both completely wolves, Miller-the-Wolf and Allegra-the-Wolf circled each other. They sniffed each other's privates. They gamboled around each other and Miller-the-Wolf trotted to his small cage with Allegra-the-Wolf close behind. He leaped at the outer door and it swung open, releasing the gold coin that had prevented the catch from catching.

The mayor shouted, "Get them! They're *both* criminals now!"

The energetic but helter-skelter efforts of Manor Tivley and his boldest followers could not prevent the two wolves from running off into the surrounding trees. Most of the crowd dispersed, adults pulling children who had more curiosity than sense.

O'Mara attempted to organize his uniformed force while Doc Kelly pointed in a direction the two wolves had obviously not gone and cried, "They went that way!" The police officers ran after the wolves, some disappearing among the trees at the place where the wolves had gone, others following Doc Kelly's spurious directions.

Chief O'Mara looked at Doc Kelly with contempt and said, "They'll never escape my trained men."

"They might," Kelly said. "It's a big country and two new werewolves in a town won't cause much of a stir."

Chief O'Mara left Doc Kelly and went to speak with a vigilante group that was clabbering among the upended chairs.

A sound stopped everyone dead. They listened hard but heard only the rattle of trees in the wind. Then, from far away came the sound that had frozen time: the howl of a wolf. A moment later another howl answered it. People stood still for a long time, waiting. But no other howl was heard that night.

RAYMOND
▼▼▼

NANCY A. COLLINS

I remember the first time I saw Raymond Fleuris.

It was during Mrs. Harper's seventh-grade homeroom; I was staring out the window at the parking lot that fronted the school. There wasn't anything happening in the parking lot, but it seemed a hell of a lot more interesting than Old Lady Harper rattling on about long division. That's when I saw the truck.

Beat-up old trucks are not what you'd call unusual in Choctaw County, but this had to be *the* shittiest excuse for a motor vehicle even to roll the streets of Seven Devils, Arkansas. The bed overflowed with pieces of junk lumber, paint cans, and rolls of rusty chicken wire. The chassis was scabby with rust. It rode close to the ground, bouncing vigorously with every pothole. The front bumper was connected to the fender by a length of baling wire, spit, and a prayer.

I watched as the truck pulled up next to the principal's sedan and the driver crawled out from behind the wheel.

My first impression was that of a mountain wearing overalls. He was massive. Fat jiggled on every part of his body. Thick rolls of it pooled around his waist, straining his shirt to the breaking point. The heavy jowls framing his face made him look like a foul-tempered bulldog. He was big and fat, but it was *mean* fat; no one in their right mind would have ever mistaken him for jolly.

The driver lumbered around the front of the truck, pausing to pull a dirty bandanna out of his back pocket and mop his forehead. He motioned irritably to someone seated on the passenger's side, then jerked the door open. I was surprised it didn't come off in his hand. His face was turning red as he yelled at whoever was in the passenger's seat.

After a long minute, a boy climbed out of the truck and stood next to the ruddy-faced mountain of meat.

Normally I wouldn't have spared the Fleurises a second look. Except that Raymond's head was swaddled in a turban of sterile gauze and surgical tape and his hands were covered by a pair of old canvas gloves, secured at the wrists with string.

Now *that* was interesting.

Raymond was small and severely underweight. His eyes had grayish-yellow smears under them that made it look like he was perpetually recovering from a pair of shiners. His skin was pale and reminded me of the waxed paper my mama wrapped my sandwiches in.

Someone, probably his mama, had made an effort to clean and press his bib overalls and what was probably his only shirt. No doubt she'd hoped Raymond would make a good impression on his first day at school. No such luck. His clothes looked like socks on a rooster.

▼▼▼

By the time the lunch bell rang, everybody knew about the new kid. Gossip runs fast in junior high, and by the end of recess, there were a half-dozen accounts of Raymond Fleuris's origins floating about.

Some said he'd been in a car wreck and thrown through the windshield. Others said the doctors up at the State Hospital did

some kind of surgery to cure him of violent fits. Chucky Donothan speculated that he'd had some kind of craziness-tumor cut
out. Whatever the reason for the head bandages and the gloves,
it made Raymond Fleuris, at least for a the space of a few days,
exotic and different. And that means nothing but trouble when
you're in junior high.

Raymond ended up being assigned to my homeroom. Normally, Mrs. Harper had us sit alphabetically; but in Raymond's
case, she assigned him a desk in the back of the room. Not that
it made any difference to Raymond. He never handed in homework and was excused from taking tests. All he did was sit and
scribble in his notebook with one of those big kindergarten
pencils.

Raymond carried his lunch to school in an old paper bag that,
judging from the grease stains, had seen a lot of use. Once I
accidentally stumbled across Raymond eating his lunch behind
the Science Building. His food consisted of a single sandwich
made from cheap store-bought white bread and a slice of olive
loaf. After he finished his meal, Raymond carefully flattened the
paper bag, folded it, and tucked it in the back pocket of his
overalls.

I felt funny, standing there watching Raymond perform his
little after-lunch ritual. I knew my folks weren't rich, but at least
we could afford paper bags. Maybe that's why I did what I did
when I saw Chucky Donothan picking on Raymond the next day.

It was recess and I was hanging with my best friend, Rafe
Mercer. We were talking about the county fair coming to town
next month. It was nowhere near as big or as fancy as the State
Fair up in Little Rock; but when you're stuck in a backwater like
Seven Devils, you take what you can get.

"Darryl, you reckon they'll have the kootchie show again?"
Rafe must have asked me that question a hundred times already.
I didn't mind, though, because I was wondering the same thing.
Last year Rafe's older brother, Calvin, got in on the strength of

some whiskers and his football-boy physique. Not to mention a dollar.

"I don't see why not. It's been there every year, ain't it?"

"Yeah, you're right." Rafe was afraid he would graduate high school without once getting the chance to see a woman in her bra and panties. He looked at the pictures in his mama's wish books, but that wasn't the same as seeing a *real live* half-naked lady. I could understand his concern.

Just about then Kitty Killigrew ran past. Both me and Rafe were sweet on Kitty, not that we'd admit it to her—or ourselves— this side of physical torture. She was a pretty girl, with long coppery-red hair that hung to her waist and eyes the color of cornflowers. Rafe went on to marry her, six years later. That fucker.

"Hey, Kitty! What's going on?" Rafe yelled after her.

Kitty paused long enough to gasp out one word. "Fight!"

That was all the explanation we needed. Schoolyard fights attract students like shit draws flies. Rafe and I hurried after her. As we rounded the corner of the building, I could see a knot of kids near the science building.

I pushed my way through my schoolmates in time to see Chucky Donothan kick Raymond Fleuris's feet out from under him.

Raymond flopped onto his back in the dirt and laid there. It was evident that the fight—if you could call it that—was pretty one-sided. I couldn't imagine what Raymond might have done to piss off the bigger boy; but knowing Chucky, the fact Raymond had weight and occupied space was probably insult enough.

"Stand up and fight, retard!" Chucky bellowed.

Raymond got to his feet, his eyes filled with pain and confusion. His bandage-turban was smeared with dirt. With his oversized canvas gloves and shit-kicker brogans, Raymond looked like a pathetic caricature of Mickey Mouse. Everyone started laughing.

"What's with the gloves, retard?" Chucky sneered. "What's the matter? You jerk off so much you got hair on your palms?"

Some of the girls giggled at that witticism, so Chucky continued pressing his attack. "Is that your big secret, Fleuris? You a jag-off? Huh? Huh? Is that it? Why don't you take 'em off so we can see, huh?"

Raymond shook his head. "Paw sez I can't take 'em off. Paw sez I gotta keep 'em on alla time." It was one of the few times I ever heard Raymond speak out loud. His voice was thin and reedy, like a clarinet.

The crowd fell silent as Chucky's naturally ruddy complexion grew even redder.

"You tellin' me *no*, retard?"

Raymond blinked. It was obvious he didn't understand what was going on. It dawned on me that Raymond would stand there and let Chucky beat him flatter than his lunch bag without lifting a finger to protect himself. Suddenly, I didn't want to watch what was going on anymore.

"Chucky, leave him be, can't you see he's *simple*?"

"Butt out, Sweetman! Less'n you want me to kick *your* ass, too!"

I cut my eyes at Rafe. He shook his head. "Hell, Darryl, I ain't about to get the shit knocked outta me on account of Raymond Fleuris!"

I looked away.

Satisfied he'd quelled all opposition, Chucky grabbed Raymond's left arm, jerking on the loosely fitted glove. "If you ain't gonna show us, I guess I'll *make* you!"

And that's when the shit hit the fan.

One second Raymond was your basic slack-jawed moron, the next he was shrieking and clawing at Chucky like the Tasmanian Devil in those old Bugs Bunny cartoons. His face seemed to *flex*, like the muscles were being jerked every-which-way. I know it sounds stupid, but that's the only way I can describe it.

Raymond was on the bully like white on rice, knocking him to the ground. We all stood there and gaped in disbelief, our mouths hanging open, as they wrestled in the dirt. Suddenly Chucky started making these high-pitched screams and that's when I saw the blood.

Chucky managed to throw Raymond off of him just as Coach Jenkins hustled across the playground, paddle in hand. Chucky was rolling around, crying like a little kid. Blood ran from a ragged wound in the fleshy part of his upper arm. Raymond sat in the dirt, staring at the other boy like he was from Mars. There was blood on Raymond's mouth, but it wasn't his. The bandage had come unravelled in the brawl, giving everyone a good look at the three-inch scar that climbed his right temple.

"What – the – blazes – is going on here!" Coach Jenkins always had trouble refraining from swearing in front of the students, and it looked like he was close to reaching critical mass. "Donothan! Get on your feet, boy!"

"He *bit* me!" Chucky wailed, his face filthy with snot and tears.

Coach Jenkins shot a surprised look at Raymond, still sitting in the dirt. "Is that true, Fleuris? Did you bite Donothan?"

Raymond stared up at Coach Jenkins and blinked.

Coach Jenkins' neck pulsed and he looked at the ring of now-guilty faces. "Okay, who started it?"

"Donothan did, sir." I was surprised to hear the words coming from my mouth. "He was picking on Raymond."

Coach Jenkins pushed the bill of his baseball cap back and tried to keep the vein in his neck from pulsing even harder. "Did anyone try to stop it?"

Silence.

"Right. Come on, Donothan. Get up. You, too, Fleuris. We're going to the principal's office."

"I'm *bleeding*!"

"We'll have the nurse take a look at it, but you're *still* going to the office!" Jenkins grabbed Chucky by his uninjured arm and jerked him to his feet. "You should be ashamed of yourself, Donothan!" He hissed under his breath. "Pickin' on a cripple!"

I stepped forward to help Raymond. It was then that I noticed one of his gloves had come off in the fight.

"Here, you lost this."

Raymond snatched his glove back, quickly stuffing his bare hand into it. But not before I had time to notice that his ring finger was longer than the others.

▼▼▼

When I was a kid, Choctaw County was pretty much like it was when my daddy was growing up. If not worse. Sure, we had stuff like television and a public library by then, but by the time I was twelve the old Malco Theatre went belly-up: another victim of the railroad dying off.

One of the biggest thrills of the year was going to the county fair. For five days in late October the aluminum outbuildings dotting what had once been Old Man Ferguson's cow pasture became a gaudy wonderland of neon lights.

If you went to the fair every night, you'd eventually see the entire population of Choctaw County put in an appearance. It was one of the few times the various ethnic groups and religious sects congregated at the same place, although I'd hardly call it "mingling." The blacks stayed with the blacks while the whites stayed with the whites. There was also little in the way of cross-over between the Baptists, Methodists, and Pentecostals. Families came by the truckload, dressed in their Sunday-go-to-meeting clothes. I never knew there were so many people in the county.

Rafe and I were wandering the booths lining the midway, looking for the kootchie show. Rafe hadn't shaved in three weeks, hoping he could build up enough beard to pass for sixteen.

We bumped into Kitty, who was chewing on a wad of cotton

candy and contemplating a banner that showed a dwarf supporting a bucket of sand from a skewer piercing his tongue.

"Hey, Kitty. When'd you get here?" I asked, trying to sound casual.

"Hey, Darryl. Hey, Rafe. I rode over with Veronica about a half-hour ago. You just get here?" There was a strand of pink candy floss stuck at the corner of her perfect mouth. I watched in silent fascination as she tried to dislodge it with the tip of her tongue.

Rafe shrugged. "Kind of."

"Seen the World's Smallest Horse yet?"

"No."

"Don't bother. It's a rip-off; just some dumb old Shetland Pony at the bottom of a hole dug in the ground." She poked her half-eaten cotton candy in my face. "You want the rest of this, Darryl? I can't finish it. You know what they say: sweets to the sweet."

"Uh, no thanks, Kitty." People keep saying that to me on account of my last name, Sweetman. I hate it, but short of strangling everybody on the face of the earth, there's no way I can avoid it. And no one believes me when I tell them I can't stand sugar.

"I'll take it, Kitty." Rafe was a smoothy, even then. Did I mention he ended up marrying her after high school? Did I mention I haven't talked to him since?

Kitty frowned and pointed over my shoulder. "Isn't that Raymond Fleuris?"

Rafe and I turned around and looked where she was pointing. Sure enough, Raymond Fleuris was standing in front of the "Tub-O-Ducks" game, watching the brightly colored plastic ducks bobbing along in their miniature millrace. Although his hands were still gloved, he no longer wore his bandage on his head, and his dark hair bristled like the quills of a porcupine.

Rafe shrugged. "I saw his daddy shovelling out the livestock barn; the carnival lets the temporary workers' families ride for free."

Kitty was still looking at Raymond. "You know, yesterday during recess I asked him why he had brain surgery."

I found my voice first. "You *actually* asked him that?"

"Sure did."

"Well, what did he say?"

Kitty frowned. "I dunno. When I asked him, he looked like he was trying *real hard* to remember something. Then he got this goofy grin on his face and said 'chickens'."

"*Chickens?*"

"Don't look at me like *I'm* nuts, Rafe Mercer! I'm just tellin' you want he said! But what was *really* weird was how he said it! Like he was remembering going to Disneyland or something!"

"So Raymond Fleuris is weird. Big deal. C'mon, I wanna check out the guy who cuts a girl in half with a chainsaw. Wanna go with us, Kitty?" Rafe mimed pulling a cord and went *rup-rup-ruppppp!*, waving the wad of cotton candy like a deadly weapon.

Kitty giggled behind her hand. "You're *silly!*"

That was all I could take. If I had to stay with them another five minutes I'd either puke or pop Rafe in the nose. "I'll catch up with you later, Rafe. Okay? Rafe?"

"Huh?" Rafe managed to tear his eyes away from Kitty long enough to give me a quick, distracted nod. "Oh, yeah. Sure. Later, man."

Muttering under my breath, I stalked off, my fists stuffed in my pockets. Suddenly the fair didn't seem as much fun as it'd been ten minutes ago. Even the festive aroma of hot popcorn, cotton candy, and corndogs failed to revive my previous good mood.

I found myself staring at a faded canvas banner that said, in vigorous Barnum script: **Col. Reynard's Pocket Jungle**. Below the headline a stiffly rendered red-headed young man dressed like Frank Buck wrestled a spotted leopard.

Lounging behind the ticket booth in front of the tent stood a tall man dressed in a sweat-stained short-sleeved khaki shirt and jodhpurs. His hair was no longer bright red and his face looked older, but there was no doubt that he was Colonel Reynard: Great White Hunter. As I watched, he produced a World War Two surplus microphone and began his spiel. His voice crackled out of a public address system, adding to the noise and clamor of the midway.

"Hur-ree! Hur-ree! Hur-ree! See the most ex-zotic and danger-rus ani-mals this side of Aff-Rika! See! The noble tim-bur wolf! King of the Ark-Tik Forest! See! The wild jag-war! Ruthless Lord of the Am-A-Zon Jungle! See! The hairy orang-utang! Borny-Oh's oh-riginal Wild Man of the Woods! See! The fur-rocious Grizz-lee Bear! Mon-Arch of the Fro-zen North! See these wonders and more! Hur-ree! Hur-ree! Hur-ree!"

A handful of people stopped and turned their attention toward the Colonel. One of them happened to be Raymond Fleuris. A couple came forward with their money. Raymond just stood there at the foot of the ticket podium, staring at the red-headed man. I expected the Colonel to make like W.C. Fields, but instead he waved Raymond inside the tent.

What the hell?

I didn't really want to see a bunch of half-starved animals stuck in cages. But there was something in the way Colonel Reynard had looked at Raymond, like he'd recognized him, that struck me as curious. First I thought he might be queer for boys, but The Great White Hunter didn't look at me twice when I paid for my ticket and joined the others inside the tent.

The "Pocket Jungle" reeked of sawdust and piss. There were raised platforms scattered about the tent, canvas drop-cloths covering the cages. Colonel Reynard finally joined us and went into his pitch, going on about how he'd risked life and limb collecting the specimens we were about to see. As he spoke, he went from cage to cage, throwing back the drop-cloths so we could see the animals trapped inside.

I hadn't been expecting anything, and I wasn't disappointed. The "jaguar" was a slat-thin ocelot; the "timber wolf" was a yellow-eyed coyote that paced the confines of its cage like a madman; the "grizzly" was a plain old black bear, its muzzle so white it looked like it'd been sprinkled with powdered sugar. The only thing that really was what it was supposed to be was the orangutan.

The ape was big, its wrinkled old-man's features nearly lost in its vast face. It sat in a cage only slightly larger than itself, its hand-like feet folded in front of its mammoth belly. With its dropping teats and huge girth, it resembled a shaggy Buddha.

Just as the Colonel was wrapping up his act, Raymond pushed his way from the back of the crowd and stood, motionless, gaping at the "timber wolf."

The coyote halted its ceaseless pacing and bared its fangs. A low, frightened growl came from the animal as it raised its hackles. The Colonel halted in mid-sentence and stared first at the coyote, then at Raymond.

As if on cue, the ocelot started to hiss and spit, flattening its ears against its sleek skull. The bear emitted a series of low grunts, while the orangutan covered its face and turned its back to the audience.

Raymond stepped back, shaking his head like he had a mite in his ear. The muscles in his face were jerking again, and I imagined I could smell blood and dust and hear Chucky Donothan squealing like a girl. Raymond staggered back, covering his eyes with his gloves. I heard someone in the crowd laugh; it sounded like was a short, sharp, ugly bark.

Colonel Reynard snapped his fingers once and said in a strong voice; "Hush!" The animals grew silent immediately. He then stepped toward Raymond. "Son . . ."

Raymond made a noise that was somewhere between a sob and a shout and ran from the tent and into the crowds and noise of the midway. Colonel Reynard followed after him, and I followed the Colonel.

Raymond made for the cluster of aluminum outbuildings that served as exhibition halls. The Colonel didn't see Raymond dodge between the Crafts Barn and the Tractor Exhibit, but I did. I hurried after him, leaving the light and activity of the fairground behind me. I could dimly make out Raymond a few dozen yards ahead.

I froze as a tall, thin shadow stepped directly into Raymond's path, knocking him to the ground. I pressed against the aluminum shell of the Crafts Barn, praying no one noticed me lurking in the darkened "alley."

"You all right, son?" I recognized Colonel Reynard's voice, although I could not see his face.

Raymond shuddered as he tried to catch his breath and stop crying at the same time.

The carny helped Raymond to his feet. "Now, now, son . . . There's nothing to be ashamed of." His voice was as gentle and soothing as a man talking to a skittish horse. "I'm not going to hurt you, boy. Far from it."

Raymond stood there as Colonel Reynard wiped his face clean of tears, dirt and snot with a handkerchief.

"Let me see your hands, son."

Raymond shrank away from the stranger, crossing his gloved hands over his heart. "Paw sez if I take 'em off he'll whup me good. I ain't ever supposed to take 'em off ever again."

"Well, I say it's okay for you to take them off. And if your daddy don't like it, he'll have to whup on me first." The carny quickly untied both gloves and let them drop. Raymond's hands looked dazzlingly white, compared to his grimy face and forearms. Colonel Reynard squatted on his haunches and took Raymond's hands into his own, studying the fingers with interest. Then he tilted Raymond's head to one side. I could tell he was looking at the scar.

"What have they done?" The Colonel's voice sounded both angry and sad. "You poor child . . . What did they *do* to you?"

"Here now! What you doin' messin' with my boy?"

It was Mr. Fleuris. He passed within inches of me, but if he noticed my presence it didn't register on his face. I wondered if this was how the first mammals felt, watching the dinosaurs lumber by their hiding place in the underbrush. The big man reeked of manure and fresh straw.

Raymond cringed as his father bore down on him.

"Raymond—Where the hell's yore gloves, boy? You know what I told you bout them gloves!" Mr. Fleuris lifted a meaty arm, his sausage-sized fingers closing into a fist.

Raymond whimpered in anticipation of the blow that was certain to land on his upturned face.

Before Horace Fleuris had a chance to strike his son, Colonel Reynard grabbed the big man's wrist. In the dim light it looked as if the Colonel's third finger was longer than the others. I heard Mr. Fleuris grunt in surprise and saw his upraised fist tremble.

"You will not touch this child, understand?"

"Dammit, leggo!" Fleuris' voice was pinched, as if he was both in pain and afraid.

"I *said* 'understand'?"

"I heared you the first time, damn you!"

The Colonel let Fleuris' arm drop. "You are the child's father?"

Fleuris nodded sullenly, massaging his wrist.

"I should kill you for what you've done."

"Here, now! Don't go blamin' me for it!" Fleuris blustered. "It was them doctors up at the State Hospital! They said it'd cure him! I tried to tell 'em what the boy's problem was, but you can't tell them big-city doctors squat, far as they're concerned! But what could I do? We was gettin' tired of movin' ever time the boy got into th' neighbor's chicken coop . . ."

"Now he'll *never* learn how to control it!" Reynard stroked Raymond's forehead. "He's stuck in-between the natures, incapable of fitting into your world . . . or ours. He is an abomination in the eyes of Nature. Even animals can see he has no place in the Scheme!"

"You like the boy, don't you?" There was something about how Fleuris asked the question that made my stomach knot. "I'm a reasonable man. When it comes to business."

I couldn't believe what I was hearing. Mr. Fleuris was standing there, talking about *selling* his son to a complete stranger like he was a prize coon dog!

"Get out of here."

"Now hold on just a second! I ain't askin' for nothin' that ain't rightfully mine, and you know it! I'm the boy's pa and I reckon that calls for some kind of restitution, seeing how's he's my only male kin . . ."

"*Now!*" Colonel Reynard's voice sounded like a growl.

Horace Fleuris turned and fled, his fleshy face slack with fear. I never dreamed a man his size could move that fast.

I glanced at where Reynard stood, one hand resting on Raymond's shoulder. Colonel Reynard's face was no longer human, his mouth fixed in a deceptive smile. He fixed me with his murder-green eyes and wrinkled his snout. "That goes for you too, man-cub."

To this day I wonder why he let me go unharmed. I guess it's because he knew that no one was going to listen to any crazy stories about fox-headed men told by a pissant kid. No one wanted to believe crap like that. Not even the pissant kid.

Needless to say, I ran like a rabbit with a hound on my tail. Later I was I was plagued by recurring nightmares of a fox-headed animal-tamer dressed in jodhpurs that went around sticking his head in human mouths, and of a huge orangutan in overalls that looked like Mr. Fleuris.

▼▼▼

By the time Christmas break came around everyone had lost interest in Raymond's disappearance. The Fleuris family had moved sometime during the last night of October to parts unknown. No one missed them. It was like Raymond Fleuris had never existed.

I spent a lot of time trying not to think about what I'd seen and heard that night. I had other things to fret about. Like Kitty Killigrew going steady with Rafe.

Several years passed before I returned to the Choctaw County Fair. By then I was a freshman at the Univeristy of Arkansas at Monticello, over in Drew County. I'd landed a scholarship and spent my week-days studying in a bare-ass dorm room while coming home on weekends to help my daddy with the farm. I had long since talked myself into believing what I'd seen that night was a particularly vivid nightmare brought on by a bad corndog. Nothing more.

The midway didn't have a kootchie show that year, but I'd heard rumors that they had something even better. Or worse, depending on how you look at it.

According to the grapevine, the carnival had a glommin' geek. Since geek shows are technically illegal and roundly condemned as immoral, degrading, and sinful, naturally it played to capacity crowds.

The barker packed as many people as he could into a cramped, foul-smelling tent situated behind the freak show. There was a canvas pit in the middle of the tent, and at its bottom crouched the geek.

He was on the scrawny side and furry as a monkey. The hair on his head was long and coarse, hanging past his waist, as did a scraggly beard. His long forearms and bowed legs were equally shaggy, coated with dark fur that resembled the pelt of a wild goat. It was hard to tell, but I'm certain he was buck naked. There was something wrong with the geek's fingers, though that might have been on account of his four-inch long nails.

As the barker did his spiel about the geek being the last survivor of a race of wild men from the jungles of Borneo, I continued to stare at the snarling, capering creature. I couldn't shake the feeling that there was something *familiar* about the geek.

The barker finished his bit and produced a live chicken from a gunny sack. The geek lifted his head and sniffed the air, his nostrils flaring as he caught the scent of the bird. An idiot's grin split his hairy face and a long thread of drool dripped from his open jaws. His teeth were surprisingly white and strong.

The barker tossed the chicken into the pit. It fluttered downward, squawking as it frantically beat the air with its wings. The geek giggled like a delighted child and pounced on the hapless bird. His movements were as graceful and sure as those of a champion mouser dispatching a rat. The geek bit the struggling chicken's head off, obviously relishing every minute of it.

As the crowd moaned in disgust and turned their faces away from what was happening in the pit, I continued to watch, even though it made my stomach churn.

Why? Because I had glimpsed the pale finger of scar tissue traversing the geek's right temple.

I stood and stared down at Raymond Fleuris crouched at the bottom of the geek pit, his grinning face wreathed in blood and feathers.

Happy at last.

THERE'S A WOLF
IN MY TIME MACHINE
▼▼▼

LARRY NIVEN

THE old extension cage had no fine controls, but that hardly mattered. It wasn't as if Svetz were chasing some particularly extinct animal. Ra Chen had told him to take whatever came to hand.

Svetz guided the cage back to preindustrial America, somewhere in midcontinent, around 1000 AnteAtomic Era. Few humans, many animals. Perhaps he'd find a bison.

And when he pulled himself to the window, he looked out upon a vast white land.

Svetz had not planned to arrive in midwinter.

Briefly he considered moving into the time stream again and using the interrupter circuit. Try another date, try the luck again. But the interrupter circuit was new, untried, and Svetz wasn't about to be the first man to test it.

Besides which, a trip into the past cost over a million commercials. Using the interrupter circuit would nearly double that. Ra Chen would be displeased.

Svetz began freezing to death the moment he opened the

door. From the doorway the view was also white, with one white bounding shape far away.

Svetz shot it with a crystal of soluble anesthetic.

He used the flight stick to reach the spot. Now that it was no longer moving, the beast was hard to find. It was just the color of the snow, but for its open red mouth and the black pads on its feet. Svetz tentatively identified it as an arctic wolf.

It would fit the Vivarium well enough. Svetz would have settled for anything that would let him leave this frozen wilderness. He felt uncommonly pleased with himself. A quick, easy mission.

Inside the cage, he rolled the sleeping beast into what might have been a clear plastic bag, and sealed it. He strapped the wolf against one curved wall of the extension cage. He relaxed into the curve of the opposite wall as the cage surged in a direction vertical to all directions.

Gravity shifted oddly.

A transparent sac covered Svetz's own head. Its lip was fixed to the skin of his neck. Now Svetz pulled it loose and dropped it. The air system was on; he would not need the filter sac.

The wolf would. It could not breath industrial-age air. Without the filter sac to remove the poisons, the wolf would choke to death. Wolves were extinct in Svetz's own time.

Outside, time passed at a furious rate. Inside, time crawled. Nestled in the spherical curve of the extension cage, Svetz stared up at the wolf, who seemed fitted into the curve of the ceiling.

Svetz had never met a wolf in the flesh. He had seen pictures in children's books . . . and even the children's books had been stolen from the deep past. Why should the wolf look so familiar?

It was a big beast, possibly as big as Hanville Svetz, who was a slender, small-boned man. Its sides heaved with its panting. Its tongue was long and red, and its teeth were white and sharp.

Like the dogs, Svetz remembered. The dogs in the Vivarium, in the glass case labeled:

```
DOG
Contemporary
```

Alone of the beasts in the Vivarium, the dogs were not sealed in glass for their own protection. The others could not breathe the air outside. The dogs could.

In a very real sense, they were the work of one man. Lawrence Wash Porter had lived near the end of the Industrial Period, between 50 and 100 PostAtomic Era, when billions of human beings were dying of lung diseases while scant millions adapted. Porter had decided to save the dogs.

Why the dogs? His motives were obscure, but his methods smacked of genius. He had acquired members of each of the breeds of dog in the world and bred them together over many generations of dogs and most of his own lifetime.

There would never be another dog show. Not a pure-bred dog was left in the world. But hybrid vigor had produced a new breed. These, the ultimate mongrels, could breathe industrial-age air, rich in oxides of carbon and nitrogen, scented with raw gasoline and sulfuric acid.

The dogs were behind glass because people were afraid of them. Too many species had died. The people of 1100 Post-Atomic were not used to animals.

Wolves and dogs . . . could one have sired the other?

Svetz looked up at the sleeping wolf and wondered. He was both like and unlike the dogs. The dogs had grinned out through the glass and wagged their tails when children waved. Dogs liked people. But the wolf, even in sleep . . .

Svetz shuddered. Of all the things he hated about his profession, this was the worst; the ride home, staring up at a strange and dangerous extinct animal. The first time he'd done it, a captured horse had seriously damaged the control panel. On

his last mission an ostrich had kicked him and broken three
ribs.

The wolf was stirring restlessly . . . and something about it
had changed.

Something was changing now. The beast's snout was shorter,
wasn't it? Its forelegs lengthened peculiarly; its paws seemed to
grow and spread.

Svetz caught his breath, and instantly forgot the wolf. Svetz
was choking, dying. He snatched up his filter sac and threw himself at the control.

▼▼▼

Svetz stumbled out of the extension cage, took three steps, and
collapsed. Behind him, invisible contaminants poured into the
open air.

The sun was setting in banks of orange cloud.

Svetz lay where he had fallen, retching, fighting for air. There
was an outdoor carpet beneath him, green and damp, smelling
of plants. Svetz did not recognize the smell, did not at once
realize that the carpet was alive. He would not have cared at that
point. He knew only that the cage's air system had tried to kill
him. The way he felt, it had probably succeeded.

It had been a near thing. He had been passing 30 PostAtomic
when the air went bad. He remembered clutching the interrupter
switch, then waiting, waiting. The foul air stank in his nostrils
and caught in his throat and tore at his larynx. He had waited
through twenty years, feeling every second of them. At 50 Post-
Atomic he had pulled the interrupter switch and run choking
from the cage.

50 PA. At least he had reached industrial times. He could
breathe the air.

It was the horse, he thought without surprise. The horse had
pushed its wickedly pointed horn through Svetz's control panel,

three years ago. Maintenance was supposed to fix it. They *had* fixed it.

Something must have worn through.

The way he looked at me every time I passed his cage. I always knew the horse would get me, Svetz thought.

He noticed the filter sac still in his hand. Not that he'd be— Svetz sat up suddenly.

There was green all about him. The damp green carpet beneath him was alive; it grew from the black ground. A rough, twisted pillar thrust from the ground, branched into an explosion of red and yellow papery things. More of the crumpled colored paper lay about the pillar's base. Something that was not an aircraft moved erratically overhead, a tiny thing that fluttered and warbled.

Living, all of it. A preindustrial wilderness.

Svetz pulled the filter sac over his head and hurriedly smoothed the edges around his neck to form a seal. Blind luck that he hadn't fainted yet. He waited for it to puff up around his head. A selectively permeable membrane, it would pass the right gasses in and out until the composition was . . . was . . .

Svetz was choking, tearing at the sac.

He wadded it up and threw it, sobbing. First the air plant, now the filter sac! Had someone wrecked them both? The inertial calendar too; he was at least a hundred years previous to 50 PostAtomic.

Someone had tried to kill him.

Svetz looked wildly about him. Uphill across a wide green carpet, he saw an angular vertical-sided formation painted in shades of faded green. It had to be artificial. There might be people there. He could—

No, he couldn't ask for help either. Who would believe him? How could they help him anyway? His only hope was the extension cage. And his time must be very short.

The extension cage rested a few yards away, the door a black circle on one curved side. The other side seemed to fade away into nothing. It was still attached to the rest of the time machine, in 1103 PA, along a direction eyes could not follow.

Svetz hesitated near the door. His only hope was to disable the air plant. Hold his breath, then . . .

The smell of contaminants was gone.

Svetz sniffed at the air. Yes, gone. The air plant had exhausted itself, drained its contaminants into the open air. No need to wreck it now. Svetz was sick with relief.

He climbed in.

He remembered the wolf when he saw the filter sac, torn and empty. Then he saw the intruder towering over him, the coarse thick hair, the yellow eyes glaring, the taloned hands spread wide to kill.

▼▼▼

The land was dark. In the east a few stars showed, though the west was still deep red. Perfumes tinged the air. A full moon was rising.

Svetz staggered uphill, bleeding.

The house on the hill was big and old. Big as a city block, and two floors high. It sprawled out in all directions, as though a mad architect had built to a whim that changed moment by moment. There were wrought-iron railings on the upper-floor windows, and wrought-iron handles on the screens on both floors, all painted the same dusty shade of green. The screens were wood, painted a different green. They were closed across every window. No light leaked through anywhere.

The door was built for someone twelve feet tall. The knob was huge. Svetz used both hands and put all his weight into it, and still it would not turn. He moaned. He looked for the lens of a peeper camera and could not find it. How would anyone know he was here? He couldn't find a doorbell either.

Perhaps there was nobody inside. No telling what this building was. It was far too big to be a family dwelling, too spread out to be a hotel or apartment house. Might it be a warehouse or a factory? Making or storing what?

Svetz looked back toward the extension cage. Dimly he caught the glow of the interior lights. He also saw something moving on the living green that carpeted the hill.

Pale forms, more than one.

Moving this way?

Svetz pounded on the door with his fists. Nothing. He noticed a golden metal thing, very ornate, high on the door. He touched it, pulled at it, let it go. It clanked.

He took it in both hands and slammed the knob against its base again and again. Rhythmic clanking sounds. Someone should hear it.

Something zipped past his ear and hit the door hard. Svetz spun around, eyes wild, and dodged a rock the size of his fist. The white shapes were nearer now. Bipeds, walking hunched.

They looked too human—or not human enough.

The door opened.

She was young, perhaps sixteen. Her skin was very pale, and her hair and brows were pure white, quite beautiful. Her garment covered her from neck to ankles, but left her arms bare. She seemed sleepy and angry as she pulled the door open—manually, and it was heavy, too. Then she saw Svetz.

"Help me," said Svetz.

Her eyes went wide. Her ears moved too. She said something Svetz had trouble interpreting, for she spoke in ancient american.

"What *are* you?"

Svetz couldn't blame her. Even in good condition his clothes would not fit the period. But his blouse was ripped to the navel, and so was his skin. Four vertical parallel lines of blood ran down his face and chest.

Zeera had been coaching him in american speech. Now he said carefully, "I am a traveler. An animal, a monster, has taken my vehicle away from me."

Evidently the sense came through. "You poor man! What kind of animal?"

"Like a man, but hairy all over, with a horrible face—and claws—claws—"

"I see the marks they made."

"I don't know how he got in. I—" Svetz shuddered. No, he couldn't tell her that. It was insane, utterly insane, this conviction that Svetz's wolf had become a bloodthirsty humanoid monster. "He only hit me once. On the face. I could get him out with a weapon, I think. Have you a bazooka?"

"What a funny word! I don't think so. Come inside. Did the trolls bother you?" She took his arm and pulled him in and shut the door.

Trolls?

"You're a strange person," the girl said, looking him over. "You look strange, you smell strange, you move strangely. I did not know that there were people like you in the world. You must come from very far away."

"Very," said Svetz. He felt himself close to collapse. He was safe at last, safe inside. But why were the hairs on the back of his neck trying to stand upright?

He said, "My name is Svetz. What's yours?"

"Wrona." She smiled up at him, not afraid despite his strangeness . . . and he must look strange to her, for surely she looked strange to Hanville Svetz. Her skin was sheet white, and her rich white hair would better have fit a centenarian. Her nose, very broad and flat, would have disfigured an ordinary girl. Somehow it fit Wrona's face well enough; but her face was most odd, and her ears were too large, almost pointed, and her eyes were too far apart, and her grin stretched *way* back . . . and Svetz liked it. Her grin was curiosity and enjoyment, and was not a bit too wide. The firm pressure of her hand was friendly, reassuring. Though her fingernails were uncomfortably long and sharp.

"You should rest, Svetz," she said. "My parents will not be up for another hour, at least. Then they can decide how to help you. Come with me. I'll take you to a spare room."

He followed her through a room dominated by a great rectangular table and a double row of high-backed chairs. There was a large microwave oven at one end, and beside it a platter of . . . red things. Roughly conical they were, each about the size of a strong man's upper arm, each with a dot of white in the big end. Svetz had no idea what they were; but he didn't like their color. They seemed to be bleeding.

"Oh," Wrona exclaimed. "I should have asked. Are you hungry?"

Svetz was, suddenly. "Have you any dole yeast?"

"Why, I don't know the word. Are those dole yeast? They are all we have."

"We'd better forget it." Svetz's stomach lurched at the thought of eating something that color. Even if it turned out to be a plant.

Wrona was half supporting him by the time they reached the room. It was rectangular and luxuriously large. The bed was wide enough, but only six inches off the floor, and without coverings. She helped him down to it. "There's a wash basin behind that door, if you find the strength. Best you rest, Svetz. In perhaps two hours I will call you."

Svetz eased himself back. The room seemed to rotate. He heard her go out.

How strange she was. How odd he must look to her. A good thing she hadn't called anyone to tend him. A doctor would notice the differences.

Svetz never dreamed that primitives would be so different from his own people. During the thousand years between now and the present, there must have been massive adaptation to changes in air and water, to DDT and other compounds in foods, to extinction of food plants and meat animals until only dole yeast was left, to higher noise levels, less room for exercise, greater dependence on medicines. . . . Well, why shouldn't they be different? It was a wonder humanity survived at all.

Wrona had not feared his strangeness, nor cringed from the scratches on his face and chest. She was only amused and interested. She had helped him without asking too many questions. He liked her for that.

He dozed.

Pain from deep scratches, stickiness in his clothes made his sleep restless. There were nightmares. Something big and shadowy, half man and half beast, reached far out to slash his face. Over and over. At some indeterminate time he woke completely, already trying to identify a musky, unfamiliar scent.

No use. He looked about him, at a strange room that seemed even stranger from floor level. High ceiling. One frosted globe, no brighter than a full moon, glowed so faintly that the room was all shadow. Wrought-iron bars across the windows; black night beyond.

A wonder he'd awakened at all. The preindustrial air should have killed him hours ago.

It had been a futz of a day, he thought. And he shied away from the memory of the thing in the extension cage. Snarling face, pointed ears, double row of pointed white teeth. The clawed hand reaching out, swiping down. The nightmare conviction that a wolf had turned into *that*.

It could not be. Animals did not change shape like that. Something must have gotten in while Svetz was fighting for air. Chased the wolf out, or killed it.

But there were legends of such things, weren't there? Two and three thousand years old and more, everywhere in the world, were the tales of men who could become beasts and vice versa.

Svetz sat up. Pain gripped his chest, then relaxed. He stood up carefully and made his way to the bathroom.

The spigots were not hard to solve. Svetz wet a cloth with warm water. He watched himself in the mirror, emerging from under the crusted blood. A pale, slender young man topped with thin blond hair . . . and an odd distortion of chin and forehead. That must be the mirror, he decided. Primitive workmanship. It might have been worse. Hadn't the first mirrors been two-dimensional?

A shrill whistle sounded outside his door. Svetz went to look, and found Wrona. "Good, you're up," she said. "Father and Uncle Wrocky would like to see you."

Svetz stepped into the hall, and again noticed the elusive musky scent. He followed Wrona down the dark hallway. Like his room, it was lit only by a single white frosted globe. Why would Wrona's people keep the house so dark? They had electricity.

And why were they all sleeping at sunset? With breakfast laid out and waiting . . .

Wrona opened a door, gestured him in.

Svetz hesitated a step beyond the threshold. The room was as dark as the hallway. The musky scent was stronger here. He jumped when a hand closed on his upper arm—it felt wrong; there was hair on the palm; the hard nails made a circlet of pressure points—and a gravelly male voice boomed, "Come in, Mister Svetz. My daughter tells me you're a traveler in need of help."

In the dim light Svetz made out a man and woman seated on backless chairs. Both had hair as white as Wrona's, but the woman's hair bore a broad black stripe. A second man urged Svetz toward another backless chair. He too bore black markings: a single black eyebrow, a black crescent around one ear.

And Wrona was just behind him. Svetz looked around at them all, seeing how alike they were, how different from Hanville Svetz.

The fear rose up in him like a strong drug. Svetz was a xenophobe.

They were all alike. Rich white hair and eyebrows, black markings. Narrow black fingernails. The broad flat noses and the wide, wide mouths, the sharp white conical teeth, the high, pointed ears that moved, the yellow eyes, the hair palms.

Svetz dropped heavily onto the padded footstool.

One of the males noticed: the larger one, who was still standing. "It must be the heavier gravity," he guessed. "It's true, isn't it, Svetz? You're from another world. Obviously you're not quite a man. You told Wrona you were a traveler, but didn't say from how far away."

"Very far," Svetz said weakly. "From the future."

The smaller male was jolted. "The future? You're a time traveler?" His voice became a snarl. "You're saying that we will evolve into something like you!"

Svetz cringed. "No. Really."

"I hope not. What, then?"

"I think I must have gone sidewise in time. You're descended from wolves, aren't you? Not apes? Wolves?"

"Yes, of course."

The seated male was looking him over. "Now that he mentions it, he does look much more like a troll than any man has a right to. No offense intended, Svetz."

Svetz, surrounded by wolf men, tried to relax. And failed. "What is a troll?"

Wrona perched on the edge of his stool. "You must have seen them on the lawn. We keep about thirty."

"Plains apes," the smaller male supplied. "Imported from Africa, sometime in the last century. They make good watchbeasts and meat animals. You have to be careful with them, though. They throw things."

"Introductions," the other said suddenly. "Excuse our manners, Svetz. I'm Flakee Wrocky. This is my brother Flakee Worrel, and Brenda, his wife. My niece you know."

"Pleased to meet you," Svetz said hollowly.

"You say you slipped sideways in time?"

"I think so. A futz of a long way, too," said Svetz. "Marooned. Gods protect me. It must have been the horse—"

Wrocky broke in. "Horse?"

"The horse. Three years ago, a horse damaged my extension cage. It was supposed to be fixed. I suppose the repairs just wore through, and the cage slipped sideways in time instead of forward. Into a world where wolves evolved instead of *Homo habilis*. Gods know where I'm likely to wind up if I try to go back."

Then he remembered. "At least you can help me there. Some kind of monster has taken over my extension cage."

"Extension cage."

"The part of the time machine that does the moving. You'll help me evict the monster?"

"Of course," said Worrel, at the same time that the other was saying, "I don't think so. Bear with me, please, Worrel. Svetz, it would be a disservice to you if we chased the monster out of your extension cage. You would try to reach your own time, would you not?"

"Futz, yes!"

"But you would only get more and more lost. At least in our world you can eat the food and breathe the air. Yes, we grow food plants for the trolls; you can learn to eat them."

"You don't understand. I can't stay here. I'm a xenophobe!"

Wrocky frowned. His ears flicked forward enquiringly. "What?"

"I'm afraid of intelligent human beings who aren't human. I can't help it. It's in my bones."

"Oh, I'm sure you'll get used to us, Svetz."

Svetz looked from one male to the other. It was obvious enough who was in charge. Wrocky's voice was much louder and deeper than Worrel's; he was bigger than the other man, and his white fur fell about his neck in a mane like a lion's. Worrel was making no attempt to assert himself. As for the women, neither had spoken a word since Svetz entered the room.

Wrocky was emphatically the boss. And Wrocky didn't want Svetz to leave.

"You don't understand," Svetz said desperately. "The air—"
He stopped.

"What about the air?"

"It should have killed me by now. A dozen times over. In fact, why hasn't it?" Odd enough that he'd ever stopped wondering about that. "I must have adapted," Svetz said half to himself. "That's it. The cage passed too close to this line of history. My heredity changed. My lungs adapted to preindustrial air. Futz it! If I hadn't pulled the interrupter switch, I'd have adapted back."

"Then you can breathe our air," said Wrocky.

"I still don't understand it. Don't you have any industries?"

"Of course," Worrel said in surprise.

"Internal-combustion cars and aircraft? Diesel trucks and ships? Chemical fertilizers, insect repellents—?"

"No, none of that. Chemical fertilizers wash away, ruin the water. The only insect repellents I ever heard of smelled to high heaven. They never got beyond the experimental stage. Most of our vehicles are battery powered."

"There *was* a fad for internal-combustion once," said Wrocky. "It didn't spread very far. They stank. The people inside didn't care, of course, because they were leaving the stink behind. At its peak there were over two hundred cars tootling around the city of Detroit, poisoning the air. Then one night the citizenry rose in a pack and tore all the cars to pieces. The owners too."

Worrel said, "I've always thought that men have more sensitive noses than trolls."

"Wrona noticed my smell long before I noticed hers. Wrocky, this is getting us nowhere. I've *got* to go home. I seemed to have adapted to the air, but there are other things. Foods; I've never eaten anything but dole yeast; everything else died out long ago. Bacteria."

Wrocky shook his head. "Anywhere you go, Svetz, your broken time machine will only take you to more and more exotic environments. There must be a thousand ways the world could end. Suppose you stepped out into one of them? Or just passed near one?"

"But—"

"Here, on the other paw, you will be an honored guest. Think of all the things you can teach us! You, who were born into a culture that builds time-traveling vehicles!"

So that was it. "Oh, no. You couldn't use what I know," said Svetz. "I'm no mechanic. I couldn't show you how to do anything. Besides, you'd hate the side effects. Too much of past civilizations was built on petrochemicals. And plastics. Burning plastics produces some of the strangest—"

"But even the most extensive oil reserves could not last forever. You must have developed other power sources by your own time." Wrocky's yellow eyes seemed to bore right through him. "Controlled hydrogen fusion?"

"But I can't tell you how it's done!" Svetz cried desperately. "I know nothing of plasma physics!"

"Plasma physics? What are plasma physics?"

"Using electromagnetic fields to manipulate ionized gasses. You *must* have plasma physics."

"No, but I'm sure you can give us some valuable hints. Already we have fusion bombs. And so do the Europeans . . . but we can discuss that later." Wrocky stood up. His black nails made pressure points on Svetz's arm. "Think it over, Svetz. Oh, and make yourself free of the house, but don't go outside without an escort. The trolls, you know."

▼▼▼

Svetz left the room with his head whirling. The wolves would not let him leave.

"Svetz, I'm glad you're staying," Wrona chattered. "I like you. I'm sure you'll like it here. Please let me show you over the house."

Down the length of the hallway, one frosted globe burned dimly in the gloom, like a full moon transported indoors. Nocturnal, they were nocturnal.

Wolves.

"I'm a xenophobe," he said. "I can't help it. I was born that way."

"Oh, you'll learn to like us. You like me a little already, don't you, Svetz?" She reached up to scratch him behind the ear. A thrill of pleasure ran through him, unexpectedly sharp, so that he half closed his eyes.

"This way," she said.

"Where are we going?"

"I thought I'd show you some trolls. Svetz, are you really descended from trolls? I can't believe it!"

"I'll tell you when I see them," said Svetz. He remembered the *Homo habilis* in the Vivarium. It had been a man, an Advisor, until the Secretary-General had ordered him regressed.

They went through the dining room, and Svetz saw unmistakable bones on the plates. He shivered. His forebears had eaten meat; the trolls were brute animals here, whatever they might be in Svetz's world—but Svetz shuddered. His thinking seemed turgid, his head felt thick. He had to get out of here.

"If you think Uncle Wrocky's tough, you should meet the European ambassador," said Wrona. "Perhaps you will."

"Does he come here?"

"Sometimes." Wrona growled low in her throat. "I don't like him. He's a different species, Svetz. Here it was the wolves that evolved into men; at least that's what our teacher tells us. In Europe it was something else."

"I don't think Uncle Wrocky will let me meet him. Or even tell him about me." Svetz rubbed at his eyes.

"You're lucky. Herr Dracula smiles a lot and says nasty things in a polite voice. It takes you a minute to—Svetz! What's wrong?"

Svetz groaned like a man in agony. "My eyes!" He felt higher. "My forehead! I don't have a forehead anymore."

"I don't understand."

Svetz felt his face with his fingertips. His eyebrows were a caterpillar of hair on a thick, solid ridge of bone. From the brow ridge his forehead sloped back at forty-five degrees. And his chin, his chin was gone, too. There was only a regular curve of jaw into neck.

"I'm regressing. I'm turning into a troll," said Svetz. "Wrona, if I turn into a troll, will they eat me?"

"I don't know. I'll stop them, Svetz!"

"No. Take me down to the extension cage. If you're not with me, the trolls will kill me."

"All right. But, Svetz, what about the monster?"

"He should be easier to handle by now. It'll be all right. Just take me there. Please."

"All right, Svetz." She took his hand and led him.

The mirror hadn't lied. He'd been changing, even then, adapting to this line of history. First his lungs had lost their adaption to normal air. There had been no industrial age here. But there had been no *Homo sapiens* either. . . .

Wrona opened the door. Svetz sniffed at the night. His sense of smell had become preternaturally acute. He smelled the trolls before he saw them, coming uphill toward him across the living green carpet. Svetz's fingers curled, wishing for a weapon.

Three of them. They formed a ring around Svetz and Wrona. One of them carried a length of white bone. They all walked upright on two legs, but they walked as if their feet hurt them. They were as hairless as men. Apes' heads mounted on men's bodies.

Homo habilis, the killer plains apes. Man's ancestor.

"Pay them no attention," Wrona said offhandedly. "They won't hurt us." She started down the hill. Svetz followed closely.

"He really shouldn't have that bone," she called back. "We try to keep bones away from them. They use them as weapons. Sometimes they hurt each other. Once one of them got hold of the iron handle for the lawn sprinkler and killed a gardener with it."

"I'm not going to take it away from him."

"That glaring light, is that your extension cage?"

"Yes."

"I'm not sure about this, Svetz." She stopped suddenly. "Uncle Wrocky's right. You'll only get more lost. Here you'll at least be taken care of."

"No. Uncle Wrocky was wrong. See the dark side of the extension cage, how it fades away into nothing. It's still attached to the rest of the time machine. It'll just reel me in."

"Oh."

"No telling how long it's been veering across the time lines. Maybe ever since that futzy horse poked his futzy horn through the controls. Nobody ever noticed before. Why should they? Nobody ever stopped a time machine halfway before."

"Svetz, horses don't have horns."

"Mine does."

There was a noise behind them. Wrona looked back into a darkness Svetz's eyes could not pierce. "Somebody must have noticed us! Come on, Svetz!"

She pulled him toward the lighted cage. They stopped just outside.

"My head feels thick," Svetz mumbled. "My tongue too."

"What are we going to do about the monster? I can't hear anything—"

"No monster. Just a man with amnesia, now. He was only dangerous in the transition stage."

She looked in. "Why, you're right! Sir, would you mind— Svetz, he doesn't seem to understand me."

"Sure not. Why should he? He thinks he's a white arctic wolf." Svetz stepped inside. The white-haired wolf man was backed into a corner, warily watching. He looked a lot like Wrona.

Svetz became aware that he had picked up a tree branch. His hand must have done it without telling his brain. He circled, holding the weapon ready. An unreasoning rage built up and up in him. Invader! The man had no business here in Svetz's territory.

The wolf man backed away, his slant eyes mad and frightened. Suddenly he was out the door and running, the trolls close behind.

"Your father can teach him, maybe," said Svetz.

Wrona was studying the controls. "How do you work it?"

"Let me see. I'm not sure I remember." Svetz rubbed at his drastically sloping forehead. "That one closes the door—"

Wrona pushed it. The door closed.

"Shouldn't you be outside?"

"I want to come with you," said Wrona.

"Oh." It was getting terribly difficult to think. Svetz looked over the control panel. Eeeny, meeny—that one? Svetz pulled it.

Free fall. Wrona yipped. Gravity came, vectored radially outward from the center of the extension cage. It pulled against the walls.

"When my lungs go back to normal, I'll probably go to sleep," said Svetz. "Don't worry about it." Was there something else he ought to tell Wrona? He tried to remember.

Oh, yes. "You can't go home again," said Svetz. "We'd never find this line of history again."

"I want to stay with you," said Wrona.

"All right."

▼▼▼

Within a deep recess in the bulk of the time machine, a fog formed. It congealed abruptly—and Svetz's extension cage was back, hours late. The door popped open automatically. But Svetz didn't come out.

They had to pull him out by the shoulders, out of air that smelled of beast and honeysuckle.

"He'll be all right in a minute. Get a filter over that other thing," Ra Chen ordered. He stood over Svetz with his arms folded, waiting.

Svetz began breathing.

He opened his eyes.

"All right," said Ra Chen. "What happened?"

Svetz sat up. "Let me think. I went back to preindustrial America. It was all snowed in. I . . . shot a wolf."

"We've got it in a tent. Then what?"

"No. The wolf left. We chased him out." Svetz's eyes went wide. "Wrona!"

Wrona lay on her side in the filter tent. Her fur was thick and rich, white with black markings. She was built something like a wolf, but more compactly, with a big head and a short muzzle and a tightly curled tail. Her eyes were closed. She did not seem to be breathing.

Svetz knelt. "Help me get her out of there! Can't you tell the difference between a wolf and a dog?"

SOUTH OF OREGON CITY

▼▼▼

PAT MURPHY

Reynal passed Jem the bottle and he took a long drink.
The warmth of the whiskey chased away the chill of the September evening. The two men leaned against the split-rail fence of
the corral, just beyond the circle of torchlight where the fiddler
played and the farmers danced on the hard-packed dirt of the
street.

"There's a pretty one," Reynal said, watching a young woman
whirl past in the arms of a young man. Her blonde hair was
twisted into curls and she wore a blue satin ribbon around her
neck. Her face shone in the torchlight, paler than any man in
the town. "Ah, she's a beauty." As she passed, Jem caught a
whiff of cloves and cinnamon, spices the women used in lieu of
perfume.

Jem did not understand these white women. Over the
scratching of the fiddle, Jem heard feminine laughter—the giggles
of young women who had traveled with their families to farm this
new land—and he froze, fearing this unfamiliar territory as
another man might fear the rapids of the Columbia. Jem took
another swig of whiskey and returned the bottle to Reynal.

Jem's father had been a trapper at Fort Vancouver. His mother had been Cayuse—a princess of her tribe, to hear his father tell it. But his father had been a liar, and Jem hadn't put much stock in what he said. His mother had died of measles when he was five, and Jem had grown up wild, eating at the trappers' table at Fort Vancouver and cared for by the trappers' squaws.

Jem's father had died in 1848—he caught an arrow between the shoulder blades in one of many skirmishes with the Cayuse. Jem was sorry for it—his father had always treated him well— but Jem was a man by then, seventeen years old and ready to live his own life. He spent a few years trapping beaver and selling the pelts to Hudson's Bay Company as his father had before him.

In 1851, Jem decided to settle. He built a cabin in a pretty valley three days south of Oregon City. He had a few head of cattle and the game was plentiful enough. He had come to town for a taste of human company and lingered for the dance. But after a day of the company of Reynal and the other trappers, he was ready to escape to the solitude of his cabin.

"Look there," Reynal said, lifting the hand that held the bottle to point unsteadily. "There she is. I heard about her."

Jem glanced in the direction that Reynal was pointing. On the other side of the corral, a slim young man in a broad-brimmed hat leaned against the railing. "What do you mean?"

Reynal leaned close to speak in a drunken whisper. "That's a woman. She dresses like a man." Reynal shook his head, scandalized. His eyes were bloodshot and he stank of whiskey. "She came riding into town yesterday on an Indian pony and allowed as how she crossed the plains by herself."

Jem studied the woman. As he watched, she turned her head and he caught a glimpse of the face beneath the hat. By the torchlight, he could see that her face was dark from the sun. Her features were those of a young woman. But white women did not dress in men's clothing. White women did not travel alone in the wilderness. As he watched, she turned away and the broad brim of her hat hid her face. She headed down the street toward Rudd's Hotel, where Mr. Rudd was selling whiskey.

"Think I'll go and get to know her a little better," Reynal said and started around the corral toward her. He walked unsteadily, reaching out now and again to lay a hand on the railing for support. Jem watched him sway as he left the railing, then steady himself, cast a sly look back over his shoulder, and follow the slim figure into the darkness.

Jem followed as far as the general store, where he sat on a wooden bench and waited. The street was dark, except for the faint light of the waxing moon. He heard the murmur of voices to his left—the lilt of French. A scuffle—boots scraping against hard-packed dirt, the clink and slosh of a bottle falling. A yelp— Reynal by the sound—then Reynal cursing in French.

Reynal was limping when he came back. He clutched his right hand in his left and Jem could see blood welling between his fingers. "She bit me," he said in a tone of aggrieved astonishment.

Jem could not help grinning. Reynal glared at him and went past him, back to the dance.

A few minutes later, the woman emerged from the darkness. She carried Reynal's bottle in her hand. She stopped when she saw Jem. "You waiting for something?"

The moonlight shone on her face. Her chin was too strong and her mouth was too wide to be called pretty. He guessed she was about eighteen.

"Just wanted to see what kind of wild critter mauled Reynal," Jem said.

She gave him a thin-lipped smile. "You've seen."

He nodded. "Hope you washed your mouth out. He's a poisonous cuss."

She did not move. "You a friend of his?"

Jem shrugged. "I wouldn't trust him as far as you could toss him, so I wouldn't really count him as a friend." He sat and watched her for a moment. The women at the dance spoke a language he did not understand—something higher and sweeter and more lilting than man talk. Jem looked at them and had no words to say. But this woman was not like them. "You could sit if you liked. I won't give you any call to bite me."

She sat on the edge of the porch, an arm's length away. He liked the way she moved: quick and graceful and a little nervous, like a high-strung horse.

"Where you headed from here?" he asked.

"South," she said.

"Homesteading?"

"Maybe."

He stretched out his legs and looked up at the stars. "People say I don't talk much. You've got me beat."

She said nothing.

"Smoke?" he asked, offering her his tobacco pouch.

She shook her head.

"I suppose traveling alone you got out of the habit of talking. And you might not have been in the habit to start with." When he glanced at her, she looked away. "My guess is you don't like people much. I can understand that. I don't like them most of the time myself. But every now and then, I get lonely. It's lonely out where I live. Pretty little valley, but it's lonely." He glanced at her again, and this time she met his eyes. He was talking to her the way he would talk to a spooked horse, soothing her, calming her, not paying much attention to what he was saying. "Seems like it must have been lonely, crossing the prairies by yourself. Worrying about the Indians and listening to the wolves howl."

"I like the Indians fine," she said at last. "And the wolves aren't a problem."

He stopped for a moment, startled that she had spoken at last. "Well, then," he said slowly, "you might like it where I live. There's a pack of wolves at the end of the valley. When the moon's up, they sing to me like a church choir on Sunday."

"You don't look like a farmer. The farmers on the trail are dull people. Like their oxen."

"Was a trapper. Gave it up. Settled down last spring. Seemed like time. I'd like to raise a family, but most of these women, they're looking for someone refined. They seem like a soft lot." He hesitated. The distant fiddle fell silent. "I'm looking for a woman with teeth."

She laughed, an unexpected musical sound. "With teeth?" She stood up. "You may find more than you bargained for."

She started for the door of the hotel. "Wait," he said. "What's your name? I'm Jem Lowell."

"Nadya," she said, showing her teeth in a sudden smile. "The Pawnee call me Crazy Wolf." She headed down the street, returning to the dance and leaving Jem to look at the stars alone.

▼▼▼

At Rudd's Hotel, for the extravagant price of a dollar a night, a traveler could rent a hard wooden cot and a straw-tick mattress, separated from the neighboring bed by a muslin curtain. A few bugs came free with the room, but the cold drove most of them out.

That night, Jem stayed in the hotel, rather than returning to the fort. He lay awake on his straw-tick mattress, listening to the grunts and snores of the man in the next cubicle.

Before the sun came up, when mist was rising from the river, he left the hotel and gathered a bouquet of the bright wildflowers that grew on the riverbank. He had heard that women liked flowers. It seemed as good a place as any to begin.

He felt like a fool, walking through the streets of town with the flowers clutched in his hand. He found her in the stable, tending to her pony. She was dressed as she had been the night before: a red flannel shirt, men's denim trousers, a broad-brimmed black hat, dusty and faded.

She was examining the pony's left hind hoof when he walked in, and for a moment, in the early morning light, she looked beautiful. He stopped in the doorway. She looked up, and the light on her face shifted. An ordinary face, nothing more. He thrust the flowers into her hands. "These are for you."

She took them, her dark eyebrows drawing together in puzzlement. The hand that held the flowers was grimy with dust from the pony's hoof, and her fingernails were broken.

He shoved his hands into his pockets and wondered what to do next. The pony turned her head to sniff at the flowers and Nadya moved them out of the animal's reach, still frowning.

"Problem with her feet?" he asked.

"She was limping yesterday. Stone bruise, I suspect," Nadya said. "Needs a rest."

"I've a liniment for that," he said. He fetched it. She set the flowers down on the stable floor, and anointed the bruise. He stood back. He did not know what to do with his hands, so he shoved them back in his pockets. She finished the job and wiped her hands on a bandanna. She glanced down at the flowers and then picked them up and held them gingerly.

"Come for a walk?" Jem suggested awkwardly.

She studied him over the scraggling bouquet. "Walk where?"

"By the river."

"All right, then," she said.

They walked down Oregon City's main street, past Rudd's Hotel. Two town women, dressed in full-length calico skirts and proper bonnets, were walking down the street toward them. Half a block away, the two women crossed to the far side of the street. Jem heard Nadya mutter something under her breath in French. He caught the phrase "mangeurs de lard," pork-eaters, a mountaineer's term for the soft-living people of the settlements.

"Don't take it personal," Jem said. "Likely as not, it has nothing to do with you."

"Why's that?"

"They do the same for me." He stopped and turned. The women were still in sight. They had crossed back. "Watch." He took a breath and whooped—a wild screeching war cry. The women jumped and clutched each other's arms. They glanced back at Jem, then doubled their pace, hurrying into a shop.

Nadya was laughing. She slapped the bouquet against her leg, scattering bright petals on the dirt track.

"They're just protecting their scalps." Jem said. "I'm half Cayuse. Never know when I might go crazy and cut loose."

Nadya looked up at him and grinned for the first time. They walked along a path that led by the river. He was aware of her walking beside him, still carrying the bouquet. She let it swing easily now, slapping it against her leg and scattering petals.

"Too crowded around here," he said at last. "Too many new settlers."

She nodded agreement.

"My cabin is three days ride south. Over the Calapooeys, not far from the Umpqua River. No towns there. Forest grows right up to my doorstep."

"When you were a trapper, what did you trap?" When he looked at her, she was watching his face.

He shrugged, puzzled by the sudden turn the conversation had taken. "Beaver, mostly. That was the best money."

"Other things, sometimes?"

"Sometimes. Bobcat, now and then. A badger or two."

They walked in silence for a while. When they came to a muddy place in the trail, he held out his hand to help her across. She stepped across without his help, then took his hand. They walked hand in hand.

"Deer ahead," she said softly, stopping in the trail. Three white-tailed deer lifted their heads and bounded away into the trees.

"Good eyes," he said.

"My father was a good hunter. I take after him."

The deer moved on, but Jem remained still in the trail, holding her hand tightly. She was not a big woman. A head shorter than he was, she had to tip her head back to look at him.

"It must have been hard, traveling across the prairie alone."

She shrugged. "No harder than for a man."

He nodded. "That's hard enough."

She studied his face, then allowed, "It was hard."

"Working a homestead alone is hard," he said. "Lonely."

"I'll do all right," she said.

He looked down at her, watching her face. "Why'd you come into town?" he asked her. "Looks to me like you could have just turned south without stopping."

She frowned at him, her expression stubborn. "I needed some supplies."

"Some company, maybe." She didn't answer. His hand tightened on hers. "I have a nice cabin on my land. I have some stock. I could be a good husband to you."

"Ah," she said, studying his face, "but could I be a good wife?"

He looked down at her small dark face, her stubborn eyes. He knew she was wild, but he liked wild things. There were things he wanted to say, but he did not know how. "Come and marry me," he said. "I'll take care of you."

"Ah, Jem," she said. "But who will take care of you?"

"I'll take care of myself. I always have," he said. He put a hand on her shoulder and pulled her close. She leaned against him and put her arms around him. He felt the warmth of her body against his.

"As you please," she said. "I will come with you."

▼▼▼

She said she had no use for preachers. And so the next day, when her pony's foot was well enough for travel, they rode south along the Willamette River, following the trail worn by emigrants who took the southern route and cut north to reach Oregon City.

The Willamette Valley narrowed and the evergreen trees grew thick and tall around them, filtering the late summer sunlight. They rounded a bend in the trail and a shaft of sunlight, like a blessing from heaven, shone on the trail ahead.

The trail climbed out of the valley, up the rocky slopes of the range known as the Calapooeys. As they came around one bend in the trail, a grouse flew up from beneath the hooves of Nadya's pony, and she brought it down with a single shot, quicker on the draw than Jem. "Dinner," she said to Jem and scrambled down the rocky slope to fetch the bird.

After they left the settled areas behind, she began to sing as they rode, lilting cheerful tunes that reminded Jem of French folksongs. He could not understand the words. When he asked her, she said they were songs her father had taught her. She would not translate the words. "Maybe later," she said. "Maybe later."

They camped that night on the lee side of a rocky ridge, where a spring burst through the earth and made a pool of clear, cool water. Jem cut branches from the cedar trees and covered them with a blanket to make a fragrant mattress. He built a fire of fallen branches. Nadya plucked and gutted the bird, then roasted it on green sticks that she cut with her Bowie knife.

As they sat by the fire, the moon rose: nearly three-quarters full, a lopsided shape hanging above the ridge. In the distance, a wolf yapped and then howled. The single voice was joined by a chorus of wailing. Nadya listened.

Jem touched her shoulder, feeling her warmth through the flannel shirt. "Come to bed," he said awkwardly.

On the bed of cedar boughs, Jem put his arms around her. She came to him, surprising him with her willingness. She unbuttoned his shirt and he felt her small cool hands against his skin. In the distance, the wolves yapped and howled. She shivered then, pressing closer to him.

"Ah, now." He was suddenly tender, knowing that her talk was partly bravado: she was not as fearless as she had seemed. "You're safe with me. Don't worry."

He caught a glimpse of her face in the moonlight: a flash of grinning teeth, a glitter of dark eyes reflecting the moonlight. "I'm not worried," she said. "Not worried at all."

Her body was pressed against his and the tension within him was concentrated now. He could feel the fabric of his trousers rub against his penis when she shifted her body. Through her shirt, he could feel the warmth of her breasts.

His fingers fumbled with the buttons of her shirt. She made a soft mewling sound that merged with the distant howling of the wolves. There was rough wool against his skin, warm breasts beneath his hands, the scent of cedar and woodsmoke, the distant howling of wolves. The wolf howls merged with Nadya's breathy cries as he pushed himself into her body and exhausted himself inside her. He fell asleep, holding her in his arms.

In the morning, he woke to find she had slipped from the bed without disturbing him. She stood by the burned-out fire, her head cocked to one side as if she were listening. Jem could hear nothing. In the dawn light, she looked as insubstantial as the white mist that curled between the trees. She could blow away with the breeze, he thought, disappear with the morning sun. "Nadya," he said, seized with the sudden fear that she would vanish.

She shifted her gaze to him, her eyes intent.

"What are you listening to?" he asked.

"The forest."

"Come back to bed and warm yourself."

She returned to him. When he kissed her, she took his ear between her teeth, growling softly.

"Crazy Wolf," he said. "Be careful with that ear."

She nipped it sharply and let loose a laugh that echoed from the trees.

▼▼▼

His cabin was a single-room building, constructed of yellow fir logs. He had carefully filled the gaps between the logs with clay from the nearby stream, packing the clay tightly to keep out the winds of the coming winter. A clapboard roof kept off the rain. The floor was hard-packed dirt.

The windows were closed with wooden shutters, and he hurried to open them and let in light and air. There was a stone hearth and a chimney to let the smoke out. For furniture, he had a single stool, constructed of roughly hewn fir, and a narrow bed platform piled with buffalo robes.

Looking at the bleak interior, Jem said quickly. "I'll build you a table first. And another stool. And a bed—we'll need a proper bed."

He glanced at Nadya's face, but she was not looking at the dark interior. She stood at the window, looking away into the trees. "Just as you said," she said. "A lovely place."

Within a week, he had built a table and a bench and two chairs and a bed of cedar wood. Nadya worked by his side. Together, they harvested the Indian corn that he had planted last spring and put it to store for the winter.

On the third day, she started out in the morning with her rifle and returned with three summer-fattened grouse. If she had asked, he would have told her not to go hunting, but she did not ask. And when he mildly suggested that perhaps it would be better if he went hunting, she gave him a long considering look.

"I don't think so," she said in a cool tone. Her eyes looked greener than they had before, or perhaps they were simply reflecting the evergreen boughs overhead. He studied her face, considered the grouse, and decided not to raise the subject again.

They had been in the cabin for just under a week when he woke alone in their new bed. The cabin's wooden door was unlatched and the night breeze had blown it partway open.

Moonlight shone through the opening, painting the dirt floor with silver. Beside him, the blankets were cold, no trace of warmth where Nadya had been.

He waited for a moment. Perhaps she had stepped out to relieve herself in the woods, not wanting to wake him. He tossed back the blankets and went to the doorway. The full moon was setting and the first light of dawn touched the eastern sky with pink. The trees were wreathed in ghostly mist that drifted in the breeze. "Nadya," he called. "Nadya." In the corral, the horses pricked their ears and watched him.

The night air chilled him and he pulled a blanket from the bed and wrapped it around him, his mind still muddled with sleep. For a moment, he wondered if she had been a dream from the start. Then he saw her shirt and trousers hanging neatly on the peg beside the door. Real enough.

The moon set, and the first light of the sun sparkled on the grass of the meadow. He called again, his voice echoing across the valley. For the space of a heartbeat, he listened to the forest, waiting.

She ran from the shelter of the trees, naked and barefoot. She was laughing and breathless. He reached out and embraced her, wrapping her in the blanket.

"Where were you?" he demanded. "Where did you go?"

"Call of nature." Her eyes were bright with amusement. "Oh, it's a wonderful morning." She pressed herself against him and he embraced her automatically. Her skin was cool beneath his hands.

"You must have heard me calling. Why didn't you come back? You're so cold."

She shook her head, her eyes on his face. "I didn't hear." She wet her lips, looking up at him. "I know a way to get warm again."

She led him back to bed where she warmed him and he warmed her. He could not stay stay angry with her for long.

When he woke again, later in the morning, she was tending the fire and heating water for coffee. Her hair was neatly braided once again, not hanging loose as it had been the night before.

That day, he chopped wood for their winter fire. He felt the axe in his hand, the smooth wooden shaft rubbing against his palm. This, he thought, is real. The sharp sound of metal striking wood. The echo returning from across the valley. This is real. The fog and the darkness of the night—that is not real. That is to be forgotten.

He watched Nadya that day and the next day and the day after. Each evening, just before the light faded, she would pause in the midst of her chores. She would set down the water bucket, stop stirring the kettle, let the fire burn unattended. For a long moment she would stand on the edge of the yard where the meadowland gave way to tall trees, and she would stare into the gathering darkness. Then, without a word, she would continue her work.

Sometimes, he listened too, struggling to hear what had caught her attention. But he could never hear anything unusual. Once, he asked her what she heard. She had smiled and shrugged and dismissed the question. "Nothing. Just listening to the birds."

At night, Nadya sat by the fire. Sometimes, she wrote in a small, leatherbound book. She said that her mother had given it to her. Jem watched her write, scribbles of dark ink on white paper. He had never learned to read; that skill had not been particularly useful around the fort. But watching her now, he wished he could read. He watched her pen move across the page and he knew that she was writing secrets. When he asked her what she wrote, she shook her heard. "Nothing important."

As the weeks passed, Jem noticed that Nadya was growing restless. When the wolf pack that roamed through the area howled, she would go to the window and listen. She tossed in her sleep and muttering in a language that he did not understand.

When he asked her what was troubling her, she shook her head and said nothing.

Late summer had turned to fall when he woke again to an empty bed. He threw off the blankets and went to the door to stand in the cold crisp air. The first snow had fallen in the night; a thin white powder clung to the ground. By the light of the full moon, he saw Nadya's footprints in the snow: bare feet crossing the yard and entering the forest. He called once, but got no answer.

He dressed quickly, took his rifle and a lantern, and followed the trail of her footprints. Just before the trail entered the shelter of the trees, the footprints changed. The delicate prints of his wife's bare feet disappeared. The trail continued unbroken but the prints were those of a wolf.

Jem squatted in the snow, examining the prints. Woman. Then wolf. He shook his head, chilled and frightened. He held the lantern high, its yellow light casting a circle on the snow.

He followed the trail of the wolf into the shelter of the trees, where the snow lay in patches. The fir trees blocked the moonlight. He held his lantern high, and it cast a circle of yellow light on the forest floor. He cast about, checking for footprints in each patch of snow. He found a few scratches where the wolf had pawed aside the pine needles to sniff at a rodent burrow beneath a fallen log. After that, just a hundred yards into the forest, he lost the trail. He could not follow the track by the uncertain light of the lantern and the moon.

"Nadya!" he called. "Nadya!" The trees swallowed his voice, giving nothing back.

He returned to the cabin to wait. He built up the fire, and sat on the wooden bench where he and Nadya sometimes sat together by the fire. He watched the fire burn and listened to the wind whispering through the chinks between the logs of the cabin. He did not know what the wind was trying to say.

The first light of dawn was shining in the cracks around the door when he heard Nadya's footsteps outside. She hesitated in the doorway, watching him warily. Snow had frosted her black hair with white.

"You must be cold," he said after a moment. "Come to the fire and warm yourself." He gave her the blanket from his lap, and she pulled it around her shoulders, still watching him steadily as she stood by the fire.

Her eyes changed color with the light. Now, in the firelight, they looked golden, like the eyes of an animal. He looked away, leaning forward to poke at the fire and make it burn brighter.

"Perhaps I'd best leave," she said. He looked up from the fire and she looked away to stare at the flames. She seemed very young just then. The firelight caught on the taut skin over her cheekbones, and she looked strangely beautiful, but not entirely human. As if the bones beneath the skin had a different shape from human bones.

"Where would you go?"

She shrugged, a quick jerk of her bare shoulders beneath the blanket. "I'll live alone. It would be better."

"Why is that?"

She turned to face him again, and her beauty shifted, fleeing with the movement of her head. Her face seemed flat and plain. "You saw the tracks," she said. Then she turned back to the fire.

"The Indians tell of medicine men who turn into animals. Birds. Wolves." He kept his voice low and even, as if he were talking about the weather. "I've heard tell of it. A medicine man puts on a wolf skin, dances like a wolf. And he becomes the wolf." He looked up from the fire to meet her eyes. "They see no harm in it. It's a sign of great power."

"Where my father came from, they tell of people who become wolves." Her voice matched his—soft and steady. He could barely hear her over the crackling of the fire. "They don't need skins. At certain times of the moon, the wolf comes to them and they become the wolf. It's not something they choose. It comes, whether they will have it or not." She was watching him now, her eyes never wavering. "I take after my father." She wet her lips delicately, like a nervous hound. The melting snow glistened on her hair and cheeks.

"What happened to your father?"

"Killed by a hunter."

"Your mother?"

"Caught in a trap and killed by a trapper who checked his line before dawn. I've been traveling alone since then." She pulled the blanket tighter around her, keeping her eyes on the fire. "You were lonely and I was lonely, too." She shrugged again.

Jem nodded. He rubbed his hands together, trying to warm them.

"I'll go today," she said.

"Sit down and get warm," he said.

"I warned you, Jem. You got more than you bargained for."

"I got what I bargained for," he said. He held out a hand. "Sit down and warm yourself."

She took his hand and sat beside him on the bench. He rubbed her hands to warm her, and put another log on the fire.

▼▼▼

Winter came, and the nights were long. The first snow melted, and the stock grazed in the meadows. When snow fell again, they carried fodder to the cattle. They lived on wild game and Indian corn. On cold clear days, Jem split rails for fences. Nadya helped with the fences. She was surprisingly strong for her size. Together they built a shelter for the milk cow and the calf that Jem hoped she would bear in spring.

The full moon came, and he woke as Nadya left the bed and slipped away in the darkness. He heard the rustle of her clothing, the soft padding of her bare feet on the dirt floor. The wooden door creaked when she pulled it open and cold wind that blew in brought a flurry of snowflakes, dancing in the moonlight. The door creaked again as she pulled it closed behind her. He lay awake in the darkness, listening to the howling of distant wolves. In the morning, she came home.

Each month, Nadya grew restless with the waxing moon. She would leave during the day, telling Jem she was going hunting. She would return late in the afternoon, when the sun was just setting, carrying a freshly killed hare and complaining that game was scarce.

The night before January's full moon, the wolves came closer to the cabin than they ever had before. Nadya sat at the fire, her book in her lap, and listened to their howls. "I'd best check on the stock," Jem said.

"I'll do it," Nadya said quickly, and she pulled on her coat and slipped out the door. Jem stood in the doorway and watched her cross the yard to the cattle shed. Snow was falling gently, the flakes catching the moonlight. Nadya paused, halfway across the yard, listening to something that Jem couldn't hear. She glanced back and him and gestured impatiently. "Close the door, Jem. Stay warm. I'll be back in a moment." She returned in a few minutes, snowflakes melting on her jacket and her hair. Her cheeks were bright and she came to him for warmth. They made love in the big bed that smelled of cedar.

The next morning, when he went out to the cattleshed, he found wolftracks. Only one wolf. A large male, he guessed from the prints. Nadya's footprints had been filled by the falling snow, but the wolf prints were fresh. The animal had lingered after the snow stopped falling. In the shelter of a bush not far from the corral, he found a place where the animal had rested, flattening the grass and leaving a few tufts of white fur caught on twigs.

He said nothing to Nadya. He spent the day splitting rails for the fence, hard physical labor that left him little time to think. That evening, Nadya stood by the cabin door at sunset, staring out into the forest.

"Looking for something?" he asked.

She shook her head. "Just restless."

That night, he woke to the open door, creaking in the wind. The latch had not caught. Jem slipped from bed, shivering in the cold. He dressed quickly, pulling on his trousers, stiff fingers lacing stiff leather boots.

In the moonlight, the split rail fence was a zigzag line of gray on the white snow, like a pencil line on white paper. The Douglas firs were black against the moonlight sky. He found her tracks under the trees and followed. His breath made silver clouds in the moonlight. A hundred yards into the trees, Nadya's pawprints were joined by the prints of a larger wolf. There was a mess of prints where the big male had approached and Nadya had retreated, where he had circled her and then she had circled him. Then the two sets of prints continued, with the male leading and Nadya following.

In the moonlight, the trail was clearly visible. Jem followed. He did not think about following. He tried not to think at all. His mind was cold and clear, like the icicles that hung from the trees, catching the moonlight and shattering it into bright and meaningless patterns. His mind was filled with bright and meaningless patterns.

About a mile from the cabin, the trail veered suddenly to the west. The distance between pawprints changed: the wolves had slowed their pace, stalking toward a dense stand of fir trees. Thirty yards farther on, the distance between pawprints had changed again, marking the place where both wolves had broken into a run.

Not far away, there was sign of deer: hoofprints in the snow, droppings, a flattened area where one animal had lain. Three deer by the look of it. Two had run west and the third had split off, running northwest with both wolves in pursuit.

Jem saw a splash of blood in the snow. A little farther on, another splash. He could imagine the big wolf tearing at the deer's flanks, ripping at its belly. He tried to imagine another wolf, a smaller wolf, doing the same—but the image of Nadya's face kept intruding.

More blood and a great confusion of tracks where the deer had tried to stand its ground, wheeling to face one wolf while the other harried it from behind. Then the deer had run again, leaving bloody hoofprints in the snow.

In a clearing, the animal had fallen. Jem stopped at the edge of the clearing, within the shelter of the trees. The wolves had caught his scent and had stopped feeding. The belly of the deer had been ripped open; blood steamed in the cold air.

The two wolves stood by the carcass of the deer, watching him with golden eyes: a big white dog wolf and a pale gray bitch. The bitch was large, almost as big as the male. Her head and muzzle were splashed with fresh blood.

Jem held his rifle ready, watching the two of them. He was not thinking clearly. He kept remembering a trapper who had found his Indian wife in bed with another man.

The male lowered his head and growled, his ruff bristling. Jem felt the trigger against his finger before he realized that he had lifted the rifle. He was aiming at the big male. The bitch—he could not think of her as Nadya—whimpered low in her throat, a complex sound that seemed close to human speech. She glanced at the male and then back at Jem. She barked once, a high yelp, then whimpered again.

She approached Jem slowly, casting frequent glances back at the male wolf. Jem shifted his aim so that the rifle pointed at her. She approached steadily, making a series of yips and whimpers low in her throat. As she moved, he followed her with the rifle. But he did not shoot. His finger was frozen on the trigger; his mind was locked on an image: Nadya, running to him across the yard.

When she was a few feet away, he lowered the rifle and squatted in the snow. She came to him and rubbed her muzzle against his hand, leaving a streak of blood on his skin. He ran his hand over her head and down her body. Her fur was warm and thick and he could feel hard muscle beneath. "Nadya," he said to her, and she whimpered low in her throat.

After a moment, she left him and returned to the carcass. The male was feeding again, though his eyes were still on Jem. Nadya stood by the carcass, watching Jem. At last, Jem turned away and retraced his steps to the cabin.

At the cabin, he wrapped himself in a blanket and sat by the fire. The trapper who had found his wife in bed with another man had fired three shots over their heads and then taken to drinking. On the third night of heavy drinking, Jem had sat with him and listened to him rant. "I couldn't kill her," he had said. "Couldn't do it. When I'm gone, she gets lonely. She needs someone to take care of her. And sometimes I'm gone." He tossed back another hit of whiskey. "Can't argue with that."

Jem fell asleep by the fire and woke to the splash of water from the kettle into a basin. Just outside the door, Nadya was washing her hands and face in warm water from the kettle on the stove. The water in the basin was tinged with red.

He went to her, took her in his arms, and looked down at her. The pale early morning sunlight shone full on her face. She always looked healthy the day after a full moon—strong and fit. Wild nights agreed with her.

He did not want to think of that. "This is real," he said to her. "Right now, standing in the sunshine with you. This is real." He could feel the beating of her heart against his skin, the warmth of her body against his. The night was gone, and he let it go.

A month passed and the winter's snow began to melt. The full moon came. He lay in bed when she went out, ignoring the soft rustling of her clothing, the creak of the door. That night, he lay awake, listening for the howling of wolves.

On a morning when the breeze carried the warmth of spring, she told him that she was with child. He had been splitting rails for the fence and he still held the broad axe in his hand. He felt the smooth shaft against his palm and tried to find comfort in it. This is real. But his hand seemed barely a part of him; the axe seemed far away. She looked up at him, her head held high, her face set in an expression that he could not read. He took the axe and struck the chopping block, so that the blade stuck firmly into the wood.

"I was thinking I might go hunting," he said. "We need fresh meat." He looked out over her head, unwilling to meet her eyes.

"We've got meat enough," she said.

"No." His voice was flat. "I'll go."

He took his rifle and his powder bag and extra shot. Nadya asked him not to go, but he did not hear her. He walked away without looking back.

He had seen wolf sign by the stream that ran from their spring: tracks in the moist soil where the snow had melted; a matted place in the grass where a wolf had bedded down.

He found wolf tracks in the mud half a mile from the cabin. The ground was soft with moisture from the melted snow, and he followed the trail into the forest. Under the trees, where patches of snow lingered in the shade, he found pawprints in the snow. The animal was heading for the ridge to the east of the valley.

From the fir branches overhead, jays scolded him. A flicker of movement made him start—a covey of quail scattered in the underbrush. The ground sloped upward, climbing to the ridge. He followed a game trail—worn by deer and elk. The soil here was dry and packed; he found no more pawprints. Once he found a tuft of white fur caught on a twig by the trail, evidence that the wolf had passed this way once—but that could have been weeks ago. The trees thinned out—the soil was rocky and only a few tough trees had managed to find a place to take root.

Halfway up the ridge, he became convinced that he had lost the trail. He stopped and thought about retracing his steps. Beside the trail was a boulder, and he sat on the sun-warmed rock, looking down over the valley. Far below, he could see a thin line of smoke rising from the cabin. His cattle were grazing in the meadow. The split rail fence was a line of gray against the new green grass. He could see Nadya clearing the underbrush from the plot of land that she had designated as her kitchen garden. As he watched, she straightened up and stretched, a graceful natural movement. She pushed her hat back on her head and looked out at the grazing cattle.

Sitting in the sun, Jem began to relax. The anger that had come to him when she told him of the child slipped away. He watched her return to work. He could see the sun flash on the blade of the grubbing hoe as she lifted it to chop at a stubborn bush. He would be a father, he thought. That was real.

He was about to turn back when he noticed a place not far from the boulder where the game trail widened. Branching off the game trail was the faintest suggestion of another trail, little more than a few scuff marks in the soil and a few bare patches of earth. Just the suggestion of a trail winding up the slope.

He scanned the slope above him. From a rocky outcropping, a raven squawked, staring Jem. A robin landed on a low bush, picked up something white in its beak, and flew away to build a nest.

Jem started up the slope, following the trail and heading toward the place where the robin had landed. He found the wolf's sleeping place first. The tough grass was flattened and white hairs mingled with the green. From here, the wolf had a clear view of the valley, the cabin below.

Beyond the sleeping place, the trail dropped a little, running down the slope and growing even fainter. He followed it for a few hundred feet to a small dark opening, just large enough to admit an adult wolf. The den was half concealed by a spreading bush and looked freshly dug.

Jem peered into the opening. The wolf had dug deep into the earth; the tunnel ended in darkness. A place where the pups would be safe and protected. He turned away, feeling as if he had invaded another man's cabin in his absence. He did not belong here. This was not his business.

He returned to the valley. Nadya saw him coming and ran to meet him. Already she was slower, heavy on her feet.

"I didn't see anything worth shooting at," he told her.

"That's fine," she said. "Just fine."

▼▼▼

Sometimes, sitting by the fire at night or lying in bed under the thick buffalo robes, he told her about the tricks that trappers used to hide their deadly steel-jawed traps. He told her of pitfalls, deadfalls, and rawhide snares that the Indians used. He told her of how trappers would lace the fresh carcass of a deer with poison. And when she went out at night, when the moon was full, he lay awake and thought of other things he had to tell her.

She seemed so small to him, little more than a child herself. Her belly swelled and her breasts grew heavy. It seemed to Jem that it happened quickly, but he knew little of the ways of women. He caressed her belly when she lay beside him in the bed, wondering at the firmness of it, the smoothness of the skin.

She stopped helping with the heavy work, went hunting less often. When the moon was full, he heard a wolf bark once, then howl. Nadya left the bed. He heard the rustle of her clothing in the darkness.

"Must you go?" he asked her.

"It's not my choice, Jem," she said softly.

"Be safe," he said. And then, shielded by the darkness, he said, "I saw the den. He'll take care of you when I can't, won't he?"

She kissed him, a fleeting warmth in the cold air. He reached up and touched her shoulder, a bare breast, but then she was gone. When she opened the door, he could see her silhouette against the moonlight, her belly rounded. She closed the door behind her.

▼▼▼

Jem plowed the land, breaking new ground and planting twice the acreage of Indian corn as the year before. Nadya stayed closer to home, planting the kitchen garden with melons and squash and pumpkins and beans.

One afternoon, Jem returned from the field to find Nadya in labor. She lay on the bed, gripping the wooden sides and panting like an animal. He filled a bucket at the spring and wiped her forehead with a cool wet cloth. He stayed at the bedside. She held his hand in a fierce grip and cried out in a rhythmic, helpless way.

The sun set and the evening came. He left the bedside to build up the fire and light the candles. In the flickering light, he saw a movement at the half-open door. The white wolf was just outside the corral fence, a ghost drifting past in the open meadow. He left the door ajar.

The first child was a girl, red and squawling with a full head of dark hair. The second was a boy, as ruddy as his sister and screaming just as loudly.

"Take them to the door," Nadya said. "Let them look outside. Let them see the moon. They need to know the moon. They'll take after me."

He carried them in his arms—they were so small, barely a weight at all. The dog wolf was in the yard, on the near side of the fence. Jem held up the babies. "Look," he said to them. "Look at the world; look at the moon."

The girl waved her tiny red hands in the air, brushing against his beard and trying feebly to grip the coarse hair. When the hair slipped from her grasp, she wailed and her brother joined in. The dog wolf barked and then lifted its head to howl with the babies.

"Sit by me," she said, and he brought the babies to her. "Beautiful babies," she said. "I'll teach them to hunt." Her eyes searched his face. "They'll take after me, Jem—I can tell already. Do you mind that?"

"They'll be fine hunters," he said.

Outside, the wolf barked once, then howled, a long lonely call as thin and cold as the light of the crescent moon. The babies startled by the sound, began to wail.

▼▼▼

Jem sat in a stump in the sun, smoothing the last splinters from a cedar toy he had carved for the babies. The grass in the meadow was lush and green. The cow had borne her calf, just a week after the twins' birth. The vegetables in the garden and the Indian corn in the field were coming up thick and green.

The day was warm and Nadya sat on a blanket on the grass. The girl nursed at her breast. The boy lay on his back, waving his hands in the air. They had named the girl Neka, after Jem's mother. The boy was Alek, for Nadya's father.

"So greedy," Nadya murmured to Neka. "So fierce." She looked up at Jem. "She will be a good hunter."

A bird flew overhead. Alek reached for its passing shadow and made a sputtering sound when he did not catch it. Jem leaned over and offered him the toy, a crudely carved figure of a running wolf. Alek closed his fingers around it, then brought the wolf to his mouth, where he proceeded to suck on its head.

"They will both be good hunters," Jem said.

SPECIAL MAKEUP
▼▼▼

KEVIN J. ANDERSON

THE second camera operator ran to fetch the clapboard. Some-one else called out, "Quiet on the set! Hey everybody, shut up!" Three of the extras coughed at the same time.

"*Wolfman in Casablanca*, Scene 23. Are we ready for Scene 23?" The second camera operator held the clapboard ready.

"Ahem." The director, Rino Derwell, puffed on his long ciga-rette in an ivory cigarette holder, just like all famous directors were supposed to have. "I'd like to start today's shooting sometime *today*! Is that too much to ask? Where the hell is Lance?"

The boom man swivelled his microphone around; the extras on the nightclub set fidgeted in their places. The cameraman slurped a cold cup of coffee, making a noise like a vacuum cleaner in a bathtub.

"Um, Lance is still, um, getting his makeup on," the script supervisor said.

"Christ! Can somebody find me a way to shoot this picture without the star? He was supposed to be done half an hour ago. Go tell Zoltan to hurry up—this is a horror picture, not the Mona Lisa." Derwell mumbled how glad he was that the gypsy makeup man would be leaving in a day or two, and they could get someone else who didn't consider himself such a perfectionist. The director's assistant dashed away, stumbling off the soundstage and tripping on loose wires.

Around them, the set showed an exotic nightclub, with white fake-adobe walls, potted tropical plants, and Arabic-looking squiggles on the pottery. The piano in the center of the stage, just in front of the bar, sat empty under the spotlight, waiting for the movie's star, Lance Chandler. The sound stage sweltered in the summer heat. The large standup fans had to be shut off before shooting; and the ceiling fans—nightclub props—stirred the cloud of cigarette smoke overhead into a gray whirlpool, making the extras cough even when they were supposed to keep silent.

Rino Derwell looked again at his gold wristwatch. He had bought it cheap from a man in an alley, but Derwell's pride would not allow him to admit he had been swindled even after it had promptly stopped working. Derwell didn't need it to tell him he was already well behind schedule, over budget, and out of patience.

It was going to take all day just to shoot a few seconds of finished footage. "God, I hate these transformation sequences. Why does the audience need to *see* everything? Have they no imagination?" he muttered. "Maybe I should just do romance pictures? At least nobody wants to see everything *there*!"

▼▼▼

"Oh, God! Please no! Not again! Not NOW!!!" Lance couldn't see the look of horror he hoped would show on his face.

"You must stop fidgeting, Mr. Lance. This will go much faster." Zoltan stepped back, large makeup brush in hand, inspecting his work. His heavy eastern European accent slurred out his words.

"Well, I've got to practice my lines. This blasted makeup takes so blasted long that I forget my blasted lines by the time it comes to shoot. Was I supposed to say 'Don't let it happen *here!*' in that scene? Hand me the script."

"No, Mr. Lance. That line comes much later—it follows 'Oh no! I'm transforming!' " Zoltan smeared shadow under Lance's eyes. This would be just the first step in the transformation, but he still had to increase the highlights. Veins stood out on Zoltan's gnarled hands, but his fingers were rock steady with the fine detail.

"How do you know my lines?"

"You may call it gypsy intuition, Mr. Lance—or it may be because you have been saying them every morning before makeup for a week now. They have burned into my brain like a gypsy curse."

Lance glared at the wizened old man in his pale blue shirt and color-spattered smock. Zoltan's leathery fingers had a real instinct for makeup, for changing the appearance of any actor. But his craft took hours.

Lance Chandler had enough confidence in his own screen presence to carry any picture, regardless of how silly the makeup made him look. His square jaw, fine physique, and clean-cut appearance made him the perfect model of the all-American hero. Now, during the War against Germany and Japan, the U.S. needed its strong heroes to keep up morale. Besides, making propaganda pictures fulfilled his patriotic duties without requiring him to go somewhere and risk getting shot. Red-corn-syrup blood and bullet blanks were about all the real violence he wanted to experience.

Lance took special pride in his performance in *Tarzan Versus the Third Reich*. Though he had few lines in the film, the animal rage on his face and his oiled and straining body had been enough to topple an entire regiment of Hitler's finest, including one of Rommel's desert vehicles. (Exactly why one of Rommel's desert vehicles had shown up in the middle of Africa's deepest jungles was a question only the scriptwriter could have answered.)

Craig Corwyn, U-Boat Smasher, to be released next month as the start of a new series, might make Lance a household name Those stories centered on brave Craig Corwyn, who had a penchant for leaping off the deck of his Allied destroyer and swimming down to sink Nazi submarines with his bare hands, usually by opening the underwater hatches or just plucking out the rivets in the hull.

But none of those movies would compare to *Wolfman in Casablanca*. Bogart would be forgotten in a week. The timing for this picture was just perfect; it had an emotional content Lance had not been able to bring into his earlier efforts. The country was just waiting for a new hero, strong and manly, with a dash of animal unpredictability and a heart of gold (not to mention unwavering in Allied sympathies).

The story concerned a troubled but patriotic werewolf—him, Lance Chandler—who in his wanderings has found himself in German-occupied Casablanca. There he causes what havoc he can for the enemy, and he also meets Brigitte, a beautiful French resistance fighter vacationing in Morocco. Brigitte turns out to be a werewolf herself, Lance's true love. Even in the script, the final scene as the two of them howl on the rooftops above a conflagration of Nazi tanks and ruined artillery sent shivers down Lance's spine. If he could pull off this performance, Hitler himself would tremble in his sheets.

Zoltan added spirit gum to Lance's cheeks and forehead, humming as he worked. "You will please stop perspiring, Mr. Lance. I require a dry surface for this fine hair."

Lance slumped in the chair. Zoltan reminded him of the wicked old gypsy man in the movie, the one who had cursed his character to become a werewolf in the first place. "This blasted transformation sequence is going to take all day again, isn't it? And I don't even get to *act* after the first second or so! Lie still, add more hair, shoot a few frames, lie still, add more hair, shoot a few more frames. And it's so hot in the soundstage. The spirit gum burns and ruins my complexion. The fumes sting my eyes. The fake hair itches."

He winced his face into the practiced look of horror again. "Oh, God! Please no! Not again! Um . . . oh yeah—don't let it happen here!" Lance paused, then scowled. "Blast, that wasn't right. Would you hurry up, Zoltan! I'm already losing my lines. And I'm really tired of you dragging your feet—get moving!"

Zoltan tossed the makeup brush with a loud clink into its glass jar of solvent. He put his gnarled hands on his hips and glared at Lance. The smoldering gypsy fury in his dark eyes looked worse than anything Lance had seen on a movie villain's face.

"I lose my patience with you, Mr. Lance! It is gone! Poof! Now I must take a short cut. A special trick that only I know. It will take a minute, and it will make you a star forevermore! I guarantee that. You will no longer suffer my efforts—and I need not suffer you! The people at the new Frankenstein picture over on Lot 17 would appreciate my work, no doubt."

Lance blinked, amazed at the old gypsy's anger but ready to jump at any chance that would get him out of the makeup trailer sooner. He heard only the words ". . . it will make you a star. . . . I guarantee that."

"Well, do it then, Zoltan! I've got work to do. The great Lon Chaney never had to put up with all these delays. He did all his own makeup. My audiences are waiting to see the new meaning I can bring to the portrayal of the werewolf."

"You will never disappoint them, Mr. Lance."

Without further reply, Zoltan yanked at the fine hair he had already applied. "You no longer need this." Lance yowled as the patches came free of his skin. "That is a very good sound you make, Mr. Lance. Very much like a werewolf."

Lance growled at him.

Zoltan rustled in a cardboard box in the corner of his cramped trailer, pulled out a dirty Mason jar, and unscrewed its rusty lid. Inside, a brown oily liquid swirled all by itself, spinning green flecks in internal currents. The old man stuck his fingers into the goop and brought them out dripping.

"What is—whoa, that smells like—" Lance tried to shrink away, but Zoltan slapped the goop onto his cheek and smeared it around.

"You cannot possibly know what this smells like, Mr. Lance, because you have no idea what I used to make it. You probably do not wish to know—then you would be even more upset at having it rubbed all over your face."

Zoltan reached into the jar again and brought out another handful, which he wiped across Lance's forehead. "Ugh! Did you get that from the lot cafeteria?" Lance felt his skin tingle, as if the liquid had begun to eat its way inside. "Ow! My complexion!"

"If it gives you pimples, you can always call them character marks, Mr. Lance. Every good actor has them."

Zoltan pulled his hand away. Lance saw that the old man's fingers were clean. "Finished. It has all absorbed right in." He screwed the cover of the jar back on and replaced it in the cardboard box.

Lance grabbed a small mirror, expecting to find his (soon-to-be) well-known expression covered with ugly brown, but he could see no sign of the makeup at all. "What happened to it? It still stinks."

"It is special makeup. It will work when it needs to."

The door flew open, and the red-faced director's assistant stood panting. "Lance, Mr. Derwell wants you on the set right now! Pronto! We've got to start shooting."

Zoltan nudged his shoulder. "I am finished with you, Mr. Lance."

Lance stood up, trying not to look perplexed so that Zoltan could have a laugh at his expense. "But I don't see any—"

The old gypsy wore a wicked grin on his lips. "You need not worry about it. I believe your expression is, 'Knock 'em dead.' "

▼▼▼

Lance sat down at the nightclub piano and cracked his knuckles. The extras and other stars took their positions. Above the sound-stage, he could hear men on the catwalks, positioning cool blue gels over the lights to simulate the full moon.

"*Now* are you ready, Lance?" the director said, fitting another cigarette into his ivory holder. "Or do you think maybe we should just take a coffee break for an hour or so?"

"That's not necessary, Mr. Derwell. I'm ready. Just give the word, see?" He growled for good measure.

"Places, everyone!"

Lance ran his fingers over the piano keyboard, 'tickling the old ivories,' as real piano players called it. No sound came out. Lance couldn't play a note, of course, so the prop men had cut all the piano wires, holding the instrument in merciful silence no matter how enthusiastically Lance might bang on it. They would add the beautiful piano melody to the soundtrack during post-production.

"*Wolfman in Casablanca*, Scene 23, Take One." The clap-board cracked.

"Action!" Derwell called.

The klieg lights came on, pouring hot white illumination on the set. Lance stiffened at the piano, then began to hum and pretend to plink on the keys.

In this scene, the werewolf has taken a job as a piano player in a nightclub, where he has met Brigitte, the vacationing French resistance fighter. While playing "As Time Goes By," Lance's character looks up to see the full moon shining down through the nightclub's skylight. To keep from having to interrupt filming, Derwell had planned to shoot Lance from the back only as he played the piano, not showing his face until after he had suppos-edly started to transform. But now Lance didn't appear to wear any makeup at all—he wondered what would happen when Derwell noticed, but he plunged into the performance nevertheless. That would be Zoltan's problem, not his.

At the appropriate point, Lance froze at the keyboard, forcing his fingers to tremble as he stared at them. On the soundtrack, the music would stop in mid-note. The false moonlight shone down on him. Lance formed his face into his best expression of abject horror.

"Oh, God! Please no! Not again! Don't let it happen *HERE*!!!" Lance clutched his chest, slid sideways, and did a graceful but dramatic topple off the piano bench.

On cue, one of the extras screamed. The bartender dropped a glass, which shattered on the tiles.

On the floor, Lance couldn't stop writhing. His own body felt as if it were being turned inside out. He had really learned how to bury himself in the role! His face and hands itched, burned. His fingers curled and clenched. It felt terrific. It felt *real* to him. He let out a moaning scream—and it took him a moment to realize it wasn't part of the act.

Off behind the cameras, Lance could see Rino Derwell jumping up and down with delight, jerking both his thumbs up in silent admiration for Lance's performance. "Cut!"

Lance tried to lie still. They would need to add the next layer of hair and makeup. Zoltan would come in and paste one of the latex appliances onto his eyebrows, darken his nails with shoe polish.

But Lance felt his own nails sharpening, curling into claws. Hair sprouted from the backs of his hands. His cheeks tingled and burned. His ears felt sharp and stretched, protruding from the back of his head. His face tightened and elongated; his mouth filled with fangs.

"No, wait!" Derwell shouted at the cameraman. "Keep rolling! Keep rolling!"

"Look at that!" the director's assistant said.

Lance tried to say something, but he could only growl. His

body tightened and felt ready to explode with anger. He found it difficult to concentrate, but some part of his mind knew what he had to do. After all, he had read the script.

Leaping up from the nightclub dance floor, Lance strained until his clothes ripped under his bulging lupine muscles. With a roar and a spray of saliva from his fang-filled jaws, he smashed the piano bench prop into kindling, knocking it aside.

Four of the extras screamed, even without their cues.

Lance heaved the giant, mute piano and smashed it onto its side. The severed piano wires jangled like a rasping old woman trying to sing. The bartender stood up and brought out a gun, firing four times in succession, but they were only theatrical blanks, and not silver blanks either. Lance knocked the gun aside, grabbed the bartender's arm, and hurled him across the stage, where he landed in a perfect stunt man's roll.

Lance Chandler stood under the klieg lights, in the pool of blue gel filtering through the skylight simulating the full moon. He bayed a beautiful wolf howl as everyone fled screaming from the stage.

"Cut! Cut! Lance, that's magnificent!" Derwell clapped his hands.

The klieg lights faded, leaving the wreckage under the normal room illumination. Lance felt all the energy drain out of him. His face rippled and contracted, his ears shrank back to normal. His throat remained sore from the long howl, but the fangs had vanished from his mouth. He brushed his hands to his cheeks, but found that all the abnormal hair had melted away.

Derwell rang onto the set and clapped him on the back. "That was *incredible!* Oscar-quality stuff!"

Old Zoltan stood at the edge of the set, smiling. His dark eyes glittered. Derwell turned to the gypsy and applauded him as well. "Marvelous, Zoltan! I can't believe it. How in the world did you do that?"

Zoltan shrugged, but his toothless grin grew wider. "Special makeup," he said. "Gypsy secret. I am pleased it worked out." He turned and shuffled toward the soundstage exit.

"Do you really think that was Oscar quality?" Lance asked.

▼▼▼

The other actors treated Lance with a sort of awe, though a few tended to avoid him. The actress playing Brigitte kept fixing her eyes on him, raising her eyebrows in a suggestive expression. Derwell, having shot a perfect take of the transformation scene he had thought would require more than a day, ordered the set crew to repair the werewolf-caused damage so they could shoot the big love scene, as a reward to everyone.

Zoltan said nothing to Lance as he added a heavy coat of pancake and sprayed his hair into place. Lance didn't how the gypsy had worked the transformation, but he knew when not to ask questions. Derwell had said his performance was Oscar quality! He just grinned to himself and looked forward to the kissing scene with Brigitte. Lance always tried to make sure the kissing scenes required several takes. He enjoyed his work, and so (no doubt) did his female co-stars.

Zoltan added an extra-thick layer of dark-red lipstick to Brigitte's mouth, then applied a special wax sealing coat so that it wouldn't smear during the on-screen passion.

"All right, you two," Derwell said, sitting back in his director's chair, "start gazing at each other and getting starry-eyed. Places, everyone!"

Zoltan packed up his kit and left the soundstage. He said good-bye to the director, but Derwell waved him away in distraction.

Lance stared into Brigitte's eyes, then wiggled his eyebrows in what he hoped would be an irresistible invitation. He had few lines in this scene, only some low grunting and a mumbled "Yes, my love" during the kiss.

Brigitte gazed back at him, batting her eyelashes, melting him with her deep brown irises.

"*Wolfman in Casablanca*, Scene 39, Take One."

Lance took a deep breath so he could make the kiss last longer.

"Action!" The klieg lights came on.

In silence, he and Brigitte gawked at each other. Romantic music would be playing on the soundtrack. They leaned closer to each other. She shuddered with her barely contained emotion. After an indrawn breath, she spoke in a sultry, sexy French accent. "You are the type of man I need. You are my soul-mate. Kiss me. I want you to kiss me."

He bent toward her. "Yes, my love."

His joints felt as if they had turned to ice water. His skin burned and tingled. He kissed her, pulling her close, feeling his passion rise to an uncontrollable pitch.

Bridgitte jerked away. "Ow! Lance, you bit me!" She touched a spot of blood on her lip.

He felt his hands curl into claws, the nails turn hard and black. Hair began to sprout all over his body. He tried to stop the transformation, but he didn't know how. He stumbled backward. "Oh, God! Please no! Not again!"

"No, Lance—that's not your line!" Brigitte whispered to him.

His muscles bulged; his face stretched out into a long, sharp muzzle. His throat gurgled and growled. He looked around for something to smash. Brigitte screamed, though it wasn't in the script. Tossing her aside, Lance uprooted one of the ornamental palms and hurled the clay pot to the other side of the stage.

"Cut!" the director called. "What the hell is going on here? It's just a simple scene!"

The klieg lights dimmed again. Lance felt the werewolf within him dissolving away, leaving him sweating and shaking and standing in clothes that had torn in several embarrassing places.

"Oh Lance, quit screwing around!" Derwell said. "Go to wardrobe and get some new clothes, for Christ's sake! Somebody, get a new plant and clean up that mess. Get First Aid to fix Brigitte's lip here. Come on, people!" Derwell shook his head. "Why did I ever turn down that job to make Army training films?"

▼▼▼

Lance skipped going to wardrobe and went to Zoltan's makeup trailer instead. He didn't know how he was going discuss this with the gypsy, but if all else failed he could just knock the old man flat with a good roundhouse punch, in the style of Craig Corwyn, U-Boat Smasher.

When he pounded on the flimsy door, though, it swung open by itself. A small sign hung by a string from the doorknob. In Zoltan's scrawling handwriting, it said: "FAREWELL, MY COMPANIONS. TIME TO MOVE ON. GYPSY BLOOD CALLS."

Lance stepped inside. "All right, Zoltan. I know you're in here!"

But he knew no such thing, and the cramped trailer proved to be empty indeed. Many of the bottles had been removed from the shelves; the brushes, the latex prosthetics all packed and taken. Zoltan had also carried away the old cardboard box from the corner, the one containing the jar of special makeup for Lance.

In the makeup chair, Lance found a single sheet of paper that had been left for him. He picked it up and stared down at it, moving his lips as he read.

Mr. Lance,

My homemade concoction may eventually wear off, as soon as you learn a little more patience. Or it may not. I cannot tell. I have always been afraid to use my special makeup, until I met you.

Do not try to find me. I have gone with the crew of *Frankenstein of the Farmlands* to shoot on location in Iowa. I will be gone for some time. Director Derwell asked me to leave, to save him time and money. Worry not, though, Mr. Lance. You no longer need any makeup from me.

I promised you would become a star. Now, every time the glow of the klieg lights strikes your face, you will transform into a werewolf. You will doubtless be in every single werewolf movie produced from now on. How can they refuse?

P.S., You should hope that werewolves are not just a passing fad! You know how fickle audiences can be."

Lance Chandler crumpled the note, then straightened it again so he could tear it into shreds, but he didn't need any werewolf anger to snarl this time.

He stared around the empty makeup trailer, feeling his career shatter around him. There would be no more Tarzan roles, no thrilling adventures of Craig Corwyn. His hopes, his dreams were ruined, and his cry of anguish sounded like a mournful wolf's howl.

"I've been typecast!"

PURE SILVER

▼▼▼

A. C. CRISPIN

AND

KATHLEEN O'MALLEY

first saw the werewolf at four A.M., Wednesday, on the A-8 Metrobus traveling from New York Avenue to my old one-room on Morris Road in Anacostia. It had been one of those days . . . there weren't any other kind with my job. I was exhausted, dozing as we lurched along, but suddenly I opened my eyes and he was there, across the aisle from me.

I knew what he was right off—but that's me. I see the animal in everyone. I'll meet someone and right away see a falcon deep inside, or a spider, maybe an otter or deer. But this was different. This guy didn't just have an animal's *spirit* inside him . . . no, no. Even though I'd never seen one before, I recognized that he was a real werewolf. I *knew* it, knew it as surely as I know I'm 5'6" and have reddish-blond hair.

His hair was pale silver, dipping low on his forehead in a pronounced widow's peak. Not just thick, it was *dense*—like a pelt. Shaggy white brows met over his narrow, hooked nose. The eyes gleaming beneath them were steel gray, ringed with black

. . . like mine. The werewolf was old, seventy at a guess, more than twice my age, but his eyes were bright . . . ageless.

His grizzled stubble of beard started on top of his prominent cheekbones, continued down over well-chiseled features, then disappeared inside the neck of an enormous, mud-colored overcoat. I glanced at his hands; they were covered with rough brindled hair. His fingernails were thick, raggedly sharp.

I dropped my eyes, wanting to ignore the werewolf, reminding myself that there were no such things, that I didn't believe in that stuff. I didn't go to horror flicks or read any scary books, and had no patience with crystals, pyramids, channeling or any of that crap. I didn't even believe in ghosts . . . and I saw those every day.

When I looked back at his face, our eyes met. Quickly, I glanced up at the "DC is a Capital City" ad, but I was too late. Now he was staring at me.

That's okay, I thought calmly, *he won't mess with me. He'll think I'm a cop.* I straightened my heavy navy-blue nylon bomber jacket with its fake fur collar. My navy pants, black vinyl shoes, blue shirt and imitation leather garrison belt completed the uniform. I made sure he could see the silver badge over my left breast. I only wished my name wasn't under it. *Humane Officer Therese* (*not* Theresa, thank you) *Norris*.

Of course, my belt wasn't studded with cop toys, just a long, black flashlight and two old rope leashes. I might look like a cop, but I worked for the S.P.C.A., enforcing the animal control and cruelty laws of the District of Columbia. To the public, I was, at best, a dogcatcher—at worst, someone who gassed puppies for a living.

Not that we gassed them. Our animals were humanely euthanized with a painless injection of sodium pentobarbitol, a powerful anesthetic pumped into the foreleg vein by a skilled technician. That it was merciful didn't make it easier.

Tonight's shift had been a *bitch*. The city's Animal Control

Facility operates around the clock. I worked the night shift, driving a big, white van Tuesday through Saturday, five P.M. to one A.M. We called it the "nut" shift; the worst time to be on the streets, with the drug dealers, prostitutes, junkies, street people, headline-hungry politicians and—worse yet—tourists.

Tonight I'd had over forty calls, picked up thirty-two animals, and had had to euthanize twenty-seven before I could go home. The paperwork had taken me until three.

I'd barely walked in the door when I'd had to kill six three-day-old kittens with feline distemper. Then I did seven healthy mixed shepherds whose time had run out. We gave animals four days more than most places, so we were always cramped for space.

Around six-thirty I picked up three seriously injured strays (no collars, no tags) hit by cars in less than an hour. One of them had been neatly eviscerated. She looked at me gratefully as I talked soothingly to her, then pushed the plunger.

At nine, Linda, the night manager, said they couldn't hold the old stray hound any longer. I'd picked her up ten days ago. In spite of our posters, and ads in the *Post*, no one had claimed her. I loved her, but couldn't take her. My cat, Alfred, had died last year at seventeen, and I'd euthanized my fifteen-year-old Dobie, Dove, just six months ago, but my landlord had slapped a "no animals" clause on me before Dove got cold.

The hound licked our hands when Linda and I came to get her. She left this earth no doubt wondering where her people were.

At ten-fifteen I killed three raccoons we'd trapped, and one small brown bat who'd had his wings shattered by a terrified second-string Redskins linebacker wielding a broom. Each would have to be checked for rabies.

But the worst thing that'd happened tonight was that damned puppy. Even hours later, I found it hard to think about him. I'd chased his mother for half an hour, finally cornering her in an alley. She was nothing but drab fur, bones, and big nipples.

She led me to the nest where I found her pup safe and warm in a tumble of rags, paper and trash. He was fat and plush, about two weeks old, eyes just barely open—mixed beagle, mostly. I picked the trash off him . . . then I saw it.

It made me sick, and after ten years on the job, not much got to me. He must've crawled through one of those plastic six-pack holders right after he was born. His head and right front leg were through one of the rings, and he was wearing it like a bizarre bandolier across his pudgy chest. Once in it, he couldn't get out, and he'd grown—but the plastic hadn't. The ring was sawing him neatly in half. Exposed muscles glistened red and swollen . . . organs clearly visible. If I'd cut the damned thing, his entrails would've fallen out. All I could think of was Linda's favorite saying . . . there are worse things than death.

I put mom in the van, then sat in the alley, finding the tiny vein by the light of the street lamp, in spite of the danger. Clean needles pull junkies out of the woodwork, crazed cockroaches after sugar, and I'd been beaten and held up at gunpoint before for them. But I couldn't let his mom watch.

Both mom and I cried all the way back to the shelter. You'd have thought it was my first week on the job. At least she'd have a warm bed for a week and an endless supply of food. Then I'd probably have to do her. It killed me to think that those seven days would probably be the best in her short, bitter life.

I remembered all this and swallowed hard. I lived with ghosts each night. In my lap was that puppy with the ring; I could feel him squirm on my legs. At my feet the old hound wagged her tail. The mixed Shepherds and sick kittens watched me sadly. The raccoons stared. On my shoulder crouched the little bat. Every night I brought a crowd home—the ghosts of all the animals I killed. Every night for ten years.

Don't get me wrong, I didn't hate my job, but I didn't love it, either. It was something I had to do because I loved animals. *Someone* had to kill the thousands of sick, injured and unwanted animals discarded annually, and who better than someone who loved them? I know. *You* love animals and *you* couldn't do it—well, that's why *I* had to.

While I was thinking this, the old werewolf touched me on the shoulder, nearly scaring me to death. He was hanging onto the overhead bar, staring at me. His expression was kindly, but I fingered my flashlight. I'd had to use it as a weapon before.

"You've had a hard night, haven't you, bubeleh?" he said in a sober, gravely voice that was laced with a thick, Old World accent. It was the last thing I'd expected. A Jewish werewolf? In New York, maybe, but D.C.?

His unexpected sympathy hit me hard; tears welled up. I couldn't speak for fear I'd start bawling with ten years' backlogged heartache, so I just nodded. Here was this old man, homeless from the look of him, comforting *me*. I took a deep breath, glanced away, trying to pull myself together. That's when I noticed the number tattooed on the underside of his hairy arm as he held the bar. It was the old, faded, concentration camp number survivors of the Holocaust wear.

"You shouldn't work so hard, a nice girl like you," the old man rumbled, still smiling. "Goodnight, Therese." Therese. Not Theresa. Everybody said Theresa. Then he got off the bus.

I was still shaking my head as I stepped down onto Morris Road. I didn't believe in monsters . . . just like I didn't believe in ghosts . . . but when I thought of that old man, all I saw was a werewolf. A kindly Jewish werewolf . . . right. Sure.

I walked home, the ghosts of twenty-seven animals trailing behind me, wondering whether there'd been a full moon tonight.

▼▼▼

"Hey, Tee, good to see you," the cop said the next night, as he opened my van door. Joseph WhiteCrane was a K-9 cop with Metro police. The shelter often supplied Metro with dogs, and Joe's dog, Chief, a big white shepherd, had been one of my finds.

Joe was part Sioux, part Hispanic, and part Irish. About 5′8″, he wasn't handsome, with his hooked nose and pock-marked face, but his dark skin, black hair and ice-black eyes were magnetic, fiercely alive. Inside, Joe was a red-tailed hawk.

A good night's sleep had erased any lingering willies I had over my odd delusion on the bus. I felt secure being back at work dealing with my normal run of real-life horrors.

"I just got the call," I said. "You impound a dog?" Drug dealers often protected themselves with bad dogs, so it wasn't unusual to be called to a crime scene to pick up animals. But this didn't look like a drug bust—for one thing, the coroner's wagon was sitting next to Joe's car. Inside the car, Chief lunged and whirled, frantically barking.

We were in the business district, the fourteen-hundred block of I Street, so at this time of night, there weren't many bystanders. Besides the handful of street people and hookers gawking at the crime scene, there were a few businessmen who must've been in the local club that served lunch to the clericals during the day, and topless shows to the bosses at night.

"No dog for you tonight—at least, not yet," Joe said, then looked at me, frowning. "What's that smell?"

I'd been hoping he wouldn't notice. "Gasoline and burnt hair. Some kids cooked a cat. I found her tied by her tail to a lamppost, still smoldering . . . and screaming." I rubbed my hands on my pants, feeling bits of her still stuck to me. Her skin had sloughed off when I hit the vein.

Joe looked away, knowing better than to show any sympathy. "Well, like you say, there's worse things than death. Look, we need an expert opinion. An old guy's been killed, maybe by animals. We called the zoo, and nothing's loose. Would you look at the body and tell the coroner what you think of the wounds?"

I nodded. After the barbecued cat, nothing could bother me. At first, the coroner only wanted to show me the bites on the arms, but finally Joe convinced him to uncover the corpse. Damn right, there's worse things than death. The man's throat was torn out, but the coroner said he survived that, only to endure the rest without being able to scream. His chest was torn open . . . his heart ripped out.

"I've seen feral dogs do stuff like this to each other," I said, "but, eat *just* the heart? Weird." I stared at the bites. "Big jaws, wide muzzles, almost flat-faced."

"Pack of pit bulls?" Joe asked.

"Maybe . . . or bull mastiffs. How big are the paw prints?"

Joe and the coroner looked at each other. "No paw prints," the cop said finally.

"Come on. This guy had to bleed like a fountain."

"*Foot*prints," Joe said. "The victim's. Nothing else."

"Are you guys sharing this with the press?" I asked quietly.

Joe shrugged. "Don't know."

"C'mon, give a poor working girl a break," I urged. "Remember the rabies outbreak? The city'll go nuts if the media talks up a crazed pack of killer dogs."

Joe smiled. "I'll talk to the captain. We might be able to keep this on low profile until we know more about the victim."

As we left the coroner's wagon, I saw Joe's still-frantic dog. "What's wrong with Chief? I've never seen him like this."

The cop shrugged. "He's been crazy since we got here. Let's take him out. You got your pole?"

"Yeah." I retrieved the aluminum rabies pole with its plastic-covered cable loop that enabled me to snag animals and hold them at a distance.

Joe put Chief on a short lead and let him out. The dog was high-strung, hackles up, whining. Normally, the big shepherd was as steady as a brick.

"Think he can smell those dogs?" I asked.

Joe shrugged. "If we spot 'em, we're going to catch them from a distance." He patted the pistol resting on his hip.

Chief pulled Joe for a few blocks, then turned up an alley.

Suddenly, he rounded on a doorway, barking furiously. A huddled form was hiding in the shadows. I moved closer. Gray eyes, silver hair, muddy overcoat . . . the old man from the bus . . . and damn it, he *still* looked like a werewolf!

"Easy, Chief, easy!" Joe said to the frenzied dog. "Hey, Grandfather, what're you doing here?"

"Resting, officer," he muttered tiredly. "Please, to hold your dog! Ach, Therese, tell him not to loose the dog!"

"You know this guy?" Joe asked me.

Something made me nod my head. "Grandfather," I said, using Joe's term, "It's not safe here. A man's been killed nearby. Did you see or hear anything?"

"Tsk, tsk." He shook his head. "Killed? *Such* a world!"

"Let us take you to the D Street shelter," Joe offered.

"In the same car with such a dog? Thank you, no."

I gazed at the old man—he seemed exhausted, weary to his soul, and my heart went out to him. Usually I only felt this kind of concern for animals, but . . . he was different. "Have you had anything to eat tonight, Grandfather? A hot meal?"

He smiled. "Say 'zeyde,' Therese. Yes. I've had a good, hot meal. Not kosher, but . . . how nice you should worry."

I wasn't sure I believed him. Impulsively, I shoved three dollars into his pocket. "Then this is for breakfast, Zeyde."

Joe and I walked back to my van. We had to drag Chief the whole way.

"So, is Zeyde his name?" I wondered to Joe.

He shook his head. "Means 'grandfather.' It's Yiddish."

Joe *would* know that. He was a mine of cultural knowledge. "What does 'bubeleh' mean?"

" 'Grandchild. It's an endearment." Joe paused. "Did you smell anything when you got near him?"

"Me? All I can smell is that poor cat. Why?"

Joe glanced back towards the alley. "I thought I caught a whiff of blood. Didn't see any, though. Might've been why Chief was so spooked. Could've been his breath."

I looked at Joe, my eyes wide. "His *breath*?"

"Lots of street people are sick . . . ulcers, whatever."

Oh, I thought, embarrassed by my weird thoughts.

▼▼▼

The next day was Friday, and by eleven forty-five P.M., Linda was helping me do my twentieth kill of the night. It was a full grown dobie, weighing thirty pounds. Should've weighed eighty. The people said they'd run out of dog food and couldn't afford more, so they just stopped feeding him. He couldn't even stand. Only his eyes looked alive.

Linda took him in her arms. "Hey, pretty dog," she crooned, petting him, her blond curls falling around her face. We ribbed Linda for looking like Jane Fonda. Lovely, quick and clever . . . inside she was a gray fox.

After filling the syringe, I turned to the dog. He had no muscles left, just hair, skin and bones. I'd found him tied in a closet, dumped like a pair of old shoes. He turned his liquid brown eyes on me and they were full of trust, ready to love again, in spite of everything he'd been through. Suddenly I saw Zeyde, ribs jutting, in the concentration camp.

"Tee, you okay?" Linda asked.

I swallowed. "Listen . . . uh, can we keep this one?"

She sighed tiredly. "He needs his own pen, vet care, it'd be *six months* before he'd be adoptable."

It was suddenly very important for me to save this dog. "I can't kill this one," I said, tightly. "He's so damned hungry."

Linda shook her head. "If we started saving every starvation case, we'd be packed to the rafters. . . ." She must've seen something in my face then, something she recognized, because she stopped, giving in. "I don't know why I let you talk me into these things. We'll put a bed behind my desk—"

The phone rang, and she nodded at me to get it as she went to settle the dog in her office and fetch him some food.

"D.C. Animal Control, Officer Norris."

"It's Joe," a familiar deep voice said. "The guy that got killed by those dogs was on the Federal Witness Protection Program. We just got the word."

"Weird," I said. "Some kind of Mafia snitch?"

"Weirder," Joe said. "He was a former Nazi. Did some favors for the State Department at the end of the war. Homicide's calling it a random wild dog attack."

My fingers tightened on the phone, thinking how odd it was to run into a Nazi and a Holocaust survivor in the same night. "Think this has anything to do with Zeyde?" I asked, finally.

"Doubt it, but if you talk to him, call me."

I fought back an urge to ask Joe if there'd been a full moon last night. Joe would know.

"Be careful on the street tonight, Tee," Joe warned me.

"I'm always careful," I said defensively.

"The hell you are. I've seen you work. You take too many chances. I mean it, Tee."

"Yeah, yeah," I agreed impatiently. "Listen, I gotta go."

"Why can't you be nicer to that poor guy?" Linda asked, when I hung up the phone. "Every straight woman in this place would *kill* to have him pay them half the attention he gives you."

"Get off my back," I said, good-naturedly.

With real pleasure I watched the dobie inhale a small meal from a soft bed of worn blankets. You had to start them slow, tiny meals every two hours, to get their systems used to food again. Maybe it was time to look for an apartment that permitted pets, I thought as I walked out to the van.

I was startled out of my mental house-hunting when I found Zeyde waiting beside the vehicle, and had the sudden, uneasy feeling that my mentioning his name had conjured him up. Just like in the movies, the old werewolf silently appeared out of the humid night air.

I gave myself a mental shake, irritated with my silly obsession about this helpless old man. The shelter was only a few blocks from the Hecht Company warehouse. All the street people knew they had the best dumpster in the city. He must've been down there foraging, and was now on his way back downtown.

"Therese, bubeleh," he greeted me warmly, like we were old friends, "still working hard?"

"Still, Zeyde," I agreed. "What can I do for you? Had anything to eat tonight?"

"Such a nice girl to worry about an old man. I was just walking by . . . I recognized your van." He must've watched me and Joe return to it the night of the murder. He smiled, and I felt funny. Why *was* I worried about him? I had enough to be concerned about taking care of the city's unwanted animals. "This is where you work, this place?" He indicated the shelter.

"Yeah, this is it."

"So, why does a nice girl like you do such a hard, dangerous job, chasing animals in the street at night?"

I shrugged. "Someone's got to do it."

"But you could get hurt by such big dogs, bitten terrible!"

"Not me, Zeyde," I reassured him. "I don't get bitten. Not in eight years. I'm good at this."

I found myself looking at the old mustard-colored cinderblock shelter. The huge walk-in refrigerator stuck out of its side garishly, all new stainless steel against the old block. That's where most of my night's work ended up, in the walk-in, waiting for the renderers. Big, plastic barrels filled with rigid animals curled in a mockery of sleep.

Suddenly I was uncomfortably aware of the similarities between the shelter and a concentration camp. We warehoused animals until we had too many, then killed the sickest, weakest and oldest. Then we sent the bodies away to become soap and fertilizer. I didn't like thinking of myself as a *humane* Nazi.

"Ach, I've upset you, being the yenta, asking questions that are none of my business."

"Zeyde, I do this work because I *have* to, because I love

animals . . . I *help* them. . . ." At least, I ended their suffering. He gave me a sad look and nodded. I thought of the dobie now sleeping behind Linda's desk who'd never again be hungry or thirsty or cold. "I'm a complete vegan. I don't eat animals or wear *any* animal products."

He looked at me gently. "And people? You love them, too?"

I gritted my teeth. On a good day, I tolerated people. After a bad shift, after picking up too many animals like that dobie, I despised them. The only reason this job existed was because of the cruelty and indifference of people. But, even before the job, I'd never had close relationships. I still hadn't recovered from Dove or Alfred's death, but my dad died ten years before, and I couldn't even remember the date.

Then I thought of Joe. I knew how he felt about me, but I didn't *want* to care. "So, how long have you been on the streets?" I asked the old man, wanting to change the subject.

"Since the war," he admitted, with an odd smile.

"*World War Two?*" Surviving that long, homeless?

"They took everything," he said softly. "Parents, wife, children, grandchildren . . . our wealth, heritage . . . everything we were. Everything we would have been."

"Other people started over, remarried, rebuilt," I said.

He nodded. "Yes, but to see your loved ones destroyed, an old family like ours . . . I did not have it in me."

"So, what've you been doing all these years?"

He smiled, showing long, yellow teeth. "Following the wind, bubeleh."

"Zeyde, what's your name?"

"Joshua Tobeck," he replied. "There are many Tobecks, but our branch of that honored line was . . . special . . . very old. Blest, we often said." He chuckled—a short, brittle sound.

"Listen, Zeyde, the other night, when that man was killed . . . weren't you close enough to hear anything?"

"Was *I* close enough?" he asked, slyly.

I watched him uneasily. "Did you know he was a Nazi?"

"Did I *know* he was a Nazi?" he repeated sarcastically.

I frowned. He was goading me. The hairs on the back of my neck stood on end. He wasn't a helpless old man anymore . . . and we both knew it. He was a werewolf. The feeling was on me stronger than ever, like instinct, like a sixth sense. "Did you kill that Nazi?" I asked softly, not wanting to know.

"Did I *kill* that Nazi?" He grinned wildly. "Did I *rip* his throat out? Did I *eat* his heart? Such a death is too *good* for a Nazi!" He spat angrily on the street. "Did *I* kill that Nazi?" His gray eyes gleamed with a feral light.

Fear made my skin crawl, but only for a moment. I got a grip on myself and felt embarrassed. It wasn't like me to let my imagination run away like that. I looked at Zeyde's thin form, his gnarled hands and stooped shoulders. He was so old, so worn.

Of course Zeyde knew about the corpse. News travels fast on the streets, and the street people who'd been there would've talked about it among themselves, sharing the grisly details. That's all it was. He was just raving, trying to scare me.

"So, how's your policeman, bubeleh?" Zeyde said, once more the sweet old man, as though nothing had happened. "Be nice to him, he has a good heart."

I watched the stooped figure shuffle away, telling myself that such conversations were typical with street people—confused memories laced with paranoia. But as I slid into the driver's seat, I switched on the radio to call Joe.

▼▼▼

I never did tell Joe much . . . just that Zeyde wasn't a reliable witness. I didn't even consider discussing my uneasy imaginings . . . I'd have sounded even crazier than the old man. I could picture Joe's face. Werewolves, yeah, sure!

However, on impulse, I did let Joe take me to breakfast. We

shared other meals over the next few weeks. We'd meet at the restaurant, go dutch, then separate from there. He had to be the world's most patient man, but I guess he could tell that was all I was up for. After the second week, I started really looking forward to seeing him and Chief, even though I suspected Joe was using my love for the dog to win me over. Linda couldn't believe I wasn't sleeping with him yet.

I kept running into Zeyde around the city. Sometimes he was lucid; others definitely not. He started telling me about his family, how the Nazis took them, how one minute they were together and the next, only he was alive. He hinted once that he'd helped other prisoners get away.

". . . when I had the strength to help them," he'd said. "The guards, they feared those bright silver nights."

"Bright silver? You mean moonli——" I'd started to ask.

"Searchlights!" he interrupted, smiling. Staring blankly, lost in memories, he muttered, "Six others, there were with me . . . three Jews, two gypsies, a political dissident . . . they hid me in the bad times, and I helped them get away . . . and revenge we tasted on sweet silver nights. . . ."

"But, Zeyde," I'd said, when he trailed off, "why didn't *you* escape?"

He didn't answer.

Yet, I couldn't shake the crazy notion that he was a werewolf. Especially when he grinned, with all those long, yellow teeth. How could a man his age not have lost any teeth, especially in the camps?

We never found any large pack of dogs to explain that Nazi's death but, with the crush of work, it was easy to forget. I was doing fifteen to twenty-five kills a night, average for fall. Then, one chilly Friday, almost a month to the day since I'd met him, Zeyde appeared at the shelter again, waiting by my van.

"Hi!" I greeted him, smiling. "Have you eaten?"

He nodded. "The people from *Bread for the City* had the

trucks out early. The soup's not kosher, but . . ." He shrugged eloquently. "Do you have a minute to speak with me, Therese?"

"*Norris!*" Linda yelled out the front door. "Phone! It's *him!*" She batted her long lashes. I flipped her the bird.

"Sure, soon as I get this call. Come inside, it's warm." I went in to grab the phone. "Norris here."

"WhiteCrane," the baritone said. "Breakfast okay?"

I smiled, then realized Zeyde hadn't followed me inside. I poked Linda, who was leaning on me, trying to eavesdrop. "Bring Zeyde in," I hissed. "Sure," I told Joe. "Can we take Chief to the park later?"

"Yeah," he said, softly. "After the park . . . can Chief and I . . . take you home? Tell us at breakfast. Be careful tonight." He hung up quickly.

So, the world's most patient man had finally lost his patience. I was surprised to find how tempted I was. Then I noticed Linda still beckoning to the old man.

"Hey, come on, Zeyde," I called. "It's warm in here!"

Reluctantly, he stepped into the reception area, glancing at the array of brightly colored posters that admonished clients to neuter or spay—it's the only way. The cat kennel was on the left behind a glass wall, so clients could see the kitties. The dog kennel was out of sight, entered through a back hallway. Two small dogs were yapping, but the other sixty were still.

"Sit down, Zeyde, and tell me—"

The quiet shelter erupted in furious sound. The dog kennel exploded with hysterical barking. Linda and I stared wide-eyed at the cats. Every one of them stood facing Zeyde, backs arched, spitting and hissing.

Grabbing his elbow, I hustled him outside. Zeyde was shivering, looking sick and ancient. I sat him in the passenger seat of the van, then turned the heat up.

"I never had much of a way with animals," he muttered.

There was a long, uncomfortable moment, until he finally said, "Therese, I've come to give you something. A gift."

I felt confused as he fumbled in the pockets of his huge coat. He pulled out something shiny, a small dagger, the blade maybe four inches long. It had a heavy handle, ornately carved.

"Pure silver," he said, touching it reverently. "It's been in my family since . . . since the family began, how far back no one knows. It's part of our legacy, this knife, like our name, and . . . our blessing. To the strongest grandson, the knife is passed from the grandfather, the zeyde. With the knife, the legacy, the blessing, is passed as well."

He took a shuddery breath and his young, gray eyes filled with tears. "Everything *they* took, but this. I hid it in the ground, and after the war, almost left it. Who needed the knife when there was no family, no legacy to pass? But, someday, I knew, I would want to pass it, so I took it. And now, I give it to you, bubeleh. I can't live much longer. If I die on the street, who gets the knife? You're all the family I have."

I didn't touch the knife, unsure if Zeyde was rational enough to give me the only thing of value he owed. "Uh . . . Zeyde, I'm honored. But . . . I'm not Jewish."

He chuckled. "Not even a little? Maybe once you went with a nice Jewish boy, we could say you were Jewish by injection?"

"Maybe once," I admitted, smiling.

"Take the knife, Therese," he begged, "with my love, my blessing. Then if I die tonight, I know the legacy is safe."

A month ago, I wouldn't have wanted that much connection to the old man. A month ago, I wouldn't have gone out with Joe. I held out my hand. He placed the handle in my palm.

"The inscription is Hebrew." He pointed to the ornately engraved letters, reading from right to left. "It is *yod, he, vau, he*. In English, it is YHVH—you would say 'Yahweh.' "

I wrapped my hand around the small, ancient knife, feeling the engraved name of God. I suddenly cared a great deal ·if Zeyde lived through the night. "Let me take you to the homeless shelter, okay?" I slid the knife into the pocket of my jacket.

His eyes glittered strangely. "No. The wind blows sweet tonight, like fresh hay sick with mold. You ever smelled that?"

I shook my head. I was a city girl, after all.

"I smelled it first in the camps. It's *their* smell, the Nazis, a smell to make you sick inside. I followed it all over the world, after the camps. In every city, I found the smell . . . I found them. But here . . . it leaks from the ground, from the big, fancy buildings. They come to make deals, and they carry the smell. Dictators come to make nice to the President. Last week, that one from South Africa—feh! The smell! And the monsters that make the bad drugs . . ." he smiled, shaking his head, lost in his memories. "To find a Nazi in this town is no easy thing. So much competition they have. Ach, tonight, the wind blows sweet and sick and I follow it."

Then, as if he'd said nothing bizarre at all, he smiled and said, "So, how's your fella, bubeleh? He's not Jewish, is he?"

▼▼▼

After Zeyde had shuffled away, I started the van and went back to work. It wasn't a bad night for a Friday. By midnight, the van was only half full—no french-fried cats, no bad hit-by-cars. The air was cold and clean smelling. I was thinking about coming in, maybe even finishing on time. Then the radio crackled.

"Tee, we've got a police call," Linda's voice said. "In the alley between Vermont Avenue and Fourteenth Street, bordered by K and L. A possible feral dog attack. Joe and Chief are on their way. He says to wait till he's on the scene before leaving the van. Says that's an order."

"Right!" I said, irritably, swinging the van around. "I'm not far away." Joe and I were going to have to talk about his mother-hen routine. A drug bust was one thing, but handling bad dogs was *my* business.

I pulled up to the alley, grabbed my pole and flashlight, then tiptoed into the darkness. I peeked around a big dumpster that blocked most of my view. If I startled them, they'd all split and I'd never catch even one. If they came after me, I could always jump in the dumpster. I heard low growling, the kind a big, heavy-chested dog makes.

Then I saw him, and my breath stopped. I blinked, confused. It was Zeyde. Hunched over somebody, his back to me. The sounds had to be coming from him. The sprawled figure was spasming feebly, while the old man squatted on his haunches, hands to his mouth, growling.

"Zeyde!" I yelled, starting forward. "What the *hell* are you doing?" The old man would get busted if he was rolling this guy, and I didn't think Zeyde could handle being in the D.C. lock up.

He stopped, and turned, rising to his feet.

All that time I had spent with him, seeing the werewolf, I'd always talked myself out of it, not wanting to really *believe* it. I couldn't see the moon, but it had to be full.

Zeyde was fully transformed. He filled up the huge coat, his thickly muscled arms thrusting out its sleeves, his coat and shirt wide open to accommodate his huge, furred chest. His clawed paw/hands were soaked with blood. He must've been six feet four, and weighed at least two hundred pounds. And his face! A wide-muzzled animal glared at me, with Zeyde's eyes shining out of thick fur. The teeth were huge, impossibly long and sharp.

As he faced me, the beast chewed the last bit of his victim's quivering heart and swallowed it.

You can't outrun him, I reminded myself, gripping my rabies pole and flashlight. I spoke quietly. "It's just me, Zeyde."

He grinned a bloody smile and I remembered Joe wondering about the smell of his breath. My knees got weak. He moved towards me, snarling. I couldn't help it. I backed up.

"Don't do it, Zeyde," I said softly. "Joe's coming. He'll kill you."

The werewolf growled a laugh and launched himself.

I swung the pole with everything I had, bending it double against him, but it had no effect. I backed away, clubbing him with the flashlight, but he ignored the blows and pulled me down. Instinctively, I threw up my left arm, protecting my throat, and he fastened his teeth into the heavy nylon sleeve, worrying it. The tough material ripped like ancient muslin. I grappled with him, trying to squeeze his windpipe one-handed, but his neck was steel, and my fingers tangled futilely in the coarse fur.

I brought my knee up, a solid blow to the groin, but he ignored it. He roared, deafening me, and his hot breath scorched my hand as I hammered my fist against his wet, black nose. He never flinched.

His claws tore my coat. "Zeyde!" I screamed. "Stop! It's Therese!" Then I shrieked as white-hot pain seared my arm.

I hadn't been bitten in eight years, and I'd *never* felt such pain. I screamed again, but he kept biting me, tearing me up. My blood filled his mouth, feeding him, giving him the hot meal he craved. Next it would be my throat, and then my beating heart.

As he clawed my coat open, I suddenly heard the clatter of his silver knife as it hit the ground. I scrabbled, searching for it blindly with my right hand.

My fingers enclosed the hilt, the name of God pressing against my palm, just as his hot, bloodied breath blew against my neck, and his teeth kissed the skin of my throat. The flare of sudden headlights brightened our bizarre coupling, as I drove the knife between his ribs right into his heart. His young, feral eyes widened, staring into mine. With a tired sigh, he sagged against me.

His expression was peaceful, just like the sick animals I killed. Hugging his body with my good arm, I wept.

▼▼▼

They released me from the hospital only a few hours later. By the time I'd reached surgery, most of the wounds had healed. By tomorrow, I knew, there wouldn't even be a scar.

Joe came by to get me, but Chief wouldn't let me in the car. The moment he caught wind of me, he went crazy, lunging and barking. I can't tell you how bad that hurt.

One of Joe's buddies came and took Chief back to the station, so Joe could take me home. We drove in silence, but finally it got to me, and I spoke. "What did the coroner say when he saw Zeyde?"

"Said it was amazing how much strength an old man can have under the right circumstances," he answered quietly.

"Like the full moon?" I asked, with a bitter laugh.

"He meant when they got crazy. All the coroner saw was an old, shriveled man."

"You knew about Zeyde," I said.

"I suspected," he said dully. "Native Americans have their own shape-changers. I was afraid you'd think I was nuts. I'm sorry, Therese." His jaw muscles tightened.

I couldn't stand his sympathy now; I'd fall apart. As we pulled up to my building, I reached for the door handle.

"You can't deal with this alone, Tee," Joe said, grabbing my arm. "Let me help you. Let me stay with you."

I choked on a sob. "Help me? How? Can you stop the changing of the moon?"

He hugged me tightly and let me cry. He smelled so good, like moonlight and nighttime, smells I'd never noticed before. Finally, I pulled away.

"The Navaho may know a rite," he insisted. "I'll find out . . ."

"Forget it, Joe," I said tiredly. "There's nothing to be done." I'd have to call Linda tomorrow and quit. I'd never be able to set foot in the shelter again. I'd lost everything. My career, the animals I loved, the man I might have had. . . .

"Joe, what happened to the knife?"

"There'll be a hearing. I'll bring it to you after that."

I saw myself as an old woman, transforming monthly into a healthy, strapping werewolf, killing and killing. The day after must be hell, as the aged body paid the price. Could I pass the knife to someone else, the way the Tobecks passed it to their strongest grandsons? "Give it to Linda," I said leadenly. "I'll get it from her. I can't see you again."

"Don't shut me out, Tee," he warned quietly.

"I *have* to. Or some night, I'll find you dead beside me."

"The full moon wanes tonight. Nothing will happen for twenty-seven days. We can . . ."

"Stop it!" I shouted. "The Tobecks carried this for centuries, generations! You're out of it, out of my life!" I stopped and took a deep breath. "I don't want your blood on my hands."

I climbed out of the car and walked away. Joe didn't call me back. As I reached my door, a silver stretch limo suddenly pulled out of a side street, then glided past, oddly out of place here in Anacostia, with its old buildings and trash-littered streets. The smell struck me like a blow, making my stomach clench. New-mown hay gone moldy. I almost puked.

After a moment I opened the door and climbed the stairs, but no animal ghosts followed me tonight. I wondered dully if, in a month, there'd be two-legged ones. Inside, even Dove's and Alfred's ghosts were gone. I thought about the long years ahead of me, doing a job that had to be done, without the warmth of a friendly animal to relieve them. Without Joe's scent to perfume the night.

I pulled out my old, battered suitcase and, ignoring the tears splashing over it, methodically filled it, wondering where I'd be during the next full moon.

There are worse things than death.

CLOSE SHAVE
▼▼▼

BRAD LINAWEAVER

"**D**ON'T let them take the natural out of the supernatural!" That's been my motto, ever since I expanded my business to include the physical side of the occult.

Allow me to introduce myself. I am Alfred Von Booten, adventurer . . . and barber for hire. Haircuts, shaves, dentistry and minor surgery are my stock in trade. I also deal firmly with monsters of every kind. Von Booten rates are reasonable, and open to negotiation if the need is great enough.

Only once have I suffered disappointment with one of my customers, but I made up for it in the end. The frustrating series of events began when I was on holiday in the mountains of central Europe. On impulse, I decided to drop in on an old friend.

Descending from the mountain, I saw the little village of Kaninsburg, partly obscured by clouds that were so low as to hug the ground. Shouldering my kit of provisions—and precision-made dental and barbering instruments—I trudged over rock and crevice with the sure-footedness of a mountain goat (a goat restricted to using its two hind legs, that is).

I had strapped my spectacles on with a fine strip of leather and could see very clearly. The last time I had visited the village,

in late Spring, it had been a thriving community of little ginger-
bread houses, surrounded by greenery, and covered in a fine yellow pollen from the many flowers that were its pride and joy.
Now I was arriving a year later, at the height of Summer, and
expected more of the same. I blamed the precipitous angle, and
the presence of so many clouds, for what must be a mistaken
impression of Kaninsburg on a dismal Winter day of washed out
browns and grays, a bleak landscape awaiting the next snowfall.
But it was when I climbed below the clouds, and had my first
unobstructed view, that I realized the place really did look *dead*—
a wasteland punctuated by trees almost leprous with black bark.

And yet only a few miles beyond the village was a verdant
testament to the season of life. It was Summer everywhere but
the village. There was only one explanation: monster trouble! I
had warned my friend, Baron Averal Tahlbot, that whenever British nobility is transplanted to small European villages, the risk of
monster infestation goes up. The Baron had won this village in
a game of whist on a Walpurgis Night, when there was a full
moon, and he had a toothache. He was in too splendid a mood
to believe in ill omens; and I wasn't about to turn down his
invitation to see him enjoying the bucolic life (he had been land-
poor back home, despite his title). When I arrived, I was to discover that Kaninsburg had no barber—as Baron Tahlbot had
driven away the previous practitioner for the crime of sorcery, and
for indifferent hair styling. I had been very busy during that stay,
and had expected renewed opportunity this time.

Upon reaching the bottom of the mountain, I set to work,
extracting clues from the unyielding cavity of life. What blight
had come to this fair village? Was it vampires? Poltergeists?
Ghouls? Frenchmen? What could it possibly be?

First, I found some wolfbane. Then I noticed a pentagram
painted awkwardly on the side of a fence. These clues, combined
with a huge sign reading BEWARE OF WEREWOLF suggested
the very strong possibility that the problem was lycanthropy.

"Von Booten, you old fraud!" It was the distinctive voice of the

Baron, whose smoky vocal chords had entertained the Queen herself (of which country I fail to recall). Unsurprisingly, he was walking his dogs whose snarling ferocity made me feel as much at home as I had been when facing the zombie legions of the Lost Jackal.

"Hello, Baron. Where are your villagers?"

"Quaking behind closed doors, I expect. We have a bit of bother at the moment."

"It wouldn't be werewolves, by any chance?"

"Astounding, dear fellow. How ever did you deduce that?"

"Elementary," I said, with a sweeping hand gesture, "it's all this damned evidence."

"Secondarily," he replied, "if it's evidence you're after, then my village is full of it. But I say, what brings you here?"

Opportunities such as this should not be wasted. Today's business reputation is only as good as yesterday's coincidence. Clearing my throat, I began in stentorian tones: "Through strange powers that defy human explanation, I felt your call for help vibrating through the ether. . . ."

"Just passing through, eh?" was his villainous reply. "Well, I'm glad you're here. Come to think of it, you're still owed money from your last visit. I'm certain that had nothing to do with your returning here. Come with me to the castle and we'll settle accounts."

We shook hands and I couldn't help noticing how he had let himself go to seed. The tweed jacket was frayed at the cuffs and it was missing buttons. This wasn't like him. Although he'd been a widower for some years, one would never know it sartorially. I also noticed that the jacket had about a dozen long, coarse animal hairs on it. Could it be . . . ?

"I can see by your expression that you're displeased over my appearance," he said.

"Oh no, it's only . . ."

"No need for dissembling, old friend. I admit it. I need a haircut badly."

As a matter of fact, he did. A shaggy mop of unkempt hair

was inappropriate to his station in life. But I would no more think of interrogating him about those hairs on his jacket than I would shave off my mutton-chop whiskers. The finest tact was called for when dealing with a Tahlbot.

"By the way," I began, as the melancholy tower of the castle loomed over the gnarled trees to mark our desultory progress, "have you been petting any werewolves lately?"

"Shiver me timbers," he said, recalling his days as a seafaring man, "you see right through me, Alfred. I can't hide a thing from your dogged ratiocination. My son is the village werewolf, and I don't know what to do."

No sooner had these words passed his lips than fog began pouring into the forest as if someone had turned on a steam-powered fog making machine. We walked in silence through the roiling mist. We walked over the moat, through the gigantic door (at which point the dogs went running off in the direction of the kitchen), past the mute English butler, by the dumbwaiter, into the den and up to the ornate fireplace.

Suddenly a beautiful woman, with hair as golden as a dou-bloon, came gliding down the staircase, in flowing gowns, and fell smack into the arms of the Baron. He introduced her as his niece. It occurred to me that I'd yet to see a villager.

"Oh darling," she said in an American accent, "who is this darling man with you?"

More introductions were made. More greetings were ex-changed. The exchange rates for various European currencies were discussed. She served drinks. She passed out cigars. She gave me a back massage and played the piano, although not in that order. Her laughter was like the tinkling of a chandelier sub-merged in a vat of ambrosia. She sang. She told my fortune.

This last diversion proved to be a mistake. Seeing the sign of the pentagram in my palm, she tried to change the subject, laugh-ing nervously, but it was to no avail. Somewhere in the night, a wolf howled. She swooned. A maid came bustling down the stairs.

The maid wasn't a villager either, but some kind of humorous Swedish person. Together, the two women sort of flowed back up the stairs, as if a tide could ebb upwards to greet the stars. Or something.

"Er, where were we?" I asked, "before, uh, what's her name again?"

"Evelyn from Idaho," answered the Baron, with a shrug. "Don't worry about it, Von Booten, she sees the sign of the pentagram in everyone's hand."

"Thank you. But what were we talking about before your niece came in?"

"My son, the werewolf,"

"He's English?"

"Born in England, of course, but raised in the great American West where two fists and a full head of hair are all that's needed to wrestle life to the ground as Davy Crockett once did with a big old grizzly bar."

"Yes, Colonials like to drink in ugly pubs . . . but please tell me more about your son."

"His name is Lonnie but the villagers have a nickname for him."

"Larry?"

"No, they call him the Horrible Beast, and since being bitten by a werewolf, they've been much harder on him."

We drank some more. At length, I popped the question: "Is he in the castle?"

"That he is."

"He's unhappy about being a monster, I take it."

"He is that."

"You know there's no cure."

"That I do."

"You've tried to put him out of his misery?"

"Yes, but none of the traditional remedies work! That's why I'm so glad you're here."

"One silver bullet ought to be effective."

"We've run out of silver bullets! He's so full of them that he sounds like a Spaniard when he walks."

I had never heard of such a phenomenon. Just what kind of werewolf was this? He could see my consternation, or else he was peering at the small mole on my left cheek. Taking me by the arm, he led me, gently but firmly, in the direction of the family dungeon.

"It will be the full moon tonight," he said, "as it has been for the last two weeks."

"Wait a moment," I said, "astronomy is not my subject, but the full moon couldn't possibly . . ."

"No time for that now," was his terse reply. "You must see for yourself what has slaughtered half the inhabitants of my village and torn Evelyn's favorite dress."

"Down into the lower depths?"

"More like the upper depths," was his curious answer. While pondering the Baron's epistemology, we descended—I had been doing a lot of that lately—past wall torches that had already been lit along the passageway. I would have preferred taking a kerosene lantern but the Baron insisted that only torches were reliable in the dungeon. The most peculiar sight was that there was a veritable curtain of spiderwebs we had to push out of the way . . . and yet not a spider in sight.

Lonnie was waiting for us, locked in the dungeon's only functional cell. He was a big, beefy man; and every bit as American as a brass band on the Fourth of July. "Dad!" he cried out. "I want to die. Please let me die. Will this man with you help me to die? I can't go through another night of eternal torment! I won't, do you hear, I won't!"

"Evelyn and Lonnie both tend to carry on," the Baron whispered in my ear. Then, in a louder voice, he announced: "This man is going to help you, my son, but first he must witness the transformation."

"Not that, anything but that!" the young man blubbered. Fortunately, the full moon put an end to his monologue.

"Now prepare yourself for a surprise," warned the Baron. I'd seen people turn into wolves before, as well as a horse (a poor peasant named Ed), a pig, several breeds of cat, snakes, and even a baboon once. But I'd never seen anything like this. Young Tahlbot retained the shape of a human being—while accumulating additional features. To see a human face take on a lupine aspect . . . to see wolfish fangs protrude from human lips . . . to see hands become—not paws, but claws, still able to grasp as well as rend . . . to see a hybrid horror that was neither wolf nor man struck me as a professional challenge, and an unparalleled opportunity to receive a larger fee.

The Baron had been speaking for some time, but I hadn't listened. There was something numb in his voice, and I heard him say: ". . . seems to die when we use silver weapons, but come the next full moon, which seems to happen awful frequently 'round here, he's alive again."

"Lycanthropy is only part of your problem," I heard myself say, "because this whole region is under a curse. When did it all begin?"

"There was an old gypsy woman who . . ."

"*Say no more!*" Any unprejudiced observer must admit that lycanthropy and gypsies go together like money and a Scotsman. "We must put an end to this damnable business tonight! Er . . . those bars are strong enough to hold your son, aren't they?"

I had good cause to ask such a question as the dirty son of a wolf was throwing himself against the bars of his cage with such vigor that drops of his saliva left spots on my spectacles.

The Baron answered: "We keep putting in new restraints . . . as he destroys the previous ones."

It was time for action! I removed my best scissors from my satchel, along with a variety of combs. The dental tools would be used later.

"We will need the assistance of several strong men," I told him, "and it would be a great help if they are stupid. If we cannot free your son through death, then we must strike at the root, no matter how painful."

It was a grim sight, watching all the young men in the Baron's household fearlessly risk dismemberment, infection and worse, as they overpowered their wolfish subject and bound him with chains. It also helped that Lonnie had exhausted himself attempting to escape.

In all the years of my trade, I'd never faced more of a challenge. Bracing myself, I laid on with scissor and comb. No amount of snarling or of staring eyes made my hand tremble. The customer deserves nothing but the best, especially when it's involuntarily. Using the razor was more difficult than the scissors, but by the time all his body hair lay a foot thick around my ankles, and my arms were numb, I felt a sense of accomplishment. But the most dangerous task remained.

He must have sensed what was next. His howling might have deterred a lesser barber from moving on to necessary surgery, but my implements were sharp and purpose clear. First, the teeth had to go—at least the nasty ones. They were more of a threat than the talons. (The incisors and cuspids remain in my possession to this day—a souvenir, one might say, sort of fangs for the memories.) Extracting the fangs was a bloody business, and it put Lonnie into such a state of shock that I encountered no resistance when it was time to give him his "manicure."

When I was finished, there was a smattering of applause. Turning around, I saw that the entire household had gathered to witness the shearing of the locks. Foremost among the assemblage was Evelyn, who was embracing an unfamiliar young man. I didn't need to ask the Baron to know that here was *another* foreigner, and probably an American to boot. This village was suffering from an identity crisis beyond anything encompassed by mere monsters.

"Well done," said the Baron.

"Simply darling," said Evelyn.

"Rrrrrrrrrrr," was Lonnie's comment in his sleep.

The young men patted me on the back. The English butler raised an approving eyebrow. A French chambermaid whom I'd somehow missed before licked her lips provocatively.

"Inform the villagers that their days of woe are over," I announced. "These stout fellows can take the glad tidings to their homes."

"Sorry governor," replied one of the lads, "but Baron Tahlbot brought us over with him." The cockney accent shouldn't have taken me by surprise. Not really. But this meant I hadn't seen a single villager! I was certain, if only because of my previous visit, that the villager had villagers in it.

As if reading my thoughts, the Baron whispered, "Easy on, Alfred. There are sufficient villagers to bring the population back up to par, if they haven't been wasting all this time behind closed doors. But the decrease in numbers will play havoc come harvest time."

I neglected to inquire what crops could possibly grow in the desolation I had witnessed. We carried the young Tahlbot upstairs. No one awaited the rising of the sun with more eager anticipation than your immodest narrator. To tell the truth, I had not the slightest idea what the next transformation would bring.

Curiosity was stronger than exhaustion. Despite a sleepless and strenuous night, I felt invigorated when, looking through a window, I saw the fog beginning to dissipate in the first light of day. Now there would be at least some answers.

Would Lonnie's natural teeth be restored, or gaps remain in his smile, putting one in mind of a village idiot? And would the small ivory substances in my hand revert to normal teeth or remain fangs? And would his natural head of hair grow back, or would he still be bald? And just how big a tip could I expect?

Then it was morning. Lonnie's face began to change. Gradually he regained all his natural features. This was good news for him *now*; but did this mean the missing features would be as easily restored when next the full moon shone? There was enough mystery here to justify a full report to the A.M.A. (Austrian Monster Association).

Only the next full moon could answer the final questions. Concerning which, I hesitated to bring up to my host the issue of his peculiar lunar problems. There is only one night of the true full moon every month, although it looks to the naked eye as if there are three consecutive nights of the full moon. That the curse of this transplanted British family could have altered all the laws of nature in this place did not occur to me at the time.

I didn't wait around to find out. After assuring the good Baron that there was nothing else I could do, I received my payment and returned to my travels. The news of Lonnie's salvation must have been transmitted by some supernatural means, for now the village square was full of singing and dancing survivors. It struck me that these people did not behave as if anything unusual or tragic had befallen them.

The story might have ended there had it not been for my damnable curiosity. I fully expected to hear news from the village eventually, but I failed to reckon on the degree of isolation involved. By late Fall, curiosity got the better of me and I decided to return before the weather made travel inconvenient.

The night I arrived, all that could be seen of the moon was a thin crescent in the sky. But as the village came into view, my vision blurred. After rubbing my eyes and putting my spectacles back on, I beheld the impossible: all 2,160 miles of lunar diameter were plainly visible as I stared at the round, silver orb. I had returned to Kaninsburg.

At least the increased luminescence made it easier to traverse the mountain path leading back to the village . . . where the werewolf was waiting for me. It was Lonnie, all right. There was hair all over his body, but it wasn't his. I recognized horse hairs, dyed all sorts of colors, and stuck at random about his body. He had fangs, too. The moonlight glinted off a full set of steel dentures. In addition, he had claws. Tied to each finger was a minature dagger in place of his talons.

With a low growl, he came for me; but a barber should always be prepared. I beat him to death with a striped pole I had used to keep my footing when negotiating the mountain pass. There was a silver knob on top.

"This is ridiculous!" I cried to the night sky. "Will I never be rid of this monster?"

"Never," came a man's voice. I turned to see an old gypsy woman emerging from the fog—there was, of course, lots of fog—but beneath the bangles and brightly colored rags, I recognized the face of a man. "You don't know me," he continued, "but the name's Basil Davies." Good God, it sounded like another transplanted Englishman. "I was the village barber before Tahlbot banished me."

I felt another deduction coming on and said: "You've been behind this all along."

"Yes, after old Tahlbot bored everyone with his stories of your splendid barbering, nobody wanted me any longer. Even the damned peasants preferred waiting for you to visit, or tried their hands at home barbering—*no matter how horrid the results*—or just let their hair grow rather than give me any business. I used black magic to try and get my business back on its legs, but nothing did any good. How I hated them. How I hated *you*!"

"So you found a way to transform Lonnie into a monster," I concluded helpfully. "Well, he's destroyed now and I'll turn you over the Baron."

He was having none of it: "You fool! I'll only escape through some ludicrous oversight on his part. And you have not destroyed poor Lonnie. He always comes back! The village of Kaninsburg is under the Universal Curse, a potent spell that guarantees monsters who return forever!"

His certainty unnerved me. "That cannot be. Nothing is forever. There must be some way to defeat you."

"You'll spend the rest of your life trying. The villagers reproduce themselves, and the Baron keeps importing Americans and Englishmen. You see, he is compelled to keep the village populated. It's part of the curse! Just as Lonnie never leaves anyone wounded and about to become a werewolf in his own right. As you may have gathered, Lonnie is one of a kind."

Laughing manically, the transvestite barber/dentist/surgeon (demonstrating a villainous lack of concern for the propriety due our profession) hurried off into the ever thickening fog. And I returned the way I had come. It was evident that if the Universal Curse was to be defeated, it would require research before any ill-considered action.

That was five years ago. In the ensuing period, I learned everything I could about the curse. There was no simple remedy. One promising method was to introduce other monsters into the werewolf's prowling grounds. It was no easy matter, imprisoning ghouls and zombies and then shipping them off to Kaninsburg. Vampires were simply too difficult a proposition or I would have employed them as well (at reasonable rates, of course).

Yet, the next time I ventured there it was to find the wolfish son of Baron Tahlbot as firmly in place as a landmark. Truly he seemed to be immortal. The Baron had lost all faith in me by then. His American niece had even left him, along with her new boyfriend, to go live with another uncle in England—some kind of scientist, I understand, who does a lot of research with electrical equipment.

It seemed that my bag of tricks was empty, insofar as dealing with this stubborn spawn of hell. But I had one last idea—and this is the one that saved the village, the Baron, and, incidentally, my reputation.

To prevail against the gravity of the lycanthrope, I turned to comedy. There was a small abbey only a few leagues distant from

Kaninsburg. In this quiet and secluded place, I found men of God who were willing to risk everything to help me. The abbot who headed the monastery persuaded one of his monks to accompany us—a short, chubby little fellow who seemed afraid of his own shadow, but who proved invaluable against the forces of darkness.

I'll never forget packing a large cloth sack with the weapons that would defeat the Ultimate Werewolf. We filled our bag with banana peels and cream pies. Nor will I forget two simple words that filled my soul with confidence; and made me believe that the Universal Curse did have an ending . . . as all things must end.

When we were leaving the monastery, the little fellow called out for us to wait: *"Hey, Abbot!"*

PARTNERS

▼▼▼

ROBERT J. RANDISI

1

FRANK Grey and Lisa Bain were partners. They had been radio car partners for three years now, and she was the best partner he'd ever had. He, in turn, was the first partner she had ever had.

Lisa Bain was twenty-five, tall and slender. Her colleagues called her skinny, but she preferred to think of herself as slender, even "rangy." She kept her hair cut short, because she never knew what to do with it. The same was true for makeup. She wore very little, because she wasn't very adept at applying it.

Lisa had spent her first year up at One Place Plaza, working in Communications. Police Plaza was Police Headquarters, which stood in the shadow of the Brooklyn Bridge. It was an unhappy year for Lisa, working first at Nine-One-One, and then as a dispatcher. After a year she was finally granted a transfer to the Six-Seven Precinct, where she was partnered with Frank Grey. After just one month in a car with Frank she knew that he was the perfect partner for her.

▼▼▼

Frank Grey was a nine-year veteran of the New York City Police Department, and he had spent five years right here at the Six-Seven Precinct. In the five years he had spent at the Six Seven, he had probably seen fifteen hundred cops come and go, as well as three Commanding Officers. He'd had four different partners: three men and Lisa Bain.

Grey—thirty-four, a hulking giant of a man at six-four and two forty—had never been a supporter of women as cops, but Lisa Bain had changed his mind within a month of teaming with her. She had proven herself extremely capable, and he felt no shame in admitting that she was the best partner he ever had.

▼▼▼

Frank Grey reached into his locker, took out his gunbelt and strapped it on. He took his service revolver out of the holster, checked the loads, and then returned it. He made sure his handcuffs and extra bullets were in place, then took his nightstick from the locker and slid it into place on the belt. He bounced the belt up and down a few times on his hips, to make sure it was riding properly. Satisfied that it was, he completed the process of readying himself for duty by taking out his hat and putting it on.

The officer in the locker next to his was a young rookie, and he had a nervous look on his face as he dressed for duty.

"It's gonna be a full moon tonight," the young officer said.

"Yeah," Frank said.

"Is it as crazy as they say?" the rookie asked. "I mean, night when there's a full moon? In the academy, they told us that there are people who go crazy when there's a full moon."

"First midnight tour?" Frank asked.

"Yeah," the rookie said. He's been assigned to the 67th Precinct for the past month, but this was his first late tour. Frank remembered his first late tour—what was it? Nine years ago? Yeah, nine years and four commands ago. He'd been in the 67th Precinct for five years, the longest he'd ever stayed in one house. This was also the one he felt the most at home in.

"Just treat it like any other tour, kid," Frank said, shutting his locker. "Be ready for anything."

▼▼▼

Lisa Bain closed her locker and looked out the window. Full moon, she thought, biting her lip. Right now it was totally hidden behind the clouds, but some time during the night it was sure to break through.

She was the only woman working this midnight shift, so she was alone in the small, makeshift locker room. For the slightly less than three years she had been assigned to the Six-Seven she—and the other two female police officers who were now assigned to the Six-Seven—had been changing in a converted broom closet on the second floor, while the men changed in the precinct locker room in the basement. They'd been promising the women a locker room of their own for the past year.

She left the room and went downstairs for roll call.

▼▼▼

Frank saw Lisa coming out of the elevator. He remembered when she was first assigned as his partner, three years ago. He never thought she'd be able to hack it, but she had fooled him. After just a month together he knew that he was going to be spoiled for any other partner.

She had four years on the job. At the moment she was one of three female officers assigned to the Precinct. She wasn't the prettiest, or the smartest, but she was the best cop. Hell, she was better than most of the men, too.

She was tall, about five ten, and she looked skinny, but Frank knew how strong she was. She had wide shoulders that made her small breasts look even smaller. Her hair was cut short, and seemed to be naturally silver. Not grey, but silver. At twenty-five, she was too young to be called grey.

Frank Grey was a big, hulking man with thick black hair, not only on his head but all over his body. He had developed body hair at a young age, and had been teased mercilessly in high school gym class until one day, when he tore into his tormenters, big fists flailing. He laid out a good half dozen of them, and they never bothered him again. Of course, he took ribbing in the locker room from his police colleagues, but he was no longer as sensitive about it as he was in high school.

He weighed in at close to two hundred and forty pounds and was usually left in the dust by Lisa whenever they were involved in a foot chase. In close quarters, however, Frank's strength usually gave him the upper hand against almost any opponent.

The late tour crew assembled in the roll call room. Frank and Lisa exchanged a glance, but while the other partners were slapping each other on the back and comparing how their days were spent, they did not have to say a word. They knew each other that well.

This was also the best crew Frank had ever worked with. They had all been steady late tour for about six months, with the odd rookie or replacement tossed in from time to time. For the most part, they were all used to working with each other, and depending on each other.

The roll call sergeant read them whatever special orders had come down, and then sent them out to do their jobs.

"Hey," he called out as they started to disassemble. They looked at him and he said, "I don't have to remind anyone that there's supposed to be a full moon tonight, do I?"

No, their silence said, he didn't. They all knew that a full moon meant they were probably in for an "interesting" tour.

More interesting for some than others.

2

Jerry Tarkenton studied his "gang."

He had known Pauly DePino for thirteen years. They had met in kindergarten class when they were both five, and even then Jerry had been able to get Pauly to do anything he wanted him to. Although the same age, the five-four Pauly had an unabashed hero worship for the six-one Jerry. Pauly—who thought that he and Jerry were "friends"—enjoyed watching the way Jerry controlled the other two members of their gang.

Jerry was the one who had nicknamed Douglas Jenks "Pudge," because Jenks was five eight and weighed over two hundred pounds, most of it around his middle. Pudge usually had some Milky Ways or Hershey Bars in his pockets.

The fourth member of this dubious group was unaffectionately known as "Stupid." Again, it was Jerry who had nicknamed the brutish, six-foot-six Willie Carson "Stupid." He and Pauly had met Carson in junior high school where, at twelve, Carson was already six feet tall. Carson's face was fixed in a perpetual frown as he struggled to understand what was going on in the world around him. It was for this reason that Jerry had dubbed him "Stupid," and Carson was actually proud of the name.

Jerry Tarkenton had chosen his "gang" well and carefully. He made sure that they were dumb enough and dependent enough upon him that he could control them. He often felt like an animal trainer, and they were his subjects.

He naturally felt that he was not only the smartest of the four, but the smartest person he knew. For all of the vacancies that showed in the eyes of Pudge, Pauly and Stupid, the look in Jerry Tarkenton's eyes could only be described as . . . crafty.

"What's in this warehouse, Jerry?" Pauly asked.

"That's what we're gonna find out, Pauly," Jerry said. "It's a big place, real busy all day long. I know there's lot of machinery inside, but it's too busy for something funny not to be goin' on."

"Funny?" Stupid asked. "What's funny?"

"Crooked, Stupid," Pauly said. "He means crooked." Pauly looked at Jerry and eagerly said, "Right, Jerry?"

"Yeah, right, Pauly," Jerry said. "All I know is, there's got to be lots of money in there, or something *worth* a lot of money."

"What about cops, Jerry?" Pudge asked.

"What about 'em?" Jerry asked, with a sneer. "I ain't afraid of cops, are you?"

"No," Pudge said, dubiously, while Pauly and Stupid shook their heads, as well.

Jerry Tarkenton, at just eighteen years of age, had a career criminal's disdain for cops. He felt they were all beneath him in intelligence, and that he could handle any situation that involved the cops.

"What about a gun?" Pudge asked. "What if we come up against a cop with a gun?"

A feral grin crossed Jerry's face as he said, "I'll have Big Stupe here feed it to the fucker, first the bullets, and then the gun! Right, Stupid?"

Stupid's eyes remained vacant as he said, "Sure, Jerry, anything you say." His eyes did not reflect even the intelligence of a dog.

Pudge took out a chocolate bar and started to unwrap it.

"Not in here, Pudge," Jerry said. "My Ma don't want no eatin' in my room."

3

Frank and Lisa rode Sector Henry, in what was generally considered the armpit of the precinct. Day or night it was a bad scene, but at night it somehow became the darkest corner of the precinct.

Frank drove while Lisa looked up at the sky. The moon may have been full, but right now it was totally hidden by a bank of black clouds.

"Six-seven Henry, 'kay."

Lisa picked up the radio handset. Frank was the Operator, and she was the Recorder. It was up to her to answer the dispatcher. She checked her watch and saw that it was 0230 hours—two-thirty in the morning.

"Henry, 'kay."

"Six-seven Henry, report of a ten thirty-four, Burglary in progress, forty-two sixty, Avenue D. Witness states he saw four males entering a closed warehouse at that location. Unknown whether they are armed or not."

"This is Henry," Lisa said. "Ten-four."

"Probably kids," Frank said. "That place has holes all over it."

Lisa nodded, then looked up at the sky. Still no sign of the moon.

Frank turned left on Avenue D. and drove the five needed blocks to get them to the forty-two hundred block. He stopped the car down the block from 4260 and doused the lights.

"Front or back?" he asked her as they got out of the car.

"Back."

They each had a foot-long, metal-cased flashlight in their hands. As well as lighting the way, it could be used as an effective nightstick.

Frank looked up at the sky, where the moon was still in hiding, and said, "Be careful."

"You, too."

Frank moved down the block towards the front of the warehouse. This block was unusual, because it held the commercial warehouse and some residences. It had probably been some insomniac resident who had called it in.

He approached the front door with his flashlight extinguished. Although the full moon had not broken through the cloud cover yet, there were enough street lamps for him to see. Also, he didn't want the glare of his flashlight to tip off the perps that he was there.

He reached for the door handle and saw that the metal door had been forced, probably with a tire iron. He opened the door as far as was necessary to enter, drew his gun, and, with one last look at the sky, went inside.

Now he wouldn't know whether the moon broke through or not. He'd have to find out the hard way.

▼▼▼

Lisa went around back, where the street lights did no good at all. She clicked on her flashlight, but shielded the glow with her hand. There were several doors back here, as well as delivery docks with corrugated metal doors that would slide upward. She tried one of the doors and found it locked. She had to climb up onto one of the docks to try the second door, which was right next to one of the corrugated metal doors. This one was locked, as well. She took a look at the metal door, and saw that the padlock that locked it was in place. She moved to the other end of the building to try another door, all the while listening intently for sounds inside the building. She wished she could use her portable radio to contact Frank, but if he was inside the noise would give him away.

After she checked the third door she'd start checking windows. She took a look at the sky and then tried the handle of the third door.

▼▼▼

This was risky. It was pitch dark inside, and Frank dared not use his flashlight for fear of giving himself away—that is, if there was even anyone inside.

He moved carefully, feeling ahead of himself with his hands and feet. He didn't want to give himself away by knocking over a crate or a set of shelves. What he couldn't have anticipated was the huge grease spot on the floor ahead of him. When his right foot landed on it, it slid right out from under him, dumping him unceremoniously on his ass in a puddle of grease. He managed to hold onto his flashlight with his left hand, but his gun slid from his right hand when he tried to use it to break his fall. He could hear the weapon skitter across the floor into the darkness like a frightened rat.

Of course, he'd made a fearsome racket, and suddenly he was spotlighted by a couple of flashlight beams.

"See?" a voice said, with great satisfaction, "I tole you I heard somethin'."

"So you did, Pudge," another voice said. "Looks like we got us a cop."

"What we gonna do with 'em, Jerry?" Pudge asked.

"I dunno," Jerry said. "Lemme think."

Frank was holding his greasy right hand up to try to shield his eyes from the flashlights. He couldn't see any faces clearly, but from the sound of their voices the perps were young, probably eighteen to twenty. He wouldn't have been worried if he'd been dealing with older, more experienced burglars. The young ones were just too unpredictable.

"Pauly, get the front door," Jerry said.

"Right."

"Jam something up against it so it stays closed. We don't want his partner surprisin' us."

"Right."

"Stupid," Jerry said, "keep an eye out for his partner."

"Uh . . . okay, Jerry."

Frank managed to identify the holders of the flashlights as Jerry and Pudge. Jerry, apparently the leader of the group, was on his left. Frank tightened his grip on his flashlight, which was behind him and out of the light.

"Get up, cop," Jerry said.

"Jerry, is it?" Frank said. "You're the leader here, right?"

"That's right. What's it to you?"

"Jerry . . ." Frank was trying to dig his heels into the floor for leverage, but they kept sliding on the grease. "Listen, Jerry, you don't want to mess with a cop."

"No," Jerry said, "you're right, I don't want to mess with a cop—I wanna *fuck* with you! Now get up!"

"I'm trying," Frank said, "but it's not easy in this grease."

Frank hadn't yet seen a gun, or any weapon, for that matter. If he could get to his feet he could put the flashlight to good use. He hadn't been lying to Jerry, though. It was very difficult to gain enough purchase on the floor even to get to his feet. He had to do it, though. He was too vulnerable sitting there on his ass.

"I shut the door," Pauly said, returning, "and look what I found."

Jerry shone his flashlight on what Pauly was holding, and when Frank saw it, his blood ran cold.

It was his own gun.

Where the hell was Lisa?

▼▼▼

Outside, in the back, Lisa had determined that all the door were locked. She was checking windows when she thought she saw a light inside. It was just a flash from the window she was looking through, so they moved to another window, and then another until the light became constant. She saw two flashlights illuminating something on the floor. That something was her partner.

She started to look around for something to pry a door open with when the area was suddenly lit up by light from the full moon.

She looked up and saw that the moon had broken through the clouds.

"Jesus," she said. Her heart began to race, and she began to sweat profusely.

She turned to the door and started kicking it as she grabbed with shaking hands for the radio on her belt.

"Ten thirteen!" she shouted. "This is six-seven Henry! Ten thirteen!"

She wanted to say more, but the radio fell from her palsied hands. . . .

▼▼▼

Inside the building the pounding was very loud. Jerry, Pauly and Pudge all turned to look in the direction of the sound. At the same time the fourth perp, Stupid, started yelling, "There's another cop in the back!"

"The back doors are locked—" Jerry started to say, but he stopped when he realized that they had all taken their eyes off the cop.

"Shit!" he said, turning back towards Frank, who was in the act of throwing his flashlight.

Jerry jerked the trigger of Frank's gun . . .

▼▼▼

The beast heard the sound of the shot. It penetrated through layers and years of bestiality, and when the second shot sounded it threw itself against the door that only moments earlier Lisa Bain had been kicking . . .

▼▼▼

Frank floundered in the center of the puddle of grease as his flashlight struck Pudge in the center of his forehead. As Pudge's eyes rolled up and he fell to the ground Jerry aimed the gun at Frank, holding it with two hands this time so he wouldn't miss.

"Die, fucker!"

Frank Grey's throat closed, and he held up one hand to fend off the bullet that was surely coming his way to end his life.

Before Jerry could pull the trigger the back door exploded inward, coming completely off its hinges.

"What the fuck—" Jerry said.

Jerry turned and saw a huge, hulking form lift the two-hundred-pound Stupid completely off his feet. He watched as the perp was literally thrown through the air into the darkness, where he landed with a loud crash.

"Jesus," Pauly yelled, "Jesus, Jerry, what the hell is it?"

Jerry didn't know, but he swung his flashlight and shined the light so he could find out. When he saw it, he wished he hadn't done so.

The light illuminated the face of a beast. Covered with brown and silver hair, a long snout, a mouthful of sharp teeth, yellow, feral eyes. It looked like a wolf, but it was standing upright.

"Jesus, Jerry—" Pauly said, but the beast swung a hand—a *paw*—at him, cutting him off in midsentence. Blood flew through the air as sharp claws slashed Pauly across the throat and chest.

A spray of blood landed on Jerry's face and chest, shocking Jerry into action. He'd frozen in his tracks at the sight of the beast, and now he raised the gun he still held in two hands and pulled the trigger as the beast advanced on him. He *knew* he had hit it, but the animal who walked like a man continued to come at him. He pulled the trigger again . . . and again . . . and again . . . until the hammer struck nothing but empty chambers.

The beast swung an arm, and Jerry's life ended with sharp abruptness. The pain was fleeting, and then he crumpled to the floor as if his bones had melted.

That left only the beast, and Frank Grey.

Frank slid and staggered his way to his feet and finally extricated himself from the grease pond he'd been floundering in for what seemed like hours.

He looked at the beast, who was standing still, head cocked, studying him.

He extended his hand to the beast. This part always frightened him the most, because he always feared that one of these days recognition would not dawn in those feral eyes—and at the same time, he always knew it would.

He heard the sirens and knew that Lisa must have called a ten-thirteen, Officer needs assistance.

"Come on," he said to the beast, "out. I'll cover it. Go on!"

As the beast went out the back door he started preparing his story. He always covered for her, always managed to make it believable. He often suspected that the others knew—their fellow cops, the patrol supervisors, even the Captain—because they always accepted his "explanations," without question—questioning looks, yes, but nothing voiced, not after the first couple of incidents almost three years ago.

Although the others may have protected their secret, it was Frank who had first had to accept the truth about Lisa Bain, and then do his best to protect her from discovery.

After all, they *were* partners.

ANCIENT EVIL
▼▼▼

BILL PRONZINI

LISTEN *to me. You'd better listen.*

You fools, you think you know so much. Space flight, computer technology, genetic engineering . . . you take them all for granted now. But once your kind scoffed at them, refused to believe in the possibility of their existence. You were proven wrong.

You no longer believe in Us. We will prove you wrong.

We exist. We have existed as long as you. We are not superstition, We are not folklore, We are not an imaginary terror. We are the real terror, the true terror. We are all your nightmares come true.

Believe it. Believe me. I am the proof.

We look like men, We walk and talk like men, in your presence We act like men. But We are not men. Believe that too.

We are the ancient evil . . .

▼▼▼

They might never have found him if Hixon hadn't gone off to take a leak.

For three days they'd been searching the wooden mountain

country above the valley where their sheep grazed. Tramping through heavy timber and muggy late-summer heat laden with stinging flies and mosquitoes; following the few man-made and animal trails, cutting new trails of their own. They'd flushed several deer, come across the rotting carcass of a young elk, spotted a brown bear and followed its spoor until they lost it at one of the network of streams. But that was all. No wolf or mountain lion sign. Hixon and DeVries kept saying it had to be a wolf or a mountain cat that had been killing the sheep, Larrabee wasn't so sure. And yet, what the hell else could it be?

Then, on the morning of the fourth day, while they were climbing among deadfall pine along the shoulder of a ridge, Hixon went to take his leak. And came back after a few minutes all red-faced and excited, with his fly still half unzipped.

"I seen something back in there," he said. "Goddamnedest thing, down a ravine."

"What'd you see?" Larrabee asked him. He'd made himself the leader; he had lost the most sheep and he was the angriest.

"Well, I think it was a man."

"You think?"

"He was gone before I could use the glasses."

"Hunter, maybe," DeVries said.

Hixon wagged his head. "Wasn't no hunter. No ordinary man, either."

"The hell you say. What was he then?"

"I don't know," Hixon said. "I never seen the like."

"Dressed how?"

"Wasn't dressed, not in clothes. I swear he was wearing some kind of animal skins. And he had hair all over his head and face, long shaggy hair."

"Bigfoot," DeVries said and laughed.

"Dammit, Hank, I ain't kidding. He was your size, mine."

"Sun and shadows playing tricks."

"No, by God. I know what I saw."

Lararbee asked impatiently, "Where'd he go?"

"Down the ravine. There's a creek down there."

"He see or hear you?"

"Don't think so. I was quiet."

DeVries laughed again. "Quiet pisser, that's you."

Larabee adjusted the pack that rode his shoulders; ran one hand back and forth along the stock of his .300 Savage rifle. His mouth was set tight. "All right," he said, "we'll go have a look."

"Hell, Ben," DeVries said, "you don't reckon it's some *man* been killing our sheep?"

"Possible, isn't it? I never did agree with you and Charley. No wolf or cat takes sheep down that way, tears them apart. And don't leave any sign coming or going."

"No man does either."

"No ordinary man. No sane man."

"Jesus, Ben . . ."

"Come on," Larrabee said. "We're wasting time."

▼▼▼

. . . How many of Us are there? Not many. A few hundred . . . We have never been more than a few hundred. Scattered across continents. In cities and small towns, in wildernesses. Hot climes and cold. Moving, always moving, never too long in one place. Hiding among you, the bold and clever ones. Hiding alone, the ones like me.

This is our legacy:

Hiding.

Hunting.

Hungering.

You think you've been hungry but you haven't. You don't know what it means to be hungry all the time, to have the blood-taste in your mouth and the blood-craving in your brain and the blood-heat in your loins.

But some of you will find out. Many of you, someday. Unless you listen and believe.

Each new generation of Us is bolder than the last.

And hungrier . . .

▼▼▼

The ravine was several hundred yards long, narrow, crowded with trees and brush. The stream was little more than a trickle among sparkly mica rocks. They followed it without cutting any sign of the man Hixon had seen, if a man was what he'd seen; without hearing anything except for the incessant hum of insects, the yammering cries of jays and magpies.

The banks of the ravine shortened, sloped gradually upward into level ground: a small ragged meadow ringed by pine and spruce, strewn with brush and clumps of summer-browned ferns. They stopped there to rest, to wipe sweat-slick off their faces.

"No damn sign," Hixon said. "How could he come through there without leaving any sign?"

DeVries said, "He doesn't exist, that's how."

"I tell you I saw him. I know what I saw."

Larrabee paid no attention to them. He had been scanning with his naked eye; now he lifted the binoculars that hung around his neck and scanned with those. He saw nothing anywhere. Not even a breeze stirred the branches of the trees.

"Which way now?" Hixon asked him.

Larrabee pointed to the west, where the terrain rose to a bare knob. "Up there. High ground."

"You ask me," DeVries said, "we're on a snipe hunt."

"You got any better suggestions?"

"No. But even if there is somebody around here, even if we find him . . . I still don't believe it's a man we're after. All those sheep with their throats ripped out, hunks of the carcasses torn off and carried away . . . a man wouldn't do that."

"Not even a lunatic?"

". . . What kind of lunatic butchers sheep?"

"Psycho," Hixon said. "Blown out on drugs, maybe."

Larrabee nodded. He'd been thinking about it as they tracked. "Or an ex-Vietnam vet, or one of those back-to-nature dropouts. They come into wild country like this, alone, and it gets to this one or that one and they go off their heads."

DeVries didn't want to believe it. "I still say it's an animal, a wolf or a cat."

"Man goes crazy in the wilderness," Larrabee said, "that's just what he turns into—an animal, a damned wolf on the prowl."

He wiped his hands on his trousers, took a drier grip on the Savage, and led the way toward higher ground.

▼▼▼

. . . We are not all the same. Your stupid folklore says We are but We're not. Over the centuries We have undergone genetic changes, just as you have; We have evolved. You are children of your time. So are We.

My hunger is for animal flesh, animal blood. Sheep. Cattle. Dogs. Smaller creatures with fur and pulsing heart. They are my prey. One here, two there, ten in this county, fifty or hundred in that state. You think it is one animal killing another—natural selection, survival of the fittest. You are right but you are also wrong.

Believe it.

We are not all the same. Others of Us have different hungers. Human flesh, human blood—yes. But that isn't all. We have evolved; our tastes have altered, grown discriminating. Male flesh and male blood. Female. Child. And not always do We desire the soft flesh of the throat, the bright sweet blood from the jugular.

And not always do We use our teeth to open our victims. And not always do We feed in a frenzy.

I am one of the old breed—not the most fearsome of Us. And sickened by the things I'm compelled to do; that is why I'm warning you. The new breed . . . it is with the new breed that the ultimate terror lies.

We are not all the same . . .

▼▼▼

Larrabee stood on the bare knob, staring through his binoculars, trying to sharpen the focus. Below, across a hollow choked with brush and deadfall, a grassy, rock-littered slope lifted toward timber. The sun was full on the slope and the hot noon-glare struck fiery glints from some of the rocks, created thick shadows around some of the others, making it hard for him to pick out details. Nothing moved over there except the sun-dazzle. It was just a barren slope—and yet there was something about it . . .

Up near the top, where the timber started: rocks thickly bunched in tall grass, the way the brush was drawn in around that one massive outcrop. Natural or not? He just couldn't tell for sure from this distance.

Beside him Hixon asked, "What is it, Ben? You see something over there?"

"Maybe." Larrabee gave him the glasses, told him where to look. Pretty soon he said, "Seem to you somebody might've pulled that brush in around the base of the outcrop?"

"Could be, yeah. That damn sun . . ."

"Let me see," DeVries said, but he couldn't tell either.

They went down into the hollow, Larrabee moving ahead of the other two. The deadfall tangle was like a bonepile, close-packed, full of jutting points and splintered edges; it took him ten minutes to find a way across to the slope. He'd been carrying his rifle at port-arms, but as he started upslope he extended the muzzle in front of him, slid his finger inside the trigger guard.

The climb was easy enough. They went up three abreast, not fast, not slow. A magpie came swooping down at them, screaming; DeVries cursed and slashed at it with his rifle. Larrabee didn't turn his head. His eyes, unblinking, were in a lock-stare on the rocks and brush near the timber above.

They were within fifty yards of the outcrop when a little breeze kicked up, blew downhill. As soon as it touched them they stopped, all three at once.

"Jesus," Hixon said, "you smell that?"

"Wolf smell," DeVries said.

"Worse than that. Something dead up there . . ."

Larrabee said, "Shut up, both of you." His finger was on the Savage's trigger now. He drew a breath and began to climb again, more warily than before.

The breeze had died, but after another thirty yards the smell was in his nostrils without it. Hixon had been right: death smell. It seemed to mingle with the heat, to form a miasma that made his eyes burn. Behind him he heard DeVries gag, mutter something, spit.

Somewhere nearby the magpie was still screeching at them. But no longer flying around where they were—as if it were afraid to get too close to that outcrop.

Larrabee climbed to within twenty feet of it. That was close enough for him to see that the brush had been dragged in around its base, all right. Some of the smaller rocks looked to have been carried here, too, and set down as part of the camouflage arrangement.

Hixon and DeVries had stopped a few paces below him. In a half-whisper DeVries asked, "You see anything, Ben?"

Larrabee didn't answer. He was working saliva through a dry mouth, staring hard at the dark foul-smelling opening of a cave.

▼▼▼

 . . . *Haven't you ever wondered why there have been so many unexplained disappearances in the past few decades? Why so many children are kidnapped? Why there is so seldom any trace of the missing ones?*

Haven't you ever wondered about all the random murders, so many more of them now than in the past, and why the bloody remains of certain victims are left behind?

You fools, you blind fools, who do you think the serial killers really are . . .

▼▼▼

They were all staring at the cave now, standing side by side with rifles trained on the opening, breathing thinly through their mouths. The death-stink seemed to radiate out of the hole, so that it was an almost tangible part of the day's heat.

Larrabee broke his silence. He called out, "If you're in there you better come out. We're armed."

Nothing. Stillness.

"Now what?" DeVries asked.

"We take a look inside."

"Not me. I ain't going in there."

"We don't have to go in. We'll shine a light inside."

"That's still too close for me."

"Do it myself then," Larrabee said angrily. "Charley, get the flashlight out of my pack."

Hixon went around behind him and opened the pack and found the six-cell flash he carried; tested it against his hand to make sure the batteries were still good. "What the hell," he said, "I'll work the light. You're a better shot than me, Ben."

Larrabee tied his handkerchief over his nose and mouth; it helped a little against the stench. Hixon did the same. "All right, let's get it done. Hank, you keep your rifle up and your eyes open."

"Count on it," DeVries said.

They had to prod brush out of the way to reach the cave

mouth. It was larger than it had seemed from a distance, four feet high and three feet wide—large enough so that a man didn't have to get down on all fours and crawl inside. The sun-glare made the blackness within a solid wall.

Larrabee stood off a little ways, butted the Savage against his shoulder, took a bead on the opening. "Okay," he said to Hixon, "put the light in there."

Hixon switched on, sent the six-cell's beam probing inside the cave.

Almost instantly the light impaled a crouching shape—big, hairy, wild-eyed. The thing snarled, a sound that was only half human, and came hurtling out at them with teeth bared and hands hooked like claws. Hixon yelled, dropped the flashlight, tried to dodge out of the way. Larrabee triggered his rifle but the suddenness of the attack threw his aim off, made him miss. The man-beast slammed into Hixon, threw him down; slashed at him, opened a bloody gash along his neck and shoulder; swung snarling toward Larrabee and launched himself like an animal as Larrabee, fighting panic, jacked another shell into firing position.

He wouldn't have had time to get off a second shot if DeVries hadn't held his ground below, if DeVries hadn't fired twice while the man-beast was in mid-lunge.

The first bullet knocked him aside, brought a keening cry out of him and put him down in the brush; the second missed high, whanged off rock. By then Larrabee had set himself, taken aim again. He shot the bugger at point-blank range—blew the left side of his head off. Even so, his rage was such that he jacked another shell into the chamber and without thinking shot him again, in the chest this time, exploding the heart.

The last of the echoes died away, leaving a stillness that was painful in Larrabee's ears—like a shattering noise just beyond the range of his hearing. He got his breathing under control and went in loose-legged strides to where Hixon lay writhing on the ground, clutching at his bloody neck. DeVries was there too, his face pale and sweat-studded; he kept saying, "Jesus God," over and over, as if he were praying.

Hixon's wound wasn't as bad as it first seemed: a lot of blood but no arteries severed. DeVries had a first-aid kit in his pack; Larrabee got it out and swabbed antiseptic on the gash, wrapped some gauze around it. Hixon was still glazed with shock, so they moved him over against one of the rocks, in the shade. Then they went to look at what they'd killed.

It was a man, all right. Six feet, two hundred pounds, black beard and hair so thick and matted that it all but hid his features. Fingernails as long and sharp as talons. The one eye that was left was a muddy brown, the white of it so veined it looked bloody. Skins from different animals, roughly sewn together, draped part of the thick-muscled body; the skins and the man's bare flesh were encrusted with filth, months or years of it. The stench that came off the corpse made Larrabee want to puke.

DeVries said hoarsely, "You ever in your life see anything like that?"

"I never want to see anything like it again."

"Crazy—he must've been crazy as hell. The way he come out of that cave . . ."

"Yeah," Larrabee said.

"He'd have killed you if I hadn't shot him. You and Charley and then me, all three of us. It was in his eyes . . . a goddamn madman."

Larrabee didn't respond to that. After a few seconds he turned and started away.

"Where you going?" DeVries said behind him.

"Find out what's inside that cave."

▼▼▼

. . . I am one of the old breed—not the most fearsome of Us. And sickened by the things I'm compelled to do; that is why I'm warning

you. The new breed . . . it is with the new breed that the ultimate terror lies.

We are not all the same . . .

▼▼▼

DeVries wouldn't go into the cave, wouldn't even go near the mouth, so Larrabee went in alone. He took the Savage as well as the flashlight, and he went in slow and wary. He didn't want any more surprises.

He had to walk hunched over for the first few feet. Then the cave opened up into a chamber nearly six feet high and not much larger than a prison cell. He put the light on the walls, on the floor: more animals skins, heaps of flesh-rotted bones, splatters and streaks of dried blood everywhere. Things had been killed as well as eaten in here, Christ knew what things.

The stink was so bad that he couldn't stand it for more than a few seconds. When he turned to get out of there, the flash beam illuminated a kind of natural shelf in the wall. There were some things on the shelf—the stub of a candle stuck in a clot of its own grease, what appeared to be a ragged pocket notebook, other things he didn't want to examine too closely. On impulse he caught up the notebook by one edge, brought it out with him into the hot clean air.

Hixon was up on his feet, standing with DeVries twenty feet from the entrance; he was still a little shaky but the glazed look was gone from his eyes. He said, "Bad in there?"

"As bad as it gets."

"What'd you find?" DeVries asked. He was looking at what Larrabee held between his left thumb and forefinger.

Larabee squinted at it, holding it away from his face because of the smell. Kid's spiral-bound notebook, the covers torn and stained, the ruled paper inside almost black with filth and dried blood. But on half a dozen pages there was writing, old writing done with a pencil pressed hard and angry so that the words were still legible. Larrabee put his back to the sun so he could read it better.

▼▼▼

. . . Believe it. Believe me. I am the proof.

We look like men, We walk and talk like men, in your presence We act like men. But We are not men. Believe that too.

We are the ancient evil . . .

▼▼▼

Wordlessly Larrabee handed the notebook to DeVries, who made a faint disgusted sound when he touched it. But he read what was written inside. So did Hixon.

"Man oh man," Hixon said when he was done, with a kind of awe in his voice. "Ben, you don't think . . . ?"

"It's bullshit," Larrabee said. "Ravings of a lunatic."

"Sure. Sure. Only . . ."

"Only what?"

"I don't know, it . . . I don't know."

"Come on, Charley," DeVries said. "You don't buy any of that crap, do you? Some kind of monster—a werewolf, for Christ's sake?"

"No. It's just . . . maybe we ought to take this back with us, give it to the sheriff."

Larrabee gave him a hard look. "The body too, I suppose? Lug it twenty miles in this heat, smelling the way he does, leaking blood?"

"Not that, no. But we got to report it, don't we? Tell the law what happened?"

"Hell we do. How's it going to look? He's got three bullets in him, two of mine and one of Hank's. He jumped us out of a cave, three of us with rifles and him without a weapon, and we blew him away—how's that going to sound?"

"But it was self-defense. The sheriff'll believe that . . ."

"Will he? I'm not going to take the chance."
"Ben's right," DeVris said. "Neither am I."
"What do we do then?"
"Bury him," Larrabee said. "Forget any of this ever happened."
"Bury the notebook too?"
"What notebook?" Larrabee said.

▼▼▼

. . . *You fools, you blind fools* . . .

▼▼▼

They dug the grave for the crazy sheep-killing man and his crazy legacy in the grass above the outcrop. Deep, six feet deep, so the predators couldn't get at him.

AND THE MOON SHINES
FULL AND BRIGHT
▼▼▼

BRAD STRICKLAND

MOONSET.

Kazak lost his claws. His fangs. His pelt.

His muscles could have driven his lean lupine form through a forest three times as fast as a man could run, but now beneath his skin they withered to strings against the bones. They could not support him, and he fell. The floor softened to receive his collapsing form, then solidified again, leaving one patch warm and yielding beneath his left side. In utter silence and without fuss, the floor grew a bed to support him, lifted him to the proper hospital height, and then stopped. The air in the room began to warm to suit his naked and unfurred body.

But the temperature was cold at first, so terribly cold. He shivered and groaned, his belly shrunken into a clenched fist of pain, his head light, spinning. His eyes, blurred and bleared from the wrenching transformation, ached at the hateful alien light. His seared lungs heaved. Icy air whistled in his nostrils, his human nostrils that only moments before had been alive to every possibility of scent, from the beast-reek of himself to the delicate spoor of Dr. Iglace.

Naked, sweating, shivering in his new form, Kazak lay on the fresh bed, gasping and only semiconscious.

The wall opened. As though in a dream Kazak heard light footsteps approaching. A warm cupped hand touched his forehead, soft fingers pried open one eye to the agony of light. "Weight," Dr. Iglace said.

In its precise child-pitched voice the room replied, "Fifty-five point eight kilos, representing a total loss of twenty-three point seven four kilos in twenty-four hours."

"Feed him," said Dr. Iglace.

The bed grew tentacles, flexible tubes that writhed and moved as if they were alive. Several pinioned Kazak's left arm, lacing it to the surface so that no movement of his could release it. Another, sharp-pointed and probing, found Kazak's brachial vein, penetrated it, and began to pump synthetic nutrients, glucose, proteins, amino acids, into his blood. The compounds reached his brain, and with a shuddering jolt Kazak felt himself yanked into consciousness. The doctor stood over him, gazing down with remote professional interest evident on his dark, ascetic features. No mercy showed in his expression or in his abnormally pale blue eyes.

"Why?" Kazak croaked.

"Because," Dr. Iglace said in a reasonable voice, "you are the world's last werewolf."

▼▼▼

He had been free once, some time before, in a place that formerly had been known by a name that marked it as a part of Central Europe. Kazak waited naked beneath an ash tree, waited for Sister Moon to rise and change him.

Parkland around him: rolling hills, trees evenly spaced, no people.

Below him, in the valley, sheep.

Sunset. Reds and golds in the west. Violet in the east.

Dark.

Darker.

Darkest.

The molten brass sphere of moonrise shone full in his face, reflected in his eyes, and led to the brief agony of change. He felt ancient forest-nurtured earth beneath his pads, springy, deep. The world had gone black and white and shades of gray, seen through new eyes. A universe rolled in through his nostrils, oh! leaf-mould and anthill, human-scent from picnickers, cold metal and *other* of their vehicles, and mutton warm, wool-clothed, bloodfull.

He felt the spring of taut muscle rippling beneath his coat, the stretch and crackle of joints, the dilating gape of a yawn. Driven by ancient instinct, he paused to lift his leg against the tree, to mark his place as his, though he had never met any others of his kind and never expected to meet any.

Then he was off, running down the slope, silent, and the moon-silvered forest glided by on either side. Scent of water wafted from farther ahead. A welcome breeze brought sheep smell, food smell. Drool pooled hot in his mouth.

His feet knew how to place themselves, to drive his body forward with only the minimum of effort, to steer him right and left around trees, around stones. They made no more noise than a patter of raindrops on the deep mould of the forest floor.

Below him drifted the sheep, stodgy, earthbound clouds. He caught the dry rotten-grass smell of dung, and in his ears rang the quavering anxious sounds of their bleats. Closer now, hidden by brush, singling one from the flock without pausing to consider—

Then bursting out, hearing the cries rise in pitch, feeling them scatter, guessing rightly that the *one* will move *this* way, the quick and merciful snap of jaws—

Kazak fed well that time. The last time.

He dreamed about it often in this place, this coldness of a

laboratory. His jaws champed in sleep, his dreaming tongue tasted the sweet hot gush of blood, the life of the flesh.

But he always awakened to disappointment, to tests, to the room that obscenely seemed to live, to the dry cheerless benevolence of Dr. Iglace.

▼▼▼

"Though you are under-educated, you are not unintelligent," Dr. Iglace said to Kazak one morning after some tests, a morning between full moons. The interview took place in Kazak's cell. The floor had grown furnishings, a table, chairs, even an ersatz window looking out into a holographic representation of a country morning. None of it made the least difference to Kazak.

When he remained silent, the doctor, seated comfortably in one freshly-grown chair, continued imperturbably: "I think you can grasp your importance to us, and your position."

Kazak paced hopelessly. "Let me go. I have rights."

A silent chuckle made Dr. Iglace bounce slightly in his place. "You have no rights. The Planetary Constitution guarantees rights to humans, and you are a lycanthrope, something rather different. *Homo sapiens ferox*, perhaps."

"I'm a man. At all times except the nights of the full moon, I am a man."

"To outward appearances. And yet you are not, really. Shall I go through the list, Mr. Kazak? Shall I enumerate the differences in DNA and RNA, in hormonal balances, in bodily systems? No? They are informative, I assure you. Do you know that lycanthropy is genetic, Mr. Kazak?"

Kazak nodded. "My family," he muttered. "Cursed. Cursed for four hundred years, since a werewolf bit my ancestor—"

"Yes," the doctor murmured. "Your family is a special case, rather."

The false window shimmered and changed, now representing sunrise over a placid ocean. Kazak gave it one disgusted glance.

"I can't stay here. I can't stand being confined. You're killing me."

"Nonsense. We're caring for you very well. Where was I?"

"The condition is genetic," the voice of the room said in its childish soprano.

"Yes, to be sure. But it is also contagious. Lycanthropes are actually genetic variants of basic human stock. The genes that make you a werewolf are scattered throughout the human species. Not everyone has them, of course—fewer than one in thirty thousand these days, according to computer analyses."

"And I happen to be one of the lucky ones."

"Mm. Different, anyway, for in your family the genes have proved dominant. In all other surviving cases, the genes are recessive, dormant. Did you know, Mr. Kazak, that the bite of a lycanthrope in lupine form carries with it a secretion of the salivary glands that alters DNA? Changes it subtly but crucially in people with that recessive lycanthrope gene? That's what makes lycanthropy communicable, though the odds of your finding and biting someone with the gene are very small indeed."

"I've never hurt a living person."

"Why not?"

Kazak looked away. "Perhaps I was never hungry enough."

"And when you were hungry, you dined on humbler fare. Sheep and forest animals." Dr. Iglace sighed. "Show us the Szamos Park," he said.

Obligingly the window expanded and elongated until it filled an entire wall of the room. The scene shifted, became the wild landscape where Kazak had roamed. Where he had been trapped.

Kazak knew that it was only holography. Yet his nostrils twitched and he had to restrain himself from flight, from a futile attempt to run into that scene. "You recognize it, I see," Dr. Iglace said. "What do you think it is?"

"My home," Kazak said. "The wilderness."

Dr. Iglace bobbed again with his silent chuckle. "Don't be

absurd. The wilderness died four hundred years ago. That is a park, and the animals are either domestic or genetically reconstructed ones, bio-engineered to be harmless to humans."

"I was free in the wild."

"You never lived in the wild. There is no wilderness left, Mr. Kazak. Oh, the government claims that the Inner Planet colonies are settlements in the wilderness, but that's a lie, a recruiting tool. Mars and Venus are only half-domesticated frontier worlds, but they have no indigenous 'wilderness,' indeed no life of their own, only such genetically engineered plants and creatures as we have provided."

The doctor leaned close, so that even in his human form Kazak could smell his delicate odor, a faint sweetness. "Would you claim those animals as wild creatures, Mr. Kazak? They are spawn of test-tube and genetic manipulators, not beasts of the wild. In fact, Mr. Kazak, 'nature' has not existed for centuries, not anywhere in the settled solar system. Least of all here."

The scene became a view from space, with the globe of the Earth hanging against the velvet black, cold stars pricking the darkness. "Earth is completely tamed, Mr. Kazak, and fully occupied already by humans. You have no right to exist on it."

"Then kill me," Kazak said. "It only takes a silver bullet."

But the scientists had something worse in mind for Kazak than killing him.

They studied him.

▼▼▼

They caught him again in dreams.

He was lupine and running, running beneath a full cold moon, sandpaper-crusted snow burning the pads of his paws, frosty air keen in his nostrils. They flew behind him in small craft a few meters above the tallest tree branches. He could not smell or hear them, could glimpse them only brokenly and momentarily, but he sensed pursuit.

The silvery eggs flashed moonlight at him, spears thrust through the black canopy of tree branch and needle. His reserves were great, his energies all but boundless, and he needed every ounce of power. To cease running, to go to ground, would doom him. Yet the pursuit was relentless.

As a wolf he did not count, but more flying things than he had legs pursued him. Time after time he broke for deeper cover, headed for darker forest, only to see ahead the telltale flash of light as a different hunter circled to forestall his flight. Even his iron will and sinew at last began to fail him. The breath seared in and out of his lungs, and his knees began to tremble with weariness. Once or twice he crossed a clearing, stood challenging them, a lone wolf waiting a chance to strike. They refused the challenge, merely came to rest in a ring around him, as high as the trees, hovering silently.

He ran again at such times, seeking forest cover and shelter. Part of him knew with despair that the chase was hopeless, that all the humans had to do was outwait him. When he lost the moon, he lost any hope of escape.

The end came swiftly. He found himself cornered, literally, in a niche of rock, part of a lofty, nearly vertical cliff. He could not climb the cliff face, and when he whirled to run he discovered that the vehicles had settled to earth. Already men had climbed out of two of them and were advancing toward him slowly, weapons shouldered and ready.

Desperate gladness rose in his heart, for men he could fight. With a snarl that rattled his throat, he leapt forward, bounding to attack the nearest one, to rend him—

A cry went up from another of the hunters, and the weapons hummed. The wolf met an invisible wall of force, impalpable but real. He felt as though he had leaped into a thick, tangling brush, as though he were struggling in nightmare to put one slow foot in front of the other.

More weapons hummed at him, and the feeling became a

physical lethargy so complete that he could not move. He fell to the snow and lay on his side, his lungs working like a bellows, his heart thudding terribly fast, rage and fear racing through his veins. Still he could not move, could not stir one voluntary muscle.

The abominable stench of the men filled his nose. One, holding no weapon, approached and knelt. He felt the touch of that one's hand on his pelt, stroking his neck. "Very good," that one had said—its was Kazak's first meeting with Dr. Iglace, in fact— "very good indeed. Load him."

Now that the wolf was down it took only one weapon's hum to keep him immobilized. Four of the others lifted him, carried him to one of the silvery eggs, waited while its side opened, slipped him into a cramped compartment. The one with the weapon shut it off, almost too soon. The second its hum died, the wolf hurled himself out of confinement—

But the hole in the vehicle's side closed, and he merely collided with a solid wall. He snarled and growled, but he was a prisoner. He did not cease trying to escape the dark compartment for hours, not until the change came over him. Then, unfed, weakened, maddened, he lapsed into unconsciousness.

Now when he waked from dreams, he was always in human form, naked, confined in the cell that somehow lived, that met his needs and yet kept him prisoner. No matter how often the dream recurred, on waking Kazak always believed, for a moment, that he was freshly captured. Then recollection came; and with recollection, hot tears of anger and grief.

▼▼▼

The change came and went, then again, and again. Kazak lost count. The wolf hours were the worst, for the boundaries of the room held him as cruelly as the steel teeth of a trap on the leg, or on the heart. After his first metamorphosis in captivity, they fed him during the change, gave him fresh meat. He ate, ravenously, because instinct drove him to eat.

Dr. Iglace explained to him later why the instinct was important. "It takes a great deal of energy, the transformation," the doctor said. "You lose biomass in changing from a man to a wolf. Some goes to the creation of your pelt, more to the rearrangement of skeleton and musculature. You must eat at least a third of your normal human weight to make the transition from man to wolf to man successfully—that is, with no ill effects."

"Live meat would be better," Kazak said.

Dr. Iglace looked distressed. "Mr. Kazak, we are stretching a point even to give you such flesh as we allow you: the carcasses of domestic park animals, dead of natural causes. Surely you must know that no human eats meat. The life-rights lobby would ruin our work if they thought you human. As it is, they view you as a carnivore, and so we have obtained a certain license from them to meet your, ah, special dietary needs." With a half-smile, the scientist added, "I suppose it's pointless to ask the question again—"

"I can't tell you how it feels to be a werewolf," Kazak insisted.

"Then you have no memory of your wolf form?"

Kazak paced. He never sat in the presence of the doctor unless specifically ordered to do so. "I have memory. I lack the words. It—it's a matter of knowing, of sensing with my entire body, of being awareness rather than intellect—" He held out his empty hands. "How would you describe a painting to a blind person, or a symphony to a deaf one? There are no words."

"And when you are a wolf? Do you then have memory of your man-like form?"

"Yes. Faint, thin, like a dream of a dream, like the morning haze in that instant when you realize that in another moment the sun will burn it off, and by the time you've thought the thought, it is gone."

"Poetic. Hardly scientific data."

Kazak stopped his pacing and spoke in a quieter tone: "Give me some dignity. Give me clothing at least, for the times—the times when I look human."

The doctor raised his eyebrows. "You believe clothing lends dignity? My word, you are old-fashioned. Surely you know that in civilized places clothing has been optional for years and years. Why not, with the climate perfectly controlled and reproduction made scientific?" He gestured at his own neatly-shod feet, his white trousers, his white jacket. "This is properly a uniform and not clothing at all. It identifies me as a member of the guild of science. If it would make you comfortable, I could be as naked as you."

"No," Kazak said. "That wouldn't make me comfortable."

"Clothing," the scientist said. "Remarkable. still, if you wish, it is possible. Lie on your bed. It has been listening, it knows."

Kazak reclined. The bed grew around him, sending a thin membrane over chest and arms, loins and legs. In a few moments he rose, dressed in white singlet and trousers, wearing soft white shoes. "Thank you," he said humbly.

"Not at all. I hope you feel more—" the thin lips stretched upward—"human now."

They gave him a "real" window, a hologram that showed a view of the great city they were in, a place of endless spiring structures and deep canyons of streets. When he was not being tested, Kazak watched the window hungrily, day after day, counting the intervals and dreading the coming of full moons.

Once he sat watching the eastern horizon through that window. He had kept careful count, and tonight was the full moon. True, he did not know which month it was, for the city was certainly "domesticated" and showed no more seasonal change than did the eternal face of the moon itself; but he knew the change was due, the sixth or eighth change since his capture.

The moon rose slowly, pale in the glare of that huge city. He shrank within as it climbed above the jagged horizon of spires and rooftops—but the change did not occur. He remained human.

Kazak shook with relief and with fear. When the moon had climbed quite high, so high that he could no longer see it through the window, the wall opened and Dr. Iglace came in. "Do you feel cured?" he asked.

"What have you done to me?" Kazak demanded.

"Perhaps a new drug. How do you feel? Do you miss the transformation?"

Kazak frowned. "I miss—" he said. "I miss—freedom."

Iglace shook his head. "Another outmoded concept."

"Please," Kazak said. "I never killed humans. I never injured anyone—"

"You injure science," Iglace replied. "By being an anomaly. By being an outrage. By being the last man-wolf. No, I am sorry." He glanced at the window. "Let him see the scene outside as it really is," he ordered.

The window brightened. The scene was not a midnight cityscape, but rather a sunset. Kazak frowned at it. "You fooled me?"

Iglace shrugged. "It was possible that the metamorphic trigger was purely psychological in nature, that you only believed the moon caused the change. Over the past month we have altered the day/night cycle of the room and have slightly speeded time for you, so that your perception is about nine hours ahead of real time. You saw an image of the full moon, not the moon itself. However, it will soon rise. Please concentrate, for my questions are not idle ones. Tell me, how did you feel when you thought you would not change?"

Kazak frowned. "I was afraid. And glad. And sorry. I wanted to be free, even if it meant I no longer heard the song of the blood."

"A lycanthrope and a poet. My friend, you are a living fossil on two counts. True sunset nears, Mr. Kazak. I must leave you now."

A door formed itself and then disappeared as Iglace stepped through it. The window winked out of existence, too, leaving just the four walls, the ceiling, the floor. Kazak paced, shaking in reaction.

The change took him in mid-stride. He felt the first grating shock, a sensation like the ends of broken bone rasping together in all his limbs, and he desperately tore away his clothing. He dropped to hands and knees, feeling his pulse race, his breath come sharp and hot. For an eternal instant he poised with all muscles locked and trembling, like a man on the brink of agony or orgasm.

The bones within him became plastic, re-formed themselves. His pelt grew, thickened, as his skull altered, as his teeth became fangs, his nails claws. Energy surged through his frame, shrinking the mass of his body as muscles altered, bones shifted, and his backbone extended into a tail.

The hateful room flowed in through his nose, aseptic smells, plastics, metals, synthetics, chemicals, nothing of the living world. In this form Kazak felt the imitation pulse of the room, sensed the throb of liquids passing through micropores, heard the hum of electricity keening like a knife kissing a whetstone ten kilometers away. The room knew him, and contained him, and was his enemy, and could not be killed, for it did not live.

He screamed, and the scream was a howl.

▼▼▼

In times past he had tried to hide from the moon, always without success, no matter how deeply he burrowed in caverns, no matter how completely he blinded himself beneath tons of earth and stone. Somehow she found him, Sister Moon, and always she called to his blood, to his urge to run and be free; and always, always, his wild blood answered the call.

He had lived a long time, a time beyond his counting, for his kind matured slowly, and their spans were longer than those of common men. His mother, whom he barely remembered, had spoken of such things years ago, in another century, perhaps: "You will live to a great age, and you will never be old or weak. And when the time comes for you to die, you will give yourself back to Brother Earth without pain, without fear."

Later, from his reading, he learned about the charm of silver against his kind. In a city on the Mediterranean he had once tested the charm, had visited an antique shop that specialized in old silver. No sooner had he stepped through the door into the cool, dim shop, smelling of garlic and dust, than he began to feel it, the pressure of the metal all around him, sharp as knives and eager for his blood. He felt decorative silver pins stir in their cases, trying to get at him, to pierce his skin, and he felt the malevolence of silver rings, trying to uncoil like snakes to strike at him.

Awareness of the hostile element had almost drowned him. The shopkeeper, fat and wearing an extravagant mustache, materialized from the depths of the shop, saying, "Silver, *signore*? Something nice in silver?"

He had fled without excuse or apology into the sunlight and the clamor of life, and eventually had retreated northward into the forests where he could live simply, could even get a position as a warden. The job demanded no advanced degree and even provided a little hermit-house in the shadow of the great trees.

His kitchen was furnished with aluminum, and all his knives and forks were steel. Silver never got its hooks into him, except for the silver moon, once a month, and that struck too deep for any surgeon to plumb.

▼▼▼

"Silver," said Dr. Iglace, "acts as a catalyst."

"I don't understand," Kazak said.

Dr. Iglace was pleased to explain. "It destabilizes at least two of your hormones. The silver is not itself affected by the reaction, but it does encourage the reaction. Normally your body repairs itself with astonishing speed, no matter what the damage. Look at your right forearm. Do you see the scar?"

Kazak stared at his arm, then raised his eyes to meet the icy blue gaze of Dr. Iglace. "What scar?"

The doctor smiled. "Precisely. We've repeatedly taken biopsy plugs from your forearm, and within hours the wounds have healed with no scarring. It might interest you to know that your body chemistry is proving useful medically. We may synthesize a serum from your blood that will accelerate healing in humans."

Kazak resumed his restless pacing, a caged animal. "But what about the silver?"

Dr. Iglace made a throw-away gesture. "It disrupts the healing process, reduces your ability to heal yourself to that of an ordinary person. So a silver knife, or a silver bullet, would kill you, because you could not counter the effects of the wound. An ordinary knife or bullet would not seriously harm you, even if it penetrated your heart. The muscle and tissue would reknit instantaneously, sealing the puncture, saving your life."

Kazak prowled the floor. "How long have I been here?"

"A lunar year tonight. Tonight is the full moon."

"I know." Kazak slumped into the other chair. "I suppose you have a theory about the moon as well."

Dr. Iglace's brown face twisted into a smile. "Of course. You are affected by radiation—a subtle form of radiation that sunlight triggers when it falls on the lunar surface. The energy of the sunlight activates a process that results in certain subatomic particles being thrown off from the moon. Forgive me, this is not my field."

Kazak shook his head dumbly.

The doctor continued: "When the moon is a quarter full, or three-quarters full, the radiation is too weak to influence you. Only when the moon is completely full does the radiation reach Earth with sufficient intensity to trigger the transformation."

"Shielding?" Kazak asked.

"My dear fellow, we have tried shielding. We estimate that you would have to be shielded by material over a thousand kilometers thick before the effect would be blunted. I suppose it would be possible for you to fly around the Earth once a month, on a fast aircraft, keeping the Earth between you and the moon. Possible, but hardly practical." The doctor consulted his wrist, where luminous red numerals, like animated tatoos, showed the time. "I must go now. I worry about you, you know. You are losing weight, in both your manifestations."

Kazak tensed in his chair. The moment Iglace approached the wall, the instant the wall dilated into a doorway, he sprang. He struck the scientist between the shoulder blades, toppled forward with him, hearing the other man's outburst of breath. They tumbled, and Dr. Iglace lay still, though he breathed.

Kazak rose and found himself in a long white hallway, not made of the artificial living stuff of his cell, but ordinary laminate and metal. He ran.

He found a window, a real one, and looked out. The city sprawled far below, but only a few meters beneath the window a skypath led from the building he was in to one opposite. Kazak tried the window and it swiveled open, just enough for him to squeeze through.

The sun was low and red.

He dropped to the roof of the skypath—and nearly slipped off, barely avoiding a fall of another ninety meters to the streets far below. But he kept his grip, crept along the sizzling hot metal to the opposite building, and then managed to swing down and inside the skypath. Crowds walked the halls of the other building, most people clothed, some nude or seminude. No one looked at him twice as he found the elevators.

Outside the sun touched the horizon.

He dropped down to street level, his heart hammering, wondering if Iglace had planted something, some remote sensor, inside his body. Wondering if Iglace had recovered, if the hunters were already in pursuit.

The street was shadowed, for the buildings allowed no sunset light to the pavement. But almost as soon as Kazak stepped out, the building fronts themselves flared into cold artificial light, ejecting dusk from a broad street where crowds of people flowed in two directions. They parted ahead of him and closed behind as he ran, ran for his life.

For theirs.

Before he knew it he burst from the crowded buildings into a green place, a place of real grass and trees, though even here the sunset was invisible behind a high cliff of buildings on the other side. With the smell of grass sharp in his nose he cut into the park, and there he felt the first agony of change.

Bushes and rocks. He crept into a nestlike place, ripped away his clothing, felt his nails hardening and sharpening. In the cool of the park the air congealed into thin ground mist, tainted with the exhalations of the city.

The moon called to him.

His breathing rasped in his throat, and its sound told him he was no longer capable of human speech. He was free of the clothes at last, free, free.

Hungry.

The stone and earth felt good against his feet. He sniffed the thickening mist and nearly gagged at the stench of the city, at the dusty, nasty smell of humans and their works that clogged even his mouth. He ran.

Now they knew him, the people who crowded the walkways that meandered through the park. They shouted and pointed, and he charged them, scattering them.

Like sheep.

His belly screamed. He cut a young one from the herd, a female, and expertly maneuvered her until her back was against a fence and her eyes were as wide as her mouth and her mouth shrieked at him—

He smelled her, smelled the meat of her, the blood, the life of her, so strong, so sharp. He smelled her fear.

Such an easy kill. Such simple prey, such warm food.

He needed her badly.

But in the dark of his mind some faint thing stirred. The dream of a dream, he had called it. The faintly glimmering recollection of something he shared with his quarry.

He had no speech to name it *humanity*, but he recognized it.

And turned away.

His back bristled and a snarl clattered in his throat.

They waited for him, a dozen or more men in white suits, each man holding a weapon. And Dr. Iglace, hands empty, at the head of them, knee-deep in the rising fog. Dimly and without human words Kazak remembered that Dr. Iglace and the others knew all about silver—

He hoped they had silver bullets.

He sprang.

▼▼▼

"It was simply another test," Dr. Iglace explained. "We had to make sure that you could resist killing before we set you free."

"Free?" Kazak asked. It was morning; he had a vague memory of the force-weapons, of the energy that seized him, slowed him, kept his jaws from Dr. Iglace's throat. They had kept him paralyzed this time until he was human again, and they had pumped his veins full of nutrients. He felt weak this morning, but not destroyed. Dr. Iglace was absorbed in reading a series of figures from a display that had appeared on the room's wall and did not respond to Kazak's question, and so he repeated it: "You're setting me free?"

Iglace stirred as though coming out of a daydream. "Yes. You were well guarded the whole time. You couldn't have hurt anyone. Though if you had fallen from the skypath even your remarkable recuperative powers might not have sufficed. We anticipated that you would use the elevators at the end of the corridor."

Kazak shook his head. "I didn't see them."

"You didn't reach them. No matter. We regrouped at once."

"You planned for me to escape."

"Of course. It was a test, as I said. To see if you would kill, or attempt to kill, a human being. You did not. I except myself." The blue eyes were cold, the smile frosty. "You scarcely regard me as human. But now we know, don't we? And so you may go free."

"Back—to the forest?"

Dr. Iglace tutted. "Dear me, no, of course not. We are a tame world, Mr. Kazak. We can scarcely allow a wolf in the fold. No, we're sending you to Venus."

Kazak blinked. "No."

"Yes. Venus is a frontier world, Mr. Kazak. Still very hot, to be sure—you'll be dropped off at the North Pole, where summer highs are only 38 degrees or so, hardly more than blood heat. The gravitational accelerators have sped the planet's rotation over the past centuries. A Venerian day is now only thirty hours. You may be the only colonist who will live long enough to see it reach twenty-four, in a hundred years."

"No," Kazak said again.

Dr. Iglace spread his hands. "Venus has rivers and lakes, admittedly small; vast oxygen-producing forests, though the trees are all bio-engineered from Earth stock; a population of, ah, individualists, happiest in a frontier setting. It's ideal for you. Who knows, there you may even hear—" the quick smile was not exactly mocking—"the song of the blood."

Kazak met the smile with a bitter laugh. "A place with none of the security of Earth? Where the men and women don't have these damned living houses to pamper and protect them? Where a wolf could kill without fear of restraint?"

"Exactly," said Dr. Iglace. 'However, you will not kill. You proved that last night. Even in your wolf form you have enough control to refrain from killing."

"I can't be sure of that. If I grow desperate, or hungry enough—"

Dr. Iglace checked the time. "You must come with me. If we don't start, we'll miss the shuttle. Don't worry, Mr. Kazak. I think you'll like the hard work on Venus, the challenge of surviving on the frontier. Why, you can enjoy a normal life, even marry—"

Kazak snarled. "The condition is genetic."

"Oh, none of your family may ever return to Earth. We will see to that."

"Are you mad? A race of werewolves on an unprotected frontier world?"

"Am I mad? Are you? Rejecting freedom?" Dr. Iglace's frosty smile flickered again. "There is, of course, one other advantage, one that you should appreciate. It really tips the scales in your favor. Given your natural abilities, your stubbornness and intellect, your stamina—I wouldn't be surprised if this last advantage doesn't make you the most powerful colonist on Venus, in time."

"And what is that advantage?" Kazak asked.

"Venus," said the scientist, "has no moon."

FULL MOON
OVER MOSCOW
▼▼▼

STUART M. KAMINSKY

KATRINA Ivanova hurried along the snow-covered Taras Schevchenko Embankment by the Moscow River. She had just finished her shift as an elevator operator in the Ukraina Hotel and when she checked the clock inside the workers' entrance, she saw that it was just before midnight, which gave her half an hour to rush down the Embankment, go under the Borodino Bridge, hurry through the garden in front of the Kiev Railway Station and get to the Kievskaya Metro Station.

If she missed the last metro, she would either have to take a cab, which she could ill afford, or go back to the hotel and ask Molka Lev to help her sneak into an empty room for the night. Katrina did not want to ask Molka Lev's help. She did not want to ask anyone's help. She had, in her thirty-two years, been less than pleased with the help offered to her by men and women alike. There was always a price to pay. Besides, Katrina carried a little bag whose contents she did not wish to share with Molka or anyone on the night staff. It was a gift, a gift she would place on Agda's pillow where Agda would find it in the morning. Katrina loved giving gifts to Agda, who truly delighted in even a small tin of lemon drops.

It was December and a light snow was falling on two days of old snow blown about by a bitter wind off the river. Katrina did not mind the cold or the snow. The colder it was the less likely she was to be bothered by a drunk or the new breed of muggers and, she noted appreciatively, at this hour and in this weather she was likely to be undisturbed.

A dog howled and the heel of Katrina's left boot struck a patch of ice under a thin spot of snow. She almost slipped but held her balance and managed to keep from falling or dropping her precious package.

Katrina was bundled tight in Agda's lined cloth coat over her own wool sweater with the high neck. A wool hat was pulled and tied to cover her ears and pink cheeks. Katrina Ivanova was no beauty. That she knew, but she was certainly not ugly. Her body was straight, solid if a bit heavy, and her skin was pink and clear. Her hair was as blonde as it had been when the photograph on the dresser had been taken on the day of her third birthday.

A sound behind her. The rustling of wind and snow in the trees or something alive, a dog, yes, a dog. The incidence of attacks on women had, since Gorbachev's new Soviet Union, risen sharply, a sixty-four percent rise in one year, a total of three hundred and six attacks inside Moxcow, including one hundred and six attempted rapes, fifty-three of which were successful.

The dog barked again, close by as Katrina moved along.

She was very good at statistics. Katrina loved statistics. There was certainty in them. Once they were established, they did not change, did not become something else. Before her, through the haze of white, she could see the lights of Bolshaya Dorogomilov-skaya Street where the bridge crossed into the heart of the city.

It was, she decided, a very large dog and it was moving toward her from behind making a very odd kind of deep wet sound as if its jowls were slapping with . . .

Moscovites own 65,000 dogs, 250,000 cats, and tens of thousands of caged birds, she thought to divert her imagination. Other animals were rare, though she had seen a few monkeys. It struck Katrina with little satisfaction that Ivanovs and Ivanovas outnumbered dogs in Moscow by 35,000. There were even 25,000 more Kuznetsovs than dogs in Moscow. The odds were better that one would be followed by a Kuznetsov than a terrier.

It was not a dog. The thought came to Katrina quite unbidden. She did not want that thought and it surprised her.

Another fifty yards to go. There was no one in sight. The street lamps along the embankment were on, though they were dimmed by the swirl of snow. She could hurry and risk falling or she could go a bit slower, a bit more sure of foot, and risk the animal closing on her before she reached the avenue.

Katrina chose to hurry. Behind her through the whoosh of a gust of wind she heard the animal bounding forth, heard the crunch of snow under its paws.

Katrina was frightened. There was no doubting that now, no lying to herself. She would never make the street. She could see that now. Some animal from the circus or a laboratory nearby had escaped. She would tell the newspapers, the television. *Pravda* was carrying all manner of complaint, now.

Katrina shifted her package under her arm, reached into her heavy red plastic purse and came out with the Tokarev 7.62mm automatic pistol Agda had given her less than a year ago when Katrina had discovered the latest statistics on attacks. Agda was incredibly superstitious, but she was also quite practical.

Katrina Ivanova dropped her purse gently in the snow, gripped the revolver in her wool-gloved hands, turned and leveled the weapon at the animal she knew would be behind her. Agda would have been very proud of her.

The creature she saw moving toward her like a sudden dark stroke of a paintbrush on the white canvas of snow was no animal that Katrina had ever seen before. It was loping toward her, the size of a large man. It was covered in coarse grey hair which quivered in the light of the full moon. Its wide mouth was open, its teeth . . . Katrina fired as the creature crouched and sprang toward her, using its thick rear legs to launch it into the air. She fired again. The creature groaned, hit the ground and landed directly in front of Katrina, raising itself above her, its forepaws held up, curved claws dark against the grey fur, teeth sharp and . . . was that blood? Katrina fired again into the creature's throbbing chest as it swung at her. Pain, like an injection of ice, ran through Katrina's shoulder, sending her stumbling backward, losing the gun in snow and fear.

She was on her back, looking up, trying to right herself with her one good arm as the creature took a step toward her, the moon haloing its head, which turned upward as it bellowed so loudly that Katrina covered her ears, screamed and closed her eyes.

She awaited the teeth, the claws, the horror of the creature's breath, but it didn't come. And then came the ultimate terror, that she would open her eyes and it would be there, inches from her face, playing a game, waiting for her to see it so it could rip her face with its teeth.

Katrina whimpered once and opened her eyes with a gasp. There was nothing before her but the snow and the top of a building. She turned on her good arm to left and then right. Perhaps it was standing behind her?

She turned her head, now expecting her throat to be torn out with a rip of those claws. But nothing. Katrina sat up and touched her torn arm, an arm which had no feeling. And then she saw it. Before her in the snow lay not a monster but a naked woman. The woman was face down and blood was coming through a hole in her back. The sight was quite unexpectedly beautiful, for the woman was slender and pale white with dark hair that billowed delicately in the wind.

Katrina crawled forward in her pain, inched her way on her

knees, holding her screaming arm to her chest, and touched the woman, who was still warm and obviously dead. It could not be. It had not been this woman who had attacked her. Katrina Ivanova believed in facts, evidence, statistics. It was Agda who was superstitious, Agda from the Ukraine who had melted down the silver candlesticks her grandfather had taken from the Summer Palace of the Tsar during the Revolution, candlesticks which had been her mother's prized possession. It was Agda who had insisted that they be turned into bullets for the gun she gave Katrina.

Getting to her feet, afraid that she would faint, Katrina looked around and decided that the closest help she could get would be on the street in front of her, the way she had been going. She staggered toward the lights, considering the possibility of not reporting this nightmare, of simply getting a cab and going home. Then she remembered her prize, her gift for Agda, and it became very important, more important than help, the touch of sanity she must have. Her foot hit the gun in the snow but Katrina did not stop to pick it up. Her eyes frantically searched the snow, took in the dead woman's body.

She felt like weeping. She could not see the package. But she could not leave it. And then, there, by the dead woman's outstretched right hand it lay on its side. She picked it up and lifted her head to thank the God that only a year ago she dared not acknowledge in public.

▼▼▼

"Her name was Olga Stashov," said the owl of a man who identified himself as a policeman.

His name was Inspector Nikulin. He never gave his first name. He had watched the woman doctor treat and suture Katrina Ivanova's arm, provide medication and announce that . . .

"Dog bite. I've given her a tetanus shot. If you do not find the animal by morning so we can check it for rabies, she will have to have rabies shots."

"There have been only two cases of rabies from dog bite in Moscow in the past four years," Katrina said weakly as the doctor helped her up. "Fourteen other cases presumed to be caused by rats."

"Most interesting," said Inspector Nikulin. "Now I will tell you something, Comrade. Do you know how old I am?"

"No," said Katrina looking over at her coat and package on the chair in the corner.

"I am almost sixty years old," he said. "I should not be working nights. I should be treated with some dignity, but I am politically what is called a reactionary."

"I don't . . ." Katrina said as the doctor interrupted with, "I have other patients," and departed from the small, hot emergency surgery room.

"I will retire next year," Nikulin said, "and I've lost all interest in the human condition. I have seen too much."

His eyes opened wide and Katrina tried to stand.

"I don't feel well," she said. "I'm tired."

"Of course you're tired. You've had a busy night. A dog bit you and you shot a naked woman in the snow," he said, sitting heavily on the only chair in the room, his hands plunged deeply into his pockets in spite of the heat. "You shot her with gold bullets."

"Silver," Katrina corrected, easing her feet to the floor.

"Yes, of course. I'm sorry. You murdered a woman who was wandering naked in the snow at midnight. You shot her with a bullet of silver. This was after the dog . . ."

"It wasn't a dog," Katrina insisted, moving to her coat. "And I didn't shoot her. I shot the . . . thing."

"Which," he said with a sigh, "ran away leaving no trail of blood but depositing the freshly shot corpse of a woman who had, coincidentally, also been shot with silver bullets."

"I do not lie," said Katrina. "As God is my witness."

"Katrina Ivanova," said the Inspector, shaking his head and

picking up a clipboard with a sheet of paper and a small photograph clipped to it. "In spite of the stupidity of the past year, I am still of the opinion that there is no God to witness what we do, but I have seen strange deaths in the past forty years. Headless corpses, secret rituals, sexual manipulations resulting in agonizing death, but this makes no sense. We could not find the woman's clothes. Did you throw them in the river? We will find them."

"No," said Katrina.

"Was she your lover?" Nikulin tried.

"What?" Katrina said, turning in indignation. The turn sent a bolt of pain through her arm now bandaged and in a sling, and she had to steady herself on the side of the bed.

"Would you like to know who this dead woman was?" he asked.

"No," said Katrina, and then, "Yes."

"Olga Stashova is a ballerina with the Bolshoi Ballet," he said with a most exggerated sigh, showing Katrina the sheet of paper on the clipboard in his hand. Katrina looked at the sheet and at the photograph pasted to it of a very pale, beautiful woman with sunken dark eyes and even darker hair. "Which means that if the newspapers and television hear of this they will be make a hell of my life and my superiors will be asking me questions I can't answer. I tell you it was easier in the days of Stalin. No newspapers would be able to touch this and we'd simply lock you up in a mental prison."

"I'm sorry," Katrina said.

Nikulin shrugged with irritation.

"Do you know why I don't simply throw you in the mad house even with your crazy story?" he asked, but before she could either answer or gesture he went on. "Because of your arm. Something did that to you and it happened near the body of the woman. The snow stopped falling. We followed your trail of blood. Did a helicopter come from the sky and take the dog? Give me answers, Ivanova. I'm not curious, mind you. I'm simply weary. Make up a lie. I'll be happy to accept it so I can go home."

"I have no lie," she said knowing that she was feverish. "I do not lie."

The Inspector stood up and brushed back the little lock of grey-black hair that fell over his forehead.

"All right," he said. "We have your gun. We have your address. You're too sick to do any harm. Go home. Ask the doctor to get you a cab. We'll come and get you when we need you, or the hospital will call you if we can't find the dog and you need shots."

"But the dead woman," Katrina said bewildered. "I . . . you think I shot . . ."

"I think she committed suicide," the Inspector said looking at Katrina. "She just returned a few months ago from a vacation in Romania. She had some kind of breakdown. It was on the television. She went to the river, threw her clothes in and shot herself."

"But the creature," Katrina said.

"Comrade Ivanova," the Inspector said with great patience. "You are not by law allowed to own and carry a firearm. The penalties are severe. Make our lives easier. Go home. If we need you, we will know where to find you. It is almost morning. In a few hours, I will go to Olga Stashov's apartment and search for evidence of both her mental state and evidence that the weapon was hers. Who knows? Perhaps I'll find bullets. I think I will, though they won't be silver. What do you think?"

"I am not feeling well," Katrina said. "I must go home and rest."

For the first time since she had seen him, Inspector Nikulin smiled, a rather dyspeptic smile but a smile nonetheless. Katrina Ivanova wanted very much to go home, to wake Agda, to tell her the tale, to receive comfort, sympathy, and to give Agda the present which she still clutched in the bag, which she picked up with her purse.

But Katrina did not go home. When Inspector Nikulin had shown her the clippboard with the photograph of the haunted face of Olga Stashov, Katrina had read the address. And though it was unlike her, something possessed Katrina Ivanova and she was quite sure that she would not sleep this morning till she knew the answer to the questions the policeman wanted to ignore. Katrina was quite sure that her sanity depended on finding that answer.

The policeman had not volunteered to drive her home, and since she was not going home this did not in the least disturb her. It was almost two in the morning when she stepped out into the street to find a cab. Fortunately, one was sitting in front of the hospital, its driver a small man with wisps of hair that stuck up from a freckled balding head. An oversized coat was bundled around his body and he was taking a secret drink from a bottle which Katrina knew was vodka when she opened the rear door. The driver, who had not noticed the potential fare, was so startled that he dropped the bottle.

Cursing as she closed the door behind her, the driver retrieved the bottle and said,

"I'm going home now. I'm through for the night. Get out."

Katrina calmly gave him the address on Malaya Molchanovka Street, not far from the embankment where Olga Stashov had been shot to death two hours earlier.

"I'm going home," he repeated turning to face her over the top of the seat. "Home. Get another cab. There are three thousand cabs in Moscow."

"There are 16,154 cabs in Moscow. The one I am in will take me to Kalinin Prospekt," she said. "I am not getting out."

The man glared at her, but Katrina did not budge. Considering what had happened to her this night, his effort at intimidation was a joke as pale as the face of the dead ballerina against the swirling snow. She placed her purse and the bag containing the gift for Agda in her lap.

"What happened to your arm?" the cab driver said, the surly edge now blunt, not sharp.

"I was attacked by an animal," she explained.

"You want a bottle of vodka? I can sell you . . ."

"Drive, please," Katrina said.

The driver shrugged, patted down a few wisps of hair, which ignored his effort, and drove. He went through the empty streets to Kalinin Prospekt, made a right turn in front of the 17th-century Church of Simon Stylites into Vorovsky Street, and then a quick left down Malaya Molchanovka Street. About a hundred yards past the house where the poet Mikhail Lermontov had once lived the driver stopped the cab and pointed at a four-story apartment building.

"That's it," he said. "Four rubles."

Katrina paid without complaint and got out. The car had been poorly heated but the slap of cold as she stepped out, arm throbbing, made her consider getting back into the cab. The driver did not give her the opportunity. He pulled away quickly, skidding tires sending the rear end of the cab swaying for a moment before he righted the car and disappeared down the curved street.

The very real possibility existed that Katrina would not be able to get into the building. Even if she got into the building it was unlikely that she could get into the apartment even if someone were inside. But she had to try. When the sun came up, Nikulin the policeman would come, would find what he wanted to find and that would be the end for him and the world, but not for Katrina. She had seen what she had seen. She was a practical woman with an arm in pain. She was a woman who needed to understand, who needed to know how that woman had appeared with Katrina's bullets in her.

Katrina moved to the door of the apartment building, pushed it, and found it open. Inside the small lobby was warm and the names of the tenants—there were not many of them—typed clearly in little slots on a neat wall. A small telephone hung on a hook near a row of buttons for each apartment. Katrina pressed the button marked "Stashov" and picked up the phone. Nothing. She pushed again. Again nothing. She was about to give up when a voice came crackling on the line.

"Thank God," said a man on the other end.

"My name is . . ." Katrina began, but the man, who seemed to be sobbing, cut in.

"Do you have a key?"

"No," she said.

"Not a key to the door, any key?" the man said through tears.

"Yes."

"Put it in as far as it will go and turn it slowly right till the lock clicks. Then pull sharply. Hurry. For the sake of God, hurry."

Katrina put the phone back on the hook and moved to the inner door, removing the key to her own apartment from her purse and placing purse and her precious bag on the floor. She did what the weeping man had told her, but it was not easy. She had only one good hand and it took two hands, one to turn the key, the other to pull the door. In spite of her agony, she removed her left arm from the sling and pulled the door toward her when the key clicked. It wasn't nearly as painful as she thought it would be, but she hoped she would not have to go through such an effort again. She picked up her things and went in.

Finding the apartment was no trouble. It was on the first floor. Even before Katrina knocked she saw that the door was slightly open. But she did knock. There was a sound, a plaintive sound within. She knocked again and the sound was repeated, but the man did not come to open the door. She pushed the door open slightly and called, "Are you there?"

This time the voice of the man, muffled by a door beyond, called, "Yes, yes, oh, God, yes. Come in."

And Katrina entered.

The apartment was dark except for a very small light in a room beyond. Katrina paused where she stood and as her eyes adjusted she could see that she was in a very large apartment indeed, that she was standing in a large foyer just before the living room of which drapes were closed tightly. She moved forward cautiously, slowly as the man called,

"Where are you? Get in here. Get in here. Hurry."

Katrina moved forward, found the partly open door from which the voice came, and pushed it open. The smell was a sour punch to her chest, animal and foul, filled with memories of dead cats and a rat she had once found behind a can of peaches in her mother's pantry.

It was from this door that the distant light had come, a light which illuminated the room in dank yellow and sent shadows that Katrina knew she would never forget. Before her stood a cage, a simple cage like those at the zoo, a cage large enough to hold an ape, with bars the thickness of of her wrists; and within the cage stood a man, a man in a suit holding two of the bars in white-knotted fists and looking at her.

"Get me out," he said. "You must hurry."

Katrina hesitated.

"Get me out," he pleaded. "I've got to find her.".

"Find her."

"Olga, my wife," the man said.

He was a tall man, about forty, with a day's growth of beard and the wild eyes of a man who was truly afraid. Katrina saw the speaker on the wall just outside the cage where the man could reach it.

"What are you doing in there?" Katrina asked, stepping forward.

"What am I . . . Get me out, damn you. Get me out, you cow," he screamed, shaking the bars, which ignored him. "I'm sorry. I'm . . . this is terrible. Please get me out. I'll beg if you like. I'll get on my knees. See, like this."

"No," said Katrina. "Why are you in there?"

The man on his knees suddenly became wary.

"Who are you?" he said without getting up. "What are you doing here in the middle of the night?"

"My name is Katrina Ivanova."

"Your arm? What . . . No," he screamed still on his knees, hitting himself with the palms of his hands. "Olga. Where is my Olga?"

"She is dead," said Katrina.

"Dead," the man said, shaking his head. "Dead. She can't be dead."

"I'm sorry," Katrina said, moving forward to stand in front of the cage door.

"No," he said. "You don't understand. She can't die. She is unable to die."

"I think I killed her," said Katrina, wanting very much to escape from this place but afraid to let her eyes wander from those of the caged madman.

The man laughed and shook his head. It was a loud, insane laugh.

"I shot her with two silver bullets," said Katrina, and the man's laughter stopped quite abruptly.

"Who are you?" he asked, looking frightened again.

"Katrina Ivanova," she said. "I am an elevator operator at the Ukraina Hotel."

"And you have a gun with bullets of silver?" he asked incredulously.

"Agda made the bullets," said Katrina. And then she understood and gave voice to that understanding. "She . . . Olga Stashova was a werewolf."

The man did not answer but Katrina could see that it was true. He sat back against the rear of the cage, his knees up, his face in his hands.

"She tried to kill me," Katrina explained, but the man did not respond. "I'll get you out."

"It doesn't matter," he said. "It doesn't matter anymore."

His head came up from his hands and he looked around the cage.

"I am a writer, Katrina Ivanova," he said. "I cannot write of such exquisite irony as this. I built this cage myself. I learned to build it. I built it so my Olga could be locked in it on the nights of the full moon. And then, this time, this one time I was late and it was I who ran to the cage, who locked myself in to keep from her claws and teeth. If she had killed me and found my body in the morning, it would have . . . I don't know."

"How did she . . . ?"

"We were in Romania, a tour, performance in Bucharest . . . What does it matter now? The animal came running out of an alley behind the theater, attacked Olga. I tried to fight the vile, rotten-smelling . . . Others came to help and it ran, climbed, no it leaped up the side of a nearby building making screaming sounds. Olga had been clawed, bitten on the neck, body. She was covered in blood. I knew she would die on the way to the hospital, but she didn't and her recovery was a miracle. A stupid nurse said she was blessed. We found on the night of the next full moon when we returned to Moscow that it was a curse. Olga killed. I was away at . . . When I came home . . . What does it matter?"

"Where is the key?" Katrina asked.

"The table by the door," he said, looking at a space near the wall not at all near the table.

Katrina moved to the table.

"There is no key there," she said.

The man shook his head.

"She took it. I don't care. With her curse Olga could have lived through eternity. How many people in Moscow live to be even a hundred? With my protection and those I would find to follow me she could have lived for centuries. Can you imagine the skill a century-old ballerina could develop? Can you imagine what her eternal suffering would have done to create an exquisite pathos in her art? The curse could have made her the greatest dancer of all time."

"One hundred and thirteen," said Katrina.

"What?" asked the man, partly rousing himself and looking at her.

"There are now one hundred and thirteen people in Moscow over the age of one hundred," she said. "The police will be here in a few hours. They will find a way to get you out. Can I get you something?"

"If you had found the key," he said, "I think I would have killed you when you let me out. I would have killed you for taking Olga from me and from the future. What would have been the loss if my beautiful Olga had taken your small life?"

Katrina moved to the door and started to push it open. Her arm wasn't hurting as much as it had when she had entered the apartment. She was about to leave the room when she saw the key on the floor and decided that she had a better gift for Agda than the curd dumplings in the paper bag.

▼▼▼

It was just before 3:30 in the morning when Katrina quietly opened the door to the apartment she shared with Agda. She put down her purse and without turning on the light she tiptoed across the very small living room-kitchen to the even smaller bedroom. The door was open and she went in by the light of the moon through the bedroom window.

Agda stirred and turned over. Katrina climbed up on the bed eager for her friend to awaken. In her hand, Katrina held her gift.

"Katrina," Agda said dreamily. "What is that awful . . . ?"

"I have something for you," Katrina said excitedly. "Something to tell you."

"You've discovered the Moscow River has two hundred tributaries," Agda mumbled.

"It has over six hundred tributaries," Katrina said. "I have something for you."

"In the morning," Agda said with annoyance. "Stop bouncing on the bed. It's the middle of the night. I've got to get to work in the morning."

"This will take a moment," Katrina said. "I promise."

Agda sat up with a sigh of resignation and looked at her friend and the present she held out, but nothing was clear, not even Katrina's voice. Agda reached over to the small table near the bed, put on her glasses and turned on the little night light.

When she turned she saw something that had once been her friend Katrina and in part still was. The creature before Agda squated on the bed on its rear legs bouncing up and down. The hands were not hands but twisted dark claws that vibrated nervously holding out the gift. But that was not the worst. The worst was the look on the face, a face which was both Katrina's and that of some hairy animal with its lips pulled back to show wide, sharp blood-stained teeth. There was no doubt. The monster was happy. The monster was smiling as it handed Agda the heart of Olga Stashova's husband.

WOLF WATCH
▼▼▼

ROBERT E. WEINBERG

"**E**VENIN'**,**" said Carl Jones, the night crew manager, as Otto came tramping through the back door. "How's the weather outside?"

"Starting to snow," said Otto, punching in on the time clock. Carl liked to make small talk before leaving each night. Usually they chatted about sports or the latest political scandal. Tonight, though, the manager had other things on his mind.

"Mr. Galliano plans to stop by tomorrow morning before the store opens," he said, the words tripping out of his mouth in a rush. "He specifically asked that you stay around till he arrives."

"He wants to see me?" asked Otto, not sure he heard the other man correctly. Carefully, he hung his threadbare overcoat in his locker. He placed the paper sack containing his lunch on the floor, near his overshoes. His thermos, filled with hot coffee, went next to that. Licking his lips nervously, he added, "He say what for?"

Drawing out his uniform jacket and cap, he dressed quickly. A short, husky man, with broad shoulders and a barrel chest, he could barely button the snaps on his coat. He had been putting on weight the last few months.

A powerful flashlight and a nightstick completed his outfit. Some night watchmen carried guns, but not Otto. He disliked weapons of all types. The billy club was only for show. He never used it.

"Not a word," said Carl, a touch of apprehension in his voice. "The boss never came around to our section before. He always left everything to me." He shook his head. "It ain't natural. Not natural at all. I don't like it."

"*You* don't like it?" said Otto, with a sigh. "He's coming to see me. I'm just a part-timer. Union rules don't protect my job. I can't even apply for membership till next week, after Christmas."

"Yeah," said Carl. "The boss always reviews a new employee's records after three months on the job," He donned his winter coat and wrapped a heavy scarf around his neck. "Seems to me you've been here that long."

" 'Bout that," said Otto. Without thought, his hands constricted into fists. "You think the old man plans to fire me? I heard he likes to hand out the pink slips himself."

"That's right," said Carl. "Mr. Galliano prides himself in delivering all the news, both good and bad. He stays on top of things."

The night watchman put on a pair of earmuffs, then covered his balding head with a fur hat. "The cleaning women all checked out a half-hour ago. See you tomorrow morning at seven. I'll keep my fingers crossed."

"Good night, Carl," said Otto, raising his nightstick in farewell. A few swirls of snow whipped into the locker room as the night manager departed. The snow outside was getting worse. "And thanks."

Otto carefully locked and bolted the rear entrance to the store. He glanced over at the time clock. It was a little before eleven P.M. For the next eight hours, until the morning crew arrived, he was the only person legally allowed in the *Big-G* department store. It was his job to keep all others out.

Most of his time he spent patrolling endless corridors, with only his thoughts for company. It was a lonely, dull routine, but Otto didn't mind. It felt good working again.

A quiet, private man, he actually enjoyed the solitude of the deserted building. He had never functioned well surrounded by people. The sounds and smells of crowds served as a constant distraction and made work difficult. Though not terribly bright, Otto recognized his limitations and tried to work around them.

Previous to this job, he had labored for thirty years on the midnight shift at the south side steel works. His wages there barely covered his living expenses. Fringe benefits consisted of a Christmas party once a year.

Last year, the company abruptly cancelled the party. On New Year's Day, a terse notice in the paper announced the mill's closing. Decades of mismanagement had thrown the corporation into bankruptcy. Hundreds of middle-aged men suddenly found themselves out of work.

The union pension fund, owed millions by the company, collapsed in ruin. Most of the members were left without a cent to their name. Otto considered himself one of the lucky ones. He owned the small cottage where he lived. Many of his old cronies lost their homes and all their possessions during the hard months that followed.

It took him eight months to find this job. Fifty years old and without any experience other than making steel, he was not qualified for most positions advertised in the newspapers. If he was terminated here, future prospects appeared grim.

Otto shrugged, as if shouldering a heavy burden. There was nothing for him to do but wait. In the meantime, he had work to be done.

Forcing the depressing thoughts from his mind, Otto began his rounds. First, he checked all the doors and windows on the first floor. Satisfied they were securely locked, he then took an elevator up to the sixth and highest floor of the store.

Patiently, he paced through the entire level, conscientiously checking behind every counter, inside every dressing room, beneath every display for intruders. He wielded his flashlight like a sword, piercing the dark shadows with its point. As expected, he found nothing out of place.

Taking the escalator down from floor to floor, he inspected each level from one end of the building to the other. The entire walk-through took a little over two hours.

Satisfied with his efforts, Otto settled down in the locker room for a cup of coffee and a chicken sandwich. He made the rounds three times each night. It was one A.M. He had an hour free. Pulling out a well-creased crossword puzzle magazine, he turned his attention to the mysteries it contained.

Otto loved crosswords. A subscriber to a half-dozen puzzle magazines, he spent most of his free time hunting for obscure words to fit the proper clues. He relished a good pun or witty phrase. Oftentimes, he copied the best of them on small stick-it notes he posted on the refrigerator at home. He savored his favorite expressions like fine wine each time he entered the kitchen.

He was a simple man with simple pleasures. Television shows did nothing for him. On his off days, he listened to classical music on the radio while struggling with the *New York Times* crossword. Good music, a cold beer, and a challenging puzzle were all he asked from life.

Twenty minutes passed without. Then, suddenly restless, he looked up, sensing something amiss. In the absolute quiet of the empty building, the slightest sound echoed like a church bell. Oftentimes, his subconscious mind picked up noises that his normal hearing missed.

Rising out of his chair, Otto walked over to the metal lockers and placed one ear against the cold steel. In seconds, the vibrations in the locker door confirmed his suspicions. There were intruders in the store.

Sighing, Otto returned to the table and cleaned off the remains of his lunch. The puzzle magazine and his thermos went to the rear of the locker. Picking up the flashlight, he pushed open the door to the main floor. The nightstick he left on the table, preferring not to carry it when trouble threatened. The heavy club only got in the way.

Movingly silently, he checked the locks and alarms on each entrance. Nothing seemed amiss. Puzzled, he stepped back. Maybe he had been mistaken.

Angrily, he shook his head. Maybe he wasn't the best night watchman around, but he didn't hear imaginary noises. Eyes narrowed in concentration, Otto checked the doors again. This time, he found the telltale marks of a break-in. The third bolt showed definite signs of tampering. The door was still locked, but tiny scratches on the metal indicated that it had been forced opened, then closed.

Investigating further, he soon discovered that the photo-electric cells protecting the entrance no longer worked. The system appeared fine, but none of the alarms were working. Otto grimaced. The equipment was pretty old. He wasn't sure if the devices had ever worked. Professional thieves might have forced their way into the store. But it was equally likely that the intruders were of a different sort.

Most of his problems with break-ins focused on elderly street people looking for shelter from the harsh night winds. Otto oftentimes permitted them to stay in the locker room for the night. It was all too easy imagining himself in the same situation. In the morning, before the day crew arrived, he sent them on their way with a stern warning, a few dollars of his own money, and directions to the nearest shelter for the homeless. Otto hated admitting it, but he was a soft touch.

Teenagers presented a different sort of problem. Otto caught at least two or three a week trying to hide in the store after hours. Drug addicts, hoping for a big score, caused him the most trouble.

To them, the world consisted of two camps—themselves and everyone else.

When apprehended, they fought, pleaded, threatened and screamed trying to escape. The girls, and sometimes the boys, usually offered their bodies in payment for Otto's cooperation. One and all he turned over to the police. He wanted no trouble with the authorities.

Not sure who had invaded his building or for what reason, Otto headed for the locker room. Located there were the main fuse boxes for the entire complex. He knew exactly which switches to throw. It only took a few seconds to cut the power to the elevators, escalators and police alarm system. By doing so, he completely isolated the store from the outside world. Only the pitch-dark emergency stairs provided escape from the upper floors. Now he could investigate without any fear of interruption.

He sat down and removed his boots. A naturally cautious man, Otto never took any chances. No reason to warn the criminals to his presence by a heel scuffing on the floor or a squeaky shoe. Besides, he liked the feel of his naked feet on the bare floor.

Moving without a sound, he cautiously ascended the unmoving metal steps of the escalator. The flashlight dangled from his belt unused. He knew the layout of the entire store by memory.

Otto discovered the burglars in the jewelry department on the fourth floor. They clustered around the display counters housing the expensive watches and diamond bracelets: four men, dressed in black, each carrying a heavy-duty, high-intensity flashlight. They whispered softly among themselves. Otto strained to hear what they were saying.

"Alarm system ain't worth a damn," declared one man. "A ten-year-old kid could take it out with a toothpick."

"I told you so," replied another. "The Old Man never replaced any of the equipment the entire time I worked for the store."

Otto recognized that voice immediately. It belonged to Jim

Patrick, the ex-manager for this very department, fired only a few weeks ago for drinking on the job. Otto sucked in a deep breath and shook his head in dismay. Company loyalty meant nothing anymore. Only old-timers like him felt an obligation to their employers, even long after they ceased working for the business.

"You almost done?" asked a third man. "We don't got all night."

"Keep your shirt on," said Patrick. "That old buzzard they use as a night watchman won't cause any trouble. He's slow and stupid and doesn't carry a gun."

"No gun?" said the first man, rummaging through a small black bag on the counter. After a few seconds, he pulled out a small glass cutter. "How can you be a night watchman without a gun?"

Otto didn't stay around to answer the question. Silently, he crept away to the men's department at the other end of the floor. None of the intruders ever realized the truth until much too late. He didn't use a gun because he didn't need one.

Carefully, he undressed, folding his clothes neatly into a stack by the door to the dressing rooms. Standing completely naked in the center of a sea of shirts, slacks, belts and socks, Otto recited the spell that called forth the monster that dwelt within his soul.

One after another, he repeated the mystic words of power taught to him many years ago by his father. His was an old family tradition, stretching back hundreds of years to the mountains of Transylvania. Moonlight and wolfbane had nothing to do with the change that turned man into beast. All that was necessary was the proper sorcery and the necessary will. Otto possessed both.

The instant he completed the chant, a powerful surge of energy slashed through his body. Otto sighed with relief. No matter how many times he used the formula, he still experienced a brief instant of doubt before it took effect. He was much too pragmatic for his own good.

Otto disliked television, but he made an effort to view the

werewolf movies whenever possible. He found their treatment of the conversion from man into beast amusing. The growls and howls of agony, the twisting and turning of bones, the sudden growth spurts—all reflected Hollywood special effects, not reality.

In truth, the change only took a few seconds. It was not a realignment or rearrangement, but an actual replacement of one physical form by another. Where once stood Otto the man, now paced Otto the huge gray wolf. Otto, the very, very hungry wolf.

The alteration always left him starving. Years ago, roaming the city park late at night, he encountered a fellow werewolf with a degree in molecular biology. The professor, a friendly sort, tried to explain the mechanism behind the magical transformation. Most of the physics went far over Otto's head, but he did grasp the fact that the change consumed vast amounts of bodily energy which needed to be replenished as soon as possible. Otto intended to handle that problem right away.

Lifting his head, he sniffed the air. Instantly, he scented his victims. They labored undisturbed a hundred feet away. A drop of slaver fell from his monstrous jaws, and his red eyes glowed in excitement. His prey smelled delicious.

With a howl of anticipation, he bounded down the corridor in their direction. Powerful legs propelled him forward with the speed of an express locomotive. The floor shook with his every step.

"What the hell was that?" yelled one of the thieves. Caught totally by surprise, they barely had time to look up before Otto slammed into their midst.

Massive teeth caught Jim Patrick's head directly below the ears. The man's shriek of agony ended abruptly as Otto's jaws clenched shut, crushing Patrick's skull like an egg. A mix of blood, bones and brains filled Otto's mouth. He growled deep in his throat. Traitors deserved no better death.

With a shake of his head, Otto sent the lifeless body skidding across the floor. He turned, to be greated by a hail of bullets. The slugs tore into his body like molten nails. He roared with pain—then hurtled forward. Only silver, the bane of black magic, could injure a werewolf.

The man who'd carried the glass-cutter loomed in front of him. In his hands, he grasped a massive gun that bellowed fire and lead. He pumped shot after shot into Otto's massive frame. It wasn't until the werewolf was nearly upon him that he finally realized his efforts meant nothing. By then it was much too late.

Rearing up on his hind legs, Otto lashed out with his right paw. Two-inch long claws ripped through the man's neck and chest like paper. Blood spurted onto the glass cabinets.

Mentally, Otto grimaced in annoyance. Claw wounds always left a mess. It took hours to clean blood stains off furniture. He needed to be more careful in the future.

Screaming, his victim staggered back, trying desperately to escape. Angry with his own sloppiness, Otto followed. Using his huge head as a battering ram, he knocked the man to the floor. Pouncing on him like a cat with a mouse, Otto sent the man to oblivion with a bite that ripped out most of his chest.

For a second, the taste of warm flesh overwhelmed him and he forgot there were two more victims to be slaughtered. Hungrily, he crunched the man's ribs, seeking out his heart and liver. Only afterwards did he remember the others. By then, there was no sign of either man in the department.

Otto howled in annoyance. He was getting old and was too easily distracted.

Trying to ignore the lure of fresh blood, he anxiously hunted for a scent. It only took a moment to latch onto the trail of one of the missing men. Hurriedly, he raced across the floor, following the smell.

He found the crook huffing and puffing his way down the unmoving escalator. "Damned attack dog," the man moaned to himself. "Never saw a dog so big. Must be some damned freak breed they raise just for guarding stores. Hell of a big dog, hell of a big one."

Otto waited patiently until the man made it to the landing.

He knew better than to try the grooved metal stairs with his claws. Wolves were not constructed for escalators.

Gathering his legs beneath him, Otto leaped through the darkness. On the floor below, the muttering crook never realized his peril. Otto dropped onto his back with devastating force. Ribs and backbone crushed, the man collapsed to the floor without a sound. One swipe from a giant paw took off most of his skull.

There was no sign of the fourth man. Nor could Otto pick up the least trace of his smell. Unable to curse, Otto growled instead. If the criminal escaped, it meant an end to these nocturnal hunts. Even the dumbest thieves were not foolish enough to venture into a store guarded by a werewolf.

Despondent, Otto paced along the floor, hunting some clue to the man's whereabouts. The thief had somehow managed to hide his scent. But the perfume department was located on the first floor. It was impossible for the man to have made there in so short a time. He had to be hiding elsewhere in the building.

Otto concentrated, mentally visualizing all of the store's many departments. None of them offered sanctuary from his powers, yet the crook was nowhere to be found. Then, suddenly, Otto knew where the man was hiding.

Playing his hunch, he hurried over to the Christmas section located at the rear of the floor. The scented wax candles and fragrant pine wreaths that decorated the area effectively shielded any other scent from his nostrils. And the displays offered a seemingly safe haven from the forces of darkness.

He found the last man, huddled at the center of a stack of holiday ornaments and religious statues. White-faced and trembling, the man clutched a small jeweled crucifix with both hands. As Otto approached, the crook started babbling a confused mixture of prayers and Hollywood werewolf lore.

"Get behind me, Satan," the man declared when Otto was only a few feet away. He held the cross straight out in front of his chest, pointing it like a spear. "Get behind me."

Otto stopped moving. Immediately sensing the werewolf's hesitation, the crook repeated the phrase, this time much louder.
"Get behind me, Satan. Get behind me."

The words rang in Otto's ears. Whining loudly, he took a step
back. Then another. And yet another.

"Get behind me, Satan!" bellowed the crook, waving his crucifix back and forth as if banishing spirits. His voice trembled
with emotion. Slowly, he moved forward, abandoning his position
amidst the toys and ornaments.

Eyes half-closed, Otto watched his enemy draw closer. Snarling in impotent rage, he retreated further, until he was far
removed from the Christmas display. His nemesis followed, bran-
dishing the ornate crucifix like a sword.

Looking around, Otto decided they were far enough away
from the delicate ornaments for his purposes. Tired of the cha-
rade, he rose to his feet and waited for his unsuspecting prey.

"Get behind me Satan," roared the crook, thrusting the cross
directly at Otto's jaws. Without hesitation, Otto opened his mouth
and bit off the man's hand, crucifix and all. Crosses might annoy
vampires, but they had no affect on werewolves.

The thief screeched out the phrase one last time before Otto
silenced him for all eternity. Then, only the gnashing of the
werewolf's razor-sharp teeth disturbed the descending curtain of
silence.

Chomping on the criminal's skull, Otto felt slightly better. In
luring the man away from the display, he had protected the fragile
ornaments from damage. His quick thinking had saved the store
a good deal of money. Satisfied with his actions, he settled down
to feast. It had been nearly a month since the last batch of intruders. During that time, he had worked up quite an appetite.

Several hours later, back in his human form, he surveyed the
scene of his final confrontation. Everything appeared in perfect
order. He had diligently cleaned the cabinets and floors until not
a trace of blood remained. The department store kept a goodly

supply of the new miracle cleaners that made such jobs a breeze. They removed the toughest stains without a bit of trouble.

The grisly remains of his four victims went into body bags he kept hidden behind the lockers. A quick call to several ghouls working the late shift at the sanitation department resulted in an unannounced early morning pickup. Otto believed in sharing his good fortune with others. The ghouls cheerfully accepted Otto's gift of the criminals' flashlights and tools as well. By the time the morning crew arrived at 7:00 A.M., all evidence of the break-in had disappeared.

A beaming Carl arrived only a few minutes after the hour. Accompanying him, dressed in an expensive charcoal gray suit, was a short stocky man whom Otto immediately recognized as Mr. Galliano. Red-faced from the wind and cold, the owner grinned when he spotted Otto.

"You must be Otto Stark," he said in a gravelly voice, coming over and extending a hand. "I'm Julius Galliano."

"Pleased to meet you, sir," said Otto, a thin line of sweat trickling down his back. Nervously, he shook hands with his boss.

"My pleasure," said Galliano, jovially. Despite his age, he had a firm, steady grip.

He peered closely at Otto, his eyes twinkling. "My coming here this morning had you worried about your job a little, didn't it?"

"Yes sir," replied Otto truthfully.

"The best workers always worry about their performance," said Galliano, chuckling. "That's what makes them the best. The lazy ones never give a damn." He paused to emphasis the fact. "I'm here to give you a raise, Otto."

Otto blinked in astonishment. "A raise?" he asked, cautiously.

"You heard me right," said Galliano. "A hefty one at that. You deserve it. Since you took over the late watch, thefts have dropped off to nothing. I'm impressed. And I back up my appreciation with cold, hard cash."

"I just do my job, sir," said Otto.

"Damned if I could handle it," said Galliano, yawning. "It's tough work, keeping alert from dusk till dawn. The graveyard shift, right?"

"Yes sir," said Otto. Night patrol had lots of nicknames—the graveyard shift, the tombstone patrol, the wolf watch. "It's tough, but I'm happy."

"Really?" asked Galliano, sounding a bit surprised. "Wouldn't you prefer working during the day?"

"Not at all," replied Otto. "I like my job. The pay is good. The hours suit me fine. And," he grinned wolfishly, "the fringe benefits are terrific."

THE WEREWOLF GAMBIT
▼▼▼

ROBERT SILVERBERG

SOME time after the fifth martini, when the barkeep was mixing them eight or nine to one and the little heap of discarded olives in the ashtray was beginning to look untidy and Keller felt his nerves starting to fray in frustration, he said: "You should see what happens when the moon is full."

The bored girl across the table yawned delicately. "What happens to the *moon* or to *you*, darling?"

"To me. I turn into a wolf."

"Of course," she said. "You don't even need a full moon for that."

Keller frowned, flicked ashes from his cigaret, fitfully sipped his drink. This evening had long since begun to look like a blank—a dead, useless, wasted blank evening. He hadn't communicated his purposes at all. Lora, sitting at the other end of the table as if there were a wall between them, was all glitter and polish, and had a marvelous way of consuming a man's money during the course of an evening—but Keller was having serious regrets about having offered to take her out. The evening's investment promised to have no returns whatsoever.

The werewolf gambit was the finale. Keller thought of it as a wry jest, an ultimate variation on the customary etchings, a desperate tactic he was employing as a final sardonic gesture toward seduction before he abandoned the night's quest.

"You don't understand," he said quietly. "*Je suis un loup-garon*. A lycanthrope. Bristles and fangs, gleaming yellow eyes. You know?"

The waxen mask of Lora's pale face seemed to show animation for the first time that evening. "You're sure you haven't had too many drinks, darling?"

"Quite on the contrary; if I'd had too many, I assure you I'd be raging on all fours up and down the cabaret this very moment. I've got myself quite thoroughly under control, though. I won't begin to change until . . . until . . ."

Arched eyebrows flickered. "*When*, dear?"

"In my flat. Later tonight, perhaps." He leaned backward, craned his neck to peer through the clinging lace of the curtains. A bright shaft of moonlight sparkled against the window. "Yes . . . tonight is the beginning. It lasts three nights. I feel it stirring within me now."

Hastily, he finished his drink. The bartender glanced inquiringly at him, but Keller signaled quickly with his left index finger that the evening's drinking was over. His campaign would stand or fall on what had already been consumed. Keller saw no reason to expend further cash in what looked like a fruitless pursuit. Besides, Lora's thirst was immense; alcohol didn't seem to satisfy it at all.

The girl leaned forward. Her clinging wrap fell away from her pale throat, creating a delightful view. "I suppose it takes five martinis to extract these confidences, darling. If you had told me earlier . . ."

"Yes?"

"We could have skipped that dreadful play. We could have gone straight to your place."

"*What?*" For the first time within his adult memory, Keller's self-composure utterly deserted him.

"I'm terribly interested in things like this," Lora said eagerly. *"Loup garous!* How fastinating!" Seizing his hand with a a passion she had failed to show all evening, she said, "Would it be asking too much . . . for you to *show* me?"

I'll be eternally cursed, Keller thought in quiet wonderment. *How To Get A Girl To Your Apartment,* he thought. *Technique 101a: The Werewolf Gambit.*

It had been only a joke to cap a wasted evening, and abruptly it had transformed a remote, passionless girl into a keenly curious and receptive woman. *Someday I must write my memoirs,* Keller thought, as he paid the check. *If only to tell about this!*

▼▼▼

"Be it ever so humble," Keller said, throwing open the door to his apartment.

Lora stepped inside and uttered a little gasp of delight. "It's a *lovely* room," she said. "A little austere, but *lovely!*"

"I like it," said Keller. "I've lived here three years."

"It's in marvelous taste," she exclaimed enthusiastically, looking around at the paneled walls, the ceiling-high ebony bookcase laden with Keller's extensive library, the kidney-shaped swirl of the dark coffee-table, the low bulk of the phonograph-tape recorder sprawling along the far wall. She slipped lightly out of her evening jacket; Keller hung it in the hall closet and tiptoed happily into the little kitchen.

"Drink?" he asked, a little tensely.

"No . . . thanks," she said. She was at the bookcase, tugging at the ponderous red-bound volume that was his copy of *Rites and Mysteries of Goesic Theurgy.* "You have strange taste in books," she said.

"Strange? Is it so strange for a werewolf to be reading Arthur Waite? Not at all." He was determined to carry the joke along as far as he could.

She chuckled lightly. "Of course not. I apologize."

He emerged from the kitchen with two oliveless martinis and set them down on the little inlaid end-table near her. As he moved toward the phonograph, he observed with professional pleasure that she had lifted one of the drinks to her lips. It was a rule he had long followed with great success in the past: *If a girl you've brought to your apartment refuses a drink, bring one anyway. She'll drink it.*

"Putting on a record?" she asked, still busy at the bookcase.

"Vavaldi. It's good music for late at night."

He turned the volume low, and as if from a great distance there issued the bright sheen of violin music accompanied by the silvery tinkle of a tiny harpsichord. "There," he said. "Just perfect."

He glanced at his watch in the dim light of the one lamp. It was quarter to three. Barring unforseen happenings, they should be safely bedded down before four-fifteen.

He crossed the room, reached agilely around her to snare his drink from the table, brushed the nape of her neck lightly with the tip of his nose as he straightened up. "Care to join me on yonder divan?" he asked, indicating the couch.

She smiled and nodded. Keller gave her his hand in formal fashion and escorted her to the couch. She kicked off her shoes and drew her knees up to her bosom, wrapping her arms around her kneecaps and letting her head droop broodingly.

"I'm not in the habit of visiting men's apartments this late at night," she remarked. "Or at any hour."

"That's obvious," he said. "I can tell by the luminous purity of your eyes that—" He let his voice trail off, then tacked on the coda: "But there's always a first time, of course."

"Of course. About this affliction of yours, this lycanthropy—"

"Oh, that. We can talk about that later." There would be plenty of time for explanations, he thought, in the morning. "Mind if I come a little closer? It's cold in here, at this distance."

Without waiting for her reply, he edged up next to her and

slid one arm suavely around her bare, cool shoulders. It seemed to him that she quivered faintly at the contact, but he decided it was just his imagination.

"They say only virgins can ride unicorns," he observed softly, letting his fingertips graze the lobe of her ear.

"There's some truth in that,' she admitted, intercepting his hand neatly as it began to slide further down her shoulder. "Unicorns have an unerring way of telling, I hear."

"It's too bad we're not all unicorns."

"Yes," she said, sighing. "It's too bad."

Through the drawn blinds, a single beam of moonlight wandered and glistened momentarily against Keller's onyx cufflink. "The moon is full," she pointed out. "You must be fighting a terrible struggle within yourself. But we're alone, now. You can change over, if you like."

"Do you really want me to?"

"Unless it's dangerous, of course. Can you control yourself when you're—you're *changed*?"

"I don't know. I never really know what I do when I'm—*changed*."

"Oh," she said. "I'll have to risk it, then. I *must* see it. Please? What are you waiting for?"

He fingered his suddenly sticky collar uneasily. The recorded ended; Vivaldi faded with an abrupt click and was replaced by a Shubert quartet. Moonbeams continued to pour into the room.

The girl was carrying the thing too far. "Let's not talk about lycanthropy now, my lovely," he whispered harshly. There had been enough talk of werewolvery; the time had come to forget the introductory gambit and get down to the main business of the evening.

He crushed up closely against her, and this time he sensed a definite shudder of repugnance as his body came in contact with hers. She was cool and distant, but permitted his caresses almost absently.

After a few moments, she wiggled away. "You promised to show me—"

Keller began to laugh, coldly at first and then almost hysterically. "Lora—darling—for a sophisticated girl, you're incredibly guillible! Can't you recognize a spoof when you fall for it?"

She drew back. "What do you mean?" she asked acidly.

"This werewolf business—did you really *believe* it?"

There was a stunned pause. Then: "I should have known you were lying. I could have told that you were no *loup-garou* . . . but yet I trusted you." "I came up here to see—to see—"

The edge of a tear glittered brightly in the corner of one eye. She had the cheated look of a maiden wronged. Keller scowled; this evening was turning into the most unmitigated fiasco he had experienced since the age of sixteen. Determined to make one last try in a valiant attempt to recoup his honor and capture hers, he took her cold hands in his.

"Lora honey, I just did it because I love you so damn much!" The words nearly stuck in his throat, but he got them out with as much sincerity as he could muster. "I wanted you so bad I'd tell you anything. Just so long as you'd come up here. Just so I could be with you for a while. Do you understand? We can go home now . . . if you like."

Her eyes pierced his. "You're *not* a werewolf, then? It was all pretense?"

Exasperated, he said, "I'm not even a ghoul, darling. I'm disgustingly mortal . . . and disgustingly enamored. You know that?"

"Of course I know that," she said suddenly, moving closer to him. She seemed to grow warmer; to his astonishment, Keller realized that he was going to succeed after all. Her arms touched his shoulders, drew his face near hers.

Looking up into his eyes, she said, "You're really not a werewolf?"

Her lips were only inches away, and triumph now seemed

near. Smiling sadly, Keller shook his head. "It was all a game
. . . a game men play some time. No, I confess I'm not and
never have been a werewolf, darling. I hope I didn't disappoint
you too much. I'm not even a vamp—"

The sentence was never finished.

He felt the sudden hot sting of tiny needle-sharp fangs meeting
in the flesh of his throat, and Lora's passionate arms gripping him
tightly, as she slaked her fearful, furious thirst.

THE WOLF MAN
▼▼▼

A SELECTED FILMOGRAPHY

First, a note and then a disclaimer.

The filmography that follows does not pretend to be complete. Rather, it is a representative list of those films which, taken together, display the range of treatments the movies have given to the theme of the werewolf.

Now, the disclaimer. "Lycanthropy in the Movies" or "The Werewolf Cinema" ought properly to be the title of this filmography but, since this volume celebrates the fiftieth anniversary of the appearance of "The Wolf Man," I have decided to let the title stand as it appears above.

It is clear, even from the most cursory look at the horror cinema, that, of the three great American film monsters in the pantheon of horror, the wolf man occupies the least glorious pedestal. There are hundreds of films dealing either with Dracula or vampirism; scores that retell the Frankenstein story, but not more than a couple of dozen films with a werewolf theme. The reason is fairly obvious. Dracula, Frankenstein, and his creature have specific identities. Filmgoers who come to see a Dracula or Frankenstein movie expect to become reacquainted with monsters they know. The "Wolf Man" film treated its protagonist, Larry Talbot—not the first werewolf to appear in the movies— as an instance of a man suffering from the disease of lycanthropy; and it is the disease as it afflicts each new hero around which subsequent werewolf films have revolved. The result is that the force of the werewolf imagery, unattached to a person with a name, has been dissipated; and werewolf films, with a couple of weak exceptions, have, more or less, to establish themselves each time on their own instead of building on the film lore that previous films have created.

THE WEREWOLF OF LONDON
1935 (B & W)   U.S.A.   75 minutes
Universal Pictures
Director: Stuart Walker
Producer: Stanley Bergerman
Screenplay: Robert Harris
Photography: Charles Stumar

An eighteen-minute "Werewolf" silent film made in 1913 in which a Navajo witch-woman, wanting to avenge herself against men, raises her daughter to be a werewolf was actually the "first" film with a werewolf theme. "The Werewolf of London" is the first full-length treatment of the myth.

The film tells the story of the botanist Henry Hull who, searching a rare plant, the *marifasa lupina* in Tibet, is bitten by a werewolf and so turned into a werewolf. We learn that the werewolf that infected him is also the Japanese Dr. Yogami, played superbly by Warner Oland (of Charlie Chan fame).

Yogami follows Hull to London determined to get the flower, which is the only known remedy for lycanthropy, from him. Dr. Yogami is killed in the ensuing struggle. The botanist in his guise as a wolf is killed by policemen.

Warner Oland is smooth and oily and properly evil-looking, but almost everything else about this film is hesitant and unconvincing. A couple of its elements, however, have become part of the stock formula of every subsequent werewolf film: the reluctance of the human to become the werewolf, and his remorse when he discovers that he has shed blood. It is a formula that, by defining the monster as victim, leaches moral authority from werewolf films. An innocent monster is essentially a contradiction in terms.

THE WOLF MAN
1941 (B & W)   U.S.A.   71 minutes
Universal Pictures
Director: George Waggner
Producer: George Waggner
Screenplay: Curt Siodmak
Photography: Joe Valentine
Cast: *Lon Chaney Jr., Claude Rains, Evelyn Ankers, Warren William, Ralph Bellamy, Bela Lugosi, Maria Ouspenskaya*

Lon Chaney Senior was known as "the man of a thousand faces"; Lon Chaney Jr. evidently inherited only one. That one has immobile, lugubrious features on which is stamped a look of hangdog bewildered sorrow for which nothing in any of the films in which he has appeared can account.

And yet that slightly pudgy woodenness serves Chaney well in this classic film. He is the truly woebegone werewolf with the look of a man who does not deserve the slings and arrows of outrageous fortune that have been discharged against him and who is un-equipped to take arms against them.

The story of the film must by now be known to almost everyone who goes to the movies or who owns a TV set: Larry Talbot, a Welshman who has lived in America, returns to his family home in Wales where, one full moon night, as he is struggling to save his fiancee Gwen's friend, Jenny, from the attack of a werewolf, he is himself bitten. The bite turns him into a werewolf.

Knowing that the only metal that can kill a werewolf is silver, and fearful that he, Larry, may attack Gwen, Larry gives his father his silver-headed walking stick. When he does attack Gwen, Larry's father, wielding the stick, beats the werewolf to death and Larry, now an innocent corpse, can be buried with honor.

Rarely in horror film history has a simple-minded story been so buoyed up by a director's lyric treatment of it. The film, in George Waggner's hands, becomes profoundly atmospheric and is made to seem like a dreamlike fairy tale with its roots in distant primordial times. Even the fake poetry that Maleva, the Gypsy fortune teller, declaims as she warns Talbot of his future, has the wonderful ring of fake truth ringing down the ages:

> Even the man who is pure at heart
> And who says his prayers at night
> May become a wolf when the wolfsbane blooms
> And the autumn moon is bright.

No doubt. And of course.

THE UNDYING MONSTER
1942 (B & W) U.S.A. 63 minutes
20th Century Fox
Director: John Brahm
Producer: Bryan Foy
Screenplay: Lillie Hayward, Michel Jacoby
Photography: Lucien Ballard
Cast: *James Ellison, John Howard, Heather Angel, Heather Thatcher*

Instead of starting with a dark and stormy night the way a proper "old dark house" film should, this one begins on a clear night on the coast of Cornwall as we hear a family retainer, Walter, worrying: "I only hope Mr. Oliver doesn't come through the lane tonight." The reason for his anxiety is is that for several generations members of the Hammond family have been involved with mysterious deaths. The family curse goes:

When stars are bright
On a frosty night
Beware thy bane
On a rocky lane.

And indeed, once again, there has been violence. A young woman, Kate O'Malley, has been ferociously attacked. A couple of Scotland Yard detectives show up, and the rest of the film plays off their scientific investigation against the possibility that there is a dark, occult explanation for the family violence. As the film ends, the solution turns out to be a hereditary disease that turns the afflicted person into a werewolf on clear, frosty nights.

Static and cold, this is not by any means a great film. What it does have are a couple of great sets and direction so shrewd that it transcends the mediocrity and the scientific banality of its script. Brahm has his camera in constant nervous motion, implying, by glimpses of sky and cloud, sea and cliff's edge, that whatever the clever folk from Scotland Yard discover, ominous ancient presences are ineradicably part of the real world.

FRANKENSTEIN MEETS THE WOLF MAN*
1943, (B & W)   U.S.A.   74 minutes
Universal Pictures
Director: Roy William Neill
Producer: George Waggner
Screenplay: Curt Siodmak
Photography: George Robinson
Cast: *Lon Chaney Jr., Bela Lugosi, Lionel Atwill, Ilona Massey, Maria Ouspenskaya*

Here is a film that is important only because it marks the signal decline in film of the compelling "Frankenstein" idea. The wolf man theme does not fare much better. If the film proves anything

---

*This review of "Frankenstein Meeets the Wolf Man" appears also in the volume *The Ultimate Frankenstein.*

it is that one can not make a fine horror movie by simply throwing great old horror regulars together. Lugosi as the monster, elicits pity, but only because his performance is so shabby. Nobody cares that Lon Chaney Jr. (as Laurence Talbot) wants medical help to escape the curse of werewolfism. Everybody is grateful when both monsters (so far as the law of sequels will permit) are destroyed at the end of the film. That end comes none too soon.

I WAS A TEENAGE WEREWOLF
1957 (B & W)   U.S.A.   76 minutes
Sunset Production
Director: Gene Fowler, Jr.
Producer: Herman Cohen
Screenplay: Ralph Thornton
Photography: Joseph La Shelle
Cast: *Michael Landon, Yvonne Lime, Whit Bissell, Tony Mar-
shall, Dawn Richard*

This is the superior twin production meant to exploit Hollywood's discovery in the fifties that there was a market for movies about teenagers.

There are a couple of things to be said in the film's favor. One of them is that it has one truly memorable scene set in a school gymnasium in which we see Tony, the highschooler who is afflicted with the werewolf disease, provoked into turning into a beast by the sight of the tights-clad and lissome Theresa doing stunts on the parallel bars. The other, related to this scene, is that, unlike *I Was a Teenage Frankenstein, I Was a Teenage Werewolf,* has some psychological validity in its favor.

The unwelcome transformation of human into wolf that is embodied in the image of the werewolf is well understood by the developing adolescent whose own body is going through surprising new changes which, often enough, can feel monstrous.

In any case, *I Was a Teenage Werewolf,* with its vaguely anti-science theme, deserves an audience for two reasons. It is indispensable for students of film werewolf lore and it is something of a time capsule in which we can find persuasive glimpses of how young people experienced the vapid fifties.

CURSE OF THE WEREWOLF
1960 (Color)   Great Britain   91 minutes
Hammer Films
Director: Terence Fisher
Producer: Anthony Hinds
Screenplay: John Elder (Anthony Hinds)
Photography: Arthur Grant

Another of Hammer Films' colorful revitalizations of the horror images Universal Pictures introduced to the world in the thirties. This one, however, is not directly based on Universal's *The Wolf Man*. Instead, its source is Guy Endore's novel *The Werewolf of Paris*, whose main theme is that no cruelty committed by a werewolf can match man's inhumanity to man.

The story, spanning generations, begins with an injustice committed by a Spanish marquis who imprisons a beggar and has him fed on raw meat which, presumably, brutalizes him. When, some years later, a servant girl who has spurned the marquis's advances is pushed into the beggar's cell, he rapes her. The child begotten by this rape is born on Christmas Eve—ironically the birth date of Christ and of werewolves—and becomes the werewolf of the film's title. For a time, his werewolf instincts are kept under control by the care he receives from his adoptive parents, but a trip to a whore house unleashes his sexual and his werewolf instincts. Though the love of a good woman calms him for a while, the beast in him bursts out when his father forcibly keeps him from seeing her. Again, as in *The Wolf Man*, it is a father who kills a son afflicted with the werewolf curse. This time the weapon, instead of being a silver headed walking stick, is a gun that shoots a bullet made from a silver crucifix.

As with Hammer films generally, production values here are high. Oliver Reed in the title role manages, despite makeup that gives him a nearly cuddly look, to be both frightening and dignified. Fisher, as he has in his previous ventures, respects the folklore materials on which his film is based. The result is a first-rate, but by no means great film.

THE HOWLING
1981, (color) U.S.A. 91 minutes
Avco Embassy
Director: Joe Dante
Producers: Michael Finnell, Jack Conrad
Screenplay: John Sayles, Terence H. Winkless
Photography: John Hora
Special Effects: Rob Bottin, Rick Baker
Cast: *Dee Wallace, Patrick Macnee, Dennis Dugan, Christopher Stone, Belinda Balaski, Keven McCarthy, John Carradine, Slim Pickens, Elizabeth Brooks*

1980 was a great year for special effects. It was then that David Cronenberg's *Scanners* stunned its audiences with scenes in which one could literally see someone's skin crawl (or at least bubble) and in which a man's head is seen to explode on camera. Like *Scanners*, *The Howling*'s first claim to our attention is its special effects.

This film version of Gary Brandner's pulp novel has a young woman TV reporter, Karen Beatty, walking the streets as a decoy, hoping to make news by attracting the attention of a sex maniac who has been terrorizing Los Angeles women. Her efforts are successful. The maniac attacks and she is raped. To recuperate from the ghastly experience she and her husband Roy, on the advice of a psychiatrist, join a psychotherapeutic colony somewhere in the northwest.

There, the second nightmare begins as we learn that the psychiatrist *and* the members of his colony are all werewolves. From here on the film becomes more and more graphic about the sex life of werewolves. We are treated to one scene in which Roy and Marcia, a nymphomanical member of the colony, begin their lovemaking as people but, as their passion moves toward orgasm, they turn into snarling, snapping werewolves.

A strange film, that on several occasions crosses the line that separates the erotic from the obscene. Much of the obscenity, strangely enough, derives from the special effects which, as they allow us to watch the transformation of human into beast, make both humans and beasts look like the kinds of caricatures adolescents encounter in pornographic booklets passed around in locker rooms and at slumber parties.

The film is graced by the presence of John Carradine howling a little bemusedly along with the other werewolves.

AN AMERICAN WEREWOLF IN LONDON
1981 (Color)   Great Britain   97 minutes
Poly Gram Pictures-Lycanthropy Films/Universal
Director: John Landis
Producer: George Folsey
Screenplay: John Landis
Photography: Robert Paynter
Special Effects: Rick Baker
Cast: *David Naughton, Jenny Aguter, Griffin Dunne, Brian Glover, John Woodvine*

Sometimes touching, sometimes terrifying, sometimes very funny, *An American Werewolf in London* is a sophisticated film that stands head and shoulders above the werewolf films that preceded it. *The Wolf Man* might be an honorable exception to that generalization, though atmosphere, not psychological truth, is its strong point.

An American Werewolf in London begins with a beautifully photographed scene in which we see a couple of young Americans making their way across a countryside on a walking tour through England. When they encounter a werewolf, one of the youths, Jack Goodman, is killed. His companion, David Kessler, is bitten and is of course infected with the taint of the werewolf.

The rest of the film neatly, poignantly and sometimes powerfully interweaves the primordial werewolf stuff with David's waning human life in modern London. In one unforgettable moment we see David trying to reach his American family via a London public telephone. For David, the phone call is sort of a deathbed farewell. His problem is that he gets his wise-cracking kid sister on the line. It is a scene at once tender, hilarious, and anguished.

The special effects for this film won Rick Baker, who also worked on *The Howling*, a well deserved Oscar.